AS BRIGHT AS HEAVEN

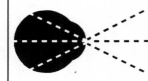 This Large Print Book carries the
Seal of Approval of N.A.V.H.

As Bright as Heaven

Susan Meissner

THORNDIKE PRESS
A part of Gale, a Cengage Company

Farmington Hills, Mich • San Francisco • New York • Waterville, Maine
Meriden, Conn • Mason, Ohio • Chicago

A Cengage Company

LIBRARY OF CONGRESS CIP DATA ON FILE.
CATALOGUING IN PUBLICATION FOR THIS BOOK
IS AVAILABLE FROM THE LIBRARY OF CONGRESS

ISBN-13: 978-1-4328-5015-9 (hardcover)

Published in 2018 by arrangement with The Berkley Publishing Group, an imprint of Penguin Publishing Group, a division of Penguin Random House LLC

Printed in Mexico
2 3 4 5 6 7 22 21 20 19 18

For my mother

Event succeeds event;
accidents, people, happenings,
one after another come toward us.
Each must be met and dealt with. . . .
For this process of adjustment is life,
and the mastery of it is the art of
living. . . .

— KARL DE SCHWEINITZ,
The Art of Helping People Out of Trouble,
1924

■ ■ ■ ■

PART ONE

■ ■ ■

CHAPTER 1

January 1918
Pauline

Morning light shimmers on the apricot horizon as I stand at the place where my baby boy rests. Stouthearted chickadees are singing in the day, just like they have done every other winter's dawn, but when this same sun sets tonight, I will be miles away from them, and inside an unfamiliar house. There will be no reminders anywhere that Henry was ever mine. Not visible ones, anyway.

I kneel on the dead grass, brittle with icy moisture. The fabric of my skirt draws in the chilled damp, as if it is parched with thirst. The growing wetness at my knees is unhurried and easy, like a clean, slow blade. I look at the little marble slab that bears Henry's name and the carving of a sweet lamb curled up among lilies, and I'm reminded again that he was my angel child,

11

even before he flew away to heaven.

From the moment I held my boy, glistening and new, I knew that he wasn't like the other babies I'd given birth to. He wasn't like my girls. They'd slipped out annoyed by the noise and chill and sharp edges of this world. Not Henry. He didn't cry. He didn't curl his tiny hands into fists. He didn't shout his displeasure at being pulled out of the only safe place he knew.

When the doctor placed him in my arms, Henry merely looked at me with eyes so blue they could've been sapphires. He held my gaze like he knew who I was. Knew everything about me. Like he still had the breath of eternity in his lungs.

He didn't care when I parted the folds of his blanket to look at his maleness and marvel at the pearly sheen of his skin against mine. I could scarcely believe I'd given birth to a boy after three girls and so many years since the last one. I just kept staring at Henry and he just let me.

When Thomas was let into the room, he was as astonished that we had a son as I was. The girls were, too. They followed in right after their father, even though it was the middle of the night, and we all gazed and grinned at the little man-child, the quiet lad who did not cry.

My father-in-law came over the next morning, as did Thomas's brothers and their wives, all of them smelling of dried tobacco leaves and spice. My parents came, too, and my sister, Jane, who was newly pregnant with her own child after several years of hoping and praying for a baby. They all marveled at how beautiful Henry was, how calm, how enchanting his gaze and how sweet his temperament. My mother and Thomas's sisters-in-law stared at him like I'd done the night before, amazed as I had been at how serene this baby was. They had known, too, without knowing, that something wasn't right.

The few months we had with Henry were wonder filled and happy. He did all the things a baby does that make you smile and laugh and want to kiss his downy head. When he needed something, like my breast or a clean diaper or affection, he didn't wail; he merely sighed a sweet little sound that if it were made of words would have started with "If it's not too much trouble . . ." We didn't know he didn't have the physical strength to exert himself. His perfectly formed outsides hid the too-small, too-weak heart that my body had made for him.

And yet had God asked me ahead of time if I wanted this sweet child for just shy of half a year, I still would have said yes. Even now, eight weeks after Henry's passing, and even when I hold Jane's sweet little newborn, Curtis, I would still say yes.

I don't know if Thomas feels this way, and I know the girls don't. Evelyn is still sad, Maggie is still angry, and Willa is still bewildered that Henry was taken from us. I can't say why I am none of those things anymore. What I feel inside, I'm not sure there are words to describe. I should still be sad, angry, and bewildered, but instead I feel a numbness regarding Death that I've told no one about. Not even Thomas.

I no longer fear Death, though I know that I should. I'm strangely at peace with what I used to think of as my enemy. Living seems more the taskmaster of the two, doesn't it? Life is wonderful and beautiful but oh, how hard it can be. Dying, by contrast, is easy and simple, almost gentle. But who can I tell such a thing to? No one. I am troubled by how remarkable this feeling is.

This is why I changed my mind about moving to Philadelphia. I'd said no the first time Thomas's uncle made his offer even though I could tell my husband was interested. Back then I couldn't imagine leaving this sleepy little town where I've lived all my life, couldn't imagine leaving my parents, though I've never been especially dependent on their subtle shows of affection. I didn't want to move to the city, where the war in Europe would somehow seem closer, didn't want to uproot the girls from the only home they've ever known. Didn't want to tear myself away from all that was familiar. Uncle Fred wrote again a couple months after Henry was born, and Thomas had said we needed to think carefully before turning down a second invitation.

"Uncle Fred might take his offer to one of my brothers," Thomas had told me.

I truly would have given the matter more serious thought if Henry hadn't begun his slow ascent away from us right about the same time. When my son's fragile heart finally began to number his days, nothing else mattered but holding on to him as long as we could. Thomas didn't bring up the matter again when the third letter from Uncle Fred arrived last week. My husband thinks I cannot leave this little mound of grass.

But the truth is, I have come out from under the shroud of sorrow a different person. I no longer want to stay in this place where Henry spent such a short time. I don't want Thomas shading a view of the wide horizon with hands calloused from binder leaves. I don't want the girls to end up mirroring this life of mine, in a place where nothing truly changes but the contours of your heart.

More than that, I want to know why Death seems to walk beside me like a companion now rather than prowling behind like a shadowy specter. Surely the answers await me in Uncle Fred's funeral parlor, where he readies the deceased for their journeys home. Thomas would've gone to his grave rolling cigars for other men to smoke, but now he will one day inherit Uncle Fred's mortuary business and then he won't be under the thumb of anyone.

I don't know what it is like to be the wife of an undertaker. I only know that I need to remember how it was to keep Death at a distance.

I kneel, kiss my fingertips, and brush them against the *H* carved into the cold stone.

And I rise from the wet ground without saying good-bye.

CHAPTER 2

Maggie

I will miss the curing barn in autumn, when the tobacco leaves hang from the laths like golden skirts in a wardrobe. I've always loved how in October the papery leaves smell like cedar, molasses, and tree bark. There won't be anything like them in Philadelphia. And we'll be long gone by the time October comes around again.

The curing barn is my favorite place because it's either as busy as a beehive or as still as a painting. After that first killing frost it's like the painting, so still and quiet you can forget there's a changing world outside. No one has to do anything in the curing barn in the fall except have a look-see now and then to make sure none of the tobacco leaves are getting moldy. In the fall, we're all in the rolling room. I'm twelve but I've the delicate hands of a young woman, Grandad says, so I roll a nice cigar. Evie

17

just turned fifteen and doesn't like rolling; she'd rather be reading under the locust tree when the weather's nice, but she likes to buy books with the money she earns. Our younger sister, Willa, is only six. It would've been a long while before Grandad told her she had hands as graceful as a dancer and rolled a cigar better than a man did.

I don't usually spend much time in the barn when the tobacco leaves are finished with their curing, but that was where I was when Mama told Papa she'd seen Uncle Fred's letter. I'd come home from school, done my chores, and then walked across the snowy field from our house to lie among the few remaining wooden slats that still held their toast-colored leaves. I'd been going to the curing barn a lot since my baby brother died, but Papa had forgotten I was there.

"I've been thinking about Philadelphia," Mama said. Papa had been checking the empty laths for rot and weak spots. He was a couple rows over from me, and I was on my back on the dirt behind a crate, looking up at the leafy ball gowns. The last time Mama had been to Philadelphia was when Henry was still alive. She and Evie had taken him to see a doctor, and they'd come home with the awful news that he wasn't going to get better. There was no doctor in the city or on the face of the whole earth who could cure Henry.

"I think we should go," Mama had said.

At first I thought Willa must be sick now, and that was why Mama wanted to go to Philadelphia again. Or Evie. Or maybe I was the sick one and I didn't even know it yet. But then Mama added she'd seen Uncle Fred's latest letter asking Papa to come work for him in Philadelphia, and now she was thinking it was a good idea after all.

"What made you change your mind?" Papa sounded surprised.

A second or two went by before Mama answered him. "Everything."

Papa paused a moment, too, before he said, "If we do this, I don't think we can undo it."

"I know."

"We won't be able to get back here that often, Pauline. Not at first."

"I know that, too," Mama said. "If I can bring the girls back to see the family for a week or two in the summer, I can be content with that."

"I don't suppose your parents will be too keen about this. Especially your mother."

"No, maybe not. But you know how she is. She'll quietly stew on it a bit, and then she'll be done. I think in the end she wants us to be happy. I know that's what I'd want for us if I were her."

A funny, spirally feeling had started to wind its way inside me as my parents talked to each other. Papa and Mama were talking about moving to the city to live with Uncle Fred, a man I had only met once. He came out to Quakertown when Granny died. Not Mama's mama, Papa's. When I was eight.

Papa had said, "Are you sure now? Are you sure this is what you want to do?"

"It's what you want to do, isn't it?" Mama replied.

"It will mean a good life for you and the girls. A much better life than what I'm giving you here."

"You've given us a good life, Tom," Mama said.

"I want to give you a better one."

Then Papa said he needed to tell Grandad and break the news to the family and they'd need to sell the house. They talked for a few more minutes, but I wasn't listening to everything they said. I was thinking about leaving my friends and the other family members and the curing barn. I couldn't remember what Uncle Fred's business was, but I was positive it wasn't growing tobacco and rolling cigars. Not in the city. It was so strange to me that my parents could just decide we were leaving and we'd leave. How could we move away from where we'd buried Henry?

When Mama left, I stood up slowly so that I would see Papa before he saw me. But he was looking my direction and he saw my head clear the laths. I'm not afraid of my father. He doesn't yell or curse or storm about when he's angry, but he can look like he wants to. He's tall like Grandad and has the same coffee brown eyes that glitter like stars both when he's happy and when he's sad. And I guess when he's surprised, too.

"I didn't know you were still in here," he said.

"I know."

"Did you hear everything?"

I nodded.

He gave me a very serious look. "You can't say anything to anybody, not even your sisters, until I talk to Grandad first. You understand?"

"Are we moving to Philadelphia?"

He hesitated a second or two before answering, like he almost couldn't believe it was true himself. "Yes," he said.

"Why? What's wrong with where we live right now?"

Papa moved from his row to mine.

21

"There's nothing wrong with where we live right now. I just have a chance to give you girls a much better home. Better schooling. Better everything. My uncle Fred doesn't have any children. He has no one to leave his home and business to. He wants to leave them to me when he dies. To us. He has a very nice house, Mags. Electric lights in every room. Hot water from the tap."

"And so just like that, we're going?"

"Mama and I've been thinking on it awhile."

"All my friends are here."

"You will make new ones. I promise you will."

"Henry's here." My throat felt hot and thick as I said Henry's name. I looked away from Papa, and in the direction of the cemetery, even though I couldn't see it from inside the curing barn.

Papa put his hands gently on my shoulders so that I would turn my head to face him again. "Henry's in heaven. He's not in the graveyard here — you know that. We're not leaving him; we're taking him with us in our hearts."

I reached up to flick away a couple tears that wanted to trail down my face.

"I need you to promise you won't say anything. Not yet," Papa said.

I didn't answer.

"Maggie, I want your word now."

"I promise," I finally whispered.

"All right, then." He took one hand off my shoulders, but left the other one as he began to lead us toward the big door that led outside. "When I tell your sisters, that's when you'll know it's okay to tell other people. Not until then."

"When will we leave?"

"I imagine it will be soon. A couple weeks. Maybe less."

And then I said, "What about the African butterflies in Allentown I've been saving for?"

I don't know why I said that. I don't truly care about those butterflies. I just saw them once under glass in a gift store, and it seemed like I should have something in mind to spend my rolling money on. And they were so pretty. When I first told Evie that was what I was going to buy when I'd saved enough, she said, "So, you know those butterflies are dead, don't you? Somebody killed them to put them on display like that." Leave it to Evie to state the terribly obvious and make you wish for a second you were Willa's age and knew nothing about anything. Evie must have felt bad about saying that, because a couple days later she told me butterflies only live a couple months anyway and not to worry too much about it.

We reached the barn door, and Papa opened it. "There are butterflies in display boxes in Philadelphia, Maggie. Far more than what's in Allentown. They have everything in Philadelphia. Everything. Wait and see."

I would have stayed in the barn awhile to ponder this move to the city, but Papa closed the door tight behind us and set off for Grandad's house next door. I went back home to the room I share with my sisters so that I could start imagining what it would be like to leave it.

When Henry died, I'd found out how fast things can change. You think you have a view of what's waiting for you just up the road, but then something happens, and you find out pretty quick you were looking at the wrong road.

CHAPTER 3

Willa

This is what I am taking to Philadelphia.

My clothes.

My dolls.

My hair ribbons.

My cigar box of pennies.

The good-bye pictures my friends Hazel and Grace drew for me.

And Henry's little rocking horse rattle that Mama said I could keep even though I'm not a baby. I'm nearly seven.

I am not bringing my bed or the chifforobe I share with Maggie, because Uncle Fred already has all the furniture we need.

We had a big get-together at Grandpa and Grandma Adler's house yesterday after church. Grandad and all the aunts and uncles and cousins came to say good-bye, and they all brought something to eat. Everyone said they were so sad to see us go.

After dessert, the uncles and older boy

cousins got out some of Grandad's best cigars, and all the men smoked them. Uncle Walt told Papa that he needed to buy a nice, new tape measure — at least six feet — and a long black coat and hat. And the men laughed like it was a very funny joke.

"You're going to miss this," Uncle Vernon said, puffing on his cigar. Like maybe they don't have cigars in Philadelphia.

I think he's wrong about that. Maggie told me they have everything in the city.

The train is coming toward us now, whistling and huffing as we stand on the platform. I grab Evie's hand, and I remind her that I want to sit by the window. I want to watch the outside zip past like it's trying to catch us and take us back to where we used to be.

CHAPTER 4

Evelyn

I've been on this train once before, when Mama and I took Henry to see a special doctor. Until that day I'd never seen streets that stretched as far as the eye could see or endless rooftops that tiled their way to the edge of the skyline or so many people on the sidewalk that your elbows touched when you passed one another. I had never ridden a streetcar or seen a building twenty stories high or gone for a whole afternoon without seeing a patch of grass.

I remember thinking as we stepped off the platform that Philadelphia was so modern and big that there had to be a hundred doctors who could figure out why Henry was sick. I wasn't wrong. That special doctor told Mama just an hour after we met him that something was amiss with Henry's heart. Just like that, the city doctor knew what was wrong. He also knew there was nothing he or anybody else could do to fix it. What Henry needed was a new heart, that doctor said, as if all we had to do was step across the boulevard to Wanamaker's Department Store and pick one out. The doctor didn't even seem that startled by his diagnosis. He was sad for us, but he wasn't surprised. Answers to big questions are so plentiful in the city that nobody is astounded by them.

You'd think I would have hated the city after that day. But it wasn't long after that train trip — even before Henry died — that I started wishing I could always live in a place where all the answers are, even the answers I don't like hearing.

In Philadelphia, I'll be able to go to a good school, and college if I want to. There's a library the size of a cathedral that I'll be able to walk to every day but Christmas, and I won't have to spend long afternoons smoothing out tobacco leaves anymore. When Papa told me these things, it was the first moment since Henry died that I felt that warm jolt of joy that comes when something good happens.

I look at my parents now across the aisle from me as the train chugs along. Papa is clearly happy. And Mama? She seems to be in a state of dreaming. Henry died in her arms and she wept for days, just like we all did. But then one day she came home from visiting his grave and she was different. She was able to sleep at nights again, and cook the meals, and read Willa bedtime stories. She does all the things she used to do, but she's not the exact same person she was before.

Maybe this is what losing a child does to you. It peels off the top layer of who you are, like a snake shedding its skin, and underneath is new skin, and because it's new, it's not the same. I don't mind that she's not curled up in her bed anymore, wrapped up in sorrow, but it's strange to me that she *wants* to live above a funeral parlor and be the wife of an undertaker.

I'm not like her. I didn't get new skin. Underneath my clothes I am still the same girl who wants to know why every feature about my baby brother was perfect except for the one thing he couldn't live without.

I want to know a lot of things.

Quakertown is falling away behind us now.

I feel like a new world is opening up to me. Scary and wonderful and amazing and fearsome. Maybe my skin is waiting for me there, in the city, in the place where answers abound.

CHAPTER 5

Pauline

Philadelphia has always been that faraway city at the end of a long road — distant and unknowable. It's a place where I would occasionally step out of my everyday life to see a show or buy a wedding dress or bring a sick baby and then I'd step back.

Even as the five of us emerge from the train station onto the very same sidewalk where I'd stood a few months earlier, holding Henry in my arms, I'm struck by how immensely foreign the city's smells and sights and sounds are to me.

I'm not thinking we shouldn't have come, but I am overcome by the sensation that we Brights will never be from here. Fifty years from now, when I am an old woman who hasn't been back to Quakertown in years, I will still feel like an outsider. We are to be lifelong strangers to each other, this city and I.

This is what I'm thinking as I get into the backseat of Uncle Fred's Overland, a shining beetle black automobile that he's only had for a week. He didn't want to collect us from the station in the funeral coach — thank the good Lord — and his Model T was too small for what is now to be a family of six, he says.

A family of six.

So, he told us, he sold the T and bought the Overland touring car, as though we needed any kind of explanation. He relays all this as he maneuvers his way into the commotion of just another busy day in the city. Willa, on Thomas's lap in the front seat with her blond mop of curls springing to and fro, clings to him as Uncle Fred wildly negotiates the streets teeming with other autos, streetcars, horses, and buggies, as well as people. Maggie, with sandy brunet hair like Thomas's, stares out a window that is half-fogged with our breath, and with the same wide-eyed expression I see on Willa's face. Evie, golden-haired like Willa, but with far fewer coils and twists, is less astonished, as she came with me and the baby to see that specialist, but she's never ridden in an automobile as fine as this one, and amid an endless stream of other vehicles all wanting the same bit of road. Fred is an old man at seventy-two, but he winds through the streets as though he's been driving an automobile all his life, jauntily and repeatedly pressing the horn if a peddler or cart or pedestrian strays perilously close to the lanes of traffic, and all without losing his place in his narration.

Fred's house, he tells us, was built in 1885 and was a banker's home. The banker and his family had only lived there for a year when he was offered a prestigious position at a bank out west. At the time, Fred worked for an undertaker across town whose family had started out in the furniture-making business as so many undertakers had, but he was ready to strike out on his own. He convinced a wealthy friend to lend him the money to buy the banker's house, and he opened Bright Funeral Home. He was one of the first in the city to offer funeral and embalming services at his place of business, rather than making house calls to the homes of the deceased. It isn't always convenient to prepare the dead at home or lay them out afterward, especially when the houses and living quarters in the city are small. Fred arranged a lovely and spacious ground-floor parlor for viewing, and for embalming to take place privately in one of his back rooms, rather than at the deceased's bedside. The business had thrived and Fred was able to pay back his friend within three years' time. That he had done so well was only partially due to his smarts as a businessman, Fred says. There are always people needing an undertaker, even in the best of times.

It seems we've no sooner gotten ourselves settled inside the Overland than the three-storied house comes into view. The main entrance is on a corner of Chestnut Street — a long, busy boulevard with tall buildings, storefronts, and other homes on both sides. A secondary entrance is located around the side of the house on a slightly less active street.

The house is dove gray stone with trim the color of cream turning to butter. Scrollwork and carvings the shade of a ripe rhubarb stalk decorate the dormers and topmost gables, and stained-glass transoms in the upper-story windows glisten like gemstones. If it had been in the open countryside instead of mere feet away from the apartment building next to it, the house surely would have had a wraparound porch that frothed with forsythia and beds of hyacinth and crocus in the springtime. The building next to it is so close, there is nary room for a person to pass in between them.

As I look up at it from the car window, it is the most elegant house I've ever seen, even set against a colorless sky that hints of snow.

We turn the corner onto the side street and into a carriage shelter that sits behind the house. Fred parks the Overland next to an even blacker Cadillac, which seems as long as a city block. The funeral coach. As we get out of the Overland, I can see that the second entrance to the house has a smaller stoop than the front but a wider doorway. It is an odd shape, this second doorway, and I realize this is where the bodies are carted inside and caskets rolled out.

The driver he'd paid to bring our cases and trunks from the train station pulls into the side yard, too, and Uncle Fred tells him to unload everything on the back stoop. He explains that he has a boy from across the street coming to haul them upstairs at the noon hour.

"Let's go around to the front, then," Uncle Fred says when we are all out of the car. "That's a better entrance for Pauline and the girls, and I'd actually prefer you ladies use that one."

Uncle Fred says this kindly enough. He is, in fact, a genial man. I've met him only twice before; he came to Quakertown for

Thomas's and my wedding, and he came again some years later when Thomas's mother died. I could tell both times that he dotes on Thomas, and Thomas has always spoken tenderly of his uncle. I think by the time Thomas came along, Fred figured he would never marry, and he decided he'd heap any affections he might have had for a family of his own on his brother's youngest child. As I see the two of them now walking side by side, there is a resemblance between uncle and nephew that I had not fully appreciated until today. Both have high cheekbones, a slender nose, and coffee brown eyes, just like Thomas's father, Eli — Fred's younger brother — has. Fred is slightly taller than Thomas and Eli but not by much. My husband could easily pass as Fred's own offspring, and that must be a comfort to Fred now that he is in his twilight years. Thomas is a fair representative of what could have been had Fred married and fathered a son. Eli said as much to Thomas when he told his father we were leaving. Though he would miss us, Eli was happy not only for us, but also for his older brother, Fred, who would live out his remaining years with family all around him.

I'd always been able to picture Fred expertly handling the delicate affairs of the bereaved with his low, comforting voice and a gray beard that is more curls than wires. Yet now I see by the way he said what he did about the two doors that despite his affection for Thomas, he thought long and hard about offering his nephew this position. Fred had decided that while his house is indeed going to be our new home, there will be restrictions for the girls and me with regard to the business. The bit about the doors is perhaps just the first one to be mentioned. As we follow him to the front of the house, I sense within me an immediate uneasiness about these restrictions. Fred wants to isolate the girls and me from the necessities and peculiarities of his job. I want the girls to have that kind of protection, of course, but I myself don't want it. I can't have it. The main reason I have come here is to shuffle Death back to the place where it belongs. That won't happen if I never get to tangle with it. I must find a way to insert myself into the goings-on at the back of the house.

Six marble steps lead from the boulevard's sidewalk to the entrance. A gilded sign fringed with tiny icicles and bearing the inscription *Bright Funeral Home, Frederick Bright, Proprietor* hangs on a brass plate from the stoop's roof, which is a decorated affair with more of the rhubarb-colored curlicues and carvings. Just below Fred's name are the words *Deliveries to the Rear.*

We step over the front door's threshold into a foyer with a high ceiling, electric lights, a slightly faded wool carpet, and woodwork free of dust but in need of polish. A staircase carpeted in a deep scarlet leads to the second story. Double-door entrances to larger rooms beckon on either side. The foyer is warm despite the chill of the day.

"The rooms here on the right side are private, just for us," Fred said. "And all the rooms upstairs are yours."

He motions us to a sitting room on the right with upholstered sofas and armchairs in celery green, sturdy oak bookshelves that Evelyn takes immediate interest in, a fireplace framed in marble and wood, lamps with cut-glass shades and etched metal pedestals, and a game table with a jigsaw puzzle of an African plain half-done in the corner by the window. A phonograph with an enormous fluted horn sits in the back on a carved table next to an upright piano. The room is clean but void of any decoration, save for a ballet figurine made of porcelain that sits on an end table. I wonder if Fred hired someone thirty-two years ago to purchase all the furniture and accessories and to place the pieces in the room and then he just left them that way. He had no doubt done the same when the house was wired for electricity. Someone else chose the lamps, arranged them in the house, and he'd simply paid for them.

On the other side of the staircase is a little hallway that leads to Fred's office and bedroom and a little privy, all of which he says we've no need to trouble ourselves with, not even the privy, as there is a very nicely appointed bathroom upstairs. His housekeeper, Mrs. Landry, takes care of these rooms as well as the rest of the house, he says.

We make our way into the dining room next, which is dusted and free of cobwebs, but boxes and books and stacks of newspapers clutter the corners and chair seats and even the dining table. There is no place to sit and eat a meal.

"Does Mrs. Landry also take care of this room?" I ask, and Thomas shoots me a look. I don't care. If we are to live here, we need a table at which to dine. Any family of six would.

Fred views the room for perhaps the first time in a long while. "Oh. I've been having League meetings in here. But I can move all that to my office."

"League meetings?" I say.

"I serve in the APL. My chapter meets here sometimes." Uncle Fred starts for the doorway to the kitchen.

"What's the APL?" Evelyn asks, ever the inquisitive one.

Fred turns to us countryfolk with a raised eyebrow. "The American Protective League, of course. We keep an eye out for German sympathizers, slackers, shows of antipatriotism. That sort of thing. It's important work." He starts to turn back around as though that is all the answer anyone should ever need about his volunteer work with the League.

Maggie tugs on Thomas's sleeve. "A German what?" she asks softly.

"Sympathizer. It's someone who sides with Germany about the war," Thomas says, but Fred apparently doesn't think that is enough of an answer.

"It's someone who is in league with the enemy!" Fred announces, with a triumphant nod.

I wonder if Fred is aware my grandparents emigrated from Germany. Would he send us back to Quakertown if he knew? I can still hear in my memory my grandmother singing *"Der Mond ist aufgegangen"* to me on

39

the nights I couldn't sleep.

Fred leads us into the kitchen. It is a colorless albeit functional room with hot and cold taps above a white ceramic sink and an icebox twice the size of what I had in Quakertown. A narrow pine table with four ladder-back chairs with woven seats sits in the center of the room on a tiled floor of black and white squares. Against the far wall is a shining Universal cookstove all piped for gas. All one has to do is light a match and turn a knob. Quite a change from the woodstove I'd always cooked on before.

"The stove is new," Fred says. "Mrs. Landry has put a pot of soup on for our dinner." He nods toward the appliance, where something bubbles on one of the burners.

I'd failed to consider that Uncle Fred would have a housekeeper. I haven't even met Mrs. Landry yet, and I already want her gone. I will never be comfortable with another woman doing for me and my family what I am perfectly capable of doing myself. But I promised Thomas that I wouldn't right away ask Fred to change anything about the way he lives.

"He's been alone for a long time," Thomas had said. "He's going to be set in his ways."

But who of us isn't set in his ways? I am also set in my ways. Everyone is. I bite my tongue so I won't speak when next Fred shows us the pantry, a mishmash of cans and jars and sacks and containers. A spider scuttles across the pantry floor, and Fred brings his booted foot down gently on top of it.

"Now, then," Fred says, and he sweeps his gaze over the girls. "Past the kitchen here and down that hallway is the business. That's just for me and your papa. You won't be needing to go into that part of the house."

I open my mouth to protest, and Thomas touches my arm. "Pauline and I would like the girls to see how the rooms are laid out so they know what they're like. They'll be curious otherwise. And if there's ever a fire and they can't get to the front door, I want them to know how to get to the side door."

Fred needs to contemplate this for a moment. And then it seems to suddenly occur to him that his favorite nephew is right. "Well. That makes sense. And now that I think on it, it's all right if they are in the viewing room when it's not being used. But it's not a playroom. None of these rooms are."

Maggie looks up at me and rolls her eyes.

I put a finger to my lips.

Fred takes us down a hallway that leads from the kitchen to the rest of the left side of the house — formerly the cook's and maids' quarters from the days of the banker and his family. The first door on the left opens to a viewing parlor. It's carpeted and wallpapered in hushed shades of wine and evergreen. Cushioned chairs line the walls, but I can easily picture them in rows facing the front window, where a treatment of lace and heavy brocade softens the light that spills on an open space just the right size for a coffin.

"I meet with the families in here," Fred says. "And if folks can't have the funeral or viewing in their home, they have it here. You older girls might be able to help with flowers and chairs and such on those days," he says to Evie and Maggie. "But the little one will need to stay in the other part of the house when there are people in here."

Fred looks to Willa with grandfatherly concern when he says this. I assure him she will cause him no trouble. Willa tosses me a look that tells me she's not "the little one." Again I put a finger to my lips.

The next door on the same side of the hallway opens to a room of caskets of different sizes and woods. The sight of them

— the first visible evidence of what is done inside this house — makes me shudder a bit.

"Families do the choosing in there," Fred says, stopping just at the doorway.

"Are those for sleeping?" Willa asks.

"They aren't beds, Willa," Maggie answers, though the question was directed to Fred.

"Now, you don't want to go climbing in those, little one. You could get hurt," Fred replies solemnly. "Those are caskets and the lids are very heavy."

"I'll explain it to her later," Thomas says.

Fred nods and we move on. Just before the mudroom and the side entrance is the third door in the hallway, this one on the right side. It's closed nearly all the way, but not quite. Through the crack, I can see a body lies on a table of some kind. I can see the stocking-covered ball of a woman's heel and the piped edge of a skirt. A peculiar odor is seeping out from the opening between door and frame.

"Now, this room is off-limits except to your papa and me. And Mrs. Brewster. This is the embalming room, and there are chemicals and such that aren't safe for you girls to be around." Fred says this in what I'm sure he imagines is a tone of paternal caution, but I can tell he is serious. I am frustrated by that seriousness, for this is the room that interests me most. It's not like the others.

I know only in part what Thomas will be doing inside it. We talked about the embalming room in the days before we came here. Thomas told me he'd visited his uncle a few times when he was younger, long before we married, and that he'd been rather fascinated by Fred's work with the dead, as perhaps only a boy could be. He hadn't had to explain in detail what he meant. I'd noticed this about my nephews as I watched them grow up. The carcass of a possum or raccoon in the road, for example, was a magnet for their attention as it decayed or was picked apart by birds. Their sisters and my girls, by comparison, would walk past with their eyes scrunched shut, noses covered. But I'd gathered from watching the nephews — not just with animals killed in the road but with a deer in someone's side yard being butchered, or a hooked fish on a line gasping for one last breath — that most boys aren't afraid to look at what death does.

I hadn't had time to ponder if my sweet Henry would have been a boy like this, heartily curious about what happens to the body when life ends. But I'd thought about it then, when I asked Thomas how he would feel about working on cadavers that had been grotesquely mangled in some way. He'd answered that he'd learn to bear it because it was a small price to pay to give us the kind of life that would now be ours. I'd wondered then if Henry would have wanted to poke at the dead raccoons and possums and peek at the little organs laid bare by tractor tires. Would he have tried to scare his sisters with them, as his boy cousins liked to do? Would he have kept coming back to the carcass as it swelled and then withered into an unrecognizable lump in the road? It surprised me to realize in that moment that I didn't mind if Henry would have been a boy like most boys. Or that he would have been Thomas's assistant when he grew up and then heir to the funeral home just like his father had been. Someone must be able to gaze on the breadth of what makes us mortal, yes? Someone has to.

Thomas had taken my silence at his answer as worry that the girls and I might somehow be exposed to those terrible cases that he would learn to bear. "You and the girls won't ever have to know what I've seen or had to do. I won't bring any part of the work into the rest of the house. I promise you that, Polly."

"All right," I'd said absently, still ruminating on thoughts of Henry and the man he might have been.

"Good," Thomas had said. "I don't want you or the girls to be afraid of anything in the house where we will be living. Especially the girls. I'll find a way to make sure they feel comfortable with what I'll be doing."

And then our conversation was interrupted by a knock at the door and another farewell that needed to be received and given.

Fred is about to say something else about the embalming room when the door suddenly opens all the way, startling us. An older woman emerges from the room, holding a basket of shears and combs and curling rods. Her expression at seeing us is as surprised as ours surely are. Behind her is the dead woman on the table, now fully visible in a midnight blue gown, as if dressed for a formal engagement. The deceased's face, the half that we can see, looks serene but slack. Her brown-gray hair has been brushed and styled and the locks gathered with hairpins. Her hands are folded across her bosom, one hand over the other. Her left hand is raised a bit like she wants to alert Mrs. Brewster to a forgotten detail. The wrist looks stiff and unyielding.

I take all this in even before I hear Maggie and Evie suck in their breath in surprise. Willa asks me what that other lady is doing in there.

"Mrs. Brewster!" Fred exclaims. "You were to come this afternoon."

"I didn't know you were back already," the woman explains, clearly flustered. "I decided to come now, as I've company coming for supper tonight."

Fred pushes past Mrs. Brewster to close the door behind her, but Thomas stops him with a gentle hand.

"I don't mind if the girls see," Thomas says. "Just here from the threshold. Just this once. I want them to know they don't need to be afraid of what's in this room."

"They can't be allowed in there!"

"Of course. I just want them to see what's inside."

Uncle Fred blinks at Thomas, apparently wondering how that is a good idea. Mrs. Brewster has the same dumbfounded look on her face. Thomas uses those seconds of stunned silence to open the door fully.

"You see?" Thomas says to the girls. "Nothing in here to be afraid of. It's just like I told you."

We peer into the room as Uncle Fred pulls Mrs. Brewster aside and mutters that he specifically told her not to come until after three and that he's tired of her deciding at the last minute to come at a time he isn't expecting her.

My girls saw Henry's body after he died, but, when everyone came to pay their respects, he'd been wrapped up cozy in the blanket I'd made for him. He'd looked as though he were only sleeping. This woman is utterly different. She lies like a mannequin on a strange kind of table. Around her are metal cabinets and carts bearing odd items. On the walls are fixtures and devices on hooks and poles. None of it is familiar, nor can I imagine what any of it is for. The woman doesn't look scary, but she doesn't look right, either. I'm not put off by her. My spectral companion for the last six months hovers near me, quiet and accommodating. I want to go inside that room, and I'm annoyed that Fred doesn't want the girls or me anywhere near it. And I wished I'd told Thomas, when we were talking about what he'd be doing in this room, that he didn't have to worry about me being afraid in the least. I wasn't. I'm not.

My daughters say nothing as we stand there, each silently contemplating in her own way the idea that the woman on the table is no longer living.

Mrs. Brewster did a fair job with the hair and cosmetics, but even from a bit of a distance, I can see that I could have done better on both. As Thomas closes the door with a gentle admonition that the girls obey Uncle Fred's rule regarding this room, it occurs to me that if I were the one doing the hair and cosmetics on the bodies, Uncle Fred wouldn't have to pay the errant Mrs. Brewster to do it. That task would get me into that room.

We head back into the main part of the house, to the staircase and our bedrooms. Upstairs, we find new, sturdy four-poster beds and bureaus and wardrobes of polished but plain cherrywood awaiting us. It is obvious that Fred values quality; he'd deemed it necessary that we have new bedroom furniture, and clearly he was willing to spend the money. But the furniture is unadorned, functional rather than decorative. I get the distinct impression that Fred isn't a miser with his money, but he's not a spendthrift, either.

If I can do for free what troublesome Mrs. Brewster is doing for a fee, and do it better than her, Uncle Fred will win on both counts. All I need to do is tell Thomas that

I want to do the hairstyling and cosmetics. I'd be good at it, I'd like to do it, and it would save him and Fred the expense of hiring someone to perform those tasks. And I'll do the work when it is supposed to be done rather than when the timing suits me. Fred surely already trusts Thomas's judgment. It's the reason we are here. When Thomas makes this recommendation, it will seem like a fine idea from his favorite nephew and newly appointed heir.

Mrs. Landry, the housekeeper, I will suffer to keep a little while longer if I must, but there again I know I have frugality on my side. One way or another, both Mrs. Brewster and Mrs. Landry will be thanked and paid and sent on their way.

This is my home now. And there are things I need to do.

CHAPTER 6

Maggie

I am standing in my new room, looking at the new furniture, when I hear the heavy footfalls of boots on the stairs and the clunky sound of something big being carried up them. We've been inside the house since we arrived, and I still feel like I'm dreaming, that this is someone else's home, and I am watching someone else's life play out upon a stage. I turn from the unfamiliar bedstead that glistens with fresh varnish to face the open doorway. I see my trunk is being hauled up the narrow stairs. Uncle Fred said the boy from the bookkeeper's across the street was coming at noon to take up our belongings, but instead of a boy, I see a young man. He is Evie's age, or perhaps a little older.

"This one yours?" he says, half out of breath. He is blond, gray-eyed, and a bit chubby, and beads of sweat sparkle on his brow. He has a nice smile.

I nod toward the trunk he's got with him. I had my choice of rooming with Willa or with Evie, but I asked if I could have my own place on the third floor. Uncle Fred apparently had thought that was an odd idea, but Mama had come to my rescue and said if she were me, she'd want to have her own little space, too. She told me I could take an attic room if Fred could be persuaded to agree, which he did. Mine is a wide, long room with a pitched ceiling and two dormer windows. Opposite my room and on either side of the little landing at the top of the attic stairs are two long, skinny spaces with little doors that look like they were built for elves. One of the spaces is filled with box after box of funeral records. The other is crammed with crates and steamer trunks and extra dining room chairs. But the rest of the attic floor is all mine.

The man-boy struggles on the landing with the trunk despite his size and strength. I help him finagle the trunk through the narrow doorway.

"Thanks," he says as we maneuver the trunk inside and by the bed. "You want to empty it now? I was told to bring it back down to the carriage house when you're done with it. Your mother and sisters are unpacking theirs."

"I guess." I reach down to unlatch the closures.

"I'm Charlie," he says. "Charlie Sutcliff. I live across the street. But I work for Fred Bright."

There is something odd about the way he tells me who he is. His words and voice and even his expression make him seem like he's Willa's age, but his body is one that's much older.

"My name's Maggie," I reply.

"I know. I remembered. Evelyn, Maggie, and Willa. And Mrs. Bright and Mr. Bright. But you call Evelyn Evie."

I give him a sideways glance as I open the trunk and start to pull out my things. I toss my clothes and quilt and a doll that was my mother's onto the bed. Then I grab the books and shoes and my hatboxes of ribbons and half-finished needlepoint projects and place them on the floor. Charlie helps me with some of these. Lastly, I pull out the painting of a sailing ship on a green-blue sea that was Grandad's and that he gave me when we were getting ready to move because he knew I'd always liked it. The ship is pointed toward a faraway horizon, and little waves are curling up its sides like bits of lace.

"I like that ship!" Charlie says, as if he were my eight-year-old cousin Liam back home in Quakertown.

"I do, too."

"Have you been to Hog Island? It's full of ships being built, not hogs. Navy ships. Big ones. They're for the war. They're huge. Have you been there? To Hog Island?"

I have no idea what he's talking about. "We just got here today."

"You should go. Jamie takes me there sometimes. To see the ships. Jamie likes trains better than ships, but he takes me there sometimes because I like ships."

"Who's Jamie?"

"He's my brother. He likes trains. But they don't have trains for war. Only ships. He's not going to the navy. He doesn't like ships. He's going to the army. But not until April. In April, he'll go."

"Jamie is older than you?"

Charlie nods. "I'm sixteen. Jamie had a birthday. He's twenty-one now. He counts with my father in the office. But in April, he'll go to the army."

"He counts?"

"You know. One. Two. Three. They count."

"He's a bookkeeper like your dad?"

"Sure."

The entire time Charlie is talking to me, he's picking up each one of my books and studying their spines. It's like he's not reading the spines, but rather just admiring the gold and silver and ebony lettering. I don't have near the books that Evie has, but I have some. *Rebecca of Sunnybrook Farm,* and the *Just So Stories,* and *The Wind in the Willows,* and *The Wonderful Wizard of Oz,* and a few others.

"You like to read?" I ask.

Charlie puts down the book he's looking at. It's *Five Children and It* by E. Nesbit. It's one of my favorites. It's about these children who find a sand fairy who grants them a wish a day. You'd think that would be wonderful, right? But when those children get what they truly want every day, trouble starts to pop up all over the place.

"You can borrow that one if you want," I tell him. "It's a good book."

Charlie shakes his head. "I'm not good at reading. I don't do the counting good, either. I work for Fred."

He looks at the book with what seems to me to be longing, despite what he just told me. "Go ahead and borrow it," I say. "The more you read, the better you'll get at it, you know."

Charlie picks up the book and turns to the first page. He has a puzzled look on his face, as if the words on the page are written in another language.

"Where do you go to school, Charlie?"

"Oh. I don't go to school anymore. No. I just work for Fred."

I can see how much he wants to be able to read those words. I feel sorry for him. To be sixteen and unable to read! If Evie were in the room, she'd probably burst into tears. I wonder how his parents could've failed him so miserably.

"Here." I pull the book from his hands; shove my pile of clothes, the doll, and the quilt to one side; and pat the bed. "Have a seat."

I sit down and wait for him. He just stands there.

I pat the mattress again. "Sit down. I'll help you get started."

He finally ambles over to me and sits down beside me. He has the most amazed look on his face, like *I* am the sand fairy about to grant him his wish for the day.

I open the book and point to the first word of the first chapter. "Can you read that?"

He smiles shyly and shakes his head.

"Sure you can. You did go to school, didn't you?"

"I work for Fred now."

"Yes, I know that. But when you were a little boy, you went to school, right? And your teacher taught you your letters?"

His grin spreads wide. "I do know my letters."

"Well. See? Words are just letters put together. If you know your letters, you can learn the words. And if you can learn the words, you can read. Here. I'll show you."

He and I pore over that first page, sounding out every word at a wretchedly slow pace. I don't know how long we are absorbed in the task. Long enough for him to be missed downstairs, I guess. Because next thing I know, there is someone else in the room — a young man with wavy brown hair, slate blue eyes, and Charlie's kind features. But this man is thinner. Taller. He is smiling down on me, and for a second I feel like all the clocks in all the world have stopped. Our eyes catch each other's, and it's a breath or two before the world starts turning again.

"Well, here you are, Charlie. We were all wondering where you were," the young man says. "Time to head back home."

"She was reading," Charlie says.

"*You* were reading." I close the book and put it in his lap. "Take it with you. Keep it

57

as long as you like."

Charlie is beaming as he stands up.

I stand up, too. The man steps forward. "How do you do? I'm Charlie's brother, Jamie," he says.

I start to answer with my own name, but Charlie fills the tiny space of silence. "This one's Maggie. Evelyn and Willa are the other two. Sometimes people call Evelyn Evie."

Jamie tips his head toward me. "A pleasure to meet you, Maggie."

I want to say something in return, anything, but my tongue seems tied up in knots.

Charlie puts the book in the crook of his arm, closes the lid on my empty trunk, and starts to drag it to the door. "Thanks for letting me borrow the book, Maggie!"

"Let me help you with that." Jamie bends to grab the other end of the trunk as Charlie hoists it over the threshold.

"Nah. I got it. It's empty now. I got it. Here, you can carry Maggie's book for me."

Jamie takes the book and then steps away to let his brother do his job. It appears to be one thing Charlie can do, and he wants to do it.

When Charlie is on the first step, Jamie turns back to me.

"That was nice, what you did for my

brother," he says softly, looking at the book in his hands and then at me.

"Pardon?" I've heard the words, but I can't make sense of them. I'm wondering just how long Jamie Sutcliff was standing there, watching us toiling over the words. The whole time?

"Not many people take the time to make him feel like he can try something new."

"Reading is new?"

"It is for him in a way."

"Why isn't he in school?"

"He went for as long as he could. He just can't retain what he learns from books and teachers. Not like you and I can. But today's the first time in I don't know how long that he even wanted to try reading a book again. So thanks. You're very kind."

Jamie turns to leave, and I find that I don't want him to.

"Wait. . . ."

Jamie pauses at the open doorway.

I search for a reason to have asked him to stop. "Um. Charlie says I should see Hog Island. He says you take him there sometimes."

Jamie smiles. "I do."

"So. Maybe . . ."

"You want to come with us next time we go?"

"Okay. Yes." I look away, embarrassed by how forward I've been. "It's just that, we just moved here and, well, I want to get to know the place."

"Sure." He turns, takes a step, and eases back around. "And I meant what I said. You were very kind to Charlie just now. I appreciate that."

He is on the third or fourth step and gone from my view before I can whisper the words *you're welcome.*

I'm alone in my room again, and my heart is beating like I've just run up the two flights of stairs to get to it. I can't explain why, but I feel like everything about my life is suddenly different. Not just the outside of it — like where I live now — but the inside of it as well. Something has begun deep within me.

I don't understand what it is. I just know I don't want it to stop, even though it scares me a little. I don't want to go back to where I was yesterday.

CHAPTER 7

February 1918
Evelyn

Everything in the city is different. The way we start our day and the way we end it, the way we eat our meals, the way we bathe and wash our clothes and say our prayers. Even the night sky seems different; because there are so many lights here, the stars are shy and shimmer less.

My school is not just a walk down a lane anymore; it is a brick building many blocks away, and I must take a streetcar to get there. It's a private academy that Uncle Fred is paying for because Papa told him I want to go to college and Uncle Fred says this school is the best. Maggie and Willa go to a different one closer to home, although Maggie can join me here next year if she wants to. I must wear a white high-collared blouse and the same dark blue skirt every day and my hair must be pulled up into a

61

neat pile on top of my head like I am already married. The boys wear vests and ties, and their hair must be slicked into place. The boys' classes are on the first floor and the girls' are on the third, and we are allowed to experiment with polite conduct toward one another on the second floor, where the dining and music and art rooms are.

On my first day, my classmates were most interested in where I'd come from and in which neighborhood I lived now and what my father did for a living. They hadn't heard of Quakertown and were thoroughly shocked when I answered that Papa is — I am still getting used to saying this — an undertaker. Maggie apparently had the same reaction at her school. Willa's new classmates don't care what someone's father does for work; they don't even ask.

My classmates allow me to keep to myself now that they all know where I live and what the family business is. There is a girl named Irene whose last name sounds German and who stays on the fringe like I do, but she and I have no interest in aligning ourselves with each other just because we are both apparently outsiders.

I like my new teachers. They are smart and they don't care what kind of work pays my tuition. Mr. Galway is especially brilliant. He is the teacher for social sciences and philosophy. He sees the other girls twittering like ducklings when I stand up to answer a question in class. He told me once, in front of all of them, that he is impressed with how thorough my answers are. If I didn't want to be a doctor, I'd want to be a philosophy teacher like Mr. Galway.

There is one boy named Gilbert Keane who is different than the rest. He told me in art class on the first day to pay the gossiping girls no mind when they had speculated among themselves if I would paint a cadaver instead of fruit in a bowl. Gilbert is handsome and well-liked at the school, and those girls were perplexed that he spoke to me so kindly. Their surprise at it occupied their whispers for the rest of the afternoon. The following day they all wanted to be my friend.

Gilbert's father expects him to go to law school and become an attorney, just like he is. But Gilbert wants to live in Manhattan and be a playwright. He showed me a few pages from one of his plays the other day. It's about a young man who buys an old house and then finds letters from a hundred years ago hidden in the attic. The man falls in love with the young woman who wrote them.

"But that woman is long since dead," I'd said. "It must be a very sad play."

He winked at me and said the dead woman has a beautiful great-granddaughter who is very much alive.

"But he will have to stop loving the one to love the other," I pointed out.

"With all great loves there is first a great struggle," Gilbert said, smiling as if he was quite happy with this cosmic arrangement.

I'm not sure I completely agree with him, and yet I can't stop thinking about what he said. Or him. Gilbert unsettles me. But in a nice way.

As for our new house, it is quite lovely from the outside. The inside is nice, too, but rather dull and lifeless, and I don't mean that as a comical reference to what Uncle Fred and Papa do in the rooms past the kitchen. My bedroom furniture is new and of exceptional quality, but it's plain. All the furniture downstairs is plainly functional, too, and at least thirty years old. The trouble with exceptional quality is that it takes a long time for it to wear out. We'll clearly live with these things forever.

The rugs and curtains are a bit faded. There's hardly any art on the walls. It all adds to the drab appearance of the house. But Uncle Fred does have a good selection of books, and not just on the art and science of embalming. On our second day here, I asked if I would be allowed to read them, and he seemed quite pleased that I wanted to, but then he cautioned me on the care and handling of his books, as if it were my current habit to lick my fingers and then dip them into the cocoa tin before turning a page. He found out soon enough that I love books and treat them with the respect they deserve. He'd come upstairs a week after we'd been there, to take a box of ledgers up to the attic storage room, and he'd seen the shelves of books just inside my bedroom door as he started to pass it.

He had stopped, the box of ledgers in his arms, and stared at them. "That's quite a collection of books you have," he'd said a second later, and I could tell it had suddenly made sense to him why I had been so interested in his bookshelves. We were both lovers of knowledge.

Uncle Fred had cocked his head as he looked at the spines, and it seemed to me he was looking at some of my books the way I had been looking at his.

"You're welcome to look at one anytime you want," I'd said, and he'd smiled. It was the kind of smile a father gives a child or an instructor gives a pupil. There was a measure of pride to it, as though he was happy that he was my great-uncle and I was his niece.

"That's very kind of you," he said. "I just may do that."

Today, when I was sitting at the little table in his office and looking at one of his books on anthropology, he came into the room, saw me there, and pulled out an enormous volume all about the human body. *Gray's Anatomy.*

"It's a marvel, what your body can do when it's alive," he said, running his hand over the front of the book. Then he leaned closer to me. "I, like you, wanted to be a doctor once." He whispered this like it was a secret just between us.

"What happened?" I asked.

He shrugged as though he didn't know what had come between him and his dreams. Or maybe he knew but it saddened him to talk about it. "It wasn't to be, for me. For a host of reasons. But you? You're smart. And you're young. And you're more than just the son of a poor tobacco farmer."

I hadn't considered too much to that point that Uncle Fred had been born and raised in Quakertown just like me. He was my grandad's older brother. He had grown up picking blossoms off tobacco plants and rolling cigars just like I had. But he'd come to the city decades before I had been born, and he'd come with a dream that had somehow been taken from him.

This was no doubt the reason why Uncle Fred was so willing to pay for me to enroll at the private school. I have the aspirations he'd once had. I wanted to say something then that communicated that I understood this, and that I was going to work very hard to accomplish my goal, but I couldn't think of how to say it without it sounding like I was going to succeed where he had failed.

He handed the heavy book to me. "My favorite section is neurology. There in the seven hundreds. You won't believe how stunning the nervous system is. Everything else fails without it. It's what makes you you. It's what makes you alive."

"I'll be careful with it," I said, nearly speechless with wonder and gratitude. "And I'll put it back where it was when I'm done with it."

He shook his head. "It's yours." And he left his office without getting whatever it was he'd come for, perhaps to recollect his thoughts or walk the house and funeral rooms and remind himself that he had done very well for himself despite the death of that dream.

I took the book up to my room.

I like having my own bedroom. Since there are electric lights in every room, I can stay up reading after Maggie and Willa have gone to bed. Willa is across the hall from me, and I can hear her singing to herself at night. I don't think she's overly happy having her own room. I told her she will feel differently in a few years. Maggie is one more flight up in one of the attic rooms and seems to feel the best thing about our move is that she now has the entire third floor to herself.

I asked Papa what Uncle Fred did with these rooms before we came, since there was only him in his house. Uncle Fred's housekeeper, a useless woman named Mrs. Landry who somehow makes everything she cooks taste like soap, doesn't live here, thank goodness. Papa said Uncle Fred had an assistant for several years, and that man lived here until he got married and moved away. Before that he rented out the rooms to single men, but he was always losing his tenants when those men met girls they wanted to impress. I doubt it was only that the girls didn't like their beaus sharing living quarters with corpses. No doubt Mrs.

Landry's cooking also had something to do with their leaving.

Mama has her sights on relieving Mrs. Landry of her duties. I would wager by this time next week she'll be gone. Mama also wants Mrs. Brewster, the hairstylist, to be given notice. I overheard her asking Papa if he might tell Uncle Fred that she could do what Mrs. Brewster does and that he wouldn't have to worry anymore about the work getting done at the wrong time, nor would he have to pay for it.

I know why Mama wants Mrs. Landry gone, but I don't know why Mama wants Mrs. Brewster's job, too. I can't ask her yet because I only overheard that conversation between my parents. I wasn't part of it. I don't want them to think I eavesdrop. But it's curious to me that Mama *wants* to be in that room where the dead are made ready for their burial. She wants to.

She seems happy to be here, but sometimes I will catch her staring off into the corner of the room, as though she is looking at a picture that isn't there. I will call to her, and sometimes I must do so three times before she will hear me. Papa is so busy trying to learn all that Uncle Fred knows, I don't think he has noticed Mama's odd behavior. Those times when I've had to

69

practically shake her to get her attention, I've asked her if she is all right, and she always says she's fine; she was just thinking.

"About what?" I asked once.

She smiled and said it was nothing I needed to be worried about.

I suppose she's missing Henry. What else could it be but that?

We have wonderful neighbors across the street. Roland Sutcliff is Uncle Fred's bookkeeper, but he's also a good friend. He and his wife, Dora, have two sons. The older one, Jamie, works with Mr. Sutcliff. Charlie is sixteen. He's a simpleminded but sweet young man who does odd jobs for Uncle Fred. Moving caskets, lifting heavy things, carting away rubbish, and that sort of thing. Jamie is slated to head off to Fort Meade for army training the first of April. Uncle Fred is very proud of Jamie and boasts about his patriotism as if he were his own child. Jamie turned twenty-one several months after the last mandated draft registration, but he volunteered to serve anyway. I guess all his friends are already off doing their part, or so I overheard him telling Maggie and Papa.

Uncle Fred is very proud of all his friends' sons who are off fighting in the war, and there are a lot of them. Every other merchant on our block is Fred's acquaintance, and it seems each one has a son either already in Europe or training to go or who has registered for the draft and will likely be called up any day. Uncle Fred reads the newspaper in our sitting room every evening, puffing on his pipe like he's a locomotive, and relaying to Papa and Mama every despicable thing the Kaiser has done, is doing, and will do if we don't stop him. Uncle Fred's American Protective League alerts the authorities when they find people loyal to Germany or who are unpatriotic about the war or who were supposed to sign up for the draft but haven't. Slackers, Uncle Fred calls them.

I'd like to ask him why we even need the APL, but I suppose I'll have to do what I always do, and that's figure things out by myself. There are plenty of books and newspapers and magazines that will tell me what I want to know. I'll find out on my own what the APL is about just like I figured out easily enough what Uncle Fred has been teaching Papa in the embalming room behind that forbidden door.

All of Uncle Fred's books on undertaking are lined up like soldiers on the bookshelves in his office. It isn't that hard to understand how something works. You just need to know which book to open and read the words inside it.

He also has a book called *Lepidoptera,* and the pages inside are filled with exquisite color drawings of butterflies. Seeing the book the first time reminded me that Maggie had once wanted a set of mounted butterflies under glass that she'd seen in a store in Allentown. She told me about them right after we'd found out Henry would not get better. I told her the butterflies are killed to be put on display like that. It was a cruel thing to say, and she looked so sad, so disappointed. I went back to her a couple days later and told her butterflies don't live very long anyway. And that I was sorry I had been so harsh to say what I had. She's never mentioned them again.

I don't know if I will show Maggie that book. So much has changed since Henry died. I hope she still thinks butterflies are beautiful. I think they are. We shouldn't think for a moment that just because their lives are short they shouldn't be here.

CHAPTER 8

Maggie

I'm not afraid to see a dead body up close.

That's not the reason I have waited until the embalming room is empty before sneaking inside it. I already saw that first body the day we got here, and then another one in the viewing room a week later, and another one the week after that.

Charlie asked me a couple days ago if I knew there were dead people in our funeral home. When I answered, "Of course," he asked me if I was afraid of them. It was almost a surprise to me to tell him I wasn't. I hadn't thought about it before, but I'm not afraid of them. I don't want to see a bloody, torn-up one, but I'm not scared of the ones that are just lying there. I could tell by the way Charlie asked that he is a bit afraid. I'd wondered if Jamie would be afraid of them, too. Probably not.

"Sometimes I have to help Fred move

them," Charlie had said. "Before your papa came here, I helped him a lot. If Fred had a heavy one, I had to come help him move it. I was afraid the dead man would reach up, grab me around the throat, and thrash me."

"You know they can't do that, right, Charlie?" I'd said. "You know dead people can't do anything."

"But they look like they can."

When he said this, that was when I decided I wanted to know what Uncle Fred and Papa actually do to dead people to make them look like they're still alive. When I heard Uncle Fred say to Papa that today's a good morning to hang the new sign out front — which now had Papa's name on it, too — I figured there were no new dead people waiting to be taken care of. The embalming room would be empty.

Uncle Fred doesn't want us to know that's where he gets the bodies ready for the funerals, but it doesn't take a genius to figure out that's what the embalming room is for. I just want to know how he gets them ready. I don't think that's too much to ask for. I know what Mrs. Brewster, the hairstylist, does, although I heard Uncle Fred tell Mama if she wanted to start doing the hair instead of Mrs. Brewster, he'd be fine with that. But he and Papa do something else to the bodies. I want to know what it is.

Papa and Uncle Fred have gone outside to the front stoop with a ladder and toolbox, and Willa is with them to watch them hang the sign. Mama and Evie have decided it's time to make sense of Uncle Fred's way of organizing the kitchen pantry, which is to say it's a mess and he has no way. I am supposed to be upstairs making my bed. It's Saturday, so I don't have to get ready for the new school Willa and I go to now, and I don't yet have new chums to play with. Papa promises I will, but city children are slow to welcome country children, especially when you live with two undertakers and dead people every day.

It is easy enough to bypass the stairs to the bedrooms and instead take a left to the kitchen, and then down the hallway that leads past the viewing parlor and casket room, to the last door at the end of the house. The door is closed, and I knock even though I know there is nobody inside, dead or alive. I hear nothing by way of response. As I open the door, I glance back down the hall to make sure I'm still alone.

I don't know what I thought the embalming room would smell like, but I wasn't expecting a mix of forgotten eggs and moldy onions and candle wax. One window with smoked glass and situated high up on the far wall lets in a sad kind of light.

The embalming room is about as big as a bedroom, but the floor is tiled like a kitchen floor. It looks a little like a doctor's office but with nothing soft in it, no blankets or pillows or curtains. Nothing that makes you think this is a place where somebody helps you get better. There is no woodstove or grate or heater to chase away the winter chill.

The table in the middle of the room is made of metal and has big wheels with long spokes. A cart with scissors and blades and needles is pushed right up next to it. There are other instruments on the cart, but their shapes are strange to me. The big electric light that hangs down over the table doesn't look anything like the pretty electric lights in Uncle Fred's other rooms. This light is big and gray, and the shade is like an upside-down mixing bowl someone forgot to paint.

Along the wall is a cupboard. Bottles the color of coffee sit on its shelves along with tins of what looks like cornstarch and lard and brown sugar, but I know that whatever is inside them doesn't belong in a kitchen. Next to that cupboard is a countertop. I see a hairbrush and a tray of creams and lotions and tubes of who knows what. Thick rubber gloves and an apron hang on a hook on the wall.

Close to the table and strapped to a tall, ladderlike frame is a copper tank with a skinny pink hose coming out of it that is looped around a brass handle. Another tank sits on the other side of the table. It is short and dark, with black tubing at its top and bottom. The bottom one leads to a grate in the floor.

I know the table is where Uncle Fred lays out the bodies and puts the suits on the men and the church dresses on the women. Mrs. Brewster surely brushed their hair with that brush and probably used those creams to make them look good. But I've no idea what the rest of the equipment is for.

I've taken two more steps inside when Evie comes up from behind me, making me jump, and tells me I'm not supposed to be in there.

I swing around, pretending she didn't startle me. "It's empty," I reply. "There's nobody in here."

"You're in here. And you know you're not supposed to be."

I'm about to tell her to mind her own business, but then I think she might be as curious as I am to know what Uncle Fred does with the bodies. "I want to see what's in this room," I say. "We live here now. It's our home. Shouldn't we at least know what Papa will be doing?"

"You already know what Papa will be doing. He told us."

Now, what Papa told us when he sat us all down was that Uncle Fred helps folks say good-bye to people who have died by making their bodies look nice for one last visit. Papa is doing that now, too. That had been an answer for Willa, not for Evie and me. I reminded Evie of that.

"What does it matter what Papa will actually have to do? We're not supposed to be in here," she says.

"Don't you want to know what all this stuff is for?" I shoot back.

But Evie has that look on her face that tells me she already does know. Somehow she's figured it out or she's gotten a book at the library and read up on whatever embalming is. Or maybe she's cornered Papa and asked him when Willa and I weren't around, and because she's fifteen and I'm only twelve, she was able to convince him she's old enough to know.

I suddenly don't care if she runs back and tells every adult in the place that I am snooping in the embalming room. Maybe

I'll get a few answers if Papa and Uncle Fred come barreling down the hallway to make sure I'm not breaking something important or setting the room on fire. I take another step. Evie sucks in her breath behind me.

"What's that for?" I point to the gleaming tank with the thin, rosy-colored hose coming out of it.

When Evie doesn't answer, I turn around to face her. She is staring at the tank.

"What's inside it?" I ask, and I know she knows the answer. She just doesn't want to tell me. I accuse her of not knowing.

Evie just shakes her head like I'm an idiot for not knowing myself. Or for wanting to know.

"Do I have to go tell them you're in here?" she finally says, in the you're-going-to-get-in-trouble way that big sisters are famous for. Except with Evie, she doesn't want you to get in trouble; she just knows you will.

"Go ahead," I say, more interested in getting answers than obeying all the rules.

She stands there a few seconds, no doubt contemplating what I'll do when she leaves to go tattle on me. I might stroll over to that cupboard and look inside the tins and drawers and learn things even she doesn't know.

But then Evie opens her mouth and says one word. I can't tell if she's gloating or not when she says it. I don't think she is.

"Formalin," she says, calmly. Quietly. Like we are in church. "That's what's in that tank."

The word means nothing to me. She could've made it up for all I know.

"What's that supposed to be?" I say.

She shakes her head like I'm a child. Like I'm Willa.

"Tell me what it is," I repeat, and when she says nothing, I point to the other tank, the darker one on the other side of the table. "And I suppose you know what's inside that one?"

Evie turns on her heel. "All right. That's it, then." Off she goes.

If I follow her, begging her not to tell, she probably won't. But I don't. My heart starts to pound inside me, but I take several more steps forward anyway. I don't care that Papa might send me to my room for the rest of the day. Or that he might even strap me, though I don't think he will. Since Henry died, Papa hasn't threatened a strapping to anyone, not even Willa, and sometimes she sure needs one.

I want to know what takes place in this room, and I'm not leaving until I find out.

It's not until I hear footsteps coming down the hall that it occurs to me Uncle Fred might be so angry with me that I won't be allowed to go with Jamie and Charlie to Hog Island after church tomorrow. Or worse, he'll tell Papa he's changed his mind and we'll have to go back to Quakertown, where we'll all be rolling cigars for the rest of our lives.

My throat feels tight and my face is warm from shame and dread as I turn toward the doorway and those footsteps. But it's not Papa and Uncle Fred both. It's just Papa. I wonder if Evie told all three of the adults where I was and it was Papa who'd said, "Let me talk to her."

"Evie said you were in here." Papa's voice is soft and hard at the same time, like it's wrong that I disobeyed but there are worse things I could've done. Still, it's a strange thing to say. He hasn't demanded to know why I am in the embalming room; he's just stated that I am, which is already as plain as day.

"I want to know what all this stuff is for." My voice cracks a little, the way it does when you're about to cry but haven't started yet.

He steps into the room to meet me fully in the middle of it and looks around. "I did, too," he says. And for a second it's like we are the same age. "I stood in here and looked at all these things, and I wondered same as you what everything was for. And I'll tell you if you want me to."

I nod.

"All of the things in here are used to make it seem that the dead person has just fallen asleep in this world and will shortly wake in the next. People have an easier time saying their farewells that way."

"But you already told us that. What is all this stuff *for*? Why do you need it?"

"Well, let's see," he says.

We step close to the cupboard, and I can see now that the tubes and bottles and tins look more like theater cosmetics than stuff in a doctor's office. Papa picks up a container and opens it. There is waxy paste the color of flesh inside.

"Sometimes when people die it's because they got hurt," Papa says. "It's too hard to look at those who got hurt so badly they died. So, Uncle Fred uses this restorative wax and the other things here to cover up injuries."

I pick up a little roundish stick with funny metal loops at either end.

"That's a modeling tool. For shaping the wax."

I point to a little brown box labeled *Eye Caps.*

"Uncle Fred puts those under the eyelids. To keep their eyes closed."

I look up at Papa, imagining someone's eyes popping open after they're dead. "Why don't they stay closed?"

"There are a lot of things about the body that start to change when a person dies and the soul leaves."

"It starts to rot," I say, and I don't know why I say it, because it makes me shudder.

He reaches out to touch my shoulder.

"What's in there?" I say quickly, pointing to the tall, shiny tank. The funny smell is coming from it; that's certain. I can't remember the word Evie said for what is inside it.

"That's the embalming fluid. It goes into the body to make it look good for just a little while longer so that everybody can gather to say good-bye. It can be dangerous to work with if you're not being careful, though. That's why Uncle Fred says this room is off-limits."

"Why is it up so high?"

"Gravity helps the fluid get inside the body."

"You have to cut the people to put that little hose in, don't you?"

"Just a little cut, Maggie. Uncle Fred fixes it when he's done. You can't even tell."

Somehow I know right then the other tank is for taking out the blood to make room for the special liquid. Farm. Farm . . .

I will have to ask Evie later to tell me again what it is.

And then I ask Papa the question he probably knows is the real reason I'm in the embalming room. "Did someone do that to Henry?"

Papa puts his arm around me. "No. We didn't need to wait to say good-bye. Everyone who loved Henry was right there. And he already looked perfect, so nobody had to fix him. Remember?"

Of course I remember. Does he really think I've forgotten? This is a room for dead people who need to look like they are only napping.

"Is Uncle Fred mad at me for being in here?" I ask.

"He doesn't know."

So Evie only told Papa, no one else. She must have whispered it in his ear.

We are quiet for a minute or two. "Is Mama going to do their hair?" I finally say, for she had told me she'd asked Uncle Fred if she could. It didn't strike me as curious when she first said it, but now that I know more about this room, I'm wondering why she wants to. Mama seems different here in Philadelphia. Happier, if that's possible, and that seems strange to me because we're here without Henry, and Quakertown — where he's buried — is so many miles away. This is the strangest room in the world to *want* to be in.

"I think so," Papa replies.

"Why does she want to?"

Papa shrugs. "Sometimes we need things to do to keep our mind off other things."

"Things that make us mad."

"Or sad. Yes."

Mama doesn't seem mad or sad to me, but she does seem like *something*. But not mad. Not sad. Something else.

"Can I help her in here sometimes?" I ask.

Papa stares at me for a moment. "What for?"

"I want to help her. Hand her the curling rods. The lipstick. That kind of thing." That's what I tell him, but really, I just want to be near Mama. I want to know why she's such a strange kind of happy. Although *happy* isn't the right word. I don't know what the right word is.

He is quiet for a moment, no doubt thinking the same thing I just was. This room is a weird one to want to be in. But it's not all bad, what happens in this room. I think it's mostly good. Ugly is made pretty again. Isn't that a good thing?

"I just want to help her," I say. "I'm not afraid of the bodies. And I won't touch anything I'm not supposed to."

"I'll need to think about it," he says, in a way that sounds more like no than yes. "Come. Let's both get back to what we were supposed to be doing, hmm?"

I ask him as we turn to leave what embalming means and he says it got its name from balm, a sweet ointment that makes a wound feel better. Like in the hymn. The Balm of Gilead. A balm that heals the wounded soul.

"Then why does this room smell so bad?" I ask as we step across the threshold and into the sweeter air of the hallway.

And Papa says he doesn't know.

I guess I don't mind not knowing the answer to that because I am not in trouble for going inside in the forbidden room. I'll still be allowed to go to Hog Island tomorrow with Jamie and Charlie. And I might be able to help Mama do the hair.

Besides, now I know everything else about that room.

CHAPTER 9

Willa

Our new house in Philadelphia has three stories and there are two front doors. The one painted gray that faces Charlie and Jamie's house is the one we're supposed to use, not the one around the corner that faces the other street. That other one is painted green. It's for Uncle Fred and Papa and the bodies.

I am not allowed to go into the funeral parlor when there are families inside, because Uncle Fred said they will be sad and maybe crying. I can go in the room where the long boxes are, but I am not supposed to touch them or climb inside them. The room at the back is the Elm Bonning Room, and I am not supposed to even touch the doorknob of that room. There are dangerous things inside that could hurt me. Maybe a tree ax or something. The dead people go in there to get ready for heaven. Maggie isn't afraid of the dead bodies, so I'm not. If they got up off the table and started chasing me with their arms stretched out, then I'd be afraid.

The kitchen is on the other side on the first floor. Mama has been painting it because it needed brightening up. Now it's yellow. Before, it was no color. The floor in the kitchen is black and white squares like a checkerboard. I like stepping on the white ones. There is a dining room that Uncle Fred has piled up with books and boxes and I don't know what else. Mama wants to clean that up next. There is also a sitting room with a big fireplace and a sofa and chairs and a phonograph. And a piano. Mama says when I'm older I can have lessons. And electric lights everywhere! Uncle Fred has a bedroom and an office next to the sitting room. I am not allowed in those rooms, either. Mama told me Uncle Fred never had a wife or a family, so I need to give him some time to get used to there being children in the house.

There's a girl who lives three buildings up the street from the gray door. She's seven like me and in my class in my new school. Her name is Florence, but everyone calls her Flossie. She lives above a bookstore. It's not hers; that's just where she lives. She has dark hair and freckles and three brothers who tease her all the time. They are older than her, so they're not like Henry. I think she will be my best friend.

There is another little girl who lives close to us, too. Her name is Gretchen Weiss. I see her at school, too. But Flossie said that girl is a Hun and her parents are Huns, and we can't be friends with her because of the war.

I had to ask Papa what a Hun is, and when I did, he asked where I'd heard that word. I just said at school. He was probably going to tell me what a Hun is, but Uncle Fred heard me ask and he turned to me and said Huns are those *damn* German savages responsible for all the misery in the world.

Papa gave Uncle Fred a look that said he can't say that one word. *Damn.*

But Gretchen doesn't look much like a savage to me. I've seen pictures of savages in Evie's *History of the World* book. Gretchen has pigtails and a little white dog and a baby doll carriage. Her parents own a bakery. They aren't savages with wooden clubs and no clothes on.

So I don't think Uncle Fred knows what a Hun is. But I don't want Flossie not to like me, so I will stay away from Gretchen.

Today I went with Jamie and Charlie and

Maggie to see the warships being built. It was supposed to be an island, but we got there in a streetcar full of shipyard workers and didn't go over a bridge or anything, so what kind of island is that? Jamie knows someone who builds the ships, so that man went with us and took us past the fences. Maggie didn't want me to come with them. Jamie had asked me if I wanted to go along, and before I could answer, Maggie said I wouldn't like to see the ships and that I would get too tired and that it was too cold for me. I told Jamie I *did* want to see the ships and that I wouldn't get tired and that it wasn't too cold for me. So I asked Mama if I could go, and she said I had to mind Jamie the whole time, and that if I promised to do that, I had her permission. She didn't say any of the things stupid Maggie did.

I did get bored after a while. The ships weren't ships. They were just big hunks that looked like funny-shaped buildings being built upside down. And I was so cold, my fingers stung inside my gloves. There was mud everywhere. Jamie said the whole island used to be mud and marshes and swarms of mosquitoes, but then the war came and we needed to build ships. There are no hogs, though, even though it's called Hog Island. Not one. There wasn't one pretty thing to look at. But I wasn't about to say a word out loud about that and have Maggie scold me for coming when she said I shouldn't have.

I'll tell you why she didn't want me to come. It's because she wants Charlie and Jamie for herself. They are always doing puzzles and games with her. Well, it's mostly Charlie who comes over to play games and do puzzles, but then Jamie comes over to fetch him and he stays. And sometimes she goes over to their apartment and visits with Mrs. Sutcliff. She likes Maggie because she has no girls. Only Jamie and Charlie. Charlie is nice, but he's not very smart. He's older than Evie and can hardly read. I read better than he can. Maggie is trying to teach him, but it's like he forgets everything she says two seconds after she says it. Mama told me his brain won't let him remember all that he's taught. She said no one knows why, but some children are born with not everything working quite right.

"Like Henry and his heart," I said.

And she nodded, kissed me, and went to the kitchen to fetch me a snack.

Sometimes I miss my old room even though I had to share it with Evie and Maggie and they never wanted me touching their things. My new room is all my own, but it doesn't feel like mine. The bed came from a furniture store, and it smells like tractor oil, it's so new. I have an electric lamp. I just turn it on with a switch. I like my new friend Flossie, and I like Jamie and Charlie, but I miss my old friends. I miss the way our Quakertown house squeaked when you walked up the stairs.

There weren't as many rules in my old house. I could go into any room I wanted. There were no caskets or crying people or an Elm Bonning Room that I had to keep away from. We only had one front door.

When I asked Mama if we had to stay here forever, she just smiled and said, "No place is forever, sweetheart."

CHAPTER 10

March 1918

Maggie

I used to be good at mathematics.

I'm not as smart as Evie — no one is as smart as Evie — but I used to be able to do all my equations without needing help from anyone. Algebra is harder here in the city. Evie says that's impossible, but I know it's not.

Today won't be the first day I walk across the street to ask Jamie or Mr. Sutcliff to help me with my math. Mama says I shouldn't be going over to the Sutcliffs' when I'm stuck on a problem when I can just have Evie show me, but asking my sister for help is like asking to be stung by bees. Somehow she makes me feel stupid. I don't think she means to, but she does.

Jamie is better at helping me than his father is. Mr. Sutcliff is probably a good bookkeeper, but he's not a very good math teacher. He can get the right answers, but he can't tell me how he got them. Evie can tell me, but she makes me feel like a dummy. Jamie gets the right answers and can show me how he got them, and I never feel stupid. I don't think Jamie even knows how to make someone feel bad.

As I grab my coat and algebra book to go across the street, Mama shouts not to stay too long from the kitchen, where she's stuffing a chicken. She's cooking all the food now. Mrs. Landry has been let go, saints be praised. I tell her I'll be back soon.

She pokes her head around the entry to the kitchen, wiping her hands on a towel. "I mean it, Maggie. You've been over there twice already this week. They have a business to run."

I don't know why she needs to tell me this. I can count how many days I've gone across the street. And I know the Sutcliffs have a business to run. "I said I won't stay too long."

I step out onto the stoop before she can say anything else.

Late March in the city is different. In the country, there might be the faintest hints that spring is here, like a shoot of green grass or an early robin or the smell of the earth as it starts to wake up from a winter sleep. But that's not how it is in the city. Snowflakes are swirling down on me like it's November as I cross the boulevard. I know there are probably flurries in Quakertown at this moment, too, but there still could be that lone blade of new grass or the smell of field dirt despite the snow. In the city, you can't tell anything's just right around the corner.

When I open the door to Sutcliff Accounting, I can see through the windows of their little offices that Roland Sutcliff is busy with a client and that Jamie is not. Beatrice, their secretary, sits up front and answers their telephone and welcomes people when they come inside. She's probably my grandmother's age but with huge bosoms that practically rest on the top of her desk. She always wears toilet water that smells like a mix of mashed potatoes and roses, but she's nice to me and never says, "You again?" when I come over with my algebra book. Behind her are Mr. Sutcliff's and Jamie's offices. A big stretch of windows separates her desk from the two offices, held up by wooden walls that come up to my waist, and the rest is glass. The doors to their offices are half wood and half window, too. Both Jamie and his father can see the front door from where they sit. You can hear their adding machines from beyond the glass if they are working them when you step inside.

Beatrice says hello to me, and both men look up to see who it is that has come in. Mr. Sutcliff just glances up and then returns his attention to the client he is talking to. Mr. Sutcliff is a bit shorter than Jamie, and thick, like Charlie. His smile and voice are like Charlie's, too. The top of his head is shiny and bare, like new skin after a sunburn, and the hair he has left rims the sides of his head like a wreath. Sometimes he will come over to the funeral parlor to go over Uncle Fred's ledgers, and he'll stay and they'll both have one of Grandad's cigars and maybe a glass of brandy.

Jamie smiles the tiniest bit when he looks up from his adding machine to see who has entered the business.

Beatrice casts a glance back at Jamie and then waves me through. She sees my algebra book.

"Again?" Jamie says, sounding like he's annoyed, but I can tell he doesn't really mind my being here. He might even like my little interruption. What he's doing looks incredibly boring. I take a chair next to his.

"It's not my fault. Algebra is hard."

He closes a ledger and moves it to make room on his desk for my book. He bumps a linked trio of little model train cars painted blue, and they start to topple over. He reaches out to gently steady them. "What are you going to do about algebra when I'm gone?" he says with a warm smile.

I've been able to put off thinking about Jamie's leaving for the army camp only until someone else brings it up. Usually it's Dora Sutcliff, who nearly always starts to cry when she does, or Charlie, who I don't think fully understands what it will be like for him when Jamie goes away. If Charlie isn't over at our place or moving things around for Uncle Fred, he's waiting for Jamie to be done with work so he can be with him.

"I don't want to talk about that," I say as sourly as I can, opening my book to the page I need help with.

"Hey, I'm the one who's going to have to put up with terrible food, a cold cot, and getting up at dawn to march for miles on end."

"Then don't go." I smooth out the page.

He finds this funny. He thinks I'm joking. I'm not. I don't know much about this war, but I know it has nothing to do with me or Jamie or Philadelphia or even Pennsylvania. I've seen all the battleships that are being built on Hog Island. I've seen Uncle Fred's magazines and files and his APL badge. I've seen the Pershing's Crusaders posters all around the city. I've glanced at the newspaper headlines telling us how terrible the Kaiser is and how wonderful our brave soldiers are. I know there's a war far away across the ocean. But it doesn't mean anything to me.

Jamie stops laughing when he sees that I'm serious. "Don't be glum, now. I'll be back to help you with your math problems before you know it."

My throat feels hot and thick with frustration, so I can't ask him how he knows that.

He helps me with the first two problems, but he does all the talking, and I just sullenly nod as he explains things. I do the third problem on my own, solving it quickly.

"I think you're getting it, Magpie," he says.

A boy in Quakertown called me that once and I wanted to box his ears. But the nickname sounds sweet and precious when Jamie says it. I can't help cracking a smile.

"So you're not angry with me, then," he says, smiling back at me.

I shake my head. I'll have to leave now. I can do the other two problems on my own, no doubt.

"I wish you didn't want to go away to the war," I finally say as I close the book.

He doesn't say anything for a second. "It's not that I want to. Sometimes duty calls us to it. Most of my friends are already on the front or getting ready to go. It's the right thing to do."

I don't see how it can be. "How do you know?"

"Because my country asks it of me. If people don't do their part to stop the spread of evil when they're asked to, it just gets stronger and then no one can stop it."

I don't know what he's talking about. And I already know I can't change anything by asking him to explain this to me.

"Will you do something for me while I'm away?" he asks when I say nothing.

"I guess."

"Look out for Charlie, will you? You're the first friend he's had in a long time. A very long time. And I'm very glad he has a friend right now. I'm not sure how much he understands about where I'm going."

I don't understand much about where you're going, I'm thinking.

"I know he's not making much progress on what you're trying to teach him, but that's not how he sees it. He loves going over to your house. Charlie being happy makes my mother happy. It might be hard for her, too, when I go."

I pull the book into my lap.

"So it would mean a lot to me if you just kept up with what you're doing for Charlie. Don't stop. Please?" he says.

Jamie is looking intently at me, and my face feels warm. His gaze is confusing me, making my heart pound. "I'm not doing anything special for Charlie. I'm just being me."

His face relaxes into an easy smile. "Then don't change while I'm gone. All right, Magpie? You just stay you."

I can't think of a thing to say. Someone who needs to speak with Jamie comes into the accounting office at that moment. Beatrice brings the man through. Jamie stands and says, "Good day, Miss Bright," like I am one of his business patrons. Beatrice, Jamie, and even the client smile wide as I make my way out. They think I'm just a twelve-year-old girl who doesn't know anything.

I'm nearly thirteen.

CHAPTER 11

Evelyn

We were moving the rest of Uncle Fred's boxes and piles from the dining room into a smaller parlor that he uses for his office — it had been a smoking room during the banker's day — when Mrs. Sutcliff from across the street called on us. We'd had to wait to do this until Uncle Fred moved all his APL documents, which were so secret, he'd said, we oughtn't even glance at them. That finally done, we could move all the other things, including Uncle Fred's stacks of old newspapers and back issues of *The Sunnyside* — a periodical for undertakers — all of which we'd promised to keep in order by date. All four of us were engaged in the task — Mama, me, Maggie, and Willa — when the door chimes rang.

Mama invited Mrs. Sutcliff inside even though we were dirty and bedraggled from pushing about items that hadn't been disturbed in ages because Mrs. Landry had been told not to touch them.

So there we were, trying to make sense of a dining room that had been treated like a storage closet for three decades, when Dora Sutcliff showed up. She had been over to the house a few times before. I had met her the day we moved in, when Charlie Sutcliff came over to haul our belongings up the stairs. She'd come over with him and brought a loaf of warm bread that we'd enjoyed at dinnertime with Mrs. Landry's flavorless split pea soup. She's been over a couple times since, to bring us a pie or homemade jam, and she's had Mama over for afternoon coffee a time or two. Dora is dark-haired and slender, with doelike eyes. She has a soft voice, like Jamie's, but she talks far more than he does. She is nearly always worried about something, whether it's a forecast of bad weather or a threat to her family's health or that we might have to start rationing sugar. She likes to start sentences with "My stars! Have you heard?" And then she'll tell us some deeply troubling fact that we *have* heard but that had seemed inconsequential to us.

After Mama apologized for the state the four of us were in — cobwebs in our hair and dust on our sleeves — she politely asked

Mrs. Sutcliff if she'd like to come into the sitting room for some coffee. Mrs. Sutcliff said she couldn't stay. They'd just found out Jamie's report date to Fort Meade had been bumped from three weeks to tomorrow. The send-off party she'd been planning and hadn't yet told us about would have to be tonight. She wanted us all to come to it.

"This will be the last time we're all together before he is shipped off to France," Mrs. Sutcliff said, her eyes filling with tears the second she said *France.* These days saying *France* is the same as saying the word *war.* It was obvious Mrs. Sutcliff didn't want Jamie to go and that perhaps she wasn't very happy that he'd volunteered when he wasn't yet required to register.

Mama thanked her and said she'd be happy to accept for all of us. She touched Mrs. Sutcliff's arm when she added we'd be honored to come. Mrs. Sutcliff flicked away a tear as she looked at all of us.

"You are so lucky to have three such lovely daughters, Pauline," Mrs. Sutcliff said. She was no doubt also thinking how even luckier my mother was that girls don't have to sail away to foreign lands to shoot and be shot at.

"We always hoped to have a girl," Mrs. Sutcliff continued with a teary smile. "I guess it just wasn't meant to be. We only had the two boys."

"We had a boy named Henry," Willa said. "But he died."

Mrs. Sutcliff turned her head to look at Mama, her mouth a perfect O shape. "Yes," she replied a second later. "I mean, oh. How very, very sad. I'm so sorry."

I could tell Mrs. Sutcliff knew this about us already. Maggie had no doubt told her about Henry during one of her many visits to the Sutcliff apartment. But Mama didn't know that Dora Sutcliff knew. It was clear to me Mama hadn't brought it up in conversation yet with Mrs. Sutcliff, and therefore our neighbor didn't know how to pretend she didn't already know about Henry. She had likely already shared the tragic news with a close friend or two. Inside my head, I could hear how the conversation must have begun. "My stars! Have you heard? That sweet little family at the funeral home lost their baby boy last autumn!"

Mama pulled away a cobweb from a wispy curl at her forehead and smiled one of those thank-you smiles that said she appreciated the words of sympathy but she wasn't going to volunteer any details. "You're very kind. What time shall we come, Dora?"

Mrs. Sutcliff stared at Mama for a second.

I think she was admiring this new neighbor of hers who had somehow survived the loss she was desperately afraid of experiencing, the death of a son. "Oh. Six."

"Six it is," Mama answered.

Mrs. Sutcliff seemed to need another second before she was able to tell us to come hungry because she was making lots of food. All of Jamie's favorites.

Mama watched her through the glass panels in the front door as Mrs. Sutcliff headed down the marble stairs and back across the street. When Mama turned back around, she said she was mighty glad Uncle Fred had lots of hot water, because we'd all need to bathe for the party tonight after working to clean up the dining room.

Even though we don't know very many people yet and the Sutcliffs don't have girls, Maggie and I were both instantly looking forward to the farewell party. The only place we'd been to so far where we got to dress up was the big Methodist church a few blocks away on Sundays. Uncle Fred has been a member of that church since he came to the city, so naturally he wanted us to join him there. We haven't been to a party of any kind since we left Quakertown, and that already seems like a long time ago.

■ ■ ■ ■

We use all of Uncle Fred's hot water getting ready, and he complains a little about it, but we don't care. Maggie and I put ribbons in each other's hair and I plait Willa's. We shine our shoes and put rose water behind our ears. Then, at a few minutes after six, we walk across the boulevard to Sutcliff Accounting and the living quarters above the shop.

We find the door to the stairs has been propped open with a chair, and there is music from a phonograph and the sound of many voices as we walk up the steps from the street entrance. When Papa knocks on the inside door at the top of the stairs, Charlie swings it open and welcomes us in.

This is my first time inside the Sutcliffs' living quarters. The apartment is bigger than our house in Quakertown but still only half the size of the second floor of Uncle Fred's house. It is nicely furnished, but not expensively so. I don't think Roland Sutcliff is a rich man, but he's been able to provide for his family. There are residents and merchants from the neighborhood whom I recognize and many other people I don't. Roland and Dora Sutcliff see us step inside, and both of them come over to us.

"Where's that brave lad of yours?" Uncle Fred says happily, and I see that he's wearing his APL badge on the inside of his suit coat like it's a medal of honor.

Mrs. Sutcliff greets him with a smile, but I see the uneasiness in her manner at Uncle Fred's question. You can almost hear her saying back to him, "You wouldn't be so jovial if it was your son being sent off to war."

"There he is," Roland Sutcliff says, motioning to the far end of the sitting room. Jamie is talking to two young women who seem to be hanging on his every word. He has a glass of punch in his hand, and it is trembling slightly at their coquettishness. At least that's how it appears to me.

We make our way through the crowd of people. Jamie looks up as we approach and seems relieved to have a reason to ease himself away from the girls' flirtations.

Despite having his mother's eyes and his father's build, Jamie Sutcliff has a voice of his own, soft and a bit like my teacher Mr. Galway's. He has the look of someone who is neither soldier — what he will be very soon — nor assistant accountant, which is what he had been before. I wonder what he might want to be if he were allowed to choose. He thanks us for coming.

"Who are they?" I hear Maggie ask him under her breath, eyeing the girls who he'd been talking to before.

He shrugs. "Just old friends from my school days."

And then Mr. Sutcliff is bringing someone else Jamie's way. We all step aside.

We eat a supper of fried chicken and succotash, beaten biscuits and coleslaw, and chocolate cake — all Jamie's favorites. Charlie, who considers Papa and Uncle Fred his employers, sits with us. After the meal, everyone stands with a glass of punch to toast Jamie and we sing "For He's a Jolly Good Fellow." The reverend from the Sutcliffs' church prays a blessing over Jamie, asking God to protect him and bring him safely home when this time of conflict is over. Then Mrs. Sutcliff hands out little cards with the address of Jamie's army unit so that we all might write him letters so he won't feel so far away. She was going to give our family just one card, I think, but Maggie holds out her hand after Mama already has one. Dora Sutcliff smiles and gives her one.

When people start to put on their hats to go, Mrs. Sutcliff begins to cry and excuses herself to the kitchen. I understand why.

Once everyone leaves, the party will be over. The next big thing the Sutcliffs must do is take Jamie to the train station in the morning and say good-bye. Dora Sutcliff doesn't want the party to end.

Once we've come home Willa wants to know where Jamie is going after training camp. I take her up to my room, get out the atlas, and show her where France is. Maggie lingers over the page, too, even though she knows the geography of Europe. Willa wrinkles her brow and says she hopes Jamie isn't afraid to go so far away from home to fight in the war.

"It's a stupid war," Maggie mutters.

"Don't let Uncle Fred hear you say that," I tell her.

"I don't care if he does hear me," Maggie says. "All wars are stupid. They don't fix anything."

"What do the Germans want?" Willa's forehead is puckered by curiosity.

"It's not just the Germans, Willa. It's . . . it's complicated." I close the atlas to end the conversation. I don't want our voices to carry downstairs and perhaps provoke a lecture from Uncle Fred.

"But what do they *want*?" Willa persists.

I have no answer other than they want to win. The assassination of some faraway heir to a foreign throne as the reason Jamie must leave his family seems impossible to explain to a seven-year-old. But Maggie seems to be waiting for my answer, too.

When I say nothing, Maggie walks to my bedroom door with Jamie's address card still in her hand. Sleet begins to fall outside as she leaves the room and I slide the atlas back into its place.

"Show me my insides." Willa points to Uncle Fred's anatomy book on the shelf. I withdraw it and open the volume to a page that shows us what we're all made of.

CHAPTER 12

May 1918
Pauline

Did you know people have been caring for their dead since the most ancient of times? I read this in one of Uncle Fred's books. He's letting Evelyn read anything in his library that she wants to, and she left a book about ancient history open on the sofa table in the sitting room a few mornings ago when the school day beckoned. Fred has an interesting array of books in his office and in the sitting room — only one shelf in the office is dedicated to publications about his trade. The rest are about nature and history and science — all the things Evie loves to study. I picked up the book to see what Evie had been reading about and saw that she'd stopped on the chapter about ancient rituals for the dead. My interest piqued, I read the chapter in its entirety.

I learned that in every culture in human

history, the living have treated their dead with honor and respect, some even with adoration. There is something sacred about the body when the soul has left it, no matter which corner of the globe or how far back you look.

You'd think the opposite would be true, that this tent of flesh, which starts to decompose within hours of the soul leaving it, would immediately be cast aside as worthless. Instead, our mortal remains are given more reverence after Death's visit than even before it.

It's as if the body is a candle and the soul is its flame. When the flame is snuffed out, all that is left to prove that there had been a flame is the candle, and even that we only have for a little while. Even the candle is not ours to keep.

And yet how we care for that candle for that stretch of time that it is still ours! How we want to remember the shape and fragrance of the little flame it held.

This fascinating thought keeps me company now when I go into the embalming room with Mrs. Brewster's basket of combs, scissors, and curling rods: this idea that what we do here is holy more than it is needful. Perhaps I see it that way so strongly because Fred and Thomas ask that I stay away until the chemical process they undertake is complete. When I am called in, the deceased are washed and waxed and dressed in their finest. All that is left to do is primp and prepare their faces and hair for their laying out.

Fred nearly always leaves the viscera intact. Some embalmers thrust a device called a trocar up the navel and tease out the insides in a terrible maneuver Fred says I would find appalling. And he says it's unnecessary. Unless the cadaver must travel a long distance, or be laid out for many days, there is no need to suck out the innards. Emptying the body of its insides is no new thing, however. I read in Fred's book that the ancient Egyptians used to remove the brain with a sharpened metal rod shoved up the nostrils. Can you imagine? The organs were also removed and then immersed in salt harvested from the dry lakes of the desert. After the organs were washed and laid to dry in the sun, they were placed in elaborate jars made of alabaster and limestone. The body cavity was then filled with a mix of resin, sand, and sawdust. Linen bandages, often made from cloth saved throughout a person's lifetime, would be used to wrap the body from head to toe. Lotus blossoms were pressed between the

113

layers of strips.

Then the body would be laid in its beautiful coffin all wrapped up in spices like myrrh and cinnamon, and the jars would be tucked right alongside it. The body would last a long time. A very long time. But the book said that mummies that have been opened and unwrapped look very little like the people they had been several millennia before. Eventually, the candle disappears, too. It just does.

"But children do not belong in the embalming room," Fred is saying. He and Thomas are getting the funeral parlor ready for a viewing, and the girls are at school. Maggie wants to help me with the hair and cosmetics, and I've come to Fred and Thomas with her request. She'd apparently asked Thomas before if she could do this, weeks ago, when he was still learning his way around the embalming room. He'd said then that he'd have to mull it over, thinking perhaps Maggie would lose interest. But she had complained to me last night at bedtime that her papa was taking too long to decide.

"She's nearly thirteen, Fred," I reply. "Not so much a child anymore. She just wants to help."

Maggie's birthday is indeed fast approaching, and she has said nothing about it. As I made her toast this morning, I asked her what kind of cake she'd like, and she merely shrugged and said any kind would be fine.

This answer and her desire to be with me in the embalming room had me wondering if my companion has been trailing her, too, like it's been trailing me, and filling her dreams like it's been filling mine, and if this is the reason why she wants to help me. My heart had begun to somersault inside me because I do not yet trust my companion even though I sense nothing but benevolence from it. How can Death be trusted? It can't. So I changed the subject and told her as I handed her a plate of toast that I'd ask about her request to help me in the embalming room. I also said that I might need to tell Fred and her papa why she wanted to, though it was I who needed to know, and she'd answered, "I just want to help fix something that will stay fixed."

"If she wants to help, why can't she just take on more chores in the kitchen?" Fred says as he sets a wooden folding chair into a row of other chairs.

"Because she wants to do *this*."

Thomas, straightening a chair in another row, looks up at me. "She really still wants to?"

I nod and Thomas furrows his brow. "Is this about Henry? Is it because she's not done grieving for him?"

This question needles me a bit, though I know Thomas doesn't intend it to. "Aren't we all still grieving for Henry?" I reply.

"I didn't mean she shouldn't be or that you and I are not still grieving. I just think being in *that* room might make it worse," Thomas says gently. "It's a room of dead people."

When he says this it's not the first time I think that grief is such a strange guest, making its home in a person like it's a new thing that no one has ever experienced before. It is different for every person. "Maybe for her it's the one way to make it better. Not worse."

Fred is looking at Thomas, seemingly waiting for him to rule on this. Thomas is thinking.

"She hasn't made new friends here, except for Charlie and Jamie," I continue. "And Jamie's leaving has made her so very sad."

"Jamie is a grown man," Thomas interjects softly, as if just to me. I can see that he's picked up on Maggie's schoolgirl infatuation just like I have, though we have not talked about it. I didn't think he had noticed, he's been so busy, and men typically don't notice those types of things.

"But that doesn't mean her feelings aren't real. Helping me might distract her from her troubles."

"Or intensify them."

"She just wants to fix something that will stay fixed, Tom. She told me this."

He ponders my words for a moment. "All right," he finally says. "We can give it a try. She can assist you from time to time if her other chores are done and she has no schoolwork."

As I leave the room, Fred reminds me in his most parental tone yet that the embalming fluid is dangerous and that Maggie must be careful around it.

With all that has recently complicated her young life — losing Henry, moving from Quakertown, having to say good-bye to one of only two friends she's made here in Philadelphia — I understand her desire to repair something that will stay repaired.

She doesn't yet realize what eventually happens to the candle. She surely will come to understand when she is older, as we all do. Sooner or later she will learn time changes everything, takes everything: sometimes in a blink, and sometimes so slowly you can't even see it happening.

CHAPTER 13

July 1918
Evelyn

The long summer days used to be filled with walking the tobacco rows and pinching flowers off the plants, rolling cigars made of last year's leaves, making afternoon trips to the swimming hole, filling up the salt and pepper shakers at Grandma and Grandpa Adler's café, and reading books under the locust tree until the evening mosquitoes chased us inside.

The summer recess is different here in the city. The days are long and hot like they were in Quakertown, but nothing else is similar. Always before, we girls spent our days together and everything we did was the same. But here in Philadelphia a person can be more of who she is individually. I can go to the library every day, practice sketching the human body, and volunteer to read to the children who are patients in the hospital. Those things don't interest Maggie. She'd rather be helping Mama with the bodies or trying to teach Charlie how to play chess or writing letters to Jamie. Willa is at her friend Flossie's every day or Flossie is here. The only thing we girls do together now is visit Philadelphia's many parks. There are four large ones close enough to walk to, all of them planned by William Penn and his surveyor back in Colonial times. They are lovely places where the thrum of the city seems far away even though it is still right there behind you and ahead of you, just on the other side of the trees. Still, even at the parks, Willa and Flossie go off on their own, and Charlie and Maggie search out something he doesn't know about and that Maggie thinks she can teach him, and that leaves me to read on a bench in the shade.

Today I did not mind in the least that when we got to the park at Rittenhouse Square, everyone left me. As I settled onto a bench with *David Copperfield* — I am rereading all of Dickens this summer — I heard someone say my name. I looked up and there was Gilbert Keane from school walking toward me with a panting spaniel on a leash. My heart jumped inside my chest. I hadn't seen him since classes let out the first of June. I'd seen some of the girls from the academy over the past weeks — one invited me to a birthday celebration where many of the girls were in attendance, and another invited me to a poetry reading, but none of the boys was at those two events. I hadn't realized how much I had missed hearing Gilbert's voice and seeing his face until that moment.

"It's you!" I said, and then after remembering my manners, "How very nice to see you."

"May I?" he said, motioning to the bench.

"Of course."

He settled down next to me. The dog plopped down at his feet, obviously ready for a rest.

"You didn't mention you had a dog," I said, wanting to say something brilliant and coming up with only that.

"It's my aunt's. She's visiting from Cincinnati and unfortunately feeling under the weather today. I offered to take Pansy for a walk. I think I may have overestimated the dog's stamina."

We looked down at the little spaniel, and we both laughed. She was resting her snout on his boot, eyes closed, pink tongue peeking out of her huffing mouth.

"I've not seen you at this park before. Do

you come often?" he said.

"Do *you*?" I hadn't pictured him as a strolling-the-park kind of fellow. I'm happy to imagine that maybe he is.

He laughed. "No."

"Oh. My sister Willa and her friend like this one best because of the fountain. It's their favorite. We come here sometimes."

He looked down at my book. "Haven't read that one. Should I?"

"You might like it. What other of Dickens's books have you read?" I said, thinking that I'd compare it for him to *A Tale of Two Cities* or *Oliver Twist*. I was also thinking how immensely wonderful it was to be having a conversation about literature in the park with Gilbert Keane.

Gilbert's grin widened. "Will you still like me if I say I haven't read any Dickens?"

Something in the way he said this filled me with warmth and instant joy. It was as though I had been sipping hot cocoa and the liquid was sliding down my throat and into my tummy on the coldest winter day. The feeling was lovely and exhilarating, even though it was surely ninety degrees in the park. It was of no consequence to me that he hadn't read Dickens. He knew I liked him. It mattered to him that I liked him.

"Of course I will still like you," I said a second later, unable to tame my own smile.

He stayed on the bench for a little while longer, and we talked about school and our teachers and the music we like and where we would go if we could visit any place on earth.

"I want to see the Valley of the Kings in Egypt," I said.

"I can see you there," he responded with a knowing look, like he knew enough about me now to imagine me in a place that fascinates me. "I want to go to London's West End and see a play every night for a week," he continued.

"That does sound lovely." It was easy to picture myself with him, my hand on his arm, as we strolled the streets on our way to a show. Gilbert in a black tuxedo and me in a shimmering gown of silk and lace. He smiled at me. Maybe he was picturing it, too.

And then too soon he rose to leave. "I'm expected back home, I'm afraid."

"Must you go?"

"Sadly, I must."

"It was so nice to see you." It was. So very nice.

"See you next month in class?"

"Yes. Yes, of course."

"Or maybe here in the park again?"

My heart did a somersault. "We're . . . we're going to my grandparents' in Quakertown for two weeks." I had been looking forward to our trip home to see the family, but I suddenly wished we were not going.

"Then at school," he said, tipping his hat to me as he and the little dog walked away. He turned after he was a few yards away, as if he knew I was still watching him walk away. He smiled.

I'll be counting the days until classes start up again.

There had been talk at the end of the term that I might be advanced to the next level when I return to school, which would put me in line to graduate a year early. Mama and Papa said the decision was mine to make.

If I made the jump, I wouldn't be in the same art and music classes as Gilbert anymore.

I hadn't decided what I wanted to do until today.

I see no need to rush things. I will stay right where I am.

Chapter 14

August 1918
Willa

Today it is too hot to do anything.

Evie said she'd take me to the park later if I want to go, but it's too hot to even do that.

If Flossie was home her mother would probably take us to their friend's house. They're rich and they have a swimming pool. We could spend the whole day in that pool, and it wouldn't bother us how hot it was. That would sure be better than sitting here in the house, making paper fans out of catalog pages. But Flossie had to go with her family to Ohio because her cousin died. He was a soldier in the army, and he got sick and died. They brought his dead body back from France all dressed up in his uniform.

I have seen lots of dead bodies since we moved here. Probably ten.

I'd sure like to go downstairs where it's

cooler, but Uncle Fred has some of his secret people over for a lunch meeting and they are talking about secret things and I am not allowed to come down until they are gone. Mama and Maggie are downstairs, in the Elm Bonning Room, but Evie and I are stuck up here.

I asked Evie what Uncle Fred and his friends are talking about down there and she said it's just war talk. I've been listening at the grate to what they are saying and it doesn't sound like it's about the war. Right now they are talking about a raid at a dance hall where five hundred slackers were arrested.

I don't even know what slackers are or why they aren't allowed to dance. Wars and dances are two different things.

It's so hot I don't care what slackers are and why they're not supposed to be dancing and why that has anything to do with the war in France.

I wish Flossie's cousin hadn't died. If he hadn't, Flossie would be here instead of in Ohio and I wouldn't be stuck upstairs with Evie. I'd be with Flossie and we'd be splashing and swimming and pretending we are mermaids.

CHAPTER 15

Maggie

The summer recess from school has been long, hot, and boring. We've lived in Philadelphia eight months, and I still feel like I'm the new girl. Going home to Quakertown for two weeks wasn't as much fun as I thought it was going to be, either. My old friends somehow filled in the gap of my leaving and are just fine without me. I suppose that's how it is when a friend moves away and you stay right where you are; you figure out how to live without that friend. We really don't have anything in common anymore, my old friends and I. They've stayed exactly the same, but I feel different after nearly a year in the city.

Before we left for our visit to Quakertown, a school chum named Sally invited me to her house along with her friend Ruby. She was probably just being nice to me, because she and Ruby are best pals, but I had fun with them. Sally is not someone I can tell all my secrets to yet, and I don't know if she ever will be. Still, it was nice to be included, and it will make returning to classes a little easier. The person I spend most of my time with these days is Charlie. He's a bit like Willa in the way he thinks, but he's kinder than Willa and only wants to make people happy. Willa just wants to make Willa happy.

Today was better than most days have been. I got a letter from Jamie Sutcliff. I've written to him five times already, but this is the first I've heard back from him. It was dated the twelfth of July and here it is mid-August and I got it today. In his letter he wrote that he had just arrived in France. He sailed to Europe on a troop ship called the *America,* and he couldn't say much about it except that they had to take turns sleeping on the cots because there were too many soldiers for the number of beds. He also said that he had to turn in his flashlight and matches when he got on board because no one was allowed to shine a light or strike a match on deck after dark. The voyage took nine days. It was strange walking on land again, he said, but he was very glad to get off that ship. He didn't say more, but I remember Charlie saying Jamie didn't care for ships, only trains. Then he wrote something that surprised me. France isn't all that different than Pennsylvania, he said. They have schoolhouses and vegetable gardens and birthday parties just like we do. They hang their laundry out to dry under the same sun. They kiss those they love and put diapers on their little ones and hold memorial services for their dead, just like we do. Germany is probably just the same, he said. Just the same. Not even the language in France seems that strange. It isn't until the marching starts that Europe seems like a different place.

In one of my letters to Jamie, I told him how hard it has been making close friends and that the summer has been especially boring. He wrote to me that sometimes people can be slow to give new things a try. He told me to be patient. The right friend will come along in due time. He said not to go sour on people just because they haven't given me a chance yet.

Reading those words that he wrote special to me made me feel light as a feather. There were only two people I could think of who would be as happy as I was at that moment to have heard from Jamie.

I open the front door and take off across

the street to show Mrs. Sutcliff and Charlie my letter. Mrs. Sutcliff comes to her door with a polishing cloth in her hand. She invites me inside, and I can see that she'd been polishing a silver tea service set atop newspaper pages on her dining room table.

"Is Charlie home?" I say as I close the door behind me, a bit out of breath from running across the street and up the stairs to their apartment.

"I'm afraid you've just missed him," Mrs. Sutcliff says, stuffing her polishing cloth into her apron pocket. "He's gone to the mechanic's with Mr. Sutcliff. The car needed servicing."

I am only momentarily disappointed. "I've a letter from Jamie!" I say, showing her the envelope, and suddenly realizing I am quite likely offering to let Dora Sutcliff read it. Why else have I brought it?

"Do you, now?" she says brightly. "We received one today, too."

She turns to a little writing table behind her on which a little stack of mail is resting, along with a tin of peppermints, an electric lamp with an emerald green shade, and a brass dish with a handful of coins in it. Mrs. Sutcliff reaches for an envelope and turns back around. The outside of her letter looks exactly like mine.

"Shall we trade for a moment?" Mrs. Sutcliff says happily.

"Sure." I hand over my precious letter and she gives me hers.

When I take her letter out of its envelope, I'm surprised and pleased that my letter is twice as long as the one Jamie wrote to his parents and Charlie. But I say nothing about that, of course. Mrs. Sutcliff takes mine out and easily sees it for herself. She looks surprised, too.

Jamie wrote to his parents about the voyage on the troop ship, just like he wrote to me. He wrote about the weather in France and the army food they were eating and how much he missed home-cooked meals. He also said there had been reports of influenza spreading from camp to camp, but that his mother needn't worry. It wasn't showing up in his regiment. He said nothing about how strangely the same we all are no matter where we live. That was something special he wrote just to me, as well as the advice about making friends at school.

"What a very nice letter," Mrs. Sutcliff says as she folds mine into thirds and slips it back inside its envelope, but her voice has a funny little lift to it, like she is saying one thing and thinking another.

"Yours is, too," I reply.

We exchange envelopes and I'm glad to have mine back.

"I'm glad you're writing to him, Maggie," Mrs. Sutcliff tells me, and this time I can tell she means what she says.

I stay for a bit longer, hoping Charlie will arrive home. But he doesn't and I need to get back myself.

Mrs. Sutcliff thanks me for coming over to show her my letter and offers to send Charlie over when he returns if I want. I tell her I do.

When I am back inside my house, my feet head to the funeral parlor without my thinking about it. Mama is in the embalming room applying flesh-colored paste to the cheeks of an older woman whose white hair looks as soft and fluffy as candy floss.

She smiles up at me. "Did you see your letter?"

I smile back. I cannot help it. "Want me to read it to you?"

"Certainly."

I read Mama the letter, and Jamie's words sound even nicer said out loud. When I get to the part where he wrote that people aren't so very different from one another no matter where they live, I look down at the dead woman Mama is caring for, and I can't help thinking that somewhere in France, somewhere in Germany, somewhere in all the places in the world, people like Mama are doing the same thing for loved ones who've just died and are being made ready for their last moments above the ground.

CHAPTER 16

September 1918
Pauline

I can't sleep.

Thomas is lying next to me for the last time before he leaves us for the army camp. I am still stunned that this is happening. He is not young anymore. He is not like Jamie Sutcliff or any of the other men who've already been called up to serve. He's thirty-six years old. A husband. A father!

I want to blame Uncle Fred and his APL for this even though I know it's not his fault. He doesn't want Thomas to leave us, either. If Thomas was my only source of provision, he wouldn't have to go. But Uncle Fred can run the business without him and also take care of the girls and me. Congress has decided the war in Europe can't be won unless more men are sent over to fight. It's not just young men they want now. All men older than eighteen and under the age of

133

forty-five must register. It would have made no difference if we had stayed in Quaker-town, Thomas told me. The draft is the draft no matter where you live.

There is a plumber here in Philadelphia whom Thomas knows who is a forty-four-year-old grandfather. A grandfather! And that man must now sign up for the draft. If he fails to register he can be arrested. The day Congress enacted the new draft law, Thomas told me he was going to volunteer so that he could ask to be placed in the medical corps. He knows so much about the human body now after working with Uncle Fred, he'd be of better use in the field hospital than in the trenches. And none of us wants him in the trenches.

So that was what he did. He volunteered and now he's headed to Fort Meade at dawn tomorrow.

The girls haven't known what to make of this. None of us knows what to make of it. And on top of all that, that dreadful influ-enza that has been killing people in Europe and the Orient is now here in the States and the paper is saying it's showing up at the navy shipyards and military camps. Places just like Fort Meade.

"I'll be careful," Thomas said to me when I told him this. We were all in the sitting room after supper.

"This flu doesn't care how careful you are," I replied quietly so that Willa playing with one of her dolls on the rug wouldn't hear me. "I've read about it."

"The flu is not a thing that can care or not care."

"This one is different," I murmured. "It seeks out the young and healthy, and there is no cure for it. You are as likely to die from it as survive."

And he kissed my forehead, something he never does if we aren't alone in our bedroom, and said, "I'm coming home to you and the girls. I promise. As soon as the war is over, I'm coming home."

But as I lie here next to him now, feeling the warmth of his body next to mine, I know he can't promise me this. He wants it to be true. But wanting something is not the same as having it.

I called my parents at the restaurant they've owned since I was a little girl to tell them Thomas was enlisting and why, and to ask them to keep him in their prayers. My mother answered and said they surely would. But the call was awkward and the conversation stilted. I suppose I shouldn't have been surprised.

I took the girls home to Quakertown to

see my parents last month before the new school term began, and our visit was greatly overshadowed by my sister Jane's remarkable news that she was again expecting, and their miracle baby, Curtis, was only just eight months old. I was very happy for my sister and her husband and had been so looking forward to seeing my sweet nephew again. The girls were, too. But as soon as we stepped off the train, I felt as though I were a distant relative who had picked an inopportune time to visit. My mother seemed hesitant to fully welcome us back home. It was as if she couldn't quite believe we were actually there. My mother and father have always been careful with their emotions, preferring a life of steadiness and calm, even when my sister and I were young, but there was a dignified happiness for Jane, and I felt on the fringe of it. A spectator. Especially around my mother. It was almost as if she wanted to punish me for having moved away by lavishing all her affection, subdued though it was, on Baby Curtis and pregnant Jane. When I hinted about how I felt, she seemed offended and in a roundabout way accused me of being jealous of my sister.

"I can understand why you might be feeling that way because you lost Henry," she'd said, "but it's not becoming, Pauline. And think of the example you are setting for the girls."

"I *am* thinking of the girls," I'd said. My mother and I were in the kitchen, speaking in hushed tones while we shelled peas. "They have missed you. We are only here for a short while, and then we'll have to go back to the city."

Her eyes had filled with tears then, something I rarely saw. But she held those tears in, blinked them all away as she held her hand motionless over the bowl of peas in the sink. "It's not my fault you and Thomas wanted to leave and take the girls," she said evenly, with the barest hint of anger. Or maybe fear. "You should have thought through how this move would affect your girls — and your father and me — before you left. You'll be back on that train before you know it, and I'll have to say good-bye all over again."

She tossed the peas she was holding into the bowl, and they rolled about every which way.

"But we'll visit again!" I replied, still unaware of what she was really telling me.

"I have laundry to bring in," she said, as if I had asked her what she wanted to get done after the peas were shelled. She pulled off her apron and left the kitchen.

There was so much I wanted to talk about with my mother on that visit. Her letters to me since we had left — as well as our few phone calls — had been short and only about things like the restaurant and the weather and what the rest of the family was doing. I thought it was because she preferred seeing someone she loved in person, so my expectation when we arrived was that she'd make up for the little she'd written in her letters with meaningful face-to-face conversations. While my parents have never displayed a great deal of physical affection toward Jane and me, I've never doubted their loyalty or love. I had always thought they would take on hell itself to save one of us. I had been looking forward to at last telling my mother about the shadow that has been following me since Henry died. My mother has the benefit of years and, with her emotional modesty, a cool head. I'd been an undertaker's wife for nine months and was still pondering why Death hovers over me like a tender shepherd, and why this doesn't alarm me. It should, shouldn't it? I'd wanted to confide in her and ask for advice.

I wanted to tell her about the job I'd insisted on having, preparing the deceased for their funerals. I wanted to tell her how I put rouge and lipstick on dead women to make them look beautiful again. I dress them in their prettiest clothes. I put toilet water behind their ears so that they will smell like verbena instead of that awful solution curdling in their veins. I talk to them and sing to them and I assure them that they look lovely and I try to guess what they were like when they were alive. I wanted to say that I tell those lifeless bodies about my day. I tell them about Henry. I wanted to tell my mother how inexplicably easy it is to go into the embalming room and do these things, often with Maggie at my side.

I wanted to say, "It's the strangest thing. I'm not afraid of Death anymore. I know I should be. But ever since Henry died, Death is not the phantom that it used to be. It is more like a quiet friend. I thought coming to Uncle Fred's funeral home would change all that, and Death would go back to being what it was before. But we've been there all these months and nothing is different. If anything, Death is more my friend than ever." I wanted to ask her what is wrong with me, and I wanted her to say, "Nothing. Nothing is wrong with you, Polly. Your child died and your mother's heart is healing the best way it can. The heart always does what it needs to do. Don't you fret, now. Everything will be all right in time."

But we never had that conversation.

My parents came to the station on the morning of our return to Philadelphia and watched us dry-eyed as we boarded our train. The girls and I waved to them as well as to Grandad, Jane, and a few other family members who had come to see us off. My mother raised one hand in farewell and kept it steady. It was more like a salute or a quiet command to stop the train. Clarity came over me as our car chuffed past the platform. My mother hadn't wanted us to move away. She was hurt that we did. And I'd failed to see it.

"She misses us. She misses *you*," Thomas said when I arrived home and told him about the visit. "Keeping you at a distance like this is no doubt how she manages it."

My mother had looked for a way to cope with our having moved away from her. And she had found one.

The heart always does what it needs to do.

CHAPTER 17

Evelyn

I've never seen so many people in one place at one time. Broad Street, which stretches as far as I can see in both directions, is a sea of faces on both sides. I can't even guess how many people are lined up for the Liberty Loan Parade. Uncle Fred told me when we first moved to Philadelphia that more than a million people live here, but I have never been able to grasp what even a percentage of that number looks like — until today. The newspaper predicted two hundred thousand will come out to watch the parade. Even the late-September sun seems determined to break through the clouds and attend.

The spectators are all packed onto the sidewalks like dominos, waving little flags and cheering. A dozen warplanes are flying overhead, the pilots pretending they are in battle, and everyone sings victory choruses as they swoop past. On the other side of the street, a man with a megaphone is asking women who've lost their husbands and sons and brothers in the war to speak to the crowd the names of their dearly departed. And then we are told that these women gave their all. And asked, what will we give?

Floats bearing cannons and massive guns and the skeletons of ships have passed us. Troops have marched by, and a truck filled with shoes has followed them bearing a sign that announces that every soldier needs a pair of new shoes every month. On what are they marching that they use up a fresh pair of boots every thirty days? I want to know. But today is not the day to ask questions. Today is only about taking out coin purses and checkbooks and breaking open piggy banks.

Parade organizers want to raise millions of dollars today to pay for the war — and the shoes. That's why we're all out here. It would be unpatriotic not to attend, disloyal not to give. Uncle Fred is planning to hand over a wad of money, but he's not his usual jolly self. He's been in and out of the city morgue all week, getting called in at all hours to undertake the final affairs of sailors who came to the Philadelphia Naval Yard last week from Boston with a killing influenza hiding inside them and who are now dead. Everyone is calling it the Spanish flu, even though it didn't originate in Spain. No one is sure where it came from. Spain has been the first to speak openly about it in its newspapers. Spain is also neutral regarding the war, Uncle Fred told me, so it has nothing to lose by being candid about how many of its soldiers and citizens are sick or dying. That openness has saddled Spain with the name of this terrible sickness.

"This is not the kind of busy I like," I heard him say to Mama yesterday. "These were our brave soldiers! These were the young men who were to defeat the Kaiser and end the bloodshed. We cannot spare them to this infernal disease."

Mama doesn't want us anywhere near the embalming room now, not that I have much notion of going in there. This influenza is apparently highly contagious and travels seemingly as easily as a housefly alights on one person and then another. Uncle Fred is not entirely sure if the flu victims in his embalming room can pass the disease on to one of us, since the deceased are no longer breathing, and that's how the virus travels — in the breath and spittle of the one who has it — but he is taking no chances. He wears a mask and keeps the connecting door from the kitchen to the funeral parlor locked so that none of us can accidentally expose ourselves.

A few days ago, the newspaper said there were six thousand cases of influenza at Camp Devens in Massachusetts and sixty-six soldiers have already died from it. That's not where Papa is, but that doesn't comfort Mama or me. The flu is wherever there are soldiers and sailors, so it's there at Fort Meade, too, she says. There is a professor from Harvard and doctors from New York who are working together to see if they can figure out how to create a vaccine, but the paper didn't say how far along they are.

I heard Uncle Fred tell one of his APL friends yesterday afternoon that the situation at Camp Devens is deplorable. The base hospital can only accommodate twelve hundred soldiers, but six thousand have the flu, so there are sick men lying in all the corridors and on the porches, coughing up blood everywhere. And there aren't enough nurses because half of them have the flu, too.

I don't know if Mama heard this conversation, but this morning she asked if we should all stay inside the house and listen to the bands from the upstairs windows. Uncle Fred might have actually let us, but

Willa didn't want to be indoors with all the fun happening a few blocks away. Maggie and I didn't want to stay inside, either. We aren't near any of the soldiers or sailors and we're outside, so Uncle Fred doesn't think we need to worry. They would have called off the parade if it wasn't safe. But Mama has asked us to stay on the steps of the milliner's store and not go down onto the sidewalk.

Easy enough. There are so many people that there is no room on the sidewalk for us.

But I worry about those soldiers at Camp Devens. And I worry that Fort Meade is just like it. Papa is training for the field medical corps, but if the base hospital there needs help caring for soldiers with the flu, won't they bring him in from training to lend a hand? If half of Fort Meade's nurses end up with the flu like the nurses at Camp Devens did, will he be called in to assist?

I know this is what Mama worries about, too. She doesn't think Papa is safe at Fort Meade. She is waving her little flag, but I can see in her eyes that she is not thinking about the parade.

She is wondering, just like I am, what the future truly holds for us. When we moved here to Philadelphia, Mama and Papa both thought they knew, but even I can see that they were wrong. None of us really knows.

CHAPTER 18

October 1918
Maggie

Empty school desks are all around me as the morning bell rings. It's been only five days since the parade, and the influenza that was at the army bases is everywhere now. At first, there were just a few sick people here and there. But by the third day every classroom was missing someone. Seven of my classmates were home sick yesterday, and there are five more absent today, including Sally. Ruby, two rows away, eyes the empty desk next to mine. A boy named Stanley usually sits there. I nod toward the seat, beckoning her to come sit by me. She looks toward the door and hesitates. Miss Darby was called out of the room and hasn't come back yet.

"She won't care," I say. At least I don't think our teacher will mind if Ruby comes to sit with the few of us remaining in the classroom. Ruby slowly makes her way to me. A boy ahead of me turns to us as she sits down. His name is Wendell, and he has enormous teeth. The other boys like to tease Wendell about his horse mouth, as they call it. But the fellows who mock him the most aren't in class today. He's easily the smartest boy in our class.

"They're going to close the school today," he says. "I heard two teachers talking about it in the hallway. They're sending us home."

"For how long?" Ruby says. She sounds afraid.

Wendell shrugs. A boy whose name is Chester says everything is being closed. All the schools. The churches. The theaters. Parks. Any place where a crowd would gather. His father, who is a custodian for the city, heard the officials at city hall talking about it. It's as bad here in Philadelphia as it is in Boston and New York and Washington, D.C. Worse, maybe.

"My neighbor said there are no more beds at any of our hospitals," says a girl named Louise, turning toward us from her seat. "He stood in line with his sick wife and waited for two hours before the nurses told him that he'd have to carry her back home. And they didn't give her any medicine."

"That's because there is no medicine,"

says Wendell.

"How can there be no medicine at a hospital?" Chester says. "It's a hospital!"

"There is no medicine for *this*," Wendell says.

"It's like one of Egypt's plagues," Louise says.

"I hear you cough up your insides," a boy says from behind me.

"I hear your lungs turn to tar and then you choke on them," says another one.

Ruby shudders next to me. "Stop it," she whispers, but I don't think anyone hears her.

"You can't choke on your lungs," Wendell says. "That's impossible."

"How do you know? You're not a doctor."

"You don't have to be a doctor to know you can't choke on your lungs."

There is a little flurry of debate about this to which Ruby says, louder this time, "Stop!"

Everyone is quiet for about two seconds. "My dad says the morgue is full," Chester continues. "The city undertakers are being told to come get the bodies to make room for more, but they won't come get them."

At this, all the heads in the room swing in my direction.

"Is that true?" Chester asks me.

149

I have no idea if it is or isn't. I know there is only so much space in the embalming room. Only so many tables. Mama has forbidden me to go back there, so I can't say for sure that we've no room for more. "I think we might be full," I venture. It both scares me and thrills me to say it because it's the first time since we moved here that I have everyone's attention.

"How many have you got?" Chester tries to sound nonchalant, but I hear the tremor of dread in his voice.

I don't know how many bodies are in Uncle Fred's embalming room. I haven't seen Uncle Fred in three days. He's been up before the sun, and he doesn't come through the house to his room until after I'm in bed. Yesterday Uncle Fred hired a man named Patek to help him move the bodies and transport them to the graveyards because Dora decided it wasn't safe for Charlie to help him anymore.

"Have you seen them?" one of the boys says. "Did they choke on their lungs?"

"I'm not allowed right now where the bodies are," I say, very aware that I can't provide the assurance that none of the deceased have choked on their own lungs. The smartest person in our class says that's impossible. If any of us could provide the proof that Wendell is right, it should be me. For the first time ever, I feel like it's to my advantage that I'm the daughter and niece of undertakers, and yet I can't give my classmates what they want.

There is silence for a few moments as they contemplate the fact that I might have been a fount of information if children weren't always kept away from everything important.

"Why is this happening?" Ruby says quietly to no one.

And none of us can answer her.

The door to our classroom opens, and Miss Darby steps inside. She tells us all classes have been canceled until further notice and that we are to head straight home. She admonishes us as we gather our things to work on our lessons on our own, but no one is listening to her. The only time school has ever been closed for more than a day was for a blizzard.

Ruby turns to me. "Do you think we're all going to die?" Her voice is but a whisper and her brown eyes are wide with worry.

But I don't get a chance to answer her. Her brother calls her name from the entrance to our classroom and tells her to come. Their mother is waiting outside to take them home.

When I step outside, I feel numb, like I'm in the middle of a dream. A little voice is telling me I need to hurry along to Willa's end of the school so that I can walk her home. But I just stand there on the street corner for a few minutes as classmates and parents rush by to get away. Some of the adults are pressing handkerchiefs to their noses and mouths. One man whisks past a streetcar signpost and a *No Spitting!* sign peels away from it at the tug of his coat. It floats away on the wind, and no one notices.

There are still little piles of parade confetti in the gutters, but they're all wet and matted now. You can't tell the clumps of mush had just a few days earlier been anything pretty to look at.

I wonder if this is what Jamie feels over there in France, this chilly, empty fear that something bad is happening and it's so quiet and quick you can't even name it. I haven't heard from him since the middle of September, nearly a month ago, even though I've written him nearly every day since the parade. The Sutcliffs would have gotten word if something bad had happened to him, and they've heard nothing, either.

I finally start to make my way toward Willa's part of the school, and I am already penning in my head what I will write to him when I get home. I won't tell him how awful it is here, nor will I lie and say it's all wonderful. I will just tell him we are all getting by and doing our best and hoping and praying every day that the flu and the war will both come to a quick end. I look down into the gutter as I walk and I see a small clump of parade confetti, tucked under some leaves, that isn't soaking wet or dirty. I instantly reach for it and slip the little cluster into my coat pocket.

I'll separate the tiny pieces of damp paper when I get home, let them dry, and then put them in the envelope along with the letter I write. When Jamie opens the envelope in some faraway field in France, the confetti will fall out and it will surprise him and he'll think of home and smile.

CHAPTER 19

Pauline

The back door into the funeral home starts to open, and I stand ready to tell whoever is on the other side of it that they cannot deposit their dead with us. Simply locking the door and putting a sign out that we will accept no more deliveries is not sufficient, as most will leave the sheet-wrapped cadaver on the stoop anyway, with a hastily written note pinned to its chest. It's been only nine days since the parade.

"Don't let anyone leave a body," Fred told me when he left for the morgue an hour ago. "I don't have any more caskets. I have no place to put another corpse. I can't keep lining the embalming room floor with them."

He looked to me with weary, bloodshot eyes, and I assured him I would do as he asked even though it meant staking my position in the mudroom amid the ghoulish rows of flu victims covered in horse blankets. There are too many here for one undertaker to attend. In a matter of days, this terrible sickness has turned our little world upside down. Bright Funeral Home had been a quiet, peaceful place for the most tender care of the dearly departed. It was almost like a library or a church. It was a calm, respected place where life was honored and hence affirmed, strange as that might sound. But now this place is like a terrible corner in someone's nightmare. Before Fred left for the morgue, I had to position Evie at the front stoop lest any desperate soul try to break down the front door and bring their dead through our living quarters.

Fred has run out of ice to keep the bodies cool, and the odor of decomposition — imagine putrid meat slathered in sugar gone rancid — is wafting about me despite the scarf tied around my nose and mouth. It is not a human smell. Nothing about the bodies smells or looks human. It's only when a stray finger or a lock of hair or a toe finds its way out of the fabric cocoon that it's clear that under the layers of blankets and canvas are people whom my bizarre companion has called to itself. At least that is what common sense would have me believe — that Death has been gorging itself on the innocent of Philadelphia since the parade. And not just Philadelphia. Everywhere. From one end of America to the other and beyond. And yet something keeps me from calling down curses on my companion. Even now I sense the enemy is not who we think it is. My companion hovers kindly in the hellish corners in the funeral home. Like a valet, like a dance partner.

The door swings open. It is on my tongue to announce in a firm voice that we can take no more dead when I see it is Fred. Instead of a handkerchief, a surgical mask he must have gotten from the coroner half covers his face. He pulls it down to speak to me.

"Only me," he says as he comes through. A welcome gust of fresh air swirls in with him, settling on the bodies closest to the entrance. The sickly scent of decay and loss rises and settles. He closes the door but doesn't bolt it.

He turns to me with the day's mail in his hand. "Three thousand are dead now in the city. Tens of thousands more are sick with it." He pulls off his coat and hangs it on a hook in the mudroom. "Too many of our doctors are away on the front. They've got first-year medical students and old washouts like me doctoring the sick!" He holds up the mail. "Thomas wants you to take the girls and go home to your parents' in Quakertown. I agree. It's not safe here."

Fred extends an envelope in my direction, and as I reach for it, I see the depth of his concern for our welfare. Thomas's absence has given me eyes to see that Fred would have been a good husband, a caring father. He has quietly looked out for the girls and me in the three weeks Thomas has been gone, asking every other day if we need anything, making sure I have enough money for groceries, double-checking the doors and window locks at night like a conscientious father would. He still has his rough edges, of course, but they are few compared to the range of his generosity toward us this past year and especially since Thomas has been gone. Making my husband his assistant and heir has reshaped all of our lives for the good. Because of Fred our girls will never want for anything.

The letter, addressed to both Fred and me, is void of any pretense of normalcy. The influenza is bad at Fort Meade, Thomas says. Nearly two thousand soldiers lie sick. They've closed the base theater, the YMCA, the Hostess House. No visitors are allowed in and no soldiers are allowed out on leave. Even so, the flu is out among the public outside the Fort, just like it is here. Civilian workers took it home from the army base with them.

"Take the girls and go home to your parents' until the plague passes," Thomas wrote in a hurried hand. "If I were home I'd take you there myself. You need to get out of the city."

I look up from the note.

"How will you manage without us?" I ask Fred, even though I know with all my being that Thomas is right. I need to get the girls home to Quakertown.

"I'll manage."

I am suddenly worried for Fred. The physical toll on him has already been immense since the flu descended on the city. Someone mentioned to him early on that he stood to make a great profit from this sickness, and Fred told that person that this was a horrific way to make a living. Some undertakers in the city have been raising their rates the last few days, charging twice as much as they usually did for their work. But not Fred.

"Do you suppose Mrs. Landry could return to do housekeeping for you?" I ask.

"No . . . no," he says, a strange tenor to his voice, as though he is afraid Mrs. Landry sports a grudge from having been let go and won't welcome an invitation to come back.

"I am sure she bears us no ill will, Fred," I say. "She understood that I wanted to run the house myself. I don't mind ringing her."

He shakes his head. "No. That's not it. She's . . . Mrs. Landry died three days after the parade. She was one of the first victims I attended. I didn't say anything for fear of distressing you."

Picturing Mrs. Landry's slate gray body — all the cadavers of the flu victims are as pale as ghosts — lying inert on the embalming table silences me for a moment.

"Just three days after?" I finally say.

"She went quick. Many of them do. It's a mercy when they do."

"I'm so sorry, Fred."

He shrugs. "I've not had time to give it much thought. It's better for me not to give any of this much thought."

I had not considered that they aren't all strangers who have been carried through the funeral home doors. Some have surely been Fred's friends, business acquaintances, people he greeted regularly at church.

"Is there another housekeeper I can call for you?" I say, wishing there were better words.

Uncle Fred shakes his head. "I will manage. This scourge can't last forever."

It is the first time since the parade that anyone has dared to suggest the flu will spend itself and then be gone. That perhaps its very viciousness is what will kill it.

"Go on back into the house and make your arrangements," Fred says as he pulls the mask up over his nose and mouth. He moves past me to the embalming room, where the rest of the day's work lies waiting for him. I wish I could help him, but I know he won't let me. The bodies are riddled with a disease that no doubt clings to them like soot from a fire. And no one is expecting my usual cosmetic touches anyway.

I return to the main part of the house. Maggie and Willa are working on a puzzle in the sitting room, and Evie has moved a chair to the foyer, where she can keep an eye on the front door while she reads. I insisted the girls continue with their lessons in the morning, but it is midafternoon now, nearly the time they would be coming home from school if classes had not been canceled.

They look up at me as I enter the room, their expressions a mix of boredom and uneasiness. It occurs to me that maybe the girls and I should remain in Quakertown not just until the flu passes but until after the war is over and Thomas returns. What is keeping us in the city, really? I am no closer to putting Death back in its proper place than I was when we first arrived ten months ago, even with all my ministrations to the dead, and the arrival of a merciless killing flu. My easy familiarity with it remains.

I look at my children — my flesh and blood — and my arms ache for Henry, gone from me for nearly a year now. What will my companion do if I take my girls and speed back to where my baby boy lies? Will it notice I have left when there is so much else to occupy itself with here?

What will it do if I stay?

There is a terrible moral rending when so many people start dying all at once and bodies begin to accumulate like plowed snow on the curbs. My girls are surely feeling this injury to humanity even though they perhaps cannot name it outright. I should have taken them the first day the schools were closed.

"I'm thinking we should go to Quakertown to sit out the flu," I say, and my voice trembles a little.

"What do you mean?" Maggie asks, her brow puckered.

"I mean, your papa and I think it's wise to go to Grandma and Grandpa's until the flu has passed. Just until the flu is gone. Unless . . . unless we want to stay longer."

"Why would we stay longer?" Evelyn studies my face, looking for unspoken clues as to why I suddenly want us to flee. She won't want to leave her school and the downtown library; Willa won't want to abandon her friend Flossie; and even Maggie, who has had the most trouble making new friends, won't want to leave the city, the Sutcliffs, and her attic room.

"Well, then, until the flu has passed," I say.

"Will we have to go to school there?" Willa asks, and I tell her not to worry about that right now.

Maggie and Evie wear twin looks of uneasiness at the thought of returning to the country life they left nearly a year ago, and for who knows how long.

"Uncle Fred said this can't last forever," I announce, wanting them to hear those words like I heard them. *It can't last forever.*

I send them to their rooms to pack, and I head to the kitchen to take inventory of our stores. If need be, I'll go to the market before we leave to make sure the shelves are well stocked for Fred. The restaurant will be busy until sundown. I'll wait to place the call to my parents until then.

I open the pantry and step into its shadows

to count the jars and packages. Alone, but not alone.

I do not fear Death for myself, but I will not allow its cold fingers to touch my girls. Not even in a slow caress.

They are mine, I whisper.

CHAPTER 20

Willa

Flossie's brother has the flu. I went to her apartment yesterday, and she told me she's not allowed to let anyone in. She's not allowed at my house because her mother is afraid of all Uncle Fred's dead bodies. We played for a little while on her stoop with her Humpty Dumpty Circus Set. It has twenty pieces, with a giraffe and a polar bear and an alligator I was afraid to touch. But it wasn't much fun, and she's supposed to stay near her house in case her mother needs her, so we ran out of things to do.

When I came home and told Mama about Flossie's brother, she said I can't go back over there until Flossie's brother is better, even though I didn't even go inside.

So there's no school, but I'm not allowed to play at Flossie's place and she's not allowed to play at mine.

Gretchen, the German girl I don't play

with, has the flu, too.

There's nothing to do here at the house, and everything is closed, like there's a snowstorm. Evie just reads her books, so she doesn't care. Maggie will sometimes play with me, but she's cross because she's not allowed past the kitchen door into the business anymore. There are dead people inside the viewing parlor now, and Uncle Fred ran out of caskets again. The place where he usually gets them hasn't had any for days. The cabinetmaker down the street is working to make some, but he says he only has two hands. The bodies in the parlor are just wrapped up in sheets and blankets. Two days ago when the kitchen door was left open a bit, I saw men bringing one in. There was black blood where the nose is. I didn't like seeing it. That night I had a nightmare that everyone had black blood coming out of their noses and nobody could stop it. I woke up before I found out if it was coming out of my nose, too.

Yesterday Mama told us we were going to go to Grandma and Grandpa Adler's to stay with them until the flu is gone. But then today Mama said she'd changed her mind. She said she'd thought about it and decided Uncle Fred would be too lonely here by himself and he doesn't have his housekeeper anymore, so he wouldn't have anyone to cook for him and do his laundry. She cried when she told us, though.

"That's because that isn't the real reason we're not going," Maggie told me later.

The three of us were in the sitting room working on sums. Mama said just because there isn't school doesn't mean we shouldn't be learning.

"Grandma Adler said we can't come because of Aunt Jane's baby," Maggie went on. "We might bring the flu to Quakertown and give it to Baby Curtis."

"But we don't have the flu," I said.

And Maggie said, "The first couple days after people catch it, they don't know they have it."

Evie told her to please be quiet. Maggie said she didn't have to be quiet — it was the truth.

"But Willa doesn't need to be hearing all that," Evie said. "And you shouldn't have listened in on Mama's telephone call to Grandma. You don't know that she said we couldn't come because we might bring the flu."

"Yes, I do," Maggie insisted. "I could tell that's what Grandma said by what Mama said."

I know I wouldn't give that baby the flu. I

don't have it. I don't feel sick. I think Maggie is wrong. I think if you catch something, you know it.

Mama is sad today that we're not going to Quakertown, and I'm a little sad, too. I think Uncle Fred should fix his own dinners and wash his own socks.

"It's not that hard," I told Mama. It's not. I'm only seven and I know how to make a sandwich.

"He's so busy because of the flu," Mama said, wiping her eyes with her sleeve. "He barely has time to sleep. We should stay and help him."

So we're not going.

Mama had some ladies from the church visit her this afternoon. They had gone to a big meeting on Walnut Street. A lot of people aren't happy with the mayor because he let the flu come, and they want to do something about it. I was listening to them talking to her. She invited them in for tea, and they sat in the sitting room. I sat on the stairs to listen because I had nothing else to do. The ladies said that at that meeting they'd all decided they needed to find a way to help.

"The school and church cafeterias have been turned into soup kitchens, and volunteers are making food for people who are too sick to cook their own meals," one of the ladies said.

And Mama said that was a good idea.

"Mrs. Bright," another lady said, "might you be willing to take some of this food down to a few people on the south side who have no one to take care of them? We have a list of names and addresses. There are so many poor souls down there who are suffering alone. Could you spare a few hours from your day to do this work of mercy? We'll provide the soup and a surgical mask."

I thought Mama would say no. She is always telling me and my sisters to be careful and not to be around any coughing people right now and to stay away, stay away, stay away from Uncle Fred's dead bodies. But she said she would go.

And the church lady said someone would be by in the morning with jars of soup. All Mama had to do was take the food to the people on the list and then bring the jars back to the church in the afternoon, and the next day it would happen all over again. They told her she might need to take a cab, though, because the streetcars might not be running. Mama said she'd find a way to get there.

"It's so nice to have you and your family at the church, Mrs. Bright," the lady said.

She said Mama was such a kind person and what beautiful girls she had and how proud her own mama must be of her that she would put the needs of others first, just like Jesus.

Mama just said, "Thank you" and "Would you care for a second cup?"

They didn't have time for a second cup. They had other ladies to visit, because they had lots of names and lots of lists.

When they left, Evie came out from the kitchen, where she'd been boiling water in case there was to be a second pot of tea.

"You're going to do it, Mama?" Evie asked. "Isn't it a bit dangerous?"

"I may as well be of use if I am to stay here," Mama said. "It's only dangerous if you aren't careful. Besides, can you imagine what it must be like to be ill and have no family to look out for you? To feel as though you've been abandoned?"

Evie didn't say anything, so I guess she can't imagine it.

That means tomorrow will be an even longer, more boring day. Mama will be gone and there's no school and Flossie can't come over and I can't even play with Gretchen.

I miss Papa. He should be here.

I miss Henry.

I wish they were both here.

I wish the flu would just go back to where it came from.

CHAPTER 21

Maggie

Mama isn't going to let me go with her.

I can see it in her eyes before she says a word. We are standing together in the kitchen, and she is gathering a basket of items to take along with the soup that the church men brought.

"I want to go with you," I say.

She turns from the pantry shelves with that look mothers have that just says *no.* I'm already deciding how I'm going to get her to change her mind; the words are right there on my tongue. I'm not a little child anymore. I'm thirteen. I want to help all those people, too. I know how to be careful. I will wear my mask. I can carry the basket.

All this is true, but the real reason is I can't spend another day at this house, pretending I don't see all the bodies piling up on the stoop and in the parlor and even in the carriage house, where Uncle Fred

171

used to keep the extra caskets, back when there were extra caskets. I am tired of Evie telling me what to do and Willa's whining and Uncle Fred's stomping about, complaining that he can't take any more bodies. I want to be where something good and right is happening, even if it's just me and Mama taking soup to a sick person lying in a bed.

I open my mouth to list all the reasons I should be allowed to go with her. But then that "you're not coming" look falls away from her face, and another one takes its place. I haven't seen her look at me that way since Henry died. Her eyes are saying things that her mouth isn't quite ready to say. Like she maybe wishes she could shield my sisters and me from what is happening and how hard it is to be a mother and yet so powerless.

"I'll be careful," I say. "I won't let anyone cough on me."

Mama doesn't answer right away, but her eyes are locked on mine. I reach out to touch her arm. She looks down at my hand on her sleeve and it's like she is measuring the length of my fingers and my ability to be of any help. She stares at me for a moment and it's as if she heard my thoughts, knows I need a glimpse of something good today.

"If I say yes, you must promise me something," she finally says.

"All right."

"You do exactly what I say. You understand me, Margaret?"

I'm not Maggie to her in that moment. I am Margaret. It's as if she is reminding me who I am. Margaret Louise Bright. Second-born daughter. Alive.

"Yes," I answer.

"If I say you can't come inside a house, you *will* wait outside. No arguments."

"I promise."

She hands me the basket, and I see what else she has put inside to do battle with the flu. Clean washcloths. Lavender soap. Rolls of cotton. Bayer aspirin. A little brown bottle of antiseptic. A flask of water.

"Get your mask and your coat," she says gently as she brushes past me. "I'll tell Uncle Fred and Evie I'm taking you with me. Wait for me on the front stoop."

My mask is in my coat pocket from when we went to the market a few days ago. It's just one of Mama's lace scarves, doubled over. It looks pretty, even wrapped around my face like I'm a bandit bent on robbing a bank. I tie it on.

I step outside holding the basket by its handle and my coat over my other arm because it isn't that cold and the morning air is so fresh and clean. When Mama joins me a few minutes later, she just looks at the coat over my arm and doesn't insist I put it on.

"We're going to walk," she says, taking the basket. "It's a bit of a ways."

"I don't mind."

She has on a new mask that was delivered with the soup a little bit ago. It makes her look like a nurse. As we step out onto the street, I look up in the upper-story windows of Sutcliff Accounting, and I see Charlie gazing down at us. I wave to him and he waves back. He looks like he wants to come to wherever it is we are going. I would ask Mama if he can join us, but I know Dora Sutcliff would never let him come. I'll go over to see him when we get back from the south side, though, and I'll tell him about it. I can ask him what he's heard from Jamie. Mrs. Sutcliff was over a couple days ago for a cup of flour — she was out — and I heard her tell Mama they'd finally gotten a new letter and she was so thankful to hear Jamie wasn't injured or sick. But she didn't say anything else about his letter and Mama didn't ask. Charlie or Mrs. Sutcliff would probably let me read the letter if I asked. I am still waiting for a new letter from him.

We turn south down Broad Street to join other people who have somewhere to be and must walk if they don't own a car or buggy. The streetcars have stopped running because people stand too close to one another on them and their breath mingles. It's not safe. People glance up at us as we walk. But nobody says, "Good morning" or "Where are you headed this fine day, Mrs. Bright?" They just nod as they take note of which direction we are headed. Most people have masks on; a few don't. Some stores we pass are open; some aren't. Some doors have red-lettered placards that read *INFLUENZA* tacked to them — which means there is flu inside — some don't. Some doors have crepe banners tacked to them — white if a child died, black if it was an adult, and gray if it was an old person whom the flu had killed — and some don't. It is like any other day, except it isn't. Broad Street is half the way it always is and half ghost town.

It's as if Philadelphia has been cut in two like an apple, and one side looks just the way the inside of an apple should and the other side is dark and wormy and makes you gasp when you see it. That side isn't an apple at all anymore but something sinister

175

and wrong.

And the worst thing is, no one's sure which side of the apple they're going to get.

I'm thinking that maybe you don't know you got the wormy side of the apple until you've already eaten half of it. You can't see the flu coming for you. You can't see when it skips you and picks someone else. You can't see anything at all except one shiny red apple that looks just fine.

Even though I'm thirteen, this thought makes me reach for my mother's hand for reassurance. And she just lets me clasp it, without so much as a glance down in wonder.

I'm not wishing I hadn't come with her. I want to be walking down this street with Mama, headed where we're headed. But her hand in mine makes me feel like I'm not alone in this world where you can't always see what's in front of you.

Chapter 22

Pauline

If Thomas weren't off training for war, he would ask why in the world I am taking Maggie with me to South Street. "Do you really think that's a good idea," he would have said, in a way that wasn't a question at all.

Truth be told, I'm not sure there are any good ideas right now. Perhaps I should turn around and take Maggie back home, but I admit I was too moved by her desire today to reconnect with life and the living. The sick people who we're off to minister to may be hovering at death's door, but they are still breathing; they are still fighting. They are still alive.

This is not the way it is at the house. There is no fight at Bright Funeral Home, only an endless influx of defeated souls.

Fred had to hire someone to watch over the most recent delivery of caskets or they would have been stolen right off the back stoop. Those coffins were claimed and then gone in a day and I never even saw who was laid in them. The dead are buried as quickly as Fred can arrange it now. The parlor isn't being used for long and tearful good-byes with open caskets and the dead all readied and beautified for the occasion. If a family uses the parlor at all, it is to weep at a safe distance over a closed casket, and none stay very long. The cabinetmaker on the next street over is working day and night to fashion impromptu coffins, having put away his half-finished highboys and sideboards to nail together simple boxes instead.

This is what Maggie wanted a few hours' respite from. I could see in her eyes her fearful need to step away from the house for just a little while. This is what I would tell Thomas if he were here and asked why I am letting her come. I would leave off my sliver of a worry that she has begun to sense my companion's shadow in the corners of our home. I don't think Death has been watching her as it watches me, but who can say what that specter is truly up to?

"And what about you, Polly? Why are you going down there?" Thomas might have said next.

I would've replied that my reason is the

same as Maggie's — I need to do something decent and useful — and yet I know he would've seen right through that answer.

You don't have to prove anything to anyone.

I hear these words in my head as if he were saying them to me this very moment as my heels click on the pavement.

I need to prove to myself I'm not selfish, Tom.

You're not.

But I feel like I am.

You did nothing wrong.

I shouldn't have asked my mother to let us come. I shouldn't have put her in that terrible place of having to say no.

You did nothing wrong.

As Maggie and I walk, I replay the telephone conversation I had with my mother when I begged her to let us come home.

"But we aren't sick," I answered when her response to my entreaty was that it was unsafe to let us come. "The girls and I have been careful. We keep to the house. We don't have it."

"But you are living right there with it! You sleep over it!" my mother replied, a rare display of emotion choking her words. "How can you even *ask* me to let you all come when you know how terrible it can be to lose a child, Polly! I can't put Baby Curtis and Jane and the rest of the family at risk like that. Jane and the baby live right next door, as you well know. I'm sorry, but I can't. You know I can't! How can you even ask me?"

You should never have left is what she'd been really saying. *You should never have left the safety of home in the first place.*

I look down at Maggie walking beside me, and I wonder if maybe my mother is right. Maybe we shouldn't have. We didn't know the war would get worse. We didn't know a plague was coming that would change forever the way my children think of life and death. But you can't get back the day you make a decision that changes everything.

"Do you know where we're supposed to go?" Maggie asks now, interrupting these thoughts. It's on my tongue to answer that I tried so very hard to get her where we were supposed to go. I tried my best. But then I realize she is only asking if I know which houses to take the soup to.

"I have a list from Mrs. Arnold." I pull the note from my coat pocket and show it to her.

The four names are foreign, long and hard to pronounce and almost exotic the way they look on paper. Mrs. Arnold told me the neighborhood where we are headed is heavily populated by immigrants from Croatia. I didn't even know where that was. Evie had to show me in her atlas, on a map that stretched across two pages.

"They don't speak much English there, but they know enough," Mrs. Arnold had said. And then she'd added that words aren't what these wretched souls need anyway. They need food and the gentle touch of compassion. The sweet attention of a selfless giver of mercy.

Maggie looks at the list, whispering the strange syllables as she sounds out the names.

"Do these people go to our church?" she asks.

"No, I don't think they do."

"Then how do we know they need us?"

I reach for the list, and Maggie hands it back to me. "Mrs. Arnold and the other ladies went to a big meeting about how to help. They made a trip down here." I slip the note back in my pocket.

"And there are others doing what we're doing with the soup?"

"Many others."

After fifteen minutes or so, we turn east on South and walk another ten or eleven blocks before we finally arrive at a stretch of streets that look so sad and dirty, it is no wonder the flu is running around this neighborhood like it's trying to burn it to the ground. Some people are out and about, but a stuttering slowness seems to characterize the speed of the automobiles and the buggies in the street and even the pedestrians on the sidewalks. The streetcars aren't running here, either. Some of the shop signs are lettered in a language I don't know. I look at Mrs. Arnold's directions for finding the first person on the list, a Mrs. Abramovic. *Turn right at the barbershop with the green awning,* Mrs. Arnold had written.

My quiet companion is with me as always, but I sense indifference as Maggie and I walk nearer and nearer to our destination. It is a strange disinterest in my task that is both welcome and disconcerting. After all this time, I should know Death's ways and wiles, shouldn't I? But I can't explain the apathy I'm sensing.

We turn into the long, narrow street by the barbershop. It is lined on both sides with brick-and-wood storefronts and row houses, three and four stories high, all of them tattered and in need of paint and window washing. There is presently a little alley off to our left as we make our way up the block, and I can see little dwellings even more dilapidated than the ones in front of us. And then there is another little alley, and more tumbledown residences, laundry lines linking them together like Christmas garland.

I find the narrow, multistory house of Mrs. Abramovic, and I knock on the door, hoping there is someone inside who will let me in, since she is sick with the flu and surely won't be answering. The rheumy-eyed old man who responds to my knock coughs when he swings the door open. It could be an innocent attempt to rid his lungs of a scattering of dust, but there are no harmless coughs anymore. I instinctively take a step back and I turn to Maggie on the bottom step and hold up a finger.

"Don't come into this one. Wait right here for me," I say quietly.

I turn back to the man. "My name's Mrs. Bright, from the Methodist church up the boulevard. And I'm here to see Mrs. Abramovic. I've some medicine and soup for her. May I come in?"

He says nothing and steps aside as he coughs again, this time into his collar. I tighten my mask around my nose and mouth and glance back at Maggie. She has moved away from the bottom step and is now eyeing a skinny striped cat strolling toward her.

"I'll be out soon," I call to her.

The foyer I step into is chilly even though it is a relatively warm day for October.

"That one," the man says, pointing to a door with the letter *B* nailed to it. He unlocks it with a key from his pants pocket and then ambles away. I had assumed this man to be Mrs. Abramovic's husband, but apparently he is just the landlord in the crumbling house. I knock on the door as I turn the knob.

"Mrs. Abramovic?" I push the door open as I peek inside. The front room is sparsely furnished and smells faintly of roasted onions, garlic, and spices I can't name. Little bits of lace lie about on the end tables, and faded antimacassars hang on the backs of the sagging sofa and an armchair. A cracked window above a tiny sink lets in a welcome draft that is probably not so welcome on cold days. "Mrs. Abramovic?" I call again as I make my way down a narrow hall that leads to the only bedroom.

I find the woman in bed with a faded quilt pulled up tight to her chin. I can't guess how old she is; her skin is so pale and drawn. She is perhaps my mother's age, late fifties. She opens her eyes and looks at me with such terror I realize I must look like I mean to do her harm with my face covered the way it is.

"I'm Mrs. Bright from the Ladies' Aid at Broad Street Methodist," I say, in as reassuring a tone as I can muster. "Mrs. Arnold was here the other day? I've brought some soup for you."

The woman stares at me blankly and I wonder how much of what I've said she understands. I approach the bed with my basket and lift out a jar of soup. It is still slightly warm. "Can you eat something?"

Her gaze shifts from me to the soup and she slowly nods. I don't know if she is in the beginning stages of the illness or if she's survived it and is now slowly making the trek back to the realm of the healthy. I hold my breath as I lean over her to help her to a sitting position against her pillows.

She is light as a feather and weak from illness. Perhaps I am meant only to leave the soup for her and go, but I wonder if she has the strength to even open the jar.

"How about if I help you eat a little? I have everything all right here," I say, glad I don't have to rummage through her tiny kitchen for a spoon. I ladle some of the soup into a small bowl from my basket.

I pull up a rickety chair next to her bed and take a seat, wondering what I should say as I help her eat. I still don't know if she speaks any English. But conversation is not needed. Mrs. Abramovic is so weak she lies back against her pillows after only five spoonsful of soup.

"Can you not manage a couple more bites, Mrs. Abramovic?" I ask her.

She shakes her head. "Thank you," she murmurs, in heavily accented English. "You are very kind."

"Is there no one to take care of you? No children or siblings?"

Again, she shakes her head. "My brother die last week. His wife, day before. Only me now."

I help her take a couple aspirins and then settle her back against her pillows. I am sad to think of leaving her, but I can't stay with Maggie waiting for me outside and three more names on the list.

"I will try to come again tomorrow, Mrs. Abramovic." I rise from the chair and put my things away, except for the half-finished soup. I set the bowl on her bedside table next to a worn Bible and a pair of misshapen spectacles. "I'm leaving the soup here for you. You try to eat it later today, all right?"

"Your dish," she says. It sounds like *deesh.* "Your spoon."

"I can get them next time I come." I pull

up her coverlet. The woman is as helpless as a little child, and she looks up at me with eyes glistening with gratitude.

"God bless you," she whispers.

As she says this, I sense that my companion is so very near to me, close as my breath, but it is not here for this woman. It does not have her name on its lips. It had hovered over her, considered her perhaps, but then it had pulled away, even before I got here.

I am suddenly overcome by my inability to understand why some will survive the flu and some won't. Why some babies live and some don't. Why some people pass away in a warm bed full of years while others have their breath snatched from them before they've earned so much as one gray hair.

I bid the woman good-bye and head quickly back to the dark, chilly foyer. I close her door behind me and lean my back against it for a moment, unable not to imagine that there is probably a person like Mrs. Abramovic in every row house on this street, and on the next street over, and on every street in this neighborhood, and in my neighborhood, and in Philadelphia, in Pennsylvania, in America, in France, in Spain, and in all the countries whose names I don't even know. This flu is like a black shroud that has been flung across everything that breathes under the canopy of heaven, and if you could stand back far enough, you wouldn't see all the people it touches, only the immense length and breadth of its expanse.

For no reason that I can see, Mrs. Abramovic was able to crawl out from underneath that shadowy veil.

"You took her brother and his wife, but you didn't take her," I whisper. "Why didn't you? Why?"

There is not so much as a tremble in the air about me. No sound or movement. No indication that I have even been heard. And then there is a startling whisper of a thought resonating deep within me: that my companion never chooses. It merely responds.

I don't know what to make of this revelation. And I don't know how I will manage coming back to Mrs. Abramovic every day until she is well enough to care for herself. But I know I must try. I've no doubt the others on the list will affect me just as greatly.

My hand is on the front door and I throw it open, eager now to see Maggie and the face of innocence. But she is not on the bottom step.

I step outside and pull the door closed behind me, gazing about for my daughter.

"Maggie?"

I see the cat that had been walking toward her when I went inside Mrs. Abramovic's building. He is sitting on the sidewalk licking his paws and washing his face, paying me no mind whatsoever. There is no other living thing on the narrow street.

"Maggie!" I shout, and my heart starts to thrum inside my chest.

My daughter is nowhere in sight.

Chapter 23

Maggie

I never would have heard the baby if I hadn't followed the cat to the street corner and the front window of the row house hadn't been broken.

The infant's little cries were like the yowls newborn kittens make or a creaky step at the top of the stairs or a little bird in a far-off tree. But I knew the second I heard it that it wasn't a kitten or a stair or a bird that made that noise. I knew it was a baby. It was as if that sunken part that had been a sister to Henry suddenly burst out of me and swirled around like a waterspout, reminding me what that sound was.

I didn't think to call out to Mama, who was still inside the woman's house. I just turned toward those cries like I was a fish hooked on a line. It drew me down a side alley with tall, skinny houses on either side and front doors with all their paint peeling off. Trash was strewn about and there were little pots of dead plants and rusted bicycle parts and broken glass and the sour smell of pee. No one was in the alley, not even a dog, even though there was dog poop every-where.

The baby's cries tugged me to the first stoop on the left, where the front door was ajar. I walked toward it and saw through a busted front window that a girl about Willa's age, maybe, lay on a sofa, sprawled out like she'd been tossed there. The baby cried out to me again as I looked at her.

I pushed the door open the rest of the way. There were stairs to the upper floors with sacks of trash on them, and another door; this one was half-open also and led into the room where the girl on the sofa was.

I didn't stop to think if I should; I just stepped inside. The room stank like garbage and outhouses, even with my mask on. I turned to the girl. She was whitish blue like someone had painted her that color. Dots of blood had pooled below her nose, like a mustache. Her eyes were closed and I couldn't tell if she was breathing. My own breath started to come in short gasps and I turned away. Across the tiny front room was a cradle and the baby who had called out to me. I crossed the room in only a few steps.

The baby looked to be nearly the age Henry had been just before he got sick. Four months or so. The baby had curls the color of dark caramel and the same sweet rosebud mouth Henry had. His eyes were half-open as I drew near and the baby poked a little fist at me as if to say, "What took you so long?" The rag that had been pinned around the baby's bottom hadn't been changed in probably days and the weight of it had made it slide down around his knees. I moved a tiny corner of the soiled blanket half covering the baby. He was a boy. He had a little birthmark shaped like a heart by his belly button.

I tossed my coat to the floor, and in one swift move I had that baby out of his filthy bed and wrapped in the folds of my coat. His disgusting diaper fell off at my feet. I scooped him and my coat into my arms and cuddled him against my neck. I didn't stop to consider that perhaps he was sick with the flu. But his skin felt cool to mine, so I was sure he had no fever.

For a couple moments, I just stood there in that little house and held the baby in my arms like it was the most natural thing in the world. I didn't think about the girl on the sofa behind me or where this baby's parents were or what I was even going to do next. I just held him and swayed a little bit with him, the way Henry had liked.

I would have stayed that way a little bit longer, but I suddenly remembered Mama would expect me to stay where she had left me. I turned toward a door by the kitchen area that I figured led to a bedroom. I tiptoed toward the half-closed door to see if there was a mother inside who was simply too weak from illness to get to her child. I poked the door open. On the bed, curled up like a rag doll, was a woman. Her splotchy skin was gray and her open eyes were unblinking. The front of her nightgown was covered in black goo that I knew she had coughed up from her lungs. Uncle Fred's bodies had been arriving wrapped in sheets, with the arms and legs neatly tucked in. Sometimes their heads weren't covered but their eyes were always closed. His bodies were dead people whom other, living people had noticed and taken care of. This woman was dead and forgotten. Her hands clutched at her nightgown like she knew she was dying all alone and her children lay in the other room. There were no signs that a father lived in this house. No boots in the corner, no coveralls draped over a chair, no can of shaving powder atop the bureau. Something deep inside me was roiling about and I knew I had to get the baby out of this house of death before I threw up on him.

I turned from the baby's dead mother and went back into the main room. I looked at the girl on the sofa one last time and, to my surprise, her glassy eyes were now open. I stood there for a second, staring at her because Papa had told me sometimes the eyes of the dead inch open as the body starts to decay.

Then the girl blinked, slowly. She was still alive.

Our eyes held each other's for a moment.

I wondered if she knew her mother was dead.

I wondered if she knew she was also dying.

Had she staggered to her front door earlier this morning to open it, hoping someone would hear her baby brother crying?

She lifted a finger toward me and pointed at the bundle I held in my arms. Poor thing. I knew the sister love that was breaking her heart in two.

"He's safe with me," I whispered, one sister to another.

And then the girl closed her eyes, and her chest seemed to heave a little. Her hand fell limp.

I couldn't get out of that house fast enough.

When I get back to the step where Mama told me to wait, I can see her way up the street, calling for me. She sounds both mad and scared. I start running toward her, but I don't want to shout to her because the baby has fallen asleep against me.

I am out of breath when I finally reach her and when I call for her in a gasp, Mama whirls around like she is a ballroom dancer and her eyes are as wide as I've ever seen them.

"I told you to stay right there and wait for me!" she says in a half yell because there are a few other people about now, and she glances at them at the same time she is glaring at me. But the very next second she sees the bundle in my arms. "What have you got there?"

"It's a little baby, Mama. His mother is dead," I say, still out of breath.

"Good Lord!" Mama heaves her basket to the ground and snatches the baby and my coat out of my arms. He makes a little sound, like he's not happy about leaving my arms for hers.

"He's not sick," I say. "He doesn't have it."

"You don't know that! I told you to stay right on the step!"

"But I heard him crying, Mama. I heard him. I could tell he needed help. I couldn't just leave him."

Mama looks closer at the baby. She sees how weak he is, smells his skin and spit-up. She makes a face, a sad one.

"The door to his house was open and he was just lying in a cradle in the front room," I say. "His mother was in the bedroom and she was dead." For the first time since I'd found the baby, tears are forming in my eyes. They are hot and they sting.

Mama's face goes pale. She is no doubt thinking she should never have brought me with her. "Show me where you found him."

I grab her basket and we turn to walk the way I'd come. I begin to worry that Mama is going to put the baby back. She almost looks like she is mad at me for finding him, even though I know she isn't. How can she be? I was meant to find him. I was supposed to have come with Mama today. That baby would have died if I hadn't come.

I don't want to take Mama back to the baby's house. I don't want to see his dead mother and dying sister, but I know I must prove to Mama that this baby needs us. We near the stoop with the half-open door and

I glance in the broken front window.

What I see makes me freeze.

The girl who'd been lying on the sofa is gone.

She isn't there.

"What's the matter?" Mama says, her question pricking me like a stick.

I only have a second to decide what to do. It's not a very long time when there's so much to ponder. That girl was near to dead. I am sure of it. That's all I can think of. She was dying. Is dying. We aren't.

"I . . . I don't think this is the right alley," I say.

"What color was the front door? Think."

"I wasn't paying attention. I don't remember." I move away from that first stoop to the second one, to the third one. To one across the alley.

"Well?" Mama says.

"I don't think this is the right alley."

We make our way back out to the street and then down the next alley. The alleys all look alike. Even Mama can see this.

"I don't know which one it is now," I say, thinking only that I was meant to find this baby.

He is crying in Mama's arms now, but it is a frail cry, like a sighing wind.

"We've got to get him some food and attention," she says. "Come on."

I follow her back out to South Street and Mama hails a taxicab that is driving by.

We settle into the seat in the back and Mama draws the baby close to her chest to shush him. He smells even worse inside the taxi. Mama looks at me and her face softens a bit. "It's all right, Maggie. We'll figure out where he belongs. One thing at a time."

Her words echo in my head the whole time we're in the cab. I can't seem to understand what she said. It isn't until we're getting out of the taxi at the funeral parlor that I realize I decided the moment I first held him that I will never let this child go.

CHAPTER 24

Evelyn

Mama's instructions when she and Maggie left for South Street were that Willa and I should not bother Uncle Fred and that we were to stay upstairs. She'd cocked her head toward the part of the house that was the funeral parlor, where we were forbidden to enter now anyway, and said, "It's very busy in there this morning."

That meant more bodies were being delivered and Uncle Fred would be pulling his hair out with where to put them. I already knew he had no more room for any. He had tried to turn some away the day before, but the people who'd brought them told him they couldn't possibly take them back home. The city morgue is full. The hospitals didn't want them because they are full, too. You'd never think in a city this size there could be a shortage of anything until people start dying every day by the hundreds and suddenly there's no place to put the bodies. That's all they are when there are that many. Bodies. Or not even that. The health department sent out a bulletin that they will begin sending around trucks to private homes to pick up the dead off the porches because undertakers like Uncle Fred are refusing to come for them. The *dead* — that was what they called them, as if it is too sad and too hard to think of them as singular beings who had names and addresses. The *dead* sounds like the *flu*. But they aren't the same. The flu is one entity who's seemingly been given a key to every house. The dead are people by the thousands — fathers, mothers, brothers, sisters.

Mama wanted us to be home in Quakertown instead of here, but Grandma and Grandpa were afraid we'd bring the flu there. I guess they didn't know they could get it from their mailman or the fellow who delivers their vegetables or the woman who stops at the restaurant to ask for directions. Anyone who breathes is a potential carrier. I said as much to Mama after she told us we weren't going and when she and I were alone with the washing.

"Grandma is afraid for Baby Curtis and Aunt Jane," Mama replied, as if I had said something completely different. "I shouldn't have asked and put her in the difficult place of telling me not to come."

"But she's not afraid for us?" I said as I hung one of Uncle Fred's nightshirts to dry.

"Of course she is. I don't want to talk about this anymore. Uncle Fred needs us here."

I truly didn't want to go back to Quaker-town, but I could see how much it weighed on Mama that she had no choice but to have us stay. Even though we've been out of school for nearly a week and no churches are meeting and no theaters are showing movies, the flu shows no signs it's letting up. The number of people dying just keeps getting bigger, not smaller. We wake up each morning wondering if maybe today's the day the flu begins to tire of us.

Willa complained at first about being relegated to the bedrooms after Mama and Maggie left this morning, but she quieted down soon enough. In fact, she is now uncharacteristically quiet. I imagined I would need to have a long list of activities with which to keep her occupied for the several hours Mama and Maggie would be gone. But once we settle into her room to look at books, that's where we stay. I let her page through my favorite book, the one with the Latin names of all the flowers and beautiful drawings of what they look like. I tell her she can find her four favorites and then we'll draw a bouquet of them and fill in the sketch with colored pencils. I am half reading a book of my own, *Anne of the Island* by L. M. Montgomery — a novel I've read twice already. My mind begins to wander and because Willa is being so quiet, I lose track of time.

I start thinking about how different everything is now with this plague covering all the earth and killing so many people, and all the while Papa and Jamie Sutcliff and so many others are off fighting in a war where more people are dying, but not from influenza — from mortar rounds and mustard gas and bullets. It is like there are two wars. And what does war even accomplish? How does one country win over another by simply killing its people? None of it makes any sense. I am missing school and Gilbert, and even the silly girls in my class who care more that all the handsome young men are coming home from the front with missing limbs than that all those limbs were lost in the first place. I am tired of sitting in the house and pretending I can't see how busy Uncle Fred is downstairs. I am tired of meatless Mondays and wheatless Wednesdays and I want Papa home with us and not heading off to France. I'm peeved that Maggie got to go with Mama when it should have been me. I'm fifteen. Practically an adult. Maggie is still just a child. When Mama came to tell me she was letting Maggie accompany her, I asked her why.

"She just needs to get out of the house for a bit," Mama had answered. "She is only coming along to keep me company. That's all."

I would have liked to get away from the funeral home for a stretch of hours. I would have liked to keep Mama company on her errand. I would have asked to accompany her if I had known she was of a mind to let one of us go.

I am ruminating on all this when Willa says she doesn't want to look at books anymore.

I pull myself out of my irritated reverie. "Shall I get us something from the kitchen?" I say to her. I toss my book onto her bed behind me. We've been sitting on the rug in her room with books all around. Morning sunshine is slanting in on us and it is almost like we're sitting outside on a day before the flu. Almost.

Willa peers up at me. Her eyes are glassy. "I don't feel good," she says.

A tiny arrow of alarm slices through me

as I move to her and put my palm on her forehead. She is hot with fever.

She coughs and makes a face. "I want Mama," she whimpers. "I don't feel good."

"Where do you feel bad, Willa?" I ask.

"All over. I want Mama."

I stand and fold back the coverlet on her bed, tamping down the temptation to assume the worst. It is just a fever, I tell myself. A bit of a cold. The kind people used to get all the time. Willa can't have the flu. We've taken every precaution with her. "Let's get you into bed, and I'll make you toast and cocoa." I turn back around to help her to her feet.

"I don't want toast," she grumbles. I expect her to fight me on getting into her bed, too. But she goes to it willingly and climbs in.

"How about just the cocoa, then?" I say, faking a cheery tone as I pull off her shoes.

She shakes her head. "I'm cold."

I pull up the coverlet around her, and my thoughts are all aflutter with what I'm supposed to do next. I dare not go ask Uncle Fred for advice. Not only would he not know what to do; he has been with the dead all morning, touching them, lifting them, moving them.

"I want Mama," Willa murmurs.

"She'll be home soon," I say reassuringly. But Mama and Maggie have been gone less than an hour. They were going to walk all the way to South Street and likely have only just arrived. Mama hasn't yet served up the soup and sympathy, and they aren't on their way back home. It will be several hours before they return. "I'll be right back," I say to Willa.

I go downstairs to get a basin of cool water and a rag for a compress. I open the pantry to get the bottle of aspirin, figuring I can crush one into some warm water if Willa refuses to swallow it, but the Bayer bottle is gone. Mama took it with her.

Maybe a warm drink will soothe Willa. I warm a little apple cider, pour it into a cup, and then take the basin and drink to Willa's room. She is already asleep and breathing heavily, as though being chased in a dream. I put the cup down and sit down on the side of her bed. I plunge the rag into the basin, wring out the excess, and place it over her forehead. The cloth is warm under my hand in an instant. The speed with which the cool cloth becomes hot scares me. I take it away and soak it again in the water. And then again.

Should I call for someone? I wonder. Should I go tell Uncle Fred? Should I run across the street to Mrs. Sutcliff? Will she have aspirin? But that would mean leaving Willa alone. Should I go? Should I stay? Is it just an ordinary fever Willa has? Or has the invader swept down on us like it has on everyone else? I refuse to admit that of course it has.

But I can't leave her to go across the street to the Sutcliffs'. What if Willa wakes and gets out of bed disoriented and feverish and falls down the stairs? What if she wakes and calls out and there is no one here?

I can't leave her. All I can do is plunge, squeeze, press — over and over and over — as I pray to God that Mama won't stay on the south side for as long as she said she would.

The Almighty surely must be looking down on me with pity, because in just a little while I hear the front door open and Mama's voice. She and Maggie have come back.

I practically fly down the stairs.

Maggie is holding the basket Mama had prepared that morning and Mama holds something else. They both turn toward me and I see that Mama holds an infant in her arms, wrapped up in Maggie's coat. It's whimpering, and the little voice is hoarse, like this child has been crying for a very long time and no one has cared. For just a second I forget what sent me careening down to them.

"What is it, Evie?" Mama says, and I realize I must have fear in my eyes.

And then I remember. "It's Willa."

CHAPTER 25

Maggie

For a couple seconds Mama just stands there frozen with the baby in her arms. It's as if she hasn't heard Evie say that Willa is running a fever and we had the aspirin with us, and that she tried to bring the fever down with a cool rag but it's not working.

But then the moment passes, and something big and fierce rises within Mama. She turns to me. "Put that basket down."

When I do, she hands me the baby.

"Don't bring this child near Willa," Mama continues, speaking to Evie and me like we are soldiers getting our marching orders. "Warm some milk in a pan and see if you can get him to take any. Squeeze it into his mouth with a dropper if you must. Then wash the filth off him. Maggie, you run over to the church when he's fed and cleaned up and ask for Mrs. Arnold. Tell her what's happened. And tell Uncle Fred he needs to go to the police and tell them we have this baby in our care. I don't want us all getting arrested for kidnapping. See if he can get one of his doctor friends to come look at him. And don't forget what I said. Don't bring him anywhere near Willa's room."

And then she picks up the basket and races up the stairs with it.

Evie watches her go and then she turns to me. "Who is that?" she says, looking at the baby.

"He's an orphan. We don't know his name. I found him. He hasn't been fed or changed in who knows how long."

Evie stares at me for a second. "How do you know all that? How do you know he's an orphan?"

I hesitate and she notices.

"His mother was dead in the next room," I finally say.

Evie looks both horrified and doubtful. "Are you sure?"

A warm ribbon of shame wraps itself about me, but I shake it off. "After all that's happened, you really think I don't know what a dead person looks like?" I drop my coat on the floor and bring the naked baby close to my body, making my arms his blanket. He tries to squall, but he can barely make a sound now, he's so weak. I move past Evie to go into the kitchen to warm up the milk.

"And you just *took* him?" she says, following me.

"What else could we have done?" I open the icebox and pull out a bottle of milk.

Evie's brow is creased with consternation, but she says nothing.

I look down at the baby in my arms, whimpering and rooting at my chest for nourishment and comfort. "Does Willa have it?" I ask. "Does she have the flu?"

"Maybe. I don't know."

Her words settle around us both as she takes the milk bottle from me and pours some in a pan. Then she lights the stove and puts it over the tiny flame.

"What was it like down there?" Evie says as we both stand there, looking at the baby.

"It was awful."

"He needs a diaper."

I think of the clothes and diapers that were Henry's and that are now folded and tucked away upstairs in Mama's cedar chest. Evie is thinking of those things, too. I know she is because when I say, "Mama won't mind, will she?" she just says she'll go get a diaper, a blanket, and something for the baby to wear.

"We'll need to put some cornstarch on

that rash," Evie says as she turns to go upstairs.

When she comes back a few minutes later, her arms full of everything that had been Henry's, my throat swells a little, and I must look away. The milk is warm now, and I blink back my tears as I take the pan off the stove and turn off the gas.

"Let's put the milk in a bowl and dip a cloth in. Maybe he can suck the milk off that," Evie says. "You can feed him while I clean him up. Maybe he won't mind so much then."

So that's what we do. We spread out one of Henry's soft blankets on the kitchen floor and put the baby on top. He screws up his little face in protest, but he doesn't have the strength to fight much. I dip a cloth into the warm milk and put it to his mouth and it doesn't take long for him to figure out if he sucks the cloth, he can get the milk. While I feed him, Evie washes his red and blistered private parts with cool water and cotton wool. Then she sprinkles cornstarch all over the redness and puts one of Henry's diapers on him. Once he's diapered and has a little milk in his tummy, he lets us wash the rest of him. As he is drifting off to a contented sleep, Uncle Fred comes in from the funeral parlor, probably to get some lunch. He sees us there on the floor with the baby now lying silent and unmoving on the blanket. He no doubt thinks someone has used the front stoop to drop off an infant dead from the flu.

"What's all this?" he shouts, yanking down his mask.

I tell my story all over again, and this time when I get to the part where I say the baby was alone except for his dead mother, the ribbon of shame doesn't feel as hot. As I repeat the same things that I told Mama and Evie, I become even more convinced that he is without a doubt a child without parents and a brother to a dying sister.

But having heard the story a second time now, Evie has another round of questions.

"Was there no neighbor you could have asked?" she asks. "Other tenants in the building? Nobody on his street knew if he only had a mother and no one else?"

"His house wasn't on a street. It was in an alley, and I couldn't recall which one it was when Mama and I went back. There are a lot of alleys and the houses all look alike." The lie is easier to say. It is getting easier all the time.

"How could you *not* remember which house?" Evie says. "You had just left it."

"I told you they all look alike!" I shoot

back. "And in case you've forgotten, I had also just seen his dead mother covered in coughed-up blood."

"All right, all right. Stop arguing," Uncle Fred says. "What are we supposed to do with him? Where's your mother?"

"Mama wants you to tell the police what happened so they don't think we kidnapped him," Evie replies.

Uncle Fred frowns like she'd just told him he is going to have to change the baby's dirty diapers for all eternity. "Why didn't your mother do it?"

"She's upstairs," I say. "Willa's sick."

Uncle Fred narrows his eyes. I see the worry there. "Sick with what?"

"She's got a fever." Evie wraps the sleeping child in the blanket as she stands up with him. She turns to me. "Go on to the church like Mama said and tell Mrs. Arnold what happened."

"Who's Mrs. Arnold? What am I supposed to tell the police?" Uncle Fred says.

"She's the woman from the Ladies' Aid who told Mama about the sick people who live off South Street. She's the one who sent Mama down there," Evie replies. "And I guess Mama wants you to tell the police what Maggie told us."

At this she turns to look at me again, and

it's like she is giving me one last chance to make sure I've not left anything out.

But I just hold her gaze and tell her that she can take out one of my bureau drawers for the baby's bed: a little reminder that he is supposed to be taken to my room, not hers.

Uncle Fred goes to make the call and I grab an apple and start for the front door, stepping over my coat as I give it a glance. The lining is smeared with filth from the baby. I have no idea how to clean it off or if it can be cleaned.

"Leave it," Evie says, nodding to my coat. "I'll see what I can do for it while you're gone. Take mine if you want."

But I don't need a coat. I step outside and turn up the boulevard. In my mind, I picture that dying girl sliding off the sofa and crawling to her mama's room to tell her that someone had come to take care of the baby, so they didn't have to worry about what will happen to him when they die. Maybe she made it as far as the bedroom and saw that her mother had gone to heaven ahead of her. Maybe she made it only as far as the kitchen before she breathed her last. But it wouldn't have mattered either way. She and I had looked at each other and I'd assured her that her brother would be safe with me.

And she had died knowing that he was.

A few more people are out and about now that it is early afternoon, but the boulevard still isn't busy. Not like it usually is. People peer at me as I walk past them, munching on my apple, perhaps because I'm not wearing a coat or my mask, and I'm not with Mama or some other adult. I see other children my age as I make my way to the church, but they are either in the company of their parents or looking out windows.

Mrs. Keller, whose family owns the stationer's, is sweeping her front step, but she stops as I near her store.

"And where you off to, Margaret Bright?" She tries to sound only slightly curious, but it doesn't work. She sounds very curious.

"To the church."

Her eyebrows float upward. "Everything all right at home?" As in, why am I trotting toward the church when it's closed unless something is wrong? I don't want to think about Willa. I can't. And the baby at the house isn't a wrong thing.

"Yes," I reply, and I just keep walking. "Everything's all right."

The church we attend with Uncle Fred is as big as a castle, and when you are inside

215

it, you are like a mouse in an echoing cavern. The hymns we sing there on Sundays are the same ones we sang at the little church in Quakertown, but here the enormously tall ceiling makes everyone sound like they are trying too hard to be opera singers. Our first Sunday I found out the reverend's name is Pope. I thought that was funny because he's not Catholic; he's Methodist. He looks like Grandad, and when I met him, he smelled a little bit like Grandad's sweetest blend of tobacco, the one that reminds me of oranges and cloves.

The week before, on the last Sunday before everything was shut down, Reverend Pope asked us all to remember in our prayers all those affected by this devastating flu. I sat there thinking that if God could split an entire sea in half so a million Hebrews could walk across dry land, couldn't he stop a little germ? Which naturally led me to pondering again why God hadn't saved Henry when we all prayed he would, knowing full well he could.

"Why doesn't God just make the flu go away?" I'd whispered to Mama that day in church, when the reverend was done praying. "He could if he wanted to."

"I don't know why," Mama had answered. She wasn't looking at me, though. I don't

216

even know if she was talking to me. She was looking straight ahead at the bright altar where the choir stood in gold robes.

It all seemed so simple to me, I remember thinking. If I were God, I'd put a stop to it. Just like that.

But now as I step inside the quiet church, I suddenly realize sometimes things aren't simple. Sometimes you do a bad thing for good reasons. Sometimes you do a good thing for bad reasons. The full weight of what I had done this morning seems to root me to the holy floor for a moment. I lied to Mama about not knowing which house I'd found the baby in and I didn't tell her that a sick girl had been there with him. But what if I had? What if I had shown her the dead mother and the dying sister? What would it have changed? We wouldn't have left the baby there. We still would have taken him. And he'd still need a home now. He would still need a family that could love him and take care of him and give him a place to grow up in. Why shouldn't it be with us? He had been born in the part of the city where the poor lived with hardly anything to call their own. Even before the flu came, it was a sad, dirty place to live. Why shouldn't we give him what every little baby deserves?

As my eyes adjust to the dimness, I see that there are a handful of other people in the sanctuary. They are scattered across the pews, bent over in prayer, doing what the reverend asked us to do. I ease my way to one of the rows and sit down. I look up at the altar, shimmering in the half-light, and I clasp my hands together. I keep my eyes open as I whisper my prayer to God.

"I don't know why you took Henry," I say. "You shouldn't have. He was just a baby. But you gave us this child now. We're going to give him everything we would've given Henry. I won't be mad at you anymore after this."

I start to say, "Amen," but then I add that he needs to keep Willa safe as part of the deal. I close my eyes at that part because it seems the right thing to do.

I get out of the pew and go to the front of the church. A door to the left of the big altar leads to a hallway where all the church offices are. A woman in an emerald green dress is coming through it just as I get close.

"Can I help you?" she asks.

"I need to find Mrs. Arnold. It's important," I reply.

"I don't know if she's still here, but we can check in the kitchen." She asks my name and I tell her.

I follow the woman down a long hallway and then through the meeting hall to a large kitchen that smells like grease and soap and lemons. Two women in aprons are drying soup pots and a third woman is talking to a man holding a box of jars with towels in between to keep them from jostling. This third woman is tiny, like a little bird, but her voice and mannerisms are quick and purposeful, as though if she really did have a beak, she'd know how to poke you with it.

"Those are all for Chinatown," the bird-like woman says. "Make sure they understand the jars need to come back tonight so we can send them out again tomorrow." She opens a door for the man, and sunlight spills into the room as he turns and heads outside with the box. "And do be sure not to let the jars knock into each other and break!" she calls out after him. The man grunts something I can't hear.

"Mrs. Arnold, I have a young lady here who needs to see you," says the woman in the green dress.

Mrs. Arnold the Bird turns to me.

"This is Maggie Bright," says the woman who'd brought me.

"Good heavens!" Mrs. Arnold blinks at me wide-eyed. "Is your mother finished already? She didn't have to send you over with the jars. Did your mother not remember that? I have Mr. Porter coming around later today for all of them." She looks at my empty hands. "Where are your jars?"

"We didn't get the chance to finish handing them out," I reply.

"We? Did your mother take you with her?" Mrs. Arnold says.

"I just kept her company while she walked down there."

"Well, what happened? Why couldn't your mother deliver the soup? Were the jars broken? Did the driver break her jars?"

"No," I say. "I . . . We found a little baby near one of the houses on your list. His mother was dead inside his house. He'd been lying in his dirty diaper and crying for a long time. We brought him home with us because there was no one else there. Mama asked that I come tell you."

"A baby? Land sakes, is your mother home with him, then? Did you notify the health services people or the Red Cross or the police?"

"I think my uncle told the police."

"Did you show them where you found him? Do they know there's a dead mother there?"

"I . . . uh . . . no. I came here to tell you."

"Oh dear, oh dear. Come on, then — let's

see if we can't find someone who knows who the child belongs to." She brushes past me and speaks to the woman in the green dress. "We need to find my driver, Heloise. I need to get back down to South Street lickety-split." She motions for me to follow her.

"I think he's an orphan," I say, rushing to keep up with them. "I don't think he belongs to anyone."

"I assure you another orphan is the last thing the city needs right now," Mrs. Arnold says, glancing back at me. "He's bound to have other family. Is his house off South Street?"

"It's in an alley. I couldn't remember which one when we went back."

Mrs. Arnold stops and I nearly run into her. "What do you mean, when you went back?"

My heart skips a beat. "I mean, I'm the one who found the baby. I picked him up and took him to my mother, who was on another street visiting a lady on your list. We went back, but I couldn't remember which alley it was. They all look alike."

She stares at me for a second. "You found him?"

I nod.

"And how do you know he was alone in

the house? How do you know his mother is dead?"

"Because I saw her."

"Go fetch Ambrose," Mrs. Arnold says to Heloise, who is also listening to my story. She walks away quickly. Mrs. Arnold pulls me into her bird-wing arms and hugs me. "You poor dear. We'll figure out which house it was. Not to worry."

"But . . . but I already tried. All the buildings look alike."

She releases me but keeps one arm around my shoulders as we move out of the kitchen into a smaller hallway. "Yes, but not all of them have a dead mother inside, right? It's important we let the officials know which house it is so they can take care of the body." She takes a coat and hat off a row of pegs where other hats and coats are hanging. "And if we can find that mother, then we can see if there's anyone nearby who knows if there are other family members, like grandparents or siblings. Maybe there's an aunt or uncle who can take the child."

But he's ours! I want to yell. I want to scream it. *You promised,* I silently remind God even though I know deep down he hadn't promised anything.

I say nothing.

"There are so many orphans in the city

right now, and it's such a pity," Mrs. Arnold goes on as she places her hat on her head. "They certainly won't know what to do with another one."

"We can take care of him," I blurt.

Mrs. Arnold stops fiddling with her hat pin. "Think so? Did your mother ask you to tell me that?"

I shrug like it is the most natural thing in the world for the Brights to take in a stranger's child. "We have the room. It's a big house. And Mama loves babies. We all do."

"Well, that would be very nice if you could, I'm sure. I can put your mother in touch with the authorities who are looking for foster homes for all the children without parents now. You wouldn't believe how dire it is."

A man in a gray suit appears in the hallway. "Ah, Ambrose. There you are," Mrs. Arnold says. "This young lady and I need to go to South Street." Then she turns to me. "But first we will stop at the funeral home. I want to see this child, and we need to let your mother know where we are going."

Mrs. Arnold's automobile is a shiny red Ford that probably sits in a carriage house all the time. Either that or Mr. Ambrose is polishing it every second when he isn't behind the steering wheel. Every inch of it gleams.

It doesn't take long to get to the funeral home. As we pull up I wonder if Mrs. Arnold will take the baby away from us if she thinks Willa has the flu. I frantically search my mind for a good reason as to why she doesn't need to see my mother as we climb the front steps. I don't want her to know that Mama is upstairs nursing my sick sister.

We step inside the house, which is as quiet as a library. I lead Mrs. Arnold to the sitting room and am about to excuse myself to run upstairs to my room to get Evie and the baby when I see Evie rise from Uncle Fred's big armchair in the corner. The baby is swaddled in her arms, and his sweet face looks like that of an angel.

"Oh!" Mrs. Arnold says softly. "What a little cherub. Poor, sweet thing."

Evie looks at me.

"Mrs. Arnold is going to take me back to South Street to see if I can find the house where the baby was," I say.

"Of course." Evie's face is expressionless. I can't tell what she is thinking.

"Yes, I've a driver, and we can get down there and back again in good time," Mrs.

Arnold says, gazing adoringly at the baby. "I'm sure we'll find the place where he lived."

"I see." Evie is still looking at me with that blank face.

Mrs. Arnold glances up from the baby, and her gaze spins around the room. "And where is your mother, Maggie? I would like to ask her permission to take you back there."

"My mother?" I echo her, sounding like a child.

"Yes. Is she upstairs? Can you fetch her for me?"

Evie turns at last from me. "Our mother is indisposed at the moment. But Maggie can get our uncle Fred for you, instead, although he's very busy in the back as you can imagine. Perhaps I can just relay the message to Mama?"

Mrs. Arnold thinks on this for only a second. "All right, then. Tell her we will be back before dark."

I don't want to stare in admiration at Evie as we leave, but I feel certain that she, too, didn't want Mrs. Arnold snatching away the baby because of Willa being sick. My sister had come up with the perfect excuse for why Mrs. Arnold couldn't speak to Mama. Mama is indisposed. Whatever that means.

It takes a few minutes to get to South Street, but it isn't nearly enough time to figure out how I am going to avoid running into someone who knows the baby and his dead mother and sister. Mrs. Arnold asks which of the four addresses on the list Mama was at when I found the baby, and I say it was the first one. She tells Ambrose to turn up the street past the barbershop and soon we are at the curb where I'd seen that cat.

"All right, then," Mrs. Arnold says. "Which direction from here?"

Once you start getting the hang of not telling the truth, it not only gets easier, but you can think up lies quicker. I no sooner open my mouth to answer her than I realize all I have to say is that I walked *up* the street, not down it. Just up from that first building that Mama went into are more alleys, on both sides of the street.

"It was up that way," I say, "but it's hard to remember which alley it was."

Mrs. Arnold pats my arm. "Take the first one to the right, Ambrose," she says. He does and we stop at the first building on the corner. It might have been the one where I found the baby, except it isn't.

"Perhaps this one?" she says.

And I say, "Maybe."

226

"You said you heard the baby from the street, so it couldn't have been farther up the alley than this, right?"

I can only nod.

A man comes out of the building then and Mrs. Arnold pokes her head out the car window. "You there! Sir! Might I have a word?"

The man just stands there, like he can't quite believe she spoke to him. He has bushy eyebrows and a thick mustache. He holds a faded tweed cap in his hands, thready in places.

"Yes. Might I have a word? It will only take a moment."

The man comes toward the car cautiously.

"Do you happen to know if there is a young mother in your building sick with the flu? A mother with a young baby? On the first floor?"

He just blinks and stares.

"Do you speak English?"

"Little." It sounds like *leetle.*

Mrs. Arnold repeats her questions slowly.

"Yes. Many sick inside," the man answers.

"A young mother with a baby, though. We're looking for a young mother with a baby. And the baby's father."

"I — not — marry," the man says, like he just learned those three words that minute.

"No, I don't mean you. I mean, is there a young mother on the first floor who has the flu?"

"Many sick for flu. Many. I have job. Good-bye." The man turns and walks away, fitting the cap to his head.

Mrs. Arnold sighs loudly and looks at me. "Wait here."

She gets out of the car, goes inside the building, and is gone for a few minutes. Then she comes back out. "I don't think this is the building where you found him. There are two families on the first floor who have no idea what I'm talking about. What about that building across the street?"

I look at the shabby structure on the other side of the car. "Maybe." I start to get out, but she tells me to stay put.

"The flu is worse here now than it was a few days ago. Let me go ask," she says. "I don't want you catching anything."

I sit and wait, knowing she won't meet with success. Four more little alleys and eight more hellish row houses, and Mrs. Arnold is weary of the search and clearly peeved at me. How can I not remember a place I had been to only hours before?

"It was just so terrible," I say. After all the lies, it is nice to finally speak the truth. "His mother was all gray and bloody. Her eyes were stuck wide open."

"All right, all right," Mrs. Arnold says soothingly as she gets back into her car. "Take us back, Ambrose. We can try again tomorrow."

Mrs. Arnold's driver pulls up in front of Bright Funeral Home as the sun is setting. She tells me she'll be by in the morning after breakfast and that this time she wants to talk to Mama about our being able to take care of the child until other family members can be found.

She drops me off and I go inside. Mrs. Sutcliff is sitting in our kitchen with a cotton mask over her nose and mouth and the baby in her arms. I quickly learn she stopped by to see if I'd heard anything new from Jamie in the last few days and was told about our finding the child. Mrs. Sutcliff then offered to run to the store for Evie to get the things we needed to care for him. New baby bottles are now boiling on the stove, and Evie is minding them with a pair of metal tongs.

"Did you find the place?" Evie asks, but I'm sure she already knows we didn't.

I shake my head.

"Then it's a miracle you were there at just the right time, Maggie," Mrs. Sutcliff says. "Just think what could have happened if you hadn't come across him. What a sweet little boy he is. Such a darling, sweet little boy." Tears make her eyelids turn silver.

"Mrs. Arnold wants to try again tomorrow," I say. "She also wants to talk to Mama about us keeping him."

"Keeping him?" Evie says. "You mean for now."

"Maybe for always. She says there are already too many orphans."

"I heard that, too," Dora Sutcliff says. "The city is begging people to take them. They can't find enough families."

Evie withdraws one of the bottles and sets it down on a dish towel laid out on the countertop next to the stove. "But this baby might not be an orphan. He might have other family."

"But what if he doesn't?" I reply.

"Or what if it's just that no one can find them?" Evie looks up from the towel.

"Then for heaven's sake you should take him in," Mrs. Sutcliff says. "I would if I didn't have Charlie to look after." She stands and hands the baby to me. "I need to go home and get supper going. And Charlie will be wondering what is taking me so long."

"We miss having Charlie over," I say as I position the baby comfortably in my arms. I do miss Charlie. Seeing his mother reminds me how much. Charlie was always in a good mood, always listened to anything I had to say, was forever willing to try my ideas for how to teach him things. And he would talk about Jamie without me having to ask about him. He would begin sentences with "One time, Jamie . . . ," and then he'd finish with telling me how Jamie once caught a fish as big as a railroad tie or how Jamie once got a black eye playing stickball or about the time Jamie took Charlie to the circus and they sat so close to the front of the ring that they could nearly reach out and touch the elephants.

"Yes, he misses coming here. But he's not as careful as he should be, you know. And he seems to get sick more often than most children. I just can't take the chance with what's beyond that kitchen door. Listen, if you girls need anything else for the baby, you come tell me. And if your mother needs anything for Willa . . ."

She doesn't finish her sentence.

"We'll be fine, but thank you," Evie says. "And thank you for going up to the store for me."

"Of course." Dora Sutcliff caresses the baby's cheek with a finger like he's her own child. "So, you'll let me know if you hear

231

from Jamie, then?" she says to me, her brow wrinkled a bit.

Jamie told me in one of his letters this past summer that sometimes it's hard for him to find a suitable place to write. And sometimes there isn't anything to say. He can't tell me where he's fighting or where his unit is headed or what they must do when they get there. I have been left to imagine what he's doing and seeing. And what it's like to be chased by the enemy and running from mortar shells and yellow gas that can kill you if you breathe too much of it.

It occurs to me that finding the baby is already filling an empty spot inside where my concern for Jamie's safety and my need to hear from him had been widening like a great hole in the ground.

"Seems like such a long time since either of us has received a letter," Mrs. Sutcliff continues, more to herself than me.

"If I get one, I'll bring it over," I say.

Mrs. Sutcliff bids us good-bye and sees herself out. The baby coos in my arms.

Evie turns to the remaining bottles, which are knocking together in the furiously boiling water. She removes them one by one as I stand there holding the child in the failing light of day.

CHAPTER 26

Pauline

No mother should ever have to hold her child in her arms, cold with fear that her baby is dying. I have already hovered in that terrible place. I made my truce there. I owe Death nothing. I should not have to remind that specter of this.

This one is not yours, I've been repeating all day, while I sponge away Willa's fever and soothe her thrashing. I have sensed her wanting to drift further and further away from me, and I have been pulling her back, pulling her back.

This one is not yours.

The hours I've spent in this room are already a blur, but I dare not leave Willa's side. I must win this contest of wills. I must stay vigilant until Death slithers away completely.

This one is not yours.

Sometime in the afternoon Fred had come

up the stairs. I heard his heavy footfalls, different from those of Evelyn and Maggie. He'd called out to me from the other side of the door.

"Don't come in," I told him. "It's not safe. Do you know if a doctor is coming?"

"I called Dr. Boyd, a good friend of mine, and he said he'll try his best to stop by this evening, but you know there's no medicine for this, Pauline."

"That doesn't mean we don't do all that we can." I placed a cool hand on Willa's brow and she whimpered slightly. "It doesn't mean we do nothing."

He'd hesitated a moment. "Yes."

"And the police? Did you telephone them about the baby?" I'd heard the infant earlier that afternoon. His cry for attention had woken an ache in my breasts that nearly felt like milk would start spilling from them. I had laid an arm across my chest to stop it, even though I knew there was nothing in my bosom to nourish a child. My milk had dried up months and months ago.

"No one's reported a missing child," Fred replied. "But they said they'd make a note of it."

"Where is he now?"

"Evelyn and Maggie are with him."

"And did Maggie tell Mrs. Arnold what

happened?"

"She went to the church earlier like you asked and then the two of them drove down to South Street in Mrs. Arnold's car to see if Maggie would have better luck remembering which house it was. She got back a bit ago. They couldn't find the house, though." He sounded like he was baffled by the idea that a stranger's baby was now staying in the house.

From somewhere above me I heard the infant's lusty wail for attention. Willa echoed it with a low whimper of her own.

"I don't know how long the baby will be with us and we need a few things," I said. "Baby bottles, rice cereal. That kind of thing. Evelyn will know what to get. Can you give her some money?"

"It's already been taken care of. Don't fret about that."

"Make sure the girls stay away from this room, Fred. I will only come out when I know no one is on the stairs. Tell Evelyn to fix me a tray later and then leave it outside the door. And I'll need some broth for Willa."

I looked down at my youngest child, wanting her to open her eyes and tell me she doesn't want broth. She wants ham loaf. Why can't she have ham loaf?

But Willa, with her eyes closed, was silent except for her labored breath.

"All right," Fred said. And then there had been a pause, before he said, "Shouldn't I call the Red Cross so that Thomas can be notified?"

A little dagger pierced my soul. "Notified of what?"

"That . . . that Willa has the Spanish flu. Shouldn't he be told?"

My youngest child trembled slightly under my hand at that moment. Of my three girls, Willa is the one least likely to throw a punch in her defense. Evelyn can wisely reason her way out of trouble, and Maggie will simply plow past it, but Willa will make friends with an enemy before realizing it desires to harm her. I hadn't wanted to admit aloud, in full hearing of my companion, that the flu that had already killed so many raged now inside her.

"No, Fred. Willa is strong. She is brave," I said, wanting my little girl to hear those words and be nourished by them. "Her papa will see her when the war is over and he comes home."

For several seconds there was no movement outside the door, and then I heard Fred taking the first step back down the stairs.

I must have dozed after he left, because twilight fills the room now and I hear far-off sounds of pots and pans in the kitchen.

Willa is moaning softly in her sleep, a dreadful murmuring that I can almost not bear to hear.

I start to sing "Let Me Call You Sweetheart" to fill the air around us with a sound other than that one. She quiets and my tears tap her coverlet like raindrops.

Chapter 27

Evelyn

Uncle Fred's friend Dr. Boyd is upstairs with Willa now, but I doubt he will suggest anything different than what Mama is already doing. He will probably tell her to just keep applying cool compresses for the fever. Give Willa aspirin. Smear Vick's Vapo-Rub on her chest. Get her to eat and drink. Pray. There is no magic pill for the Spanish influenza, though everyone wishes there was one. I was on the landing earlier to leave a tray for Mama and Willa. I could hear Willa's strange new cough from behind the door. She sounded like an old woman and it scared me.

"Is the baby all right?" Mama asked, her voice floating out to me from the tiny seam of space between door and frame. "Did he eat something? Did you take care of that rash?"

"Yes. He's sleeping with a full tummy," I

said. "We dressed him in a few things that were Henry's. That's okay, isn't it?"

She paused only a second. "Yes. Yes, of course."

The baby already looked and smelled so much better than he did when Mama and Maggie first brought him home. The diaper rash was not such an angry red anymore and he hadn't howled when I changed him the second time. He even smiled and cooed at me at one point, though mostly what he had done today was sleep.

"He's resting quite comfortably now, Mama. Truly."

She thanked me and sent me away, not opening the door for her tray until I was on the bottom step.

After his supper, Uncle Fred came into the sitting room while Maggie, the baby, and I were playing on the floor. He decided after lunch that with the baby here and Willa coming down with the sickness, he would start eating all his meals in the hallway off the kitchen. He doesn't know if the flu that killed all the people he has been attending clings to his work clothes. He is taking no chances.

I had brought him clean trousers and a shirt earlier, which he hung on hooks that funeral-goers used to hang their coats on, and which are as far from the bodies as they can be. He had come into the sitting room because he'd wanted to hear for himself what Mrs. Arnold told Maggie we were supposed to do with the child.

Maggie repeated to him what she had told Dora Sutcliff and me when I was boiling the baby bottles. I already knew that Mrs. Arnold had said there were more orphans in Philadelphia than people willing to take them, so I watched Maggie's face instead of listening to her words.

A girl can always tell when something is not quite right with her sister. I know there is something Maggie is not telling us about how she found the baby. She says she can't remember in which row house the baby lay crying because finding his dead mother upset her. Mrs. Arnold, Uncle Fred, and even Mama believe her. But I don't. I think she does remember where she found him. I just can't figure out why she is pretending she doesn't.

At first I thought maybe it was because she *did* see evidence that a father lived there, and she'd lied about not seeing any. I was thinking all the rest of the afternoon we'd hear from the police that a distraught father had come home from work to find his poor wife dead and his baby missing.

But there has been no telephone call like that. No father has contacted the police to report a missing baby and apparently no grandparent or aunt or neighbor or friend has, either.

I've been wondering how that can be. When that woman's body was carted away by the authorities — surely someone noticed she was dead — didn't they see the cradle in her front room and wonder where her baby was? And since there has been no telephone call from the police, does that mean no one has found her yet, or have they found her but no one cares that there is an empty cradle in her house? Or maybe they think her baby already died. Uncle Fred told me seven thousand people in Philadelphia are dead from the flu. Seven thousand people in just eleven days. What's one more immigrant woman and her fatherless child?

The baby grins at me now and gurgles a sweet, little sound. Maggie leans down and snuggles him, and his smile widens. He is so very much like Henry. Not in the shape of his nose or chin or mouth. It's that smile and innocent gaze that are Henry's. I look at this baby and I want to forget what I've been pondering all day. I want to push away any and all questions about why no one has reported him missing and why Maggie says she can't remember where she found him. I want to forget that the plague that so disinterestedly brought him to us is at this very minute wanting to snatch away Willa. I just want to forget every terrible thing that is happening in the world right now and love this little child whom Maggie rescued.

Maggie looks up at me. "Isn't he precious?"

And the words "Tell me why you're lying," which sit unspoken on my lips, just fall away like they'd never been there at all.

CHAPTER 28

Maggie

I don't want Evie's help with the baby during the night, but when he starts crying a little after two and I'm struggling to hold him and get a bottle ready, I'm glad when she comes downstairs to help me. So is Uncle Fred. He comes out to the kitchen ahead of Evie, looking like Ebenezer Scrooge in his long underwear, and asks me if I've dropped the baby in hot oil, for the love of God.

"That's just how babies cry when they're hungry!" I tell him, feeling a little exasperated by his question with the baby in one arm while I fiddle with getting a saucepan onto the stove. I have no idea how I am going to light the burner, because Uncle Fred is already turning to go back to his bedroom. But then Evie appears in the kitchen, passing Uncle Fred as he shuffles out. She doesn't say a word; she just takes the baby so I can light the stove and pour the milk in the pan.

"Thank you," I say.

"I wasn't asleep anyway." She pats the baby's back and shushes him, swaying back and forth like she's a hammock in a breeze.

"Suppose Mama is awake, too?" When I came down the stairs with the crying baby, I couldn't hear anything else but the baby's wails.

"I don't think so. It's been quiet in Willa's room, so a little while ago, I opened the door a tiny bit and peeked inside."

"You did?" That surprises me. Evie always follows the rules. Mama had clearly told us to stay out of Willa's room.

"I just wanted to see if . . . if she needed anything," Evie says.

I stir the milk and wait.

"Mama is asleep, half in a chair, half on Willa's bed," she continues.

"And Willa?"

"She's asleep, too."

"You're sure?" I can't look at her. I just keep my eyes on the milk.

"She's sleeping."

Evie hums softly to the baby as I fill the bottle and then test the temperature on my wrist. I reach for the baby and she hands him to me without a word. I stick the nipple into his mouth and he starts to suck greedily. As I walk into the sitting room to sit in Uncle Fred's big, cozy chair, I hear Evie wash up the milk pan and then head back upstairs.

I don't mean to fall asleep in that big chair with the baby in my arms, but that's what happens. When I wake, it is just before dawn. I can hear Willa coughing above me.

When I take the baby into the kitchen to start warming his milk before he starts crying for it, there is Mama, standing at the stove waiting for the teakettle to whistle. I come to a stop at the doorway. She snaps her head in my direction.

"Stay right there, Maggie," she says, softly but urgently. "I don't want you or him near me. I'll be done here in just a minute or two."

"How is Willa?" I ask.

"Her fever doesn't seem quite as high this morning. So. There's that." She purses her lips together like she doesn't want to say anything that might change that fact somehow. The kettle begins to sing and she takes it off the flame and pours the hot water into a teacup where she has a little brass steeper waiting. The steeper is in the shape of a pudgy cat. I've always liked it. She sets the kettle down on the stove and twirls the steeper. I smell Earl Grey. Then she looks at me. "You're going back out with Mrs. Arnold today?"

"She said she'd be back for me first thing this morning."

"I know yesterday was a difficult day for you, but it's very important that you try to remember which house it was. Do you understand?"

"Yes, Mama," I say, very glad that she didn't ask me to promise that I will do my best to remember. She asked me if I understood. I understand perfectly. "He may not have anyone else, though," I add.

"I know that. But we must make sure. Because we know what it's like to lose a child, don't we?"

I nod. I understand that perfectly, too. "No one has called the police department about him."

"Yes. Uncle Fred told me that."

The baby makes a little waking sound. Soon he'll be fussing for a bottle. Mama withdraws the steeping ball even though it hasn't been in the cup long enough.

"Mrs. Arnold told me the city has too many orphans and not enough foster families to care for them," I say. "The orphanages are all full."

"Maggie —"

"They are! He's going to need a home, Mama!"

She lets out a long breath as she sets the pudgy brass cat on a saucer. "That doesn't necessarily mean we're the ones who should be giving him one."

"Why? Why shouldn't it be us? We have the room. We even have the clothes and the diapers!"

I hadn't meant for that to hurt her, but I think it did a little. She flinches, same as when you touch something that is hotter than you think it will be. I want to say I'm sorry, but she speaks again before I can.

"Let's just consider all this one day at a time. If Mrs. Arnold thinks the authorities would appreciate us taking this child, then —"

"She already told me they would."

Mama goes on as if I hadn't rudely interrupted her. "Then we can talk to Uncle Fred and we can write to Papa and we can see if it's the right thing to do for the child. It has to be about what's best for him, Margaret, not about what's best for us." She picks up her cup. "You need to step aside now so I can get back upstairs."

I move away from the entrance to the kitchen. Mama comes through the doorway and looks down on the baby from several feet away. Despite the motherly smile, I see exhaustion and worry and distress on her face.

"Willa's going to be all right, isn't she?"

Mama just nods and turns from me to head for the stairs.

I wait all morning and half the afternoon for Mrs. Arnold and she never comes for me. Uncle Fred finally sends me down to the church to see what is keeping her. I find Miss Heloise in the kitchen with a group of ladies who are washing up soup jars just brought back from their mercy missions. Boxes of groceries have just been delivered and more dirty jars are being brought in by old men in felt caps.

"Oh!" Miss Heloise says when I ask for Mrs. Arnold. "She's not here. She's home sick. I'm afraid she took ill last night."

"She's sick? With the flu?"

"I'm afraid so. What is it you need, dear?" She moves about the kitchen like it is on fire.

"Well, I . . ." My voice just falls away when I realize Heloise is now so busy with all Mrs. Arnold's responsibilities heaped on her that she's forgotten all about the baby.

"Did you come to tell me your mother can resume taking food down to South

Street? We missed her today."

"She can't right now. My sister's not feeling well."

Someone calls her name. She pats my shoulder. "Oh. I see. Sorry to hear that. All right, then. I'm sure I can find someone else."

She tells me, sweetly, to run along home, she is so very busy.

When I get back to the house, Evie is playing with the baby in the sitting room and Uncle Fred is making coffee for himself and a crew of grave diggers the city has sent over to load up a truckload of decaying bodies.

"Well?" he says, but I can tell he is too busy to talk to me about what to do with the baby, which is fine with me because the answer to the problem is clear as day. The adults are making it much too complicated.

"Mrs. Arnold wasn't there."

"So now what?" He pours coffee into a cup. "I haven't heard back from the police, you know. No one's asking about that child."

"Mama said this morning we need to think about keeping him," I answer. "The orphanages are all full and he probably doesn't have any other family. We're all that he has now."

"I suppose," he says, and turns from me

to pour more coffee.

I can't help smiling a teensy bit at those two words as I make my way to where Evie and the baby are.

There will be no more trips to South Street with Mrs. Arnold — or anyone else. Willa is going to get well, the flu is going to go away, the war is going to be won, Papa and Jamie will be coming home, and the baby is going to be ours.

CHAPTER 29

Willa

I'm so cold. Is it still daytime? Where's Evie?

I want Mama.

I'm so cold.

Mama touches me and I don't want her to. Her hands are like fireplace pokers.

Don't touch me. Why is there ice in my bed?

She holds a cup to my lips, but I don't want a drink. Leave me alone.

I want Papa.

Make it stop.

Someone pulls back my blanket and it hurts. My heart hurts. My arms. My neck. Someone tries to bend close to me and I push them away. My throat hurts. My heart. My head.

Flossie, how did you get in here?

She has a new parasol. Pink with lace and

ribbons. She laughs and runs through the grass. I see birds.

Don't touch me.

It is nighttime.

It is daytime.

Flossie?

Shhhh, Mama says, I'm right here.

I hear a baby crying.

Henry.

I try to sit up. I want to see Henry. I want to see him!

But a dragon pins me to my bed with his sharp claws. His mouth is full of fire.

Henry!

I cough out fire.

I'm the dragon.

CHAPTER 30

Pauline

Three days after falling into the abyss, Willa climbs out. She had at last heard me calling, felt my strong arms around her, and obeyed my command that she find her way back to me. I haven't left her side except to fetch food and water and use the toilet. It was my duty to stay at the very edge of where she'd fallen and, if need be, dive in after her.

When she wakes just now, I can tell the sickness has released her. She has come back to me.

The scarlet glassy-eyed stare is gone, and her eyes once again shine clear like the sky, blue and beautiful. The gray tinge to her skin, which is now cool to my touch, is gone, too. The cough lingers, but it no longer sounds like the screeching of a wounded animal. The worst is over, and though she is as weak as a newborn kitten, my darling Willa has survived.

As I cry tears of joy at her whispered request for pancakes with blackberry syrup, I know this time I have not failed. I battled for my child and I prevailed. With Henry I had beseeched the heavens — for days on end — that he might be spared. But it was as if I had voiced no protest at all. Death had come for him anyway. Willa returned to me is the proof that I have somehow convinced my companion to leave her be. Perhaps during these months that Death has trailed me, and as I've labored to understand its nature, it has grown to care for me. Is such a thing even possible? It seems profane to even think it. After all this time together, and despite all that has happened, I am sure now that Death is not the enemy, but something else surely is. My companion has been suggesting to me month after month since Henry died that it spreads its reach with the tender embrace of an angel, not the talons of a demon. But I still don't understand why.

I am so grateful Willa was spared, but why does it come for the young and innocent at all? Why does it not wait until the body is old and gray and full of years? As a dull ache in my bones and heat under my skin starts to spread, I want to call out to the room,

"What is it you *want*?"

Because I still do not know.

I can feel the fever creeping over me as just outside Willa's door, the orphan child makes a happy, cooing sound. Maggie or Evelyn is taking him downstairs for a bottle or breakfast or maybe just to hold him and sing nursery songs to him.

"I hear a baby," Willa whispers now. "Is it Henry? Am I in heaven?"

I smile down on her. "No, sweetheart. You are not in heaven. You are home. And we have a guest with us. A little baby. He's not Henry, but he's very sweet. He's staying with us right now."

Interest gleams in her eyes. "I want to see him."

"When you're all better."

"What's his name?"

I shake my head, the simplest of moves, but arcs of pain spiral across my head and shoulders. "I don't know. We might have to give him one while he's here."

Willa thinks on this for a moment. The room begins to sway.

"I like Alex. Can we call him Alex?" she says.

I want to grab Willa's blanket and wrap it about me. A chill in the room has turned to an icy blast. "Alex is a nice name," I mumble as I try to stand.

"Mama?"

"I need to see about your pancakes, love. You just stay put and I'll —"

Then I hear the shattering of porcelain.

I've fallen across the nightstand where a teacup had been sitting. As the room tilts, I remember it had been one of Fred's mother's teacups and I am sad that I've broken it.

The flu has released my daughter, but now it has sunk its teeth into me. I feel its jaws tightening, and my body's inability to deflect it. As the world goes sideways, my companion seems to lean toward me as if to cushion my fall.

Just before my head hits the floor, I whisper the question I had seconds earlier wanted to shout. "What do you *want*?"

And as the room darkens I hear the answer.

I will show you.

CHAPTER 31

Evelyn

I am woken by the sound of china breaking and the thump of something heavy hitting the floor in Willa's room. Tendrils of daylight are spilling onto my coverlet from the gaps in the curtains. The street below my bedroom window is quiet.

What comes to mind first is the sickening image of Willa lying unmoving in her bed and Mama rousing from sleep to find that our little girl has died in the night. The bedside table has overturned as Mama throws herself upon Willa's lifeless body and the contents atop it have flown off, some of them breaking. I have no sooner pictured this horrible scene than I hear Willa cry out Mama's name, rather than the other way around.

I spring from my bed and throw open my bedroom door, nearly crashing into Maggie, who is flying up the stairs with a wide-eyed baby in her arms.

"Stay there," I command, and Maggie takes a step back as I yank open Willa's bedroom door.

Mama is crumpled on the floor by Willa's bed. Pieces of a broken teacup lie around her head. Her face is pale and a tiny trickle of blood is seeping out of a thin line on her forehead where a porcelain shard has cut her. Willa is half sitting up in her bed, her pale face creased with worry. But even in a swift glance, I can see my sister is better. Her eyes are bright and clear and her skin a faint peach color.

"She just fell over," Willa whispers, her voice full of fear.

"Mama?" I kneel to touch her shoulder, shaking it just a little.

She moans softly and raises a hand toward me, not for me to help her get up but in protest. She is trying to shoo me away.

"Mama!" I say again, and I put my hand to her forehead. It is hot with fever. I see no sign of her mask anywhere about her. She had been caring for Willa without wearing it.

"She was getting up to go to make me pancakes and she just fell over," Willa whimpers.

"Mama?" This comes from Maggie, hovering at the doorway with the baby in her arms.

Mama opens her eyes and looks past me to Maggie. "Go," Mama murmurs.

"Run and get Uncle Fred!" I say to Maggie.

Maggie turns away without a word and I hear her footfalls fast on the stairs.

"Mama, can you sit up?" My heart is thumping in my chest, pounding away like it is caged and wishes to be free. Why hadn't she worn her mask? How could she have been so careless? As I lean over Mama and try to wrap my arms around her, I realize I'm not wearing mine, either.

"Go, go!" she says, fighting me off with weak limbs.

"Why can't she get up?" Willa whines.

"She's just resting a minute, Willa. Hush now and go back to sleep."

"I don't want to go back to sleep. Make her get up!"

"Please. Evelyn. Just go," Mama whispers.

"Uncle Fred is coming, and we'll get you into your bed, Mama. Just lie still." I stroke her forehead and she turns her head away from me.

Far below us I hear Maggie pounding on Uncle Fred's bedroom door. Her voice carries up the stairs.

"Mama has fallen!"

"Uncle Fred is coming," I say to Mama, patting her shoulder gently.

A moment later Uncle Fred is in the room wearing his bedclothes. He has a blue plaid kerchief in his hand that he ties around his nose and mouth as he comes toward me.

"Move out of the way," he says, and I scoot to the side, raising my arm so that the sleeve of my nightgown now covers the bottom half of my face.

Uncle Fred hoists Mama into his arms as if she weighs nothing. He is out the door with her in a blink, and I scurry to follow him into her and Papa's bedroom. Maggie, who has sprinted up the stairs behind Fred, stands helplessly at the top step watching while downstairs the baby starts to wail.

Mama hasn't been in her own bed for three nights, and all the covers and pillows are neatly in place. I yank back the coverlet, wool blanket, and sheet, sending the decorative pillows flying. Uncle Fred lays Mama on the mattress. She curls into a ball and begins to shiver. Uncle Fred pulls up the covers.

"You're bleeding," Fred says, and his voice sounds strange. He is frowning at the little cut on Mama's forehead. It is nothing compared to the flu now furious inside her and he knows it. We all do.

"It doesn't hurt," she murmurs, and then she turns her head so she can see me. "Willa needs you right now, Evelyn. She's past the worst of it, but she's weak. She can't be allowed to get up yet."

"I'll take care of her, Mama. Don't worry. You just rest."

"Don't come in my room again," she continues. "Do you hear me? You girls stay out."

"But, Mama . . ." I can't finish. How can we stay away when she will need care just like Willa had? Does she really expect us to do nothing for her? It is an impossible request.

Uncle Fred doesn't like that idea, either. "I can't be running up here all the day to look after you, Pauline. It's like a madhouse downstairs." Now Uncle Fred sounds as if he is about to cry. Maybe he is. Maybe after days and days of sorting out the dead by the dozens, some of whom were friends and neighbors, he is past the point of being able to shoulder the terrible weight of the situation. Maybe what he is really saying is, "I can't do this anymore."

Suddenly I understand how his occupation had a measure of sacredness to it before the flu, almost as though Uncle Fred was as much a minister to the living as an embalmer to the dead. I'd seen the way he cared for the bodies when I happened upon him as he brought a cadaver in or carried one out. He treated them as if they could still see, hear, and feel. And I witnessed many times his care over the mourners who wept in his funeral parlor: how he spoke so gently to them about the glories of heaven, the gates of pearl, and the absence of pain and suffering and tears in that bright place where their loved ones had flown.

The flu had taken all that from him. He was at the moment charged merely with getting the ghoulish victims into the ground as soon as he possibly could.

"I don't need you to look after me," Mama replies, but she barely whispers this. "Just bring up the aspirin bottle and some water. And then leave me. All of you."

She closes her eyes and is asleep in an instant. I motion for Uncle Fred to follow me.

"Maggie and I will find a way to take care of her," I say, when we are on the landing outside Mama's bedroom. "And we'll be careful. You don't need to worry about this."

But Uncle Fred points a finger at me and works his brow into one long line. "Don't tell me what I don't need to worry about," he growls, but his voice is riddled with emotion, not anger. "You girls don't have any idea what you're dealing with." He moves past me but turns his head in my direction when his foot is on the first stair. "You need to get that baby out of this house. He never should have been brought here. I've got more bodies piling up beyond the kitchen door than I know what to do with and you girls bring home a baby!"

Deep down I know he is probably right. I think I have known since the moment the child arrived and Willa was already sick that our house isn't safe for a baby. But I shout something entirely different as Uncle Fred takes the first step. "What else could Maggie and Mama have done?" I say.

He starts down the rest of the staircase and I follow. Maggie is at the bottom step with the crying baby in her arms, a look of dread on her face.

She'd heard what we'd both said. The thought of sending the baby away is a crushing thought. He's only been with us for four days, but already he has woven himself into my soul. Maggie's, too. He is, at this moment, our only thread of evidence that the entire world isn't collapsing into itself in ruins. This child is perfect and beautiful and innocent and fully alive. In the middle of all the death surrounding us, he seems our last grip on life.

As Uncle Fred passes Maggie at the foot of the stairs, he again says, this time to Maggie, that the baby needs to go.

"But the orphanages are full!" Maggie protests.

"That's not my problem," he says as he heads toward the small hallway that leads to his rooms. "This is a funeral home. And we're in the middle of a plague."

"But he has nowhere to go," Maggie implores as she follows him, with me right behind her.

Uncle Fred stops and turns to us. "This is *not* the place for an infant," he shouts. He sounds mad, but I see the shimmer of tears in his eyes. "You know it's not."

He is right, he is right, the voice of reason whispers to me.

"But he has nowhere to go," Maggie says again, her voice softer this time. She, too, is on the verge of tears. Uncle Fred doesn't say anything else. He doesn't have an answer for any of our problems. A second later he turns for his bedroom. He closes the door, no doubt to dress for another appalling day in a funeral parlor that is more of a mausoleum now than anything else.

My insides feel like they are being pulled

in all directions. Our house, filled with the dead and now the flu itself living here, clearly is unsafe for the baby. But are there completely safe places anymore? And who else can take a helpless orphaned child? Dora Sutcliff could probably care for him for a little while, but she already said she didn't think she could care for a baby along with Charlie. The thought of handing this child over to some stranger — even only temporarily — fills me with dismay.

Maggie looks at me with pleading eyes.

"We can't just think about what we want," I tell her, knowing what I will have to do. I will have to go across the street and beg Dora to take him.

I brush past my sister to go into the kitchen and start warming the milk. "Maybe Mrs. Sutcliff should take him for a while," I say as I take a bottle off the draining towel.

"I don't want her to," Maggie mutters.

The baby is now fully distressed at the delay in getting his breakfast. Maggie is cuddling him close and bouncing up and down to distract him. "We can keep him safe here. I won't take him upstairs anymore. At all. I'll sleep on the sitting room sofa. I won't take him anywhere near Mama and Willa. Or Uncle Fred's bodies. I can keep him safe!"

I pour the milk in the pan and say nothing. I don't tell her that no one can guarantee anyone's safety. Not the way death is swarming this city, this house. We can only do the best that we can at the moment we can do it.

When the bottle is ready, I hand it to Maggie and she takes the baby into the sitting room to curl up in Uncle Fred's big armchair and feed him.

I fix oatmeal for Willa, of which she eats only half while telling me she wanted pancakes. I upright her fallen bedside table, pocket the bottle of aspirin, which had fallen off it, and pick up the pieces of the broken cup. I help her to the toilet and then tuck her back into bed. I assure her that Mama is resting and I tell her that when she is all better Maggie will show her the sweet little baby we are taking care of. She then drifts off to sleep.

I leave Willa and return to the kitchen. I pour cool water into a basin, grab some cotton wool, and put on my mask before heading back upstairs. When I step into her room Mama is sleeping, which I'm glad of because she can't command me to leave. But it also means she isn't awake to take the aspirin. I set the bottle on her bedside table.

I sponge away the bit of dried blood on her forehead and then I sit with her for a long while, cooling her fever with the compress, just as I had done with Willa. And just like Willa's, her fevered skin heats the cool cloth with terrifying rapidity. This flu is like Goliath — enormous and evil and strong — and I am like David but without a slingshot, without a stone. I have only the desire to fight it and no weapon. Mama moans as if to tell me my observations are correct.

Ours is not a safe house.

I rise, wash my hands in the upstairs bathroom, and then head downstairs, grabbing my cape off the hook by the front door.

Maggie, playing on the parlor floor with the baby, calls out to ask where I am going.

I don't answer her.

I yank open the door and run across the street. Dora Sutcliff answers the bell looking like she hasn't slept in a month. Her clothes are rumpled, her hair askew, and her eyes are shadowed by dark circles.

In tears she tells me she cannot take the baby.

Charlie has the flu.

CHAPTER 32

Pauline

In my dream, I am back home in Quaker-town. I am young again. Seventeen. Thomas Bright, the son of the cigar maker, is looking at me from across the straw-strewn dance floor.

I know him from school and church socials and from the times his family has occasionally come to my parents' restaurant. He is nice-looking. Tall. Taller than his three brothers even though he's the youngest by five years. I've seen him staring at me before. He doesn't stare at any of the other girls, only me. And that makes my heart pound a little. My friend Carrie whispers to me that I'm probably going to have to be the one to ask him to dance because everyone knows he's too shy and quiet to come over and ask himself. She says that because she thinks I won't do it. But I do. I walk over to Thomas Bright. And his eyes grow wider with every step I take toward him.

"Are you going to or aren't you?" I say when I reach his side of the barn. I look down at my clothes and I see that I'm wearing a yellow dress with tiny white flowers all over it. It's the one I saw in a store window in Allentown and that Mama said was too expensive.

"Am I what?" Thomas Bright says, and when I look up again, I see that he is also more handsome than his brothers.

"Are you going to ask me to dance?"

"If . . . if I did, would you say yes?" he asks.

"Ask me and see."

He smiles at me and says, "Will you marry me, Pauline?"

I look down at my clothes again, and I'm wearing a creamy white dress with lace trim and pearl buttons. The one I bought in Philadelphia. I have a bouquet of asters and mountain laurel in my hands. We're not in the barn anymore; we're in the Quakertown Community Church and Mama is sitting in the front pew with my daddy. She is dabbing her eyes with a pale violet handkerchief.

I look up at Thomas and I say, "I will."

He kisses me and when his lips come away from mine I tell him Willa is going to live.

"Oh!" he says.

He is looking away from me now, at something in the distance.

"Here it comes," he says.

And then I am awake and my body is ablaze.

CHAPTER 33

Willa

I'm not allowed to get out of bed yet, but at least Maggie let me see the baby. She brought him to my bedroom door and let me look at him, but she didn't think it was a good idea to let him get too close to me. He can't come into my room until it's for certain the flu from Spain isn't inside me anymore.

I had the flu for three days, but I don't remember much about them. I remember looking at Evie's flower book on the first day and then feeling really bad and lying in my bed, hot and cold at the same time and wishing I could just disappear. Then the flu left me yesterday, but it made me sleepy. Seems like all I do is take naps. I am tired of naps.

That sounds like a funny joke.

I must do whatever Evie says because she's in charge while Mama's sick. Mama

271

has the flu now, too. Evie's taking care of me and Mama. Maggie is taking care of the baby. It's better for the baby if one of my sisters takes care of Mama and the other one takes care of him. Maggie probably got the baby because she found him. He's an orphan. That means his mama and papa are dead. Maggie says we might get to keep him because he needs a family and we have the room.

"I told Mama I like the name Alex," I said to Maggie, when she was standing there at the door with the baby so I could get a look at him.

"Alexander was Henry's middle name," Maggie said, and I wasn't sure if that meant she liked the name Alex or didn't.

"But we would call him Alex."

She just nodded. It was a nod that said she'd heard me, not that the baby's name is now Alex. "We'll see," she said a second later.

The baby smiled at me from the door. He's got brown hair and dark eyes — not like Henry — but he's still sweet as can be. I wanted to hold him and Maggie said soon. He was wearing one of Henry's outfits. I remembered it was the one Grandma Adler had made.

"Does Mama know he's wearing Henry's

clothes?" I said.

"She does," Maggie answered.

I wanted to see Mama then. I missed her. She had promised me pancakes with black-berry syrup.

"I want to see her." I started to get out of bed.

"Not right now, Willa." Maggie started to rush into the room even though she still had Baby Alex in her arms.

But I was all woozy and I had to plop back down onto my pillows.

"You're not well enough yet." Maggie had stopped halfway to my bed. "You need rest right now. And so does Mama. Promise you won't try to go to her room alone, Willa."

Well, I hadn't thought of that yet, but I probably would have.

"Willa?"

I was thinking about it.

"Willa!"

"What?"

"Promise me."

But I wasn't going to promise her. "I'm tired." I rolled over so my back was to her.

"Mama wants you to stay in bed and rest," Maggie said a second later.

Baby Alex said, "Goo."

"I bet Mama wants you to make us pan-cakes with blackberry syrup," I said.

"Stay in your bed and I will."

She left without me having to promise anything.

CHAPTER 34

Maggie

It's the fourth day since Mama came down with the flu. Today she will start to feel better. This is the day when Willa woke up with cool skin and clear eyes. Today will be different. I already feel like it will be.

I've been sleeping in the sitting room with Baby Alex to avoid the stairs and the second floor. Mama's bedroom is right above me and I heard her coughing all through the hours of the night.

But last night was still only the third full day. Today is the fourth day and today will be different.

Uncle Fred heard Mama last night, too.

I heard him go up to her room twice while we were all trying to sleep. The second time he said aloud to the whole house as he climbed the stairs that we girls and Mama should have been allowed to go to Quakertown when she asked. Then early this morning, when the sun was just barely up, I heard him on the telephone to Fort Meade. He said they must let Papa come home. It's an emergency.

It doesn't feel like an emergency. It just feels like the fourth day. And it's quiet now. Mama is asleep. Evie, too, I hope.

Baby Alex slept through it all, and now he's sucking on a bottle and staring up at me.

Willa started calling him Alex, short for Alexander. Alexander suits him. I think Mama will like that name. She and Papa had given it to Henry for a middle name, so she must've liked it enough for that. Alex needed a name. We couldn't just keep calling him "the baby," as though he were a thing like the house or the war or the flu. So that's what it will be.

I'd written Jamie yesterday and told him about the baby, but we hadn't settled on Alex yet. I told him the same story I told everyone else. Writing it down made it seem more like the truth than how I'd really found Alex. As I wrote down the words that the baby was alone in the house except for his dead mother, I felt as though my story of how it happened was really how it happened. He was alone. I couldn't find the house a second time. And no one has called the police about him. I also wrote that Willa had the flu but was much better, and that Mama had it now but would certainly start feeling better very soon. I didn't tell him Charlie was sick with it now. I figured that was something Mrs. Sutcliff was supposed to tell him. Or not tell him.

I'm so very sorry Charlie is ill, but I'm not sorry Dora Sutcliff couldn't take Alex when Mama came down with the sickness. Alex doesn't know her. She's a stranger to him. It's us who feel like family to him now.

Uncle Fred seems to have forgotten that three days ago he said that Alex had to go. Or maybe when he found out Charlie Sutcliff had the flu he realized our house is as safe as anywhere at the moment. I don't care what his reason is for not demanding to know why Alex is still here. If Evie tries again to send Alex away, I'm going to take him and board the first train to Quakertown. He and I can wait out the flu in the curing barn among the leafy tobacco dresses. I dare anyone to send us back here if it comes to that.

Alex has just made a little cooing sound, and now he's smiling at me, breaking the seal he has on the nipple of the bottle. A bit of milk dribbles down his chin. It's like he knows I am thinking of him.

"You're mine," I whisper to him, and he smiles wider as I kiss his forehead. I let my mind pretend that I am eighteen, not thirteen, and I'm married to someone kind and brave like Jamie Sutcliff and Alex is our child. We live in a big house in the country with lots of apple trees. And there is no war and no flu.

Willa's voice above slices into my imaginings. She is calling out for Evie to come to take her to the toilet. I can do that for Evie. Alex is fed and has a clean diaper, and Evie's been up all night with Mama. I don't think Willa is in danger of giving the flu to anyone anymore, but she still can't walk more than a few paces without help.

I make a cozy place for Alex on a blanket by the hearth, surrounding him with toys and the fronts of picture books that I set up against the side of the bureau drawer I've been using for his crib. He likes all the pictures on the book covers. He kicks his legs and tries to punch the pictures with his little fists. He thinks they are real and that if he just tries hard enough he can pluck them off.

At the second-floor landing, I see that Evie has just emerged from Mama's room. The door is partially open and her hand is still on the knob. Evie pulls down her mask.

She looks terrible.

"What are you doing up here?" she says.

"I can help Willa to the toilet. I'm sure it's fine now if I go in. You can go back to bed if you want."

Evie opens her mouth to answer me, and I bet she's going to send me back downstairs, but it's Mama's voice that fills the little stretch of silence between my words and Evie's.

"Maggie." I know it's Mama's voice, but it sounds so strange. Like an old woman's. Like a scary witch's.

Evie turns toward the sound, and her eyes fill with tears.

I don't know that voice and I take a step away from the door. Evie lays her hand on my arm as if to stop me from running away.

"Maggie," Mama says again, in a whispery growl.

I look up at Evie.

"Just stay by the entrance," she says.

And then Evie crosses the hall to Willa's room.

I take a step toward Mama's door and then another one. I push it open, and as my eyes adjust to the dimness, I see that Mama is propped up with pillows. Her hair is slick with sweat, and she's as pale as Alex's dead mother. Her skin is splotched with dark spots that look like berry stains. I cannot take another step.

She turns her head toward me and raises a hand. "Don't come any closer, Maggie." Mama's voice floats across the room to me like fireplace smoke. I don't think she realizes I am frozen where I stand by the sight of her. Something heavy is swelling inside me, ballooning like bread dough. It feels like fear, and yet it's bigger than fear.

"Are you feeling better?" These words tumble out of my mouth because I woke up thinking she would be. She should be. But I don't think she is. I don't think she is feeling better.

"Maggie, listen to me," Mama says, and then she coughs into a handkerchief spotted with something dark. I don't want to think about what has made those marks.

"Maybe you should rest, Mama." The heavy thing inside me wants to push me out the door and back down to the sitting room where Alex is cooing and kicking and trying to grab happy pictures off the covers of books.

"Listen." Mama takes away the cloth from her face. "You did the right thing, Maggie. That baby . . . he would have died if not for you. You did the right thing. I should have told you that the first day. I'm sorry. . . ."

Her words fall away and a barking cough takes their place. I can't think of a thing to say. I want to reply, "It's all right, Mama. I'm not mad at you. You don't have to say you're sorry." But it's like there's a door at the back of my throat where the words get out and it has just slammed shut.

"Tell your papa I said that," she says. "Tell him I want the baby to stay. I want him to be ours."

Why can't you tell him? These five words just won't come. I think them but I cannot say them.

"I want you all to raise him and care for him and never let him think for a moment that there was a time when someone did not love him," Mama says. "All the love you still hold in your heart for Henry, you give it to that little boy. Will you do that?"

Tears are spilling down my cheeks. I want to say yes. I want to say, "Stop talking like that!" Nothing gets past that door in my throat except a sob. Just one.

"You're my brave girl, Maggie," Mama says when I say nothing.

Inside my head I am shouting "Mama," but no sound comes from me. In an instant and before she can tell me not to, I run to the foot of her bed. The only parts of her that I can reach are her feet. They barely shudder under her blanket when I fall across them. One of her big toes fills that triangle spot at the end of my neck and as I cry, it feels like that toe is trying to help me stop. I know I can't stay here. I know for Alex's safety I must leave her. I must.

"Don't go!" I finally sputter, as if she is the one about to leave the room.

"You're my brave girl," Mama whispers, and then she pulls her feet up and away from me. The front half of my body is now lying across just bed and blanket. Mama has curled up into a ball and turned to the wall.

She will get better, I say to myself as I back away from her bed. It's the fourth day. Later today she will start to feel better. I turn toward her door.

I am almost at the doorframe when I turn back around. "We named him Alex. Is that all right?"

I wait for a response. It seems like a long time goes by before I get one.

"It's perfect," Mama whispers, and then those two words are lost in an avalanche of coughs that chase me the rest of the way out of her room.

Papa arrives by train from Fort Meade, near Baltimore, in the late afternoon. The army let him get on the first train to Philadelphia after Uncle Fred's phone call. He is wearing a uniform that makes him look like he belongs to other people in some other place. When he left for the camp in September, we all went to the station to see him off. Today, Uncle Fred went alone to pick him up. When I hug Papa, he doesn't smell like my father; he smells like new wool and metal and train smoke. He has only been gone from us for a month, but it seems like so much longer.

"Mags," he whispers into my hair when he puts his arms around me. His embrace is light and quick. He has an eye toward the stairs, and the bedrooms, where Mama is.

He hugs Evie next. Tears spill from her eyes at his touch, and she pretends that she's not starting to cry. She's trying to be brave. He breaks away quickly from her, too.

Next, he bends down over Willa, who is lying on the sofa in a pile of blankets and whimpering for him. He bends down to kiss her forehead and says, "How's my little Willow?"

His voice sounds stiff with emotion. Willa starts to cry, too. "Did you bring me a present?" she says. And Papa smiles and says she can have the Hershey's bar in his travel bag if she takes a little rest.

Baby Alex, lying awake in his bureau drawer by the hearth, had been kicking his little legs quietly when Papa came in. Now he makes a gurgling sound that is nearly a laugh. He is amused by his own feet. Papa looks down at him now and I can't read what my father is thinking.

"This is the poor orphan baby Mama and I found," I say, sensing the need to come to Alex's defense.

"I told your father all about this child on the way home from the train station," Uncle Fred says, frowning. I can just imagine what Uncle Fred said about Alex.

"We don't know his name, but we've been calling him Alex," I continue.

"I named him," Willa says in a hoarse voice from the sofa.

"Yes," Papa says, but he's just staring at the baby with no expression on his face. He's not angry or happy. I don't know what he is.

For a second everyone is just watching Papa watching Alex.

And then the silence is broken by terrible coughing from upstairs.

We all turn our heads toward the staircase. A second later Papa is on the steps and heading up to his bedroom, pulling out of his pocket a white surgical mask that the army must have given him.

At sunset, Evie takes up a tray of food for Papa and Mama, but when she brings it back down after we've eaten our own supper, the food on the tray looks untouched.

The next few hours slink by as we wait in the sitting room for Papa to come back down. Alex falls asleep, but I keep him in my arms rather than put him in the bureau drawer by the hearth. Willa dozes curled up on Evie's lap.

Just after the clock in the hall strikes nine o'clock, we all notice that it's suddenly very quiet upstairs. Uncle Fred goes up to Mama's room. He comes down some minutes later and stands at the entrance to the sitting room. He exhales long and slow like he's smoking a pipe. But there is no pipe.

"I think you girls need to come up and say your good-byes," he says softly.

"No," Evie whispers.

"What?" Willa says, half-asleep. "Where are we going?"

I don't say anything. A tingling sensation instantly creeps all over my body and a rush of hotness fills my ears. Alex startles and then slips back into deep slumber.

"You can bid her farewell from the bedroom door," he continues. "She won't want you to come any closer."

The three of us just stare dumbly at Uncle Fred.

"Come on, then," he says, trying to sound gruff, but his voice is high and airy, like an old woman's. He steps over to Willa and scoops her up to carry her up to our parents' bedroom. Evie trails behind them, crying into a handkerchief.

I get up off the sofa and lay Alex in the drawer and tuck the blanket in around him. He is so little and helpless.

My feet feel leaden as I climb the stairs. Evie and Uncle Fred with Willa in his arms are already just inside the bedroom when I get to the second floor. A single table lamp is on and its faint light throws tall shadows over the room. "We're here, Mama. We're all here," Evie is saying.

As my eyes adjust to the dimness of the room, I can see that Papa is at Mama's bedside, his mask over his face. He's still in his uniform, like he only just got here. He is leaning forward in his chair as he holds one of Mama's hands. The breath in Mama's lungs doesn't sound like air but rather sloshing water. She is so pale she looks like a ghost.

Willa, in Uncle Fred's arms, can't seem to believe the figure on the bed is Mama. I can scarcely believe it. Willa stares at the bed and Mama, frowning. After a second or two she lays her head against Uncle Fred's chest. "I want to go back downstairs," she murmurs.

As Uncle Fred and Willa leave, Evie takes another step into the room, filling the empty space. Tears are running down her face. "We love you, Mama," she says. "You can go. We'll be all right. We'll always remember you. You were so good to us."

If there is a word of farewell I am supposed to add to this, I can't find it. I can't think of one thing I want to say. Mama turns her head slightly toward Evie and me, and she raises a finger on the hand my father isn't holding. But that's all she does. She doesn't speak, doesn't raise her head. Doesn't do anything but hold up that one finger. Maybe she is saying "Hello" with it. Maybe she is saying "Good-bye." Maybe she is just pointing to the ceiling, where on the other side of the roof is the starry October sky and beyond.

Or maybe she is saying, "Just one second there! Uncle Fred is wrong. I'm not going anywhere."

I want to believe this is what she is saying. I think about all the kind words she has spoken to me over the years of my life, all

the motherly touches, the gentle correc-
tions. I think of how she said I could have
the room in the attic when we moved to
Philadelphia, how she let me join her in the
embalming room so that I could help give
back to all those poor dead souls the look
of life, and how she allowed me to go with
her to South Street, where I found and
saved Baby Alex and brought him home to
us.

I think of all these things and I choose to
believe she is telling us Uncle Fred is
mistaken. He is mistaken.

I raise my hand in return. I think she sees
it. She lowers the finger lifted off her
coverlet, and every part of her save her lungs
goes still again.

Evie is weeping.

I turn from the room without saying anything.

Chapter 35

Pauline

I had no idea the gap between earth and heaven is narrow, no wider than a jump over a brook. I'd always thought heaven was so far from the living, no one could measure its distance from earth. Even the wisest person ever born couldn't look up at the night sky through the most powerful telescope and catch a glimpse of heaven — it was that far off.

That was the only part of knowing there is a heaven that used to frighten me — how far away it was. And when Henry died, that was what pained me the most. I was his mother and he was just a baby and how could heaven be Paradise for him if I was so far away no mortal could gauge the distance that separated us?

This is why Death stayed with me after Henry left. Not to haunt or accuse or disturb me, but because I was always meant to follow my little boy. Death knew that in just a short time, I would cross over, just like Henry did, and so it has been hovering, gentle and benevolent, waiting for me. All this time my companion has been trying to show me that the space between the two worlds is not so vast. Heaven is just on the other side of waking.

Death is not our foe. There is no foe. There is only the stunningly fragile human body, a holy creation capable of loving with such astonishing strength but which is weak to the curses of a fallen world. It is the frailty of flesh and blood that causes us to succumb to forces greater than ourselves. We are like butterflies, delicate and wonderful, here on earth for only a brilliant moment and then away we fly. Death is appointed merely to close the door to our suffering and open wide the gate to Paradise. If we were made of stone or iron, we would be impervious to disease and injury and disaster, but then we could not give love and receive love, could we? We'd be unable to feel anything at all, and surely incapable of spreading our wings and flying. . . .

Henry is near to me now. I can feel the canopy lifting, and I am not afraid. If I were orchestrating the events, I would have us all be together at this moment I join my baby boy. But I shall fly ahead of Thomas and the girls, just as Henry did, and I know with all my heart that we shall all be together again. Perhaps on that fine day it will even seem that we've drifted heavenward only moments apart from one another, not years or decades. . . .

Oh, Thomas!

I see you there at my bedside, holding my hand, saying my name. The army let you come home to me! How I've missed you. I wish I could tell you how much, but I am strangely not inside that shell of a woman whose hand you are holding. I am right beside you, leaning in close. Can you feel my arms around you? Can you hear me? I am going to our precious Henry. Don't weep. You and I had a happy life. We had seventeen good years. Some people never see seventeen days of the same measure of happiness. I don't think my parents were ever as happy as we were. Don't hate them now, my darling, for stopping us from going home. They did what they thought they had to.

The girls will be all right, Thomas. I know you are already worried for them, but Willa has Evelyn, Maggie has Alex, and you all have the love that I leave here for each one of you. It is spilling out of me even at this moment and finding its way to you all. There is even love for Alex that is gushing out of me, Thomas. I held him for just a short while, but in those few minutes my heart was linked to his.

That child needs you and the girls, Thomas. And you may not know it yet, but you need him, too.

Tell the girls this, will you? Tell them that all the love that had been tucked inside this mortal heart of mine remains with you all. That's how I will stay close. My love for you all is right there now. Just under your skin. And there it will always —

Oh! Oh, Thomas!

Look! Can you see it? It's so beautiful! Look!

So beautiful!

Beautiful.

CHAPTER 36

Evelyn

I keep thinking I'm having a bad dream and soon I'll wake up and everything will be back to the way it was before the flu.

She is gone. Mama is dead. The flu took her just like it wanted to take Willa. Just like it took Alex's mother and Mrs. Landry and thousands upon thousands of others.

Why, if it could let Willa go, did it not do the same for Mama? Why does it choose to take some and not others? Why doesn't it just kill us all? I am not asking for the scientific reasons. I know those. I don't want the medical reasons. I want to know the *real* reasons.

We were all in the sitting room when Papa came down the stairs several hours after we were told to say our farewells. Uncle Fred was standing by the window, looking out into the darkness. I was on the sofa and Willa was asleep with her head in my lap.

Maggie had Alex in her arms, and she was singing to him even though he was asleep. When Papa stepped into the room, she stopped.

He didn't have to say anything. We knew. Mama had left us. I started to cry and Willa stirred on my lap but didn't wake.

"I'll take care of her," Uncle Fred said a minute later, his voice soft and gruff at the same time.

Papa shook his head. "No. I want to."

"Let me do her hair," Maggie said, and all of us looked at her.

"Maggie," Papa said.

"Please. I want to do her hair!" Maggie said, louder this time, and Alex whimpered in her arms. "Not you, Papa. Not Uncle Fred. Me. Please?"

"I don't think —" Uncle Fred began, but Papa cut him off.

"Let her do it, Fred."

Uncle Fred was quiet for a moment. "You want to take her to Quakertown when we're finished?" he said to Papa.

"Pauline stays here," Papa said. "Her home is here. With us." His eyes were rimmed with tears of grief but also anger.

I thought maybe he would gather us all in a wide embrace and we'd cry together for a little while, but Papa just turned and left the room. I think he wanted to be alone to cry, maybe because he wanted to be strong for us. Maybe because he doesn't like crying in front of people.

Or maybe it was because he wanted to punish Grandma and Grandpa Adler by burying Mama here with us instead of there with them, and he wanted to be alone with those dark thoughts.

When he left, Maggie bolted out of the chair she'd been sitting in. She ran up the stairs with Alex, all the way to the top of the house and her room. Her door slammed shut. Uncle Fred turned to me. He looked so very tired.

"It's late. You should both be in bed," he said, nodding to Willa in my lap.

"Do you really want to talk about *should*s?" I snapped. I regretted those disrespectful words the second I spoke them. But I was seething inside. Mama *should* be alive. That was a *should* I was willing to talk about!

But I couldn't trust myself to speak again. Uncle Fred had been so kind to me in so many ways, not the least of which was paying for my schooling and letting me — even encouraging me to — read his many books whenever I wanted. I should have said I was sorry. But I didn't. He set his pipe in its little tray on the table by the bay window.

"I'm sorry, Evelyn. Do whatever you need to. Stay here as long as you like," he said softly. He walked away from me, into the foyer and toward the little hallway that led to his rooms. He coughed a few times on the way to his bedroom.

Willa opened her eyes and squinted up at me. "Is it morning?"

"Shhh. No. It isn't."

She settled back to sleep and I let my head fall against the back of the sofa. I hadn't the strength to climb the stairs. I hadn't the strength to do anything.

I didn't think I would be able to sleep, but I must have dropped off at some point. The next thing I know the room is suddenly bathed in ghostly light from the rising sun outside the windows.

I ease myself away from Willa and head into the kitchen. Papa is sitting at the table with a whiskey bottle and a coffee cup. The door to the funeral parlor is ajar. He'd been back there already, but I don't want him to do anything to Mama just yet. I look at him and I'm ready to tell him it is too soon. She's only been dead a few hours. It is too soon.

He meets my gaze and then nods toward

the half-open door that leads to the funeral rooms. "Roland was just here," he says, his voice void of strength. "Charlie Sutcliff died last night, too."

I feel for the back of a kitchen chair and close my eyes against the assault of those words. It is too much. Too much.

When I open my eyes, I see that Papa has brought the morning paper in and set it on the table. A skinny column of type on the bottom of the front page announces the influenza is abating. The number of cases being reported is at last decreasing, and not just in Philadelphia, but elsewhere, too. But like the monster it is, the flu is madly grabbing for its last victims as it pulls away like a tidal wave headed back out to sea.

"Is Uncle Fred up?" Papa says tonelessly.

"I don't think so."

Papa takes a drink from his cup, grimaces as he swallows, and then sets it down. "He and I need to get started." He looks up at me.

I know what he is saying. Mama needs to be brought down and made ready for her burial.

I shudder for a moment at the thought of this, but then I remember Maggie will fix Mama's hair and cover the awful splotching on her skin and apply rouge to her cheeks and color to her gray lips, such that when I see my mother for the last time, she will look like herself and not the phantom I saw last night.

"I'll go see if he's awake," I reply.

He nods. "I can tell him about Charlie. You don't have to."

"All right."

I make my way to Uncle Fred's bedroom, feeling numb. I hear no sounds from the other side of his door. I knock lightly.

"Uncle Fred? It's Evie. Are you awake?"

I receive no response.

I knock again, a bit louder. "Uncle Fred?"

Nothing.

I open the door a crack. "Uncle Fred. It's Evie."

I peek around the door. Uncle Fred is still in his bed, eyes closed, his skin a dull gray.

"Uncle Fred?" I hear a tremor of fear in my voice. He is not moving. There is no rise and fall of his chest. He is as still as stone.

For a second I can only stand there in disbelief.

And then my feet carry me to his bedside and my hand, seemingly of its own will, reaches out to touch his face.

It is cold to my touch.

I run back to the kitchen and Papa turns

from the sink where he is rinsing out his cup.

"What is it?" he says.

I can barely squeak out the words. "Uncle Fred is . . . He's gone."

Papa doesn't understand. He thinks Fred has left the house. "Gone where?"

"He's dead, Papa!"

My father brushes past me and I follow him to Uncle Fred's bedroom.

Papa calls Fred's name, feels for his pulse, bends down to listen for the sound of a beating heart.

But there is no pulse, and Uncle Fred's heart is not beating.

"What happened? Was it the flu?" I ask, remembering how he coughed last night on his way to his bedroom.

"Maybe. I don't know," Papa says in a shallow voice I've never heard from him before. "I don't know. He was old. He was exhausted. Perhaps it was all those things. I don't know. I don't know."

I lean into my papa and put my arm around him, much like he might have done for me. He looks so empty and weak as he stands there staring at Uncle Fred, and it's as though if I don't hang on to him, he might disappear like a vapor. My father loved my mother. Deeply. They were modest and quiet about their love for each other in front of other people, but I could see the depth of their affection for each other in so many little ways, even in the way they held hands when grace was said at suppertime. And Uncle Fred had been as kind to Papa as Grandad — his own father — perhaps even more so. And now both of these people had been taken from him.

And from me. My father seems to realize this at the same moment, and his arm comes around my middle like mine is around his. It's like we are each holding the other up.

We stand silent that way for a moment. I can see in Papa's dazed expression that it has not yet occurred to him that the funeral business, the house, everything that Uncle Fred owned, is now his. Or maybe the dazed expression is there because this thought *has* occurred to him, and that now Mama won't be here to share in the joy and responsibility of that ownership.

"I'll go get Roland to help me," Papa finally says. "Close the door."

Papa leaves me to fetch our neighbor.

After my father is gone, I stand over Uncle Fred's body, serenely posed in the guise of sleep. "I'm sorry I was short with you last night," I whisper to him. "I should've said so when I had the chance. Please forgive me."

I begin to cry for him, for Mama, for Charlie, and for every single future moment they should have all been granted.

Death doesn't ever look at *should*s, though, does it? Death looks at nothing. It just does what it's meant to do.

CHAPTER 37

Willa

When I woke up this morning, I found out Mama had gone to be with Henry.

I got very angry when Papa told me this. I was already not in a good mood because I'd woken up on the sitting room sofa and nobody was around, and when I tried to get up, I fell. Evie and Papa heard me and came into the room. That was when Papa sat me on the sofa and told me Mama isn't with us anymore. She is in heaven with the angels. And Henry.

I don't like it one bit that Mama is with the angels. I know about heaven. I know if you go to heaven you don't ever come back to earth. Ever.

Mama is supposed to be here. Mothers aren't supposed to leave their children. Doesn't she know that?

Papa was sitting next to me. In front of us was an empty candy dish on a table. I grabbed it and threw it as hard as I could and it broke into a thousand pieces. I wanted Papa or Evie to yell at me for doing that because that's what grown-ups are supposed to do. They were both right there and neither one did. And that scared me a little. I had my eye on the china ballet dancer on the end table next to me and I was about to grab it and hurl it, too, when Papa put his hand over mine. He didn't slap it like I wanted him to; he just covered it.

"Breaking things won't bring her back," Papa said.

"What will?" I said.

He pulled me into his arms but didn't answer me.

Evie sat down on the sofa next to us and put her head in her hands.

"I don't want her to be in heaven with Henry. I want her here," I said.

Papa held me tighter and still said nothing.

I heard creaking on the stairs and for just a second I thought Papa and Evie were wrong about everything. I thought Mama was coming down the stairs and she was going to come into the room and say she'd only been fooling.

But it was Maggie with Baby Alex. She had his blanket and a diaper and some toys in her arms, too. And a bottle, half-empty. Maggie's hair was pulled back tight away from her face, and the mask she wears when she goes outside was tied loose around her neck.

Evie looked up when they came into the room. She didn't say anything. She just held out her arms and Maggie walked over and put Alex on Evie's lap. Then Maggie set down all the baby things on the rug by the hearth.

Papa leaned away from me but kept one arm around my shoulders. "We need your help for a little while this morning, Willa. Maggie is going to be with me in the funeral parlor. Can you help Evie look after Baby Alex for a few minutes? Would you do that?"

I looked over at Alex. He has the name I'd wanted him to have. He grinned at me. I turned from him to face Papa again because everything else about this day was starting out wrong, wrong, wrong.

"Why does Maggie get to go in the funeral rooms with you?" I said. "Maggie isn't supposed to be in there now. Only Uncle Fred."

"I need her help."

"Uncle Fred won't let her go in there."

Papa looked down at the floor and then up at me again. "Uncle Fred went to heaven last night, too, Willa. And Charlie across the street."

None of this was making any sense. Why was this happening? I had the flu. I didn't go to heaven. Why was everybody else?

Maybe I would, though. Maybe later today I would or the next day. Or maybe I'd wake up tomorrow and the whole house would be empty because Papa and Evie and Maggie and Alex would have all left for heaven without me.

"I don't want to be here alone!"

Papa pulled me into his arms again. "You're not alone. Evie will be right here. Maggie and I will just be in the other room."

"Don't go without me!"

"I'm not going anywhere without you. I just need to take care of Mama and Uncle Fred and Charlie. And Maggie is going to help me. Evie and Baby Alex will be right here with you."

I knew what he meant then. He was taking Mama into the Elm Bonning Room.

"Is Mama a dead body?" I could barely say those words. But I had to know.

"No," Maggie answered before Papa could say anything. "You can come and see her when we're done, and I'll show you that she's not."

Evie looked up at Papa like she wasn't

sure Maggie had given me the right answer.

"That's right," Papa said, so I guess she had. "When we're done, we'll show you."

"Uncle Fred and Charlie, too?"

"If that's what you want."

Evie laid Alex on the blanket by the hearth, and Papa stoked the fire that had gone out. I lay back down on the sofa, tired already. Then Papa and Maggie left. Evie went out of the room for a minute, too, but it was just to get a broom and a dustpan. When she came back, she swept up all the pieces of the candy dish.

You can't even tell that I threw it unless you notice the empty spot on the table, and that it looks like something that belonged there is gone.

CHAPTER 38

Maggie

Papa and Roland Sutcliff move the other bodies that were already in the embalming room into the casket closet, and they lay out Mama, Charlie, and Uncle Fred, side by side by side on three tables. While they are doing this, I fetch Uncle Fred's church clothes out of his wardrobe and Mama's prettiest dress — the white lace one with yellow ribbons. Before Roland Sutcliff returns home, he leaves Charlie's best suit with us. Papa tells him that Mama, Uncle Fred, and Charlie are going to be honored the way the deceased used to be, before the flu.

The city has said there can be no more public funerals, no more viewings, no more careful readying for satin-lined caskets.

Remove the dead as quickly as possible from your homes and get them into the ground. That's what the city leaflets said.

But that's not what we're going to do for Mama, Charlie, and Uncle Fred.

"When we're all done here, we'll take them into the parlor," Papa says. "And we'll honor them."

Roland Sutcliff nods and says nothing. But in his eyes I see that he likes this idea very much. When he leaves, Papa tells me he's not going to use the tank with the foul-smelling formalin. He's not going to make the cuts and insert the tubes. He is going to leave the blood inside Mama, Uncle Fred, and Charlie because they will be buried this very day.

I reach for Mama's apron on a hook, but Papa lays a hand on my arm.

"I need you to leave me while I dress them in their burial clothes. I'll let you know when I'm ready for you to come back."

I blush slightly and wish I could rub the color out. I won't look at Uncle Fred's and Charlie's private parts, if that's what he's worried about. I can look away. "I'm thirteen," I begin, but Papa cuts me off.

"It's not that, Maggie. Their bodies are becoming stiff. You'll think I'm being too rough with them. I don't want you to see what I might have to do."

I open my mouth to protest that I am not afraid of what happens in the embalming room. I've never been afraid. But I don't get the chance to say this.

"Do as I say, Mags. Now."

I turn for the kitchen.

I stand at the sink for what seems like a long time. I can hear Evie reading a story to Willa in the sitting room, and Alex cooing. I imagine he is cuddled against Evie's chest as she reads, trying to make sense of the pictures in the book she holds.

When Papa finally calls for me to come back, he looks tired and worn out even with half his face covered behind his mask. It's as if the effort to make the bodies obey has exhausted him. Mama and Uncle Fred and Charlie are now lying clothed on the tables. Their nightclothes are in a heap in the corner, ready to be burned, no doubt. The vents in the room are fully open and the room is chilled like it's a huge icebox.

This time when I reach for the apron, Papa doesn't stop me. I pull my mask out of my skirt pocket, tie it on, and join Papa at Mama's side.

"Are you sure you want to be here?" he asks in a weary voice.

"I do. I know what to do, Papa. I know how to do the hair and cosmetics. I watched her do it a dozen times before the flu came. I know how to do it. I *want* to do it. I can take care of Charlie and Uncle Fred, too."

He nods and then reaches for the canister of flesh-colored paste on a cart with all the other items he uses to fix and preserve the bodies. There are horrible berry-colored stains on Charlie's and Mama's faces. The flu somehow did that to them. I watch Papa for a few moments as he works to cover up the stains on Mama and when I ask if I can take care of Charlie, he extends the canister to me. I use a little wooden stick to get the paste out and then I rub it onto Charlie's face and hands with a small sponge, the way I saw Mama do it. The skin on his face feels strange under the sponge, like a mask made of cold leather.

When we're done with the flesh-colored paste, Papa tells me I can do Mama's hair while he takes care of Uncle Fred's beard and hair.

Mama's hair is a tangled mess from her sweating and shivering and writhing. I have never seen her with her hair in such a state. I wet the hairbrush with lavender water and gently smooth out all the snarls, trying not to tug too hard. I use the curling rods and I style Mama like she is going to a party. I find myself talking to her, just like she talked to the deceased people she worked on. I let her know her hair is back to the way it is supposed to be, and that the rouge I put on her cheeks is just the right shade, and that I was very careful with the lipstick and brow pencil so as not to make wiggly mistakes. This is my way of saying good-bye, I think to myself. A much better way than how I was supposed to have said it last night when she seemed to be drowning right there on her bed.

Papa glances over at me now and then. Perhaps my talking to Mama like this is comforting to him. I hope it is.

Every minute I am with her, she looks more and more like Mama again. When I'm done with her hair and cosmetics, she looks like she could open her eyes, hop off the table, and ask me to set the table for dinner. But then I touch her hands that are crossed over her waist and they are now like marble, cold and hard. The finger she had raised the night before is clamped down against the rest of her hand, and when I try to move it, I can't. This is when I know in my soul Mama is truly gone from me and the body that looks like her isn't her at all.

When I had helped Mama before in this room, I had only ever handed her things. She was the one who touched the bodies. I had not known how much like stone the dead became.

"The stiffness will pass," Papa says gently. He has turned around from Charlie's body to stand next to me. He saw me try to move Mama's hand. "But not before it gets worse."

"Why? Why is she like that?" I say, not looking up from Mama's statuelike hands.

"I don't know why this happens. I only know that it does."

I look up at him and I see a tear sliding down his cheek. He is staring at Mama. He touches one of the curls I made. Her hair at least is still feather soft, like always.

"You did well, Mags. She looks beautiful."

"She looks like Mama," I say. But I know this body is not Mama. She is not inside it anymore.

I turn to fix Charlie's hair and to allow Papa some moments with Mama. Though Papa covered the stains of illness, Charlie is still so pale. I put a little rouge on his cheeks and just a tiny bit of color on his lips. Then I comb and slick his hair into place. Soon he looks like Charlie again. And because he does, I am struck anew that he, too, is gone. He was my first friend here in Philadelphia, and Jamie's only brother. Jamie had asked me to look out for Charlie while he was away and now he must be told that Charlie is dead. A new sorrow is expanding inside me. I didn't think there was room for more sadness today, but there is.

Jamie should be here today to say good-bye to Charlie and it makes me angry that the war has him a world away. I will say good-bye for him and I will let him know that I did this. That way I will have fulfilled my promise.

I lean over Charlie's body. "Good-bye," I whisper into his ear. "Jamie sends all his love to you. You were a good brother and a good friend."

I step away from the table and use my sleeve to wipe away the tears that have started to fall. I want to collapse or scream or pound my fist into the wall. Papa has also moved to the center of the room, but he has done so to survey the three tables. We are finished. All that can be done for these people we loved has been done.

"Run across the street and fetch Mr. Sutcliff," Papa says to me. "Tell him I'm ready for him. Tell him Dora should come over in a little while, too, after we've changed and washed up. I'll get the caskets ready." He moves past me to do this next thing he must do. I pull off my mask and apron and hang them as I follow him out of the embalming room.

On my way to the mudroom I pass the

casket room, which contains just a few hastily made caskets and a dozen of yesterday's dead. I can smell the bodies through the seam in the closed door. The odor reminds me of rotten apples and kerosene. A welcome blast of cold air meets me as I step out onto the back stoop. There are automobiles out today and delivery carts and people walking about in masks and heavy coats. But no one seems to notice me as I cross the boulevard, without a coat, without a mask. Everyone is intent on their own reason for being out on the street in the middle of a plague.

The accounting office is closed, so I take the stairs to the Sutcliffs' apartment, realizing afresh that I will never again see Charlie coming down them or waving to me from the window. Jamie will come back from the war to a home without Charlie in it.

Roland Sutcliff answers my knock. I have never seen him look so careworn.

"Papa is ready for you now. And he says Mrs. Sutcliff should come over in a little while, too."

"All right," he says heavily, as if those two words weigh a hundred pounds each.

An idea pops into my head. A way for Jamie to be here today, to pay his respects.

"Could I have the baseball Jamie and Charlie used to play catch with? I've seen it on Charlie's bureau. I think Jamie would be happy if Charlie was laid to rest with it."

Roland Sutcliff blinks and then stares at me for a moment. It seems to take a second or two for him to understand what I am asking for and why. Then the faintest of smiles tugs at his mouth. "Yes. Yes, I think Jamie would like that."

He leaves me at the door to go get the baseball. From where I stand, I can see the closed door to their bedroom. Dora Sutcliff is no doubt on the other side, curled up in grief. Mr. Sutcliff returns a moment later with the ball. It is more dirt-colored than white, and the red laces have faded to a rosy pink. It has been thrown and caught and hit and chased many times. His eyes fill with tears as he hands it to me.

"Tell your father I'll be right over." He casts a glance over his shoulder to the bedrooms. "And Dora will be along shortly."

A few minutes after I return to the house, Mr. Sutcliff comes over and he and Papa move Mama, Charlie, and Uncle Fred into the viewing room one at a time. We are out of nice caskets again. We only have pine boxes made by the cabinetmaker down the street, but they are smooth and warm and they smell like Christmas. I like them better than the coffins that smell like varnish anyway. Papa has lined them with quilts to cover up the shavings meant to pad the inside. Charlie's hands are getting stiffer by the minute, but I am able to place the baseball in his grasp. Roland Sutcliff puts a hand on my shoulder for a moment as we stand at Charlie's casket and then he returns home to change his clothes and get his wife.

Papa and I head to our rooms to take off our working clothes and put on church clothes. Evie plaits my hair and then gets Willa ready. Alex doesn't have any dark clothes to wear, so I just dress him in a yellow romper because yellow is Mama's favorite color.

At noon, we open the front door to the boulevard and let whoever has gotten word come in to see our beloved dead, if they want to. There are a lot of people who have learned of our losses. People from church come, from the APL, from up and down the street. Nobody asks where Mama's family is because they all figure her people live too far away and we can't wait. They don't know Papa hasn't called Grandma and Grandpa Adler yet. Only Mr. Sutcliff asks why he hasn't and Papa just says, "I can't talk to them right now."

316

For a couple hours the people come. Some bring flowers. Some bring food for us to eat later. Some sit in the chairs for a long time, as if waiting for something to start. Some folks I know, but many I don't. It is like each one of them has lost someone in the last few days and they haven't been able to do what we are doing now, so they are lingering in honor of their own dead. Charlie and Mama and Uncle Fred are suddenly not just their own persons anymore: they are a young man, a woman at midlife, and an old man. They are everyone's beloved dead.

Willa hangs on Evie, never letting her out of sight, and Alex — afraid of all the strangers — clings to me, and his need for my arms takes my mind off the deep ache inside my heart. Papa is the one who greets those who come. He is the one who must respond time and time again to people who say, "We're so sorry for your loss." I grow tired of hearing it. It is like listening to the words *She's dead* over and over and over. Dora sits in a chair the whole time, crying into a handkerchief, but she manages to thank everyone, through her tears, for coming.

By two o'clock, the crowd thins. Willa and Alex are both asleep — Willa in Evie's lap and Alex in my arms. Papa tells us it is time

317

for Mama and Charlie and Uncle Fred to be buried. What comes next we don't need to be a part of, he says. Papa arranged by telephone for Reverend Pope to come pray over the quickly dug graves and commit Mama and Charlie and Uncle Fred to the ground. Uncle had purchased a lot for himself some time ago at a big cemetery across the Schuylkill River, and the lot is large enough for him and Mama, and Papa one day, too. Mr. Sutcliff is taking Charlie to the cemetery that belongs to the church they attend.

As much as I want this terrible day to be over, I know this moment is the last time I will see Mama. After today she will exist only in the memories I have of her. Memories tend to fade, even the ones that mean the most to you, and this thought scares me. I touch one of her curls with my free hand, cementing the image of my doing so in my head and heart. Brokenhearted Dora Sutcliff has already been escorted home, so I say good-bye to Charlie, too, and I reposition the baseball in his hands. It had scooted out of his grasp a bit.

Evie scoops up Willa and leaves the room in tears. I start to follow her, but I stop at Uncle Fred's box. We are the only family he had in Philadelphia. He had made Papa the heir of everything he had: the business, the house, the cars, everything. This big house is now all ours and the funeral business is all Papa's. Surely the army won't insist on Papa's going back now that we girls have no mother and no uncle. Papa will surely have to stay home now.

"Good-bye, Uncle Fred," I murmur to him. He looks younger somehow in death. I hadn't realized just how much he'd physically changed since the flu arrived. He'd begun to look so haggard and old, older than his seventy-two years. It is not until this moment that I see how very much at peace he looks now. Happy, even.

And then I leave the viewing parlor to join Evie in the kitchen. I close the door that leads to the funeral rooms, but I still hear the nails being driven into the tops of the boxes. She hears it, too. My sister and I run into the sitting room to get away from the sound, but we still hear the faint tapping. We lay the sleeping children down on the sofa and cover our ears.

When at last the hammering stops, Evie drapes a shawl over Willa, who still has not stirred. "I suppose I should see to all that food," she says, wiping away the tears from her face with her sleeve. Nearly everyone who visited brought some kind of food with them — roasts and bread and desserts. I have no appetite for any of it. What I hunger for is the way our life was before.

I transfer Alex to his bureau drawer by the hearth and stoke up the fire. When it is burning nicely again, I go into Uncle Fred's office, to his desk, and I sit down at it. His APL papers and issues of *The Spy Glass* are all in a pile off to the side, like he suddenly decided he couldn't be bothered anymore with slackers and unpatriotic people and Hun sympathizers. I have never seen his desk so uncluttered.

I pull out a piece of stationery from inside the drawer. Uncle Fred has a nice selection of fountain pens. I choose one, smooth out the paper, and date it to be sent two days from now.

Dear Jamie,
I trust you have received word from your parents about Charlie. They probably told you that my dear mama and uncle Fred also passed.

I just want you to know that I helped take care of Charlie when your father brought him over. My papa dressed him in his nicest clothes and I combed his hair and saw to it that he looked as though he had only just closed his eyes in sleep.

I put the baseball you and Charlie played with in his hands. And even though we're not supposed to, we had a visitation here. So many people came. Today was a terrible day, but this one good thing happened — people came and kept coming to let us know Mama and Charlie and Uncle Fred had mattered.

I know you would've liked to be here. When the war is over and you come back, I will tell you anything about this day that you would like to know.

I don't know what it will be like to not have my mother with me anymore. I only know that right now I feel like she wasn't supposed to go. I thought Mama was stronger. I thought she would beat the flu like Willa did. I thought Uncle Fred had been wrong last night when he told me I needed to say my farewells. But it's me that had it wrong. I had to say good-bye to Mama after she was already gone, while I combed the tangles out of her hair. She was so cold and stiff, like a statue. I don't know if she heard me. But perhaps she saw me. Perhaps she was allowed a glimpse of me caring for her as she sailed up to heaven.

I'm so glad we have Alex — that's what we named the baby I wrote you about. He is the opposite of the war and the flu. He is sweet and beautiful and alive. Alex is the war and the flu and death all turned upside down. When you come home, I will introduce you to him.

I pray for you every day, Jamie. I pray that you stay safe and that the Germans will be beat and that you can come home.

Yours very truly,
Maggie Bright

When I cap the pen, I hear the faint sound of the funeral car being started outside.

Papa and Roland Sutcliff are taking Mama and Charlie and Uncle Fred away.

CHAPTER 39

Evelyn

When Henry died, losing him was all any of us had to think about. The all-consuming, singular focus seemed needful and appropriate. The rest of the world had to wait for us to catch up with it because we had been in mourning. *In* mourning. It was a thing we went inside, and we didn't have to come out until we wanted to.

But with Mama and Uncle Fred and Charlie, the world doesn't stop. It just keeps spinning, with all its troubles, yanking us into its wild revolutions. There is no stepping into mourning, all secluded with nothing but much-warranted sorrow for company. Instead it's as if the train we're all on switched tracks at full speed and now we are racing forward in a completely new direction with no time to think about the destination we'd been headed toward before and now will never see.

Papa now must be what Uncle Fred was, the undertaker.

I must be what Mama was, the keeper of the house.

Maggie must be what I had been, the older sister to the little ones.

The influenza is still rampant, the war still rages, and there is a business to run and a house to manage and there are young children to take care of. The train is still charging ahead, and whoever is conducting it expects us to fall into our new duties without so much as a backward glance.

And so we do.

I think Papa is glad there will be no quiet reprieve to grieve Mama's death. He begins to attend to Uncle Fred's grisly tasks the moment he returns from seeing those three pine boxes safely into the ground. While he was at the graveyards, the bell on the back stoop was rung four times. I did not have the heart to turn the people away. Each time, I answered it, and I instructed those who had brought their dead to bring them into the embalming room. At least the number of dead this day is fewer than it has been, even counting our own losses.

When Papa returns from the cemeteries, he records the new deliveries. Maggie and I push the chairs back against the wall of the viewing parlor and take the flowers our neighbors brought into the main part of the house. Papa needs the viewing room again to become a staging area in which none of us girls is allowed.

When he finally comes into the sitting room hours later, he is exhausted, and still wearing his church clothes from the funeral. He had come in through the back door when he came home from the burials, and in the back he'd stayed.

"Has it really been like this the whole time?" he says to me as he washes up at the kitchen sink. I am warming up some baked chicken brought to us by the Kellers, who live up the boulevard.

"Yes." I don't say it has been worse.

"What did Fred do when he ran out of caskets?"

"He . . . he waited for more."

"With the bodies just lying there?" A look of disgusted worry crosses Papa's face.

"The morgue hasn't had room. The city opened a storage facility on Twentieth, but it's been full, too."

Papa turns and points toward the door that leads to the funeral parlor rooms. "You girls are forbidden to go anywhere near that door."

He says it like it's a new edict, never

before uttered.

"We know, Papa."

None of us is very hungry when I call everyone to the table. I put away most of what I had laid out for supper. And when we are done Papa goes back to work. Maggie feeds Alex, bathes him, and then takes him and his bureau drawer upstairs to her room.

It isn't until I'm putting Willa to bed that I realize the only other beds in the house are Mama's and Uncle Fred's, and Papa can't sleep in either one until the bedclothes have been boiled and the mattresses aired. Willa begs me not to leave her, but I tell her I'm just going to take care of a few things after she falls asleep and that I'll be back to spend the night in her room. This comforts her greatly.

"Sing me 'Daisy Bell,' " Willa says. "Sing it like Mama does."

I don't have Mama's singing voice, but it doesn't matter. Willa holds my hand and fights to stay awake as I sing to her, but slumber overtakes her in only a few minutes.

I leave her room and make up my bed with fresh linens and then put on my mask and a pair of gloves and take the bedclothes off Mama's and Uncle Fred's beds. I'm downstairs with the big bundle in my arms and am about to take it to the washroom when Papa comes into the kitchen. He looks at what I hold.

"I made up my bed for you. I can sleep on the floor in Willa's room," I say. "I'll boil these tomorrow and then air out the mattresses."

Papa holds out his hands. "I'm burning those. Give them to me."

I open my mouth to protest, but Papa repeats his command. I give him the bundle.

"Stay away from the mattresses. I'll haul them away. We'll get new ones."

He turns from me to head back into the funeral rooms. When he comes back, his arms empty, he heads into Uncle Fred's office — his office now — and closes the door. I hear him pick up the receiver of the telephone and ask to place a call. It is urgent, he says. He has a death notification to relay.

Papa tells the operator he needs to place a call to Quakertown. I linger near the door because I know who he is calling. Not Grandad. Papa called him earlier in the day to tell him the sad news that his brother had died. He's calling Grandma and Grandpa Adler.

"I buried your daughter today," he says when the call is put through.

A few seconds of silence follow. I can imagine what is happening on the other end. I must close my eyes to stop imagining it.

"She died of the flu, Eunice!" Papa says, his voice raised.

More seconds of silence.

"No, *you* killed her. *You* did. She'd still be alive if you had let her and the girls come. . . . You should have thought of that before. . . . How do you think they are? They've just lost their mother. Of course they know she had wanted to come home to you. . . . No . . . No, Eunice! *This* is what it's like to want to be somewhere and be told you're not welcome."

The phone's receiver hits the cradle and I take to the stairs to fly up them as quickly as I can.

I tiptoe into Willa's bedroom, fully clothed, not wanting to meet Papa on the stairs and intrude on what might be the only solitary moments of grief he will have this day. I can't think about my grandparents. I don't want to think of them the way Papa is right now. Who can really say if we'd have brought the flu to Quakertown like Grandma Adler had feared? Was it already hiding inside Willa when Mama asked if we could come and they'd said no? No one really knows. I push away thoughts of my grandparents from the folds of my mind. I will contemplate how I feel about their decision on another day. Not this day. Not now.

I lay out a down comforter on the rug near Willa's bed and stretch out upon it. Her bedsheets haven't been laundered since she recovered and remnants of the flu might be clinging to them and I've now a house to run. I can't run any risk of catching this sickness. Despite the ample feathers sewn inside the comforter, the floor beneath me feels hard as stone.

Today, the first full day without Mama, it was announced that a Philadelphia doctor named Paul Lewis has created a vaccine for the flu. From the moment the killing influenza descended, doctors and scientists everywhere have been looking for a way to immunize people against it. In New York, another doctor has come up with a vaccine, too. And so has a doctor in Boston and a team of doctors at an army hospital in Washington, D.C. The newspaper doesn't say if the Philadelphia vaccine works, only that a limited number of doses is available. The board of health sent ten thousand doses of Lewis's vaccine to our local physicians. Papa took us to get vaccinated — me,

Maggie, Willa, and Alex — making the case that we live in a funeral home and are daily exposed to the menace. Even though Willa already had the flu, Papa wanted her to get the injection as well in case she isn't fully immunized. Some flu victims are having relapses.

As we wait now in the doctor's office, I hear one patient whisper to another that he'd heard this new vaccine won't stop the flu; it just makes people think that it will.

"What good is that?" says the other patient, clearly displeased.

"It will make you think you are strong, so you will act strong," the first patient replies. "People who are weak fall faster than people who aren't."

I look over at Papa. He heard the two people talking, too. I can tell he did when our eyes meet.

It does seem too much to hope for that an effective vaccine could be ready so quickly when Louis Pasteur, for example, spent nearly a year working on the rabies vaccine. But who of us in that waiting room wants to look hope in the eye and challenge it to prove itself worthy of trust? I can see that Papa does not wish to challenge it. He wants to embrace it, frail and untested as it might be. His gaze tells me he wants me to

330

embrace it as well.

The nurse calls our names.

Papa stands first and then we all follow.

CHAPTER 40

Willa

Today is the twenty-seventh day of October, and the flu is finally leaving.

It must be, because yesterday all the churches were open again, and today so were all the schools.

It had been a long time since Papa was at church, because he was at the army camp. People kept coming up to us to talk to Papa and give us hugs and sad looks. They asked if there was anything they could do and he said, "No, thank you," and then they all made silly faces at Alex and asked if we were going to keep him.

"We're looking into what we need to do to let him stay with us," Papa said, and they said what a wonderful thing that was to do. I don't know what Papa meant exactly. Alex is an orphan. He doesn't have any family but us. What's so hard about keeping him?

Some of the church ladies wanted to know

if Papa can stay home now or if the army is going to make him go back. Papa said he asked for extended leave. I don't know what that is or why he needs it to stay home. He only had one more week of training anyway. Plus, Maggie told me the newspaper says Germany will surrender. I do know what that means. No more war, and Papa can stay home.

After church yesterday we came home and Evie made us dinner and Maggie helped and it was me and Papa who watched over Alex while they got it ready. It was strange watching Papa hold Alex and play with him. It was like Henry had never left. Everything Papa would have done for Henry he was doing now for Alex. And Alex liked it. It was strange but it was not strange. I wanted to tell Mama this and it made my throat hurt that I couldn't. She's been dead nine days. I looked at that china dancer. It would have felt really good to smash it against the wall.

At first Papa said I didn't have to go back to school right away if I didn't feel well enough yet. Mrs. Sutcliff already said she'll watch Alex while we girls are at school, so she could mind me, too. But I didn't want to stay home another minute. I was tired of it. Three weeks of no school when it's not summer is too long. I missed Flossie. I missed art class and reading time and lunch with my friends. Mrs. Sutcliff is nice, but she's not Mama and she's not Evie.

So I went today. Maggie had to walk slow with me because I get tired fast. I was so glad to see Flossie. She got the flu, too, but not as bad as me. She got it from her brother. And I probably got it from her. I guess that means Mama got it from me. But I don't want to think about that.

Some schoolchildren got the flu like I did. Some got it like Mama did. Some didn't get it at all. I was sad to hear that the German girl Gretchen Weiss got it and she died. I spent the whole day wondering who's looking after her little white dog. When we walked home I asked Maggie if she thought we could ask that German family if they need someone to take that dog. If we are taking Alex, why can't we take a dog, too? She acted like she hadn't heard me. Or maybe she really didn't. The girl who was her friend wasn't in school today, only the other girl she likes, Ruby. The other one is Sally. She got the flu and died.

When we got home, Maggie ran over to the Sutcliffs' to get Alex and she stayed there for a while. Evie was already home and she was sad. Her favorite teacher, Mr.

Galway, is dead. And a boy she liked named Gilbert. She didn't say she liked him, but I can just tell she did.

That was what it was like going back to school. You found out who is still alive after the flu and who isn't.

CHAPTER 41

November 1918
Maggie

Yesterday started out mostly wonderful and ended mostly terrible.

We thought the war was over.

Somehow all the newspapers got word that Germany surrendered and everyone took to the streets to celebrate. And I mean everyone. The last time I saw so many people all at once was that Liberty Loan Parade that brought us the flu and nearly killed all of Philadelphia. And that was only two hundred thousand people. This time it was probably a million. There were whistles and bells and cannon fire and every scrap of white paper that could be found was torn into paper snowflakes and thrown into the air.

"It's over! It's over!" everyone was shouting. Mr. and Mrs. Sutcliff came outside to stand with us on the street and I know Dora

Sutcliff was thinking what I was thinking — that the fighting was over and Jamie had been spared.

I'd been spending part of every afternoon with her since school started up again. She watches Alex for me and I go fetch him every day when classes are over. She'd been showing me Jamie's photographs from when he was a child, the sketches of trains he drew, and telling me all the things he did when he was little. One time we'd gone into Charlie's room and she did the same thing, but I think it hurt her too much to talk about Charlie the way she likes to talk with me about Jamie. It hurt me, too. So I know just how marvelous it was for Dora Sutcliff to hear that Germany had surrendered.

That was what made the day mostly wonderful. The war was over and Jamie had survived it. Something good had finally happened.

But then we heard that it wasn't over. Not really and not yet. It was a news service that had reported the Germans signed an agreement, not the government. The news service was wrong. And that was what made the day end up terrible.

I've been reading the newspapers each night after putting Alex to bed — Papa had bought him a proper crib — looking for news of Jamie's regiment, the 315th Infantry, and I know the Americans have been marching closer and closer to Germany and that the Huns can't stop them. The Americans are near Verdun. I looked at the map in Evie's atlas. Verdun is a city in France that is nearly all the way to Germany. That's how close the Americans are getting. And while the paper made it seem like that was good news, Papa said just before a war ends, the fighting is at its most awful. The Germans are putting bombs in churches along the way so that when the Allied soldiers step inside to thank God for getting them so far, they'll be blown to bits.

When I thought the war was over, I was so happy to imagine that Jamie would not have to step inside any church on the road to Germany. He could just turn around now and head back the way he'd come. Naturally when we heard that the news was not true, I couldn't stop myself from picturing him kneeling in prayer after a long day's march and being ripped apart as the church he was in exploded.

So now we are back to waiting and hoping.

It's been three weeks since Mama and Uncle Fred died. I ache for Mama's voice and her touch and just the sound of her footsteps on the stairs. Alex and I have moved into the room where she died. It's a bigger room for us and Papa wants to sleep in Uncle Fred's old room. When Alex is a little bigger he can share Willa's room with her — she can't wait — and then when he's older still, he can have my old attic room on the third floor if he wants it.

Mama's room will be my room now. I like having it. The bed is new and all the linens, but her things are still in her wardrobe and dressing table. And they will stay there. I miss her so very much, even though now that she is gone, I realize she was a different person after we moved here. It was like she had been keeping an enormous secret from all of us. Not a terrible secret, but not a wonderful one, either. I'm sure that secret was the reason she wanted to be in the embalming room. Papa had said Mama liked to do the hair and cosmetics on the deceased to get her mind off things, but I don't think that was what it was. I think she was putting her mind *on* something. She was there to think about her secret, not escape from thinking. Even now I can't explain what I mean. All I know for sure is, Mama was drawn to that room. And I find myself likewise drawn. I'm not sure I will ever know why she was, but it's enough for me now that she was. We had that in common, and she alone understood why I wanted to be in there. In time, if the flu hadn't taken her, Mama might have told me her secret. I have imagined that some future day she would have, and it's made me a little sad because I know I could never have told her mine.

I don't know if the vaccine worked or if the flu just ran out of gas, but the funeral parlor isn't something out of a nightmare anymore. Papa still gets bodies brought to him — and still too many for one person to take care of properly — but it's not like it was. He has caskets again. They aren't fancy, but they are here. And he doesn't have to worry that they will be stolen off the back stoop. The streetcars are running again, the cinema is open, the wreaths are coming off doors.

Evie says it's like we are getting back our humanity.

That's not how I would describe it. You don't get back what a thief stole from you unless he gives it back. Mama, Uncle Fred, Charlie, Mrs. Arnold, Sally, and so many others — they are all still gone. And they will stay gone. And who knows now when the war will be over and if Jamie will come home? I'd rather have the people taken from me returned than our humanity.

Evie says I am wrong about that. She says the flu wanted to make barbarians of us, to have us think life is not precious and the dead are not worthy of our kindest care. Our humanity is what made what happened to us so terrible. Without it, nothing matters. Nothing is awful. But nothing is amazing, either.

The one lovely thing about our days is Alex. He is happy and chubby and is turning over now, all on his own. Everyone loves to hold him and play with him and feed him, even Papa. The day after we buried Mama I told Papa that it was her wish that we keep Alex and make him part of our family. No one had claimed him, I'd reminded him, and I knew no one would. He said he knew that had been Mama's wish and he was going to go to the authorities to make it official but that he wanted me to remember Alex isn't Henry.

"Of course he's not," I'd said. I didn't need to be reminded of that.

Tomorrow I am going to ask Ruby if she wants to come over to the Sutcliffs' after school with me to get Alex. Ruby seems kind of lost without Sally. They had been playmates since they were three years old. Ruby sits next to me in class now and eats her lunch by me and is never more than an arm's reach away. I'm not happy that Sally died, but I must confess it is nice to have a close friend again.

I might tell Ruby that I write letters to Jamie Sutcliff and that I think about him all the time. That's the kind of thing you can tell a good friend. She won't say, "He's too old for you." She will look at his picture — Dora Sutcliff gave me one — and say how very handsome he is. Or she might not say anything at all, which would be all right, too.

Grandma Adler wrote us girls a letter, begging us to forgive her and telling us she misses us so much and that she wants us all to come for Christmas.

I know for a fact that Papa won't take us there. Not this year anyway. I don't think the return of your humanity means you forget what broke your heart.

CHAPTER 42

Evelyn

This time it's true. The war has ended, three days after that first report threw us all into a whirl. At the eleventh hour on the eleventh day of this eleventh month, the armistice was signed. The cessation of hostilities was declared. The Allied Forces are victorious, and Germany has been defeated.

The bells began to peal before dawn. The cover of night still blanketed the city when the news came, official this time. The clanging was joined by factory whistles and the sharp crack of small arms and the banging of pots and pans and any other noisemaker a person could fashion. In our pajamas and nightshirts we all took to confetti-strewn streets to witness the heralding of the end of bloodshed and the beginning of peace over all the earth.

The Great War is finished.

When the day finally broke a few hours

later, throngs of people began to march toward Independence Hall in commemoration. School was canceled; work was canceled. Everything but the celebration of life itself was canceled.

Papa asked if we girls wanted to join the marchers. He had three bodies waiting to be cared for — only three now — but he would take us if we wanted.

Willa didn't want to. Having been woken like the rest of Philadelphia at three a.m., she was tired and wanted to stay home — that is, unless Flossie came over and said she was going. Then she'd go. Maggie wanted to take Alex over to the Sutcliffs' and celebrate the day there. I knew Papa would rather stay home and mark the day quietly with work. He had come home in uniform poised to join the fight in this war that had just ended, and instead he'd been made a widower. He was not in the mood to revel and so I told him I was fine with staying home and watching the people stroll by from the window.

I had no burning desire to go with the crowd. I was still getting used to the changes we'd all had to make and how different things were at school. Gilbert is gone. He died the same day Willa started to get better. One of the other boys at school, who was his closest friend, told me this. I've had to push away my sorrow at losing him. I don't know what he was to me. Just a friend? Was that all he was? I feel like in time he could have been more to me, but I'm not sure, and now I will never know. I only know my heart aches for him in a wholly different way than it does for Mama, or even Uncle Fred or Charlie Sutcliff. The part of me that knew and liked Gilbert feels scraped raw.

Mr. Galway also died from the flu. And two of the girls who'd always derived much pleasure from snubbing me. The flu flattened all the differences between me and the other girls who remained, though. They sought out my friendship the first day we returned to classes and counted our number. Death had touched us all in one way or another and we now had far more in common than not.

Maggie is putting on her coat now to take Alex over to the Sutcliffs'. I know why she spends so much time over there. Dora Sutcliff, still wrapped in grief over losing Charlie, finds comfort in caring for our orphan baby, and when she is experiencing that solace with this beautiful child, she talks of Jamie. If I were to let on to Maggie that I know this, she would accuse me of sticking my nose into her business.

That she is somewhat infatuated with a man eight years older than she is not a concern of mine. I am far more interested in why she continues to lie about how she found Alex. I've no doubt most of her account of that day is true. The fact that no one ever went to the police to report Alex's disappearance is ample proof that Alex's mother died of the flu and there is no father or other immediate family.

I believe that part of her story.

But she is not one to forget details. Not Maggie.

She knows in which row house she found Alex. She is purposely withholding that information.

It can only be because she thinks if she were to reveal it, Alex might be taken from us.

This is not my dilemma, I tell myself. *This is not my lie.* If there is someone to whom Alex belongs, they would come forward, wouldn't they?

The front door opens and shuts and Maggie heads across the street with Alex. I walk to the front windows to watch them, and confetti swirls about their heads like ash.

CHAPTER 43

December 1918
Willa

Today is Christmas, but it doesn't feel like it.

Evie tried to make a ham the way Mama did, but it didn't taste like Mama's ham. Mr. and Mrs. Sutcliff came for supper. Dora Sutcliff spent a lot of time just holding Alex on her lap. Even though the war is over, Jamie Sutcliff isn't home yet. Maggie asked them why not. Mr. Sutcliff said it takes a while for the dust of war to settle.

"What dust?" I asked.

But Mr. Sutcliff just sipped his sherry like I was asking Maggie instead of him. But Maggie didn't say anything. She doesn't know what kind of dust he's talking about, either.

Grandma and Grandpa Adler came on Christmas Eve, but they didn't stay over.

When they got here on the train, Papa

took us all over the river to the cemetery where Mama and Uncle Fred are buried. Charlie is buried in some other graveyard. Mama's cemetery is called the Woodlands, which sounds pretty, but because it's December all the trees were like skeletons and the big white statues and towers looked sad and cold. There's no stone with her and Uncle Fred's names because Papa is having one made out of marble, like the steps to our front door, and it's not done yet. Grandpa and Grandma wanted to put flowers on Mama's grave. All that's there on her spot is dead grass and a little wooden sign painted white that says *P. Bright.* They put the flowers, little white roses, under the *P.*

But it was cold and windy and we didn't stay long. Evie had made a big pot of stew for dinner, so we came home and ate and then we opened presents.

That part didn't feel like Christmas, either. Grandma and Grandpa were still sad from going out to the graveyard, so Grandma kept dabbing her eyes and blowing her nose. And Grandpa kept looking sideways at Alex. When Grandma Adler asked Papa if he thought it was wise to take in another person's child when there was no mother in the house, he said, "What goes on in this house is not your concern, though, is it, Eunice?" And her mouth dropped open like a fish's.

"There's no cause to speak that way, Thomas," Grandpa Adler said, his voice real low, but his eyebrows all scrunched.

"What way?" Papa said, in his normal voice with normal eyebrows. "I am only stating what is true. You decided what was best for your house, and now I am deciding what is best for mine. If you will excuse me."

Papa stood up and went into Uncle Fred's office to go smoke one of the cigars Grandad — his papa — had sent him.

I think Papa is mad at Grandma and Grandpa Adler.

I got a new doll and mittens and a necklace and a miniature tea set for Christmas. Evie got books and two hair combs and perfume. Maggie got a bracelet and ice skates and a fur muffler. Alex got toys and a cuddly blue elephant with a curly trunk. There was fruitcake and peppermints and punch and oranges. There was music on the wireless. There was a tree in the sitting room with garlands and lights. There were stockings at the fireplace.

But it still didn't feel like Christmas. Not without Mama.

I wanted this day to end. I wanted Christmas to stop. After the Sutcliffs left I took my new doll and tea set up to my room and I shoved them under my bed. I threw my new mittens in the corner by my toy shelves. I took my new necklace and dropped it into one of my old shoes that doesn't fit me anymore.

I didn't know that Maggie was at the doorway watching me. She had Alex in her arms and he was asleep.

"Go away," I said.

And she said, "Come with me."

"No."

"Come with me," she said again. "I have a present for you from Mama."

"No, you don't," I said.

She cocked her head toward her new room. Mama's old one. "Come and see."

I followed her into the room. She laid Alex in the baby crib that Papa had bought and then she turned toward Mama's dressing table. She opened a drawer and took out the jewelry box with the roses carved on it. Mama's jewelry box.

Maggie sat on her bed and patted the space next to her. I walked over and sat down.

She opened the box. All of Mama's pretty things were in there. Necklaces, brooches, earbobs, hair combs, bracelets.

"Which one do you want for Christmas?"

Maggie said.

At first I wanted to say that those were all Mama's. But Mama is in heaven, where you don't need jewelry.

I had always liked the hat pin with the blue butterfly. It has a sharp point at the bottom, though, so Mama never let me touch it. That was what I wanted. The butterfly hat pin. I pointed to it.

"It's yours, Willa. Merry Christmas."

I felt a smile tug at me, and I lifted the hat pin from the velvety place where it had been lying. It felt warm in my hands. And not dangerous at all. I ran my finger across the butterfly's silvery blue wings. Each side looked like half a heart.

I looked up at Maggie. "Which one do you want?"

Maggie looked into the box. She took out a cameo pin. The little lady made of white had pretty hair, all piled on her head like a queen. Mama told me once her grandmother had given her that pin.

"And Evie?" I said.

"Which one do you think Evie would like?" Maggie said.

I pointed to a hair comb with pale roses on it. I knew Evie had just gotten two new hair combs, but they weren't like this one. This one had been Mama's.

"Perfect," Maggie said, and she handed it to me. "Let's go put it by her bed so she will see it when she comes upstairs tonight. You can take some of your drawing paper and color a little Christmas tree and I'll write, 'Merry Christmas, Evie. With love, from Mama,' on it."

So we did.

Then I took the hat pin to my room. I sat with it for a while. I got my new doll out from under my bed, and I slid the pin into her curls. So now she has a sparkly butterfly in her hair. And she looks beautiful.

Chapter 44

January 1919
Maggie

Finally, finally, I've a new letter from Jamie. It's been so long since the last one, so very long. I'd hoped Jamie might write home right after the armistice or after he got the notice about Charlie, but it wasn't until nearly Christmas that he finally wrote to his parents. Dora Sutcliff showed me that letter. It was short. Jamie had gotten word that Charlie had died and he was so very sorry and he wished he could have been there when his brother was laid to rest.

He didn't say much of anything else in that letter. Not how he was. Not where he had been when the Germans surrendered. Not why he hadn't written anybody in weeks and weeks. Not even when he was coming home. He didn't seem like he was himself. It was like someone else had written that letter. And he didn't write one to me.

"You're still writing to him, aren't you?" Mrs. Sutcliff had said, when she took the letter from me after I'd finished reading it. I told her I was.

I had in fact gone back home and written him that very day. I had already written him about what Philadelphia was like when the war ended — the parades, the noise, the celebrations. And that I missed my mother but that I had a good friend in Ruby now. That time, though, I decided to write that I'm doing the hair in the embalming room now that the flu is gone, just like Mama had done. I didn't know if he would find that bizarre. I was hoping he wouldn't. Ruby thinks it's bizarre. I also told him how much Alex likes being over at Jamie's house when we're all in school and that his mama, "Auntie Dora," as she calls herself, spoils him. I wrote that Alex is going to be our permanent foster child when all the papers come through and after the city people make sure sufficient time has gone by for any of Alex's extended family to inquire about him.

I'd sent it off the next afternoon, and I'd written him twice more since.

But today is the first time I've received a

letter in return since just before the Liberty Loan Parade back in September.

I come inside from having spent the afternoon at Ruby's and there it is on the table inside the front door with the rest of the day's mail. I can't get my mittens off fast enough. I tear the envelope open and I stand there reading the letter in the foyer with my boots dripping melted snow all over the rug.

Jamie's letter to me fits on just one side of the thin piece of paper:

Dear Maggie:

I am very grateful for what you have done for my family even in the midst of your own loss. Mother has written to me about how much she loves caring for your orphan child during the day. Thank you, too, for the special attention you gave Charlie, before he died and afterward. I still can't believe he is gone. I fear I'll be coming home in the spring to a different world. I wonder if it will even seem like home.

I wish the war had never come, but I am grateful for all your letters.

I remain,

Yours sincerely,
Jamie Sutcliff

When I finish reading, my eyes travel back to the line "I wonder if it will even seem like home."

I'm glad he is grateful for all my letters, but that line pokes at me. And the one before it, too. The one about coming home to a different world, which somehow makes it sound like it's not a good thing. Different doesn't have to mean things can't be made good again, does it?

Besides. Home isn't a place where everything stays the same; it's a place where you are safe and loved despite nothing staying the same. Change always happens. Always. Surely Jamie knows that.

We adjust to it. Somehow we figure out a way. We straighten what we can or learn how to like something a little crooked. That's how it is. Something breaks, you fix it as best you can. There's always a way to make something better, even if it means sweeping up the broken pieces and starting all over. That's how we keep moving, keep breathing, keep opening our eyes every morning, even when the only thing we know for sure is that we're still alive.

All these thoughts are tumbling around in my head as I hold Jamie's letter. I'm a second away from writing him back this very moment when I realize these thoughts have shaken loose something I haven't wanted to think about since the day I found Alex. I suddenly know what I must do before I can write those words to Jamie and know beyond all doubt they are true.

I look at the grandfather clock ticking away the minutes. Alex is asleep for his nap. It's a Saturday and Willa is at Flossie's house. Evie is making bread even though it's her birthday today. She's sixteen now, and Dora Sutcliff is having us all over for cake later. Papa is at a meeting with other businessmen. I poke my head into the kitchen where Evie is, kneading a mound of dough. She looks up at me.

"Can you listen for Alex? I need to run over to Ruby's for a little bit," I say. "It's for school. I won't be long."

"I suppose," she says, and goes right back to her task.

I turn from her and then feel in my coat pocket for streetcar fare. I have enough. I go back outside. I pull my scarf tight around my neck and lower face and hurry to the streetcar stop down the block. Some minutes later I am on South Street, standing by the barbershop with the green awning. Even though it is icy cold and snow threatens, the streets and alleys are bustling with people. Old men, teenage boys, mothers, children in tattered wool coats. People are shopping and talking and yelling and selling. The scene is very different from how it had been on that day in October when Mama and I walked all the way down here. I turn up the street where I had seen the cat, and to the tumbledown row house that Mama left me outside of to wait for her. I know which alley to turn down after that. I know which building to stop in front of. Which window to look in.

I stand in front of Alex's old home, silently challenging anyone inside that front room window to see me, talk to me, ask me what I am doing there.

But no one does. The broken window has been replaced. New curtains are pushed to the sides. A tall woman with jet-black curls caught up in a ribbon is just on the other side of the new glass. She is standing over a little boy about seven and cutting his hair with long scissors. A man sits in a chair behind them, looking at a newspaper.

The woman looks up at me, and our eyes meet for just a second. Then she looks back down at the child. She doesn't care who I am.

This woman and the man and the boy are new to the building.

The busted window has been fixed.

New curtains have been hung.

A new family now calls the little apartment home because its previous occupants are gone, victims of the killing flu.

Life has remade itself here.

You see? I'm right. We find a way to move forward, even if it means starting all over.

That's how it is.

That's what we do.

I make my way back to the streetcar stop. When I'd arrived on South Street just minutes earlier, I'd felt like I'd been carrying heavy rocks in my pockets that had been weighing me down for weeks. But now they are gone.

Everything is setting itself to rights again, as best it can. Jamie might not believe me if I tell him all this in a letter, though. Maybe he will need to see it for himself, like I just did.

I can tell him the truth. I can tell him the whole truth about what happened the day I found Alex. I can bring Jamie here when he's home at last and show him that life begins new again every time we think all is lost, because that's what life does.

I will trust him with my secret.

Until then, I will keep writing to him. I will tell him every good and lovely thing that happens, even if it's just that I saw a chickadee or that Alex got a new tooth or that his mother made a fudge cake.

And then when he gets home in the spring — spring! — I will prove to him there is always a way to make right again what has been skewed wrong.

Chapter 45

Evelyn

Jamie Sutcliff is finally home. He arrived today with the remainder of the 315th on the USS *Santa Rosa.* Dora and Roland asked us to stand with them at the Snyder Avenue Dock to greet the ship and welcome him.

Two weeks before, the 28th Division had arrived to a parade and cheers and speeches. City officials had offered to do the same for Jamie's regiment, but he and the other soldiers aboard the *Santa Rosa* had opted to forgo the fanfare. They said they just wanted to go home.

It had been a year since we'd seen Jamie, but it seemed like more time than that when we saw him. He had changed so much. He strode slowly toward his parents, dazzling in his uniform, yet as one hindered by a ball and chain around his leg. His countenance seemed to have been thinned by his experience somehow, like taffy stretched too far. His eyes looked vacant to me, as though some of the color in his irises had been squeezed out. He held on to his mother for a long time. Or maybe it was Dora who could not let go.

Maggie waited patiently for the Sutcliffs to break from their embraces and for Jamie to turn to us. When he finally did, Jamie seemed both glad and glum that we were there. His expression was a strange mix of both. He shook Papa's hand and said hello to Alex, who was hoisted in the crook of Papa's left arm. He kissed me on the cheek first — his lips were as light as a moth — and then Maggie. He then bent down to say hello to Willa.

"Thank you all for coming," he said to us. "You didn't have to."

"It's our pleasure," Papa said. "We're all very grateful for your service."

Jamie seemed frozen by Papa's words for a second, as though he needed a moment to figure out what he'd done that we Brights should be thankful for.

"Thank you, sir," Jamie finally said. But I could tell it was good manners speaking. He was still pondering my father's expression of gratitude.

Dora linked her arm through Jamie's, and Roland Sutcliff picked up Jamie's duffel. We made our way through the pockets of reunions happening all around and walked to our vehicles.

Dora had earlier invited us to come back to their house for a welcome-home lunch. Maggie had made a banana cream pie for the occasion, and so after parking the Overland at home and getting the pie, we walked across the street and up the stairs to the Sutcliffs' living quarters.

"Let's not stay long," Papa said quietly on the way, Alex still in his arms. "Jamie looks tired."

"Yes, I agree," I said.

Maggie said nothing.

It is so obvious to me how lovestruck she is. Perhaps no one else can tell. At least no one else let on today that they could. And I can't help feeling some concern for Maggie. I don't want her to get hurt. It is one thing to have written letter after letter to Jamie during the war; it is another to have him home again, living right across the street, and yet with such a spread of years between them. Even newly at fourteen, Maggie is still a child. She has seen more horrors than any young person should — we all have — but her being infatuated with a twenty-one-

363

year-old man is proof to me she is still just a girl.

Maggie sat next to Jamie at the meal, hanging on every word that he said — not that there were many. She barely ate anything herself. She behaved as one who had something important to tell Jamie and was just waiting for the right moment. Having us all in the room with her was messing with her plans.

Jamie saw none of this. He didn't seem to be seeing anything. If possible, his eyes were more empty now than when he had stepped off the ship that morning.

After the meal, Dora asked Maggie to come help her get the desserts ready. Willa and Alex started playing on the floor with some of Charlie's old toys, and Papa and Roland went into the living room to smoke cigars Papa had brought to mark the day. They had invited Jamie to join them, but he'd declined.

In a matter of seconds, I was alone at the table with Jamie. He was staring at the children playing on the rug in the other room.

"We'll leave right after dessert," I said, wanting him to know I could tell how much he wanted to be alone.

He looked up. "Thank you for coming."

There wasn't an ounce of genuineness in his words, and yet he was not being insincere, either. He hadn't heard what I'd said. Not really.

"Maggie made a pie," I added, those words popping out from nowhere other than that I wanted him to be mindful of Maggie's tender feelings.

"She didn't have to go to that trouble."

"Maggie's very fond of you, Jamie." I locked my gaze onto his. Or tried to. His eyes seemed made of paper. What in God's name had he seen over there? I knew the trenches had been awful. I had read what the Allies had been up against. I knew that Jamie's regiment, like so many others, had been exposed to mustard gas — a quiet poison that could blister the inside of your throat and lungs so that you'd suffocate on your own tissue if you breathed enough of it. I also knew the Germans' mortar shells could rip a man in two. I knew Jamie had marched with a rifle, and that he'd likely had to fire it again and again and again.

"Maggie doesn't know me," Jamie replied quietly. "She doesn't know who I am."

"You're a man who has miraculously come home from the war in one piece and to people who love you."

"In one piece," he said vacantly, as though

he were still a world away from us. "Is that what you see?"

Words of response froze in my throat. I could think of nothing to say.

Maggie came in then and placed the pie she'd made in front of Jamie.

"Would you like to cut it?" Maggie held the knife toward him. Jamie looked at the handle of the knife for a long moment and then shook his head.

"You do it," he said. "I'd just make a mess of it."

I saw then, as clear as crystal, that Jamie still had his arms and legs, still had his sight and hearing, but he'd been gravely wounded somehow, and the wound must have been so deep inside him, none of us could see where to press a hand and stop the bleeding.

And then with equal clarity, I realized that all of us in that room were like that, in one way or another. All of us. Me. My sisters. Papa. Little Alex. Roland and Dora. And Jamie. We were all wounded inside where no one could see. None of us had survived the last year unscathed.

We had all been dealt crippling, devastating blows that had crushed us to the core. Jamie was the only one of us brave enough to admit that we'd all been transformed.

The world was different after the flu and the war. And so were we.

Chapter 46

June 1919
Willa

I am dreaming of Mama, and it's like she is alive again. I'm so happy to see her I call out her name, and my own voice wakes me up.

When I open my eyes, I don't know at first that it was only a dream. I get out of bed and look for Mama on the stairs, in the kitchen, in the sitting room.

She isn't in the house, though, and I feel so empty inside.

But then I see Gretchen's father through the sitting room's big front window. He is walking that little white dog even though the sun is barely up. After the flu, I walked up the street several times to stare at the apartment above the bakery where Gretchen had lived. I hoped each time that I'd see that little dog in the window barking down at me, or on the street as Gretchen's mama or papa took him outside to pee. But I never did see him. And now there he is.

I run to the front door, unlock it, and walk outside. Gretchen's father is walking fast. He is already stepping onto the next corner. I want to chase after him so I can pat that dog. I want to so very badly. But I don't have any shoes on and I can't think of Gretchen's last name, so I can't call out for her papa to wait, and I'm mad that he can't tell I am behind him on my top step wishing he would stop and turn around.

He just keeps walking.

I stand there in my nightgown, watching them. I suddenly remember his name is Mr. Weiss, but it's too late. He's too far away. I'm sad now and I wish I was back in my bed again dreaming of Mama.

Then I hear a door opening across the boulevard from me.

Jamie Sutcliff is coming out of his house. He carries a fat duffel bag and he's wearing his cap. He looks like he is going on a long trip. He closes the door quietly and then turns around. Jamie is surprised to see me standing there across from him, and he startles like he's been caught doing something he's not supposed to be doing.

We look at each other for a second, and then he just tips his hat to me and starts to walk away without saying anything.

"Where are you going?" I yell.

He turns toward me. "Go on back inside, Willa. It's too early to be out."

"But where are you going?"

I can tell he is off for somewhere. No one carries a duffel like that unless they are going on a trip. Jamie just got home after being at the war all that time. And now he's leaving?

He stares at me for a moment. Then he looks back at his house and then up at the bedroom windows of my house. He crosses the boulevard easy and quick because it's too early for streetcars and automobiles and carriages. Only the milkman and Mr. Weiss are out and about.

When he gets close he hikes up his duffel onto his shoulder and looks up at me. I'm taller than him because I'm on the top step and he's on the bottom one.

"I have to go away." He looks sad.

"But you just got here."

Jamie looks down the boulevard for a second. Gretchen's dad is so far away now. The dog is just a little white dot.

"I can't stay here," he says.

I know for a fact that Jamie still has his old bedroom and his father still has a desk for him in the bookkeeping office. "Why not?"

He shakes his head. "I just can't."

"But your mama has waited all this time for you to come home."

For a couple seconds, he doesn't say anything. "I'm not the person she has been missing. I'm not him."

I don't know what he means by that, so I ask him again where he is going.

"Good-bye, Willa," he says, not answering my question at all. His eyes are shining into mine. "Be good."

And then he turns and walks away.

I watch him go in the opposite direction of Gretchen's dad and her dog. Pretty soon he is a speck, too. And then he is gone.

What a rotten morning this is turning out to be.

I sit down on the top step, hoping Gretchen's dad will be coming back this way so I can pat the dog on their way home. I wait and wait, but they don't come. Autos and people and streetcars start to go by. A lady walking past our house sees me sitting on the stoop and she stops and frowns at me.

"Child, does your mother know you're sitting out here in your nightdress?" she calls out.

I don't know. I don't know if Mama can

see me here.

So I stand up and go back inside the house. I'm hungry now. I go into the kitchen, and I'm glad Maggie is up with Alex, because she'll make me something to eat. Her eggs aren't as good as Evie's, but they are better than nothing.

She frowns at me, too, when I step inside. "Was that the front door?" she asks. "Were you outside just now?"

I nod. "Can we have breakfast? I'm hungry."

Maggie sets Alex into his high chair. He picks up a wooden spoon that he likes to play with and bangs it on the tray. He is one year old now. We gave him Maggie's birthday — May 15 — because he needed to have one and she wanted him to have hers. I wanted him to share mine with me — I'm eight now — but my birthday was in February and it wouldn't have worked for him to be one back then. His birthday had to be in May or June, Maggie and Evie said. Even Papa said it.

"What on earth were you doing outside in your nightgown?" Maggie says.

It occurs to me right then that Maggie might want to know Jamie has left. She is friends with him. I saw all the letters she posted to him when he was in the war.

"Jamie's gone," I say.

Maggie is opening a box of Post Toasties. I guess we aren't having eggs. "Gone where?"

"He didn't say."

Alex points the spoon at me and says, "Gah da!"

"What do you mean, 'he didn't say'?" Maggie is frowning again. She puts the box of cereal down.

I pull out a chair at the kitchen table and sit down. "I mean, he didn't tell me."

Maggie looks from me to the front door and back to me again. "You talked to him out there in your nightgown?"

Jamie didn't say a word about my being in my nightgown. He hadn't even noticed. Why was everyone else making such a big commotion about it?

"I was watching Gretchen's dad go by with her dog, and I saw him come out of his house. And then I talked to him."

Maggie looks like she wants to send me to my room, but she can't because I haven't done anything wrong. But that's the look she has on her face.

"You're not making any sense," she says.

I'm done with her. "*You're* not making any sense." I get up out of the chair. I'll go back up to my room and wait for Evie to wake up and make me breakfast.

"Wait!" Maggie says, grabbing hold of my arm. "What do you mean he's gone? Tell me."

I pull my arm away from her. "I mean, he said he can't stay here. He went away. He had a duffel bag, and it was full."

Maggie's eyes get wide and the mad look slips away. Another look comes over her, but I don't know how to describe it.

"What did he say to you?" Maggie's voice says *please* even though her words don't.

I can't quite remember what Jamie said about his mama not missing him. I try to think of how he said it, but I can't.

"He told me to be good."

Maggie slowly turns toward the front door. Alex babbles some made-up words, but it's like she doesn't hear him at all. Maggie tears out of the room, into the foyer, and throws open the door. I follow her.

A second later she is the one standing on the stoop in her nightgown in the full light of day, instead of me.

She is the one staring up the boulevard.

She is the one wanting so very hard to have something that's not hers and not having any way of getting it.

■ ■ ■ ■

PART TWO

■ ■ ■ ■

CHAPTER 47

September 1925
Maggie

She's the same age Mama would have been, this woman lying before me. Forty-two. Papa has already glued the eyes shut, but the photograph the family provided hints that the deceased's eyes were the type to catch sunlight, just like my mother's were. Mama's were blue, like Henry's had been.

I remove the last curling rod from the woman's hair and position the lock with an heirloom comb before bending close for one last check on the cosmetics I applied. Papa reduced the swelling on the woman's forehead and reshaped the delicate socket bone above her left eye. I covered the fix and the sutures from the embalming process with flesh-colored foundation. The penciled, chocolate-hued eyebrows make her look like she's very much enjoying her third day in Paradise. There are no telltale signs of the

377

injuries that claimed her mortal life.

"You look lovely, Mrs. Goertzen." The rigor has finally released her after three days of stiffness, and I'm able to fold the woman's hands across her bosom without any bodily resistance. "No one will see that nasty bruise from your fall. And the hair comb your daughter brought is beautiful."

I hear a noise just outside the half-open embalming room door. Alex is peering in. His coffee brown curls are tousled and his shirt untucked, and I wonder what he and Willa have been up to while I've been busy with the morning's work.

"Aren't you done yet?" All four words are laced with breathy impatience. He hangs on the door, one foot sneaking over the threshold. Papa and I have kept the same rule about the embalming room that Uncle Fred had insisted on. No children inside. I'd been annoyed with my great-uncle when we first arrived in Philadelphia and he'd been so worried about my sisters and me being in that room. I understand his caution so much better now that Alex is seven and curious about nearly everything. The world can be a dangerous place. Even so, I'd wanted Alex never to feel afraid or unwelcome to come to me or Papa while we are working back here. When the embalming room door is closed, however, it means he must knock. When it's half-open, like now, he can hover at the doorframe as long as he wants.

"Nearly," I answer.

"You're taking too long. You promised we'd go to the park after lunch. I already had lunch. A long time ago."

I glance down at the watch pendant just below my collar. One o'clock. The morning has flown. "I just need to wash up, and I'll be right out."

"Promise?"

"Promise."

The front bell rings from far down the hallway and past the kitchen, and he scampers off to answer it.

I toss the curling rod into the basket with the rest of them and push my cart with all my restorative tools to the corner of the room so that Papa will see that I am finished with Mrs. Goertzen when he returns from the cemetery. I pat the dead woman's hand. "Nice chatting with you."

I wash up and then hang my apron on its peg next to Papa's. I'll grab an apple or a slice of bread on my way to find Alex so that I can keep my promise. We've a play-date at the park.

Most days Alex seems as much a child of

Papa and Mama as I am, and it's not until someone says something like "Did your mother have those dark eyes, too?" that I suddenly remember he is not. It's when I'm jolted by a random question like this from someone who never knew Mama that I'm reminded Alex had another name for the first four months of his life, and that his real mother was a European immigrant. Foreign. Croatian, maybe. Only God knows.

God knows.

I have never again gone back to that building off South Street where I found him, but I visit it in my mind now and then. The remembrance of that time in my life always leads to nightmarish images of Alex's dead mother and dying sister, closely followed by those of my own mother. Uncle Fred. Charlie. It's an effort to push away the unwanted visions from the last days of the flu and replace them with happier images of the heart-shaped birthmark that winked at us every time we bathed Alex or changed his diaper, or the way he'd reach for my father at the end of the workday and how we all cried when the first word Alex said was "Papa."

I don't know what would have become of us — of me — had we not had Alex during those first years when we were all learning how to live again. It was Alex who gave us reasons to get up in the morning, to sing silly songs and play games, to forget how the flu and the war had twisted every notion we had about the sacredness of life. When I missed Mama so much it physically hurt, Alex soothed the sting. When I wanted to run away to wherever it was that Jamie Sutcliff had escaped to, Alex made me stay. When I wanted to just close my eyes and never wake up, having Alex persuaded me to welcome each new day like a fragile blessing instead of a curse.

He was and is the only good thing to come to us after the flu and after the war. Or maybe it's just that he showed us good things still existed. And while it's obvious he loves us all, and Papa especially, I am still his favorite.

When he was four, I told him that he'd been brought to our doorstep like a precious gift and that I was the one who found him. We had decided — Papa, Evie, Willa, and I — that Alex didn't need to know he'd been found a few feet away from his dead mother. It was bad enough that I still had that horrific image of her in my head, so it was my idea that he be spared the worst of the details. We'd decided when he was old enough we'd tell him his sweet mama, when she knew she was dying, had secretly picked us out special because she was certain we would love him and give him a happy, forever home.

Sometimes when I'm tucking him in, he'll say, "Tell me how you found me." And I'll tell him I got up early one morning during the terrible flu, and there he was on our doorstep, all snug and warm in a basket. Willa, who sorely wanted to embellish that story, had to be told we weren't going to be making up any more particulars than those basic ones. We were able to get our way with her when she asked if she could at least give him the rocking horse rattle that was Henry's and tell Alex that he'd had it in his hand when I found him, and we conceded. It turned out to be a good idea, because the little rattle is the only thing Alex has of his first life — or so he thinks — and it comforts him.

He believes that rattle is something his sick mother had placed in his little hand when in tears — he's asked if she cried when she left him and I always say that of course she did — she'd set him on our stoop and then run away, perhaps coughing into a handkerchief. Papa and the others can tell Alex the made-up story of how he came to us. Even Dora Sutcliff, who adores him, can relay the account we concocted. But Alex never asks them to retell it, only me. I guess it's because I'm the one who found him.

For the first year and a half he was with us, he slept in a crib in my room. When he was two, he moved across the hall to share a room with Willa, but only for a year. She wanted a room of her own again when Alex turned three and she was eleven. She took my old room on the third floor. Evie's at the university or the asylum most of the time these days, and Papa's on the first floor in Uncle Fred's old room, so it's often just Alex and me on the second floor. When he has a bad dream, I'm the one who goes to his bedside to console him. I tuck him in at night. I make his breakfast in the morning. I'm the one he runs to when he's scared or hurt. Evie is like a mother to him, too, when she's around, but she's not the one he calls for first. It's my name that flies off his tongue when he's got something important to say. Last year, when he was six, he asked me if I could be his mama instead of his sister. And it took me several seconds to find my voice and tell him that I loved him just like a mama would.

"But I don't have a mama and I want one," he'd answered.

"You did have one, though," I'd said.

"And she loved you very much."

"She's not here!"

"Oh, but she is." I'd placed one hand over his heart. "Right there. Just like my mama's right here in my heart." And I'd placed my other hand over my own chest.

He had asked to see my mother's photograph then, the one in a gilt frame and sitting atop the mantel in the sitting room. I went and got it and he took it up to his room.

Papa asked about the photograph later that night when he noticed it was gone and I begged him to please just let Alex have it for a while. "You have other photographs of Mama," I'd reminded Papa. Alex has nothing by which to remember his mother's face.

My father said nothing. He was probably thinking, "But that's not his mother." He didn't say that, though. He just nodded and then headed down the little hallway to his rooms at the back of the house. Alex still has that photograph on his dresser.

He knows Mama was not his mother, but he can't remember anything about the woman who did give birth to him. Mama's photograph reminds him he *had* a mother and she loved him. Sometimes you need a little help imagining something that used to be yours but which you have no memory of.

I, however, remember everything about my mother. Her voice, her fragrance, the way she swirled the cat-shaped tea infuser in her cup, the soft tap of her heels on the stairs, how much she liked birdsong and the color yellow, how she called Papa "Tom," and the way she talked to the dead in the embalming room as she made them look beautiful again.

I suppose these are the reasons I also love the sound of birdsong in the morning, and sunny yellow hues, and tea made with the cat infuser, and why I chat to the people in the embalming room when I am getting them ready for their grand good-bye. All of these are echoes of Mama's beauty and mystery. These things keep me close to Mama, close even to that part of her I hadn't yet come to fully know because I was too young and we simply ran out of time.

I hear a man's voice now beyond the kitchen as I step into the hallway that leads to the rest of the house — then the sound of the sitting room piano.

The voice is Palmer Towlerton's, and my heart takes a little stutter step. Palmer is my current suitor. He works for the city as a facilities manager. He is from New Jersey and he's tall like Papa but with darker eyes and hair and he's five years older than me. I met him at the library on Locust Street on one of my trips with Alex to borrow books. It is one of the many city buildings over which Palmer's department has oversight. We've only been courting for a couple months, but I like Palmer very much. So does Papa. Actually Willa likes him, too.

He is not like Jamie Sutcliff, whom I haven't seen in six years. Palmer is talkative and energetic and spontaneous. Jamie Sutcliff is quiet and even-keeled and more thoughtful. At least he was. I guess I don't know what he is now. He's only come back to visit Philadelphia once, and I didn't see him then because we were all in Quakertown for the holidays that year. Dora and Roland have traveled to visit him, sometimes having to go as far away as San Francisco. Dora has said that the war, just those few months Jamie fought in it, changed him. He doesn't like being at home now or around anything that reminds him of home, which includes his parents and us and anything related to the man he was before he shipped to France.

I asked Evie quite a while ago what might have happened to Jamie in those few months that ruined home for him. At the time, she was in her last year of college before medical school to become a psychiatrist. She said it's not how short or long an experience is; it's the depth to which it touches the core of who you are that matters.

"You and I don't have to be told how quickly one's world can change, Maggie," she'd said.

Palmer Towlerton had a draft number, but it had been issued in the last weeks of the war when the registration age was lowered to eighteen. He never got called. I'm glad he didn't.

I'd forgotten now that Palmer had said he was going to try to arrange his Saturday afternoon so that he could join Alex and me on our outing to the park today. He knows how devoted I am to Alex, and it doesn't seem to rankle him. I do wonder, though, if he understands that if we should marry, Alex surely comes with us. Papa can't raise a seven-year-old boy with just Willa for help, and Evie is hardly ever home. And Alex thinks of me as a mother figure. He would miss me too much. I'll need to be ready to work all this into a conversation with Palmer about our future together, if we are to have one.

I admit I have lain awake some nights imagining what it would be like to be

Palmer's wife. He is not the first man to want my affection — there have been a few others — but he is the first to capture it. He is the first to measure up to Jamie Sutcliff, or at least Jamie as I remember him. Every young suitor who has asked me to a dance or a concert or a party, I have compared with Jamie. And even though I wish I didn't, the fact is, I do. I still have Jamie's letters from France. There are only four of them, and goodness knows I wrote ten times as many to him, but they still whisper to me the kind of person he was before he left for the army, and the kind of person I still want to believe he is — underneath all those terrible memories of the war.

Palmer doesn't remind me of Jamie, not in the least. But he does make me think less about Jamie. More so than anyone else ever has.

I make my way into the sitting room now. Willa is at the piano and she's singing "Moonlight and Roses." She is golden-haired and beautiful, and her voice is angelic. If she were a few years older, I'm sure Palmer would be positively smitten with her. I should be jealous of her constant flirtations with my beau. If she were seventeen and not fourteen, I no doubt would be.

Palmer stands just inside the sitting room, which I'm happy to say we updated with new furniture and decor a year after the flu. He is politely listening to my sister, who no doubt coquettishly asked him to listen to her play and sing. Willa began taking piano lessons the summer after Mama died. She caught on quickly. It was as if she had been born to excel at music. She can play and sing just about anything and rarely needs the sheet music. She is a natural, as Dora Sutcliff likes to say.

Alex is a few feet away from them, absently kicking a little red ball on the carpet, obviously bored. He will see me in a moment or two standing just beyond the open doors. When he does, he will run to me and beg for us to go now that Mr. Towlerton is here. Palmer will turn then and smile at me, and Willa will stop and pout. I'll ask her if she wants to join us, and the frown will slip off her face as if it's made of water.

But I wait for Alex to catch that glimpse of me. I want Willa to continue with "Moonlight and Roses" a few seconds more. I want to hear her sing how the smile of a long-ago love can still haunt your dreams.

CHAPTER 48

Evelyn

"I'm so very sorry," Dr. Bellfield says, kindly but in a way that suggests he's said this before to other people. He no doubt has.

The man to whom he speaks, Conrad Reese, slowly turns his head to look out the window. His wife, Sybil, only three years older than me, is sitting on a chaise in the garden just on the other side of the glass, unaware of the high fence fifty yards away, or that she's wearing a bathrobe in the noonday sun, or that she's at Fairview Hospital for the Insane rather than at home. The beauty of her physical body masks the invisible disease that has wrapped itself around her mind.

Sybil is Dr. Bellfield's patient, but the diagnosis I make as a second-year resident, that she suffers from dementia praecox, a psychotic disorder that only gets worse, was confirmed by him. Her symptoms supported no other conclusion. Many months of erratic behavior, followed by delusions and hallucinations, followed by paranoia, followed by her current near-catatonic state, point to no other finding. I've seen this terrible malady before, not just in the pages of my textbooks but here at the asylum, where I've been working and studying as part of my residency.

The progression of Sybil's illness is the only constant in her life. Her mind is like an onion whose layers are peeling off all by themselves. And just like there is no way to reattach an onion's layers, there is no way to stop Sybil Reese from mentally disappearing.

This has been the most sobering fact I've learned in my residency. The mind, like any other part of the body, has crippling limitations.

"Is there nothing else you can try?" Conrad Reese says, now looking from Dr. Bellfield to me to the doctor again.

Dr. Bellfield reiterates that we've utilized every remedy we know: bathing therapies, sleep cures, barbiturates, hypnotics, alkaloids. No cure exists at present for dementia praecox. Sybil Reese is going mad, and there is no stopping it. Ours is the third hospital he has tried in his search to cure his wife.

"I'd like to see her," Mr. Reese says a moment later, and there is something in his voice and manner that tells me he already knew that his wife would never return to him. I think maybe he has known this for a while but didn't want to admit it.

Dr. Bellfield starts to clear his throat, preparing, no doubt, to tell Mr. Reese that his wife has stopped communicating. Sybil speaks to no one now, makes eye contact with no one, recognizes no one. But her husband has asked to see her, not have a conversation with her.

"Of course," I tell him. "I can take you to her."

Dr. Bellfield closes his mouth and nods in acquiescence.

I lead Mr. Reese out of the building and into the early-September sunshine. The lawns on the grounds are still lush, the hydrangeas are still in bloom, and the leaves on the sugar maples are still green. Hard to believe that in a month, everything will look different. And yet the hospital grounds blanketed in snow will be lovely in another way. Our hospital is a haven compared to the other asylum, on the east side of Philadelphia, where the patients are chained like criminals to their disease. There are no lawns or flowering shrubs or happy canaries in cages or interior walls papered in paisley prints. I could never work there. The east-side asylum is not a place in which to get well; it's a place to be forgotten in. Here at Fairview, every attempt is made to cure. There, the objective is only containment.

There are other patients out on the lawn as we step outside. Most are sitting in chairs or on lounges. Some are strolling about with a nurse by their side. Were it not for the hospital gowns and bathrobes, they would all look like vacationers at a quiet hideaway. As we draw near to Sybil, a girl about Willa's age — and stretched out on the same kind of chaise as Mr. Reese's wife — raises her head to look at us. The girl arrived yesterday. A necklace of angry bruises across her throat reveals the method of her suicide attempt. The orderly who sits beside her is there to make sure she does not run headlong into the reflecting pool to drown herself or attempt to scale the wall and die jumping off it. But he is reading to her, I notice. He also looks up as we pass, and I smile at him. He'd likely been told he had to do nothing more than watch the young girl, and yet he's reading aloud to her. He smiles back.

When we reach Sybil Reese, I lean over and touch her hand, gently. Were I to pull on her arm, she would rise willingly and follow me like a sleepwalker. "Sybil, you have a visitor," I tell her. "Your husband is here."

She blinks languidly but does not turn toward him.

Mr. Reese exhales heavily and then sits down on an empty chaise next to his wife. He takes her hand.

"Can she hear me?" he asks.

Medically there is nothing wrong with Sybil Reese's ears. She can hear. But I know what Conrad Reese really wants to know is, will his wife understand anything he says?

"I think you should say whatever your heart tells you to say, Mr. Reese," I respond.

He nods. "Thank you."

"You're welcome. Take all the time you need. I'll wait for you there by the door." I turn to walk away.

Before I can take a step, a question is off his lips. "How do you do it, Miss Bright? How do you work day after day in this place?" He is looking over at the young girl with the rope burns around her neck. The girl is staring at her hands.

I doubt Mr. Reese is truly expecting an answer, but I offer one anyway. "Because I believe someday, if we work hard enough, we will discover how to help someone like your wife."

"You really think there's a cure out there for this?"

I know from reading Sybil's file that she has been ill for a long time, the first symptoms beginning when she was a new bride five years ago, and that Mr. Reese kept her at home as long as he could. "I do."

Mr. Reese nods once. "I won't be long."

I first wondered what it might be like to study psychiatry when Uncle Fred gave me his anatomy book and showed me his favorite chapter, on neurology. Not long after that day, everyone I knew — including myself — had to scramble to make sense of what the flu and the war had taken from us. Millions upon millions of people had died around the globe from the flu, far more than in the war itself. The simple reclaiming of delight and goodness and joy had been a staggering endeavor that took place inside our minds, in the tangles of neurons that have always distinguished us from brutes and beasts. Our injuries were hidden deep within our psyches. That was where we needed the balm that would heal us.

Papa was the first person I told, in my first year of college, at the age of seventeen. He didn't think psychiatry was a wise choice for me. Not because he didn't think I would excel at it but because so few women went into the field of medicine aside from nursing, and fewer still studied psychiatry. He was afraid I would work myself to the bone getting the doctorate only to find I wouldn't be hired anywhere. My weaker sex is still believed by most to be highly susceptible to fits and hysteria. I, being a woman, had better odds of becoming a future mental patient than of becoming a psychiatrist. I persisted, though, and Papa finally gave me his blessing — but not before he asked me why I wanted to pursue this kind of medicine when there were so many others to choose from.

"I want to understand," I'd said.

"Understand what?"

"Everything."

My course of study is nearly over — one year remains — and I am astonished that for all I know now about the human mind, there is so much I don't know. Dr. Bellfield doesn't know everything. Nor do Dr. Freud or Dr. Jung or any of the other great minds in the universe who are considered the pioneers of this new field. The human mind is so complex, sometimes it seems the more we study it the less we understand.

Papa is glad that my schooling and residency will soon be complete and I can then concentrate on being properly married off. He doesn't say it quite like this, but it concerns him that I will be twenty-three in January and I've no suitors. Maggie has Palmer Towlerton calling at the house now, and Willa is forever talking about the boys she likes. But I spend all my waking hours at an asylum full of the mentally ill. Not a suitable place to find a husband. Papa's words, not mine.

It's not that I don't want to be married. I do. But I want to experience again that electrified sensation I felt with Gilbert all those years ago, when the way he looked at me made my heart flutter. That feeling had been real and wonderful and different and very new. I had only just started to love Gilbert when the flu snatched him away from me.

I remember what it was like, though. I remember how that sensation swirled inside me for those months I was the new girl and Gilbert was still alive. I knew I had sampled something rare and divine.

I think if Mama were here she'd tell Papa not to worry about me. I have my studies. I have my work. I have Papa and Maggie and Willa and dear Alex. And I have my memories of what that first bloom of romance is like. Sometimes I think I can hear her voice assuring me that she is proud of who I am. Other times I'm convinced it is only my own voice inside, telling me I don't need anything else — or anyone else — for my life to be complete. I came through the crucible, and it did not reduce me to ashes.

I survived.

CHAPTER 49

Willa

Piano music drifts up from the grate in the sidewalk, faint and airy, as if in a dream. Someone down there below the concrete is practicing. I know the song being played. It's "What'll I Do" by Irving Berlin. The grate where the music is coming from leads to a speakeasy far under the city street. A vent has been left open. I crouch on the metal slats and tilt my head toward the darkness while the city's pace at three thirty in the afternoon swirls about me. Autos, trucks, carts, walkers, strollers, cyclists, and peddlers dash and scurry past. I doubt anyone else hears the music but me.

"What are you doing?" Howie says.

He is a classmate of mine at the academy that Evie and Maggie attended and that Papa has insisted I must also go to. He and I ride the same streetcar to get to class every day, but Howie is lucky. He doesn't have brilliant older siblings who have gone to the school before him. All right, so only Evie is truly brilliant. But Maggie was no slouch. What she lacked in outright genius, she made up for in determination, or so I hear. My teachers, when they aren't telling me to hush and pay attention, are probably still trying to figure out how to motivate me to study.

Howie is my age, freckled and pudgy, and he adores me. He moved to Philadelphia after the flu. Several years after.

I have no idea if my voice will carry into the shadows beyond the grate the same way the notes of the piano are floating up to me. But I open my mouth to sing, and I jump right in where the lyrics speak of there being only a photograph to tell my troubles to.

The piano stops. Whoever is playing it can hear me. I look up at Howie standing next to me, and I laugh.

"Willa! Come on," Howie implores. "We shouldn't be here!"

He looks about, half-panicked. There are dozens of people up and down the sidewalks, some in suits and fine dresses, some in weatherworn work clothes, and some — the beggars — in rags. Most haven't given us a second glance. The vegetable vendor across the narrow street is scowling, however — she is big and red-faced and her disdain at my bending over the grate of a speakeasy that no one is supposed to know about but everyone does is as clear as glass. A man leaning up against the brick wall of the building next to the grate and puffing on a cigar is staring down at me, too. But he looks surprised, not disgusted.

The music starts up again, slow and tentative, inviting me to join in like a hopeful partner at a dance. It pauses, waits for me. So I sing the words about being alone with dreams that won't come true. The man with the cigar takes a step toward us and Howie grabs my hand and pulls me to my feet and we dash off, the music of the piano falling away.

We run for several blocks before we stop, breathless, holding our sides. Howie looks behind to see if we're being chased by the police or gangsters with machine guns or the woman with the cabbages. But no one is coming after us.

"What'd you do that for?" Howie says.

I flick back a curl. What a ridiculous question. Why does anyone do anything?

"Did you hear how that piano player waited for me to keep singing?" I reply instead.

"If my parents find out I was hanging around the door to that place . . ."

Howie doesn't finish. I don't know what his mother and father do to dole out punishments, but Howie just shakes his head back and forth like it's just too terrible to contemplate. If Papa found out I was singing into the grate of a speakeasy, he'd give me a stern look and tell me that's not acceptable behavior. He might extract a promise that I never do that again even though I'm not so good at keeping promises, even to him. And anyway, I could easily make a vow never to sing at the grate of that speakeasy again and uphold it. If I wanted to try my luck at another grate of another speakeasy, I wouldn't have much trouble finding one. This is Philadelphia. Worse than New York and Chicago, if you ask Dora Sutcliff. I didn't, by the way; she is just always ready to tell people that.

"But how would your parents find out?" I ask as we start to walk again, and the air in our lungs is now going in and out at the regular speed.

"What if someone saw us?"

"We were just listening at a grate."

"You were *singing* down a grate! And not just any grate." He leans in close to me. "Those places are illegal."

He says the word *illegal* like it's illegal to say it.

"It's just what they sell that it is illegal," I offer back.

"That's what I mean."

"No, you said the place is illegal."

"It's all illegal."

"So your father doesn't have any whiskey in your house?" I loop my arm through his, knowing my question will make him gasp. Howie's father is a deacon at his church and a prominent businessman. It's unthinkable that an upstanding, law-abiding gentleman such as he would have bootleg liquor in his house, except that it happens all the time. I bet even Papa has some in his back office.

"Of course not," Howie sputters, turning about to see if anyone on the street is close enough to hear our conversation.

"I bet he does."

"He does not," he growls. "And I'll kindly thank you not to suggest that he does."

I laugh and kiss him on the cheek. "That's you being kind, is it? I'd hate to see you being heartless."

He is so flustered now he doesn't know what to think. "I'm not sure I should be walking you home from the trolley stop anymore," he says, but I don't believe him.

"I completely understand," I say as piously as I can. "But I do hope you change your mind. You are very handsome when you're being stern. Good-bye, my dear Howie!"

I turn from him to continue walking on my own, knowing he is most likely fixed to the pavement, torn between running after me and stomping off in the direction of his own house.

"So, I'll see you tomorrow?" he yells after me.

I turn to him and wave.

As I start to walk the last few blocks alone, I realize I don't care so very much if Howie walks me home tomorrow. I'd like to swing by that grate again and listen and this time I'd rather he wasn't beside me.

For a tiny moment there, I felt like I was the only person in the world besides that piano player. It was just me and the piano man and the music. And it was as if the piano man knew who I was, and what I've seen and done, and yet he wanted me to sing for him anyway.

That moment lasted only a few seconds, but I can still hear the echoes swirling inside me. When I get home, they will no doubt float away like feathers on the wind. Alex will want to play a game, Papa will want to know if I've schoolwork to do, Maggie will want help with supper or sweeping up flower petals in the funeral parlor. We've a cleaning lady now, but she comes only on Tuesdays and Saturdays. There's always plenty to do when I get home from school. I know the spell will be broken when I open the door and go inside the house I both love and hate.

I do sometimes wonder if Mama would still be alive if we'd never come to live in that house. Papa says only God knows what would have happened if we'd stayed in Quakertown. She could have died from the flu there — people did, just not so many — or been in a terrible accident or who knows what else. We're not like God, he says. We can't know. We can't live like we do know or should have known.

"She got the flu from me," I told him once. And he said no, she did not. The flu came here all on its own like a plague of grasshoppers that had nothing to do with me. But I know the truth. I came down with it, and then she came down with it. I caught the flu from Flossie. Mama caught it from me.

The swirling echo of that moment with the piano man is starting to lift from me and I slow my pace to keep it if I can. When

I get to the corner by the Weiss Bakery, I stop and look for the little white dog at the front window above the shop. Gretchen's parents still have him, and because he's white, the color of his fur doesn't tell you how old he is. I know dogs don't live much past their twelfth or thirteenth birthdays. But I figure if Gretchen's dog was two when we moved here, then he is only nine now. Only nine. Lots of dogs live to be older than nine. He sees me on the sidewalk looking up at him. I can't hear him, but he is yapping fiercely while standing on his hind legs and with his front paws on the glass. And yet his little stub of a tail is wagging. He knows me now. I've been looking up at that window for years. I smile up at him and his little body trembles with the happy force of his barking.

If I stay too long, Gretchen's parents will come to the window to see what the dog is so upset about, so I blow him a kiss and resume my slow stroll home.

Maybe Mr. Towlerton will be staying for supper tonight. That would make the approaching evening not so dreary. I like Maggie's beau. Or maybe Evie will come home at a decent hour and I can get her to tell me about all the crazy people she looked after today. You wouldn't believe some of the stories she tells when I'm able to pry them out of her.

Maybe Alex will want me to play the piano for him while he pretends to be an opera singer. It's truly awful and hilarious when he tries to sound like a virtuoso. And maybe Papa will come in early from the funeral rooms and for once not look so sad and alone.

I start to hum "What'll I Do" as I turn down our street. The words just fall off my lips like I wrote them myself because what I had before the flu is broken and cannot be mended.

Chapter 50

Maggie

The coffin is small and white with gold trim. Inside it is the body of a three-year-old girl who died of scarlet fever and whose hair I styled into corn silk curls held fast now by white satin bows.

She is such a little thing. Papa won't need his hired man for this one. I will be able to help him move her.

Most of the time Papa relies on a fellow named Gordon Luddy, a man who delivers milk in the early mornings but who is free the rest of the day, to help him do what I cannot. Gordon helps Papa transport the caskets from the parlor to the hearse and assists him at the cemetery with getting the coffin to its place near the freshly dug hole in the ground. Gordon is not here yet, but it does not matter. I push the short casket on its cart down the hall to the rear entrance. I help Papa carry it down the four steps to the hearse's opened back end so that he can deliver it to the church for the memorial and then to the cemetery. It is the eighth of September and the early afternoon is warm and humid as I push the hearse door closed.

"Don't wait supper on me," Papa says as he heads for the driver's-side door. "And there will be plenty of people able to help me get the casket back into the hearse and out again at the cemetery. You don't need to come down later."

"All right."

I watch him leave with the small casket and the little girl named Lucy inside it before I head back inside.

Preparing the very young for their funerals has been the hardest thing to get accustomed to since I've become Papa's assistant. It is difficult to find a snippet of beauty in preparing a child or an infant for burial. The only word of solace I can whisper to these little ones as I cover up the pallor of death is that my mother and brother are there in heaven, that Mama is sweet and kind, and that her name is Pauline, so that if they want to, they can find her there.

"You don't have to do this," Papa had said when I told him two years ago that I wanted to be his official assistant.

I had been nearing my graduation from the academy, and Papa's full-time apprentice at the time, a man named Wilbur with a pronounced lisp, had just gotten married and moved to Virginia to be closer to his new wife's family. I'd never had the college aspirations that Evie did, and while I could easily have set my sights on a position behind the perfume counter at Wanamaker's or courses at a secretarial school, those pursuits had never interested me. I was already doing the hair and makeup at the end of the preparation process, but Papa and Wilbur did the embalming and suturing and restoration work. They did all the important repairs. My contributions were nothing compared to what they did. I wanted to do more.

"But I want to. It's what I want to do," I'd said.

We had been going over the ledgers in the little office off his bedroom. He had been smoking a cigar from a box that Grandad had sent him. Business had been steady for us. More and more people had been discovering they much preferred the embalming of their loved ones to take place at the mortician's place of business rather than the beloved deceased's bedroom. And fewer people all the time had large parlors in their

410

homes for viewings. We offered a homelike atmosphere for both, with all the up-to-date conveniences of a modern-day mortuary. Papa was officially a mortician now, not just an undertaker. He'd enrolled in a special school to become licensed in what he pretty much already knew how to do.

"It's not the most cheerful room to work in, you know," he'd replied. "The things we do and see . . ." He hadn't finished the thought. He was right in that we saw our share of tragic circumstances, day in and day out. There were some cadavers Papa flat-out refused to let me view. The human body is amazing and wonderful but so delicate. And there are so many ways for a person to die, especially if the death has had something to do with a crime or gangsters. There had been more murders since Prohibition was enacted. A lot more. Papa said it was because when something is illegal but people still want it and will pay for it, there are other people who will do whatever it takes to provide it. They will even fight over who is going to be the supplier. They will kill to be the one who controls the supplies. Sometimes there is not even a body for Papa to embalm. Or not much of one.

"But it isn't all sad, what we do. Part of it

is needful," I'd answered. "Part of it is . . . pleasant."

He'd smiled as he stroked his chin. "Now, there's a word we didn't hear much in mortuary school."

"But it is," I'd replied. "It's the only part of death we can control. The farewell."

He'd puffed on his cigar, thinking on this.

"You have your own life to consider, Maggie," he'd said a moment later. "Marriage, children."

I hadn't met Palmer yet, and my heart was still tender toward absent Jamie Sutcliff. I had written him many times at postal boxes provided to me by Dora. One in Missouri. One in Colorado. One in California. He had never written back. I'd finally stopped writing at that point even though I hadn't forgotten about him. And as far as children went, I had Alex. He was my brother, true, but he was more than just my brother.

"I'm only seventeen, Papa," I'd answered. And then to put him at ease about my future, "There's still plenty of time for all that."

He had tapped his cigar onto an ashtray, contemplating a thought that he then voiced. "Do your peers find it distasteful, what you do?"

After changing schools following Jamie's

return and then escape, I'd been surrounded by new classmates and had to make all new friends. Evie was there only the first year, and then she graduated early and was off to the university. The next two years at the academy, I had a circle of friends who enjoyed my company and I theirs, but I spent most of my after-school free time with Ruby, who still clung to me, even though we were no longer attending the same school. She never got over losing Sally. Ruby also never wanted to hear any details about what I did at the funeral home, which didn't bother me because there were always plenty of other things for us to talk about. I hadn't known what my academy classmates thought about what I did because I didn't tell them and they didn't ask if I helped my father in his business. It likely never occurred to them that I did.

So when Papa had asked me this, I'd said that my peers didn't care, which hadn't been a lie.

After I graduated from high school and Wilbur left, if Papa needed help lifting someone heavier than I could help him handle, he'd call for Roland Sutcliff to come over or he'd wait for Gordon to finish his milk route to help him. There were — and are — plenty of times he and I could handle a body just fine.

Now, three years after high school, I help Papa with just about everything. Not with the embalming so much, but with the restoration work and helping families choose a casket and getting the flowers ready in the viewing parlor and sometimes just putting an arm around a grieving widow or mother or lover and letting her cry.

Occasionally, when I've an arm around someone in a half embrace, he or she will ask if I have ever lost someone. When I tell them I lost an infant brother when I was a child and that I said good-bye to my dear mother in that very room, they will invariably lean into me and cry a little harder. They will always later thank me for that excruciating moment. Always. This is something Gordon cannot do for them: stand beside them — in every sense of the phrase — in their loss and grief.

Palmer isn't put off by my occupation. If he were, he'd say so. Palmer always says what he wants to say. But I know he sees my work with my father as temporary. To him, this is what I am doing right now, not what I *do.* I think he might be hoping I will fall deeply in love with him and that when that happens, I will leave all this behind like it was someone else's life.

There are times that scenario woos me. But it's only the part about being deeply in love that has me intrigued. I could choose making a beautiful life with someone over making someone's dead body beautiful if there were that kind of love between us.

I could leave behind the embalming room if I had that.

I do want to fall for Palmer. I do. But I also feel a tugging to stay upright, to remain where I am with my feet planted. A pull to keep from pitching forward and tumbling into a world I don't know.

Perhaps this is how it is for everyone who stands poised to unite her heart and flesh to another. Or perhaps this is just how it is for me. I am not one to step off a ledge and trust there is a net in good repair to catch me.

I am not one to let herself fall.

The hearse is gone from view now.

I head back into the embalming room to put away the curling rods and hair ribbons and all the other traces of a little girl gone too soon.

CHAPTER 51

Evelyn

My days at the asylum are all the same, and yet not the same. The other second-year residents and I sit in on sessions with the patients and meetings with the families; we make rounds with Dr. Bellfield and other doctors; we study the current case records, read the archived files, write reports, send correspondence, and also observe the nurses and orderlies as they go about the daily care of people whose illnesses range from moderate melancholy to full-blown madness. And yet no two patients are exactly alike, even the ones who have the same malady; hence no two days are exactly alike.

I completed my university studies in three years instead of four, and Fairview is close enough to home to hop on a streetcar to get to. When I applied for this residency, Dr. Bellfield was interested in me because I had been the first woman from the university to come his way, and he chose me for my insights into the female brain, as he put it. He keeps me busier than the other residents — there are four others, all male — but I don't mind. On nights when I've stayed past the last streetcar, I sleep on a cot in the doctors' lounge.

I don't mind the long hours, nor the added responsibilities Dr. Bellfield sometimes heaps on me. I really do want to find a way to help people like Sybil Reese. It is too late for her, but there will be more like her down the road. And someone must find a way to help people like Sybil. Someone must.

Dr. Bellfield asked me specifically to weigh in on Sybil Reese's case, but he also asked me a few days after that to peruse the file of that girl who tried to hang herself. He told me after rounds to read the girl's medical history, analyze her symptoms, visit with her, and recommend to him a course of action that I could adequately defend in front of him and the other doctors.

So a few days after Conrad Reese was given the sad, official news, and after I'd stopped in the solarium to say hello to Sybil — I'd decided I would find the time to say hello to her every day, even if it seems she cannot hear me — I pulled the girl's file and sat down to read it.

There wasn't much there. Her name is Ursula Novak. She is fifteen, barely, and apparently has no family. She'd been working as a kitchen maid for a wealthy Philadelphia couple when the housekeeper discovered her in the cellar, swinging by the neck from a rope poorly slung across a floor joist. The butler had cut her down and then telephoned for help. She was still alive. Ursula's employers had taken pity on her and insisted on paying her medical bills at the hospital and then sending her here instead of the state asylum on the east side — the one that gives me nightmares.

Ursula has no history of hysteria or depression or mental illness. She'd been working for the family without incident since she quit school at fourteen. This attempt on her life had apparently been her first. She was otherwise healthy. Strong lungs, clear skin and eyes, good hearing and sight. She exhibits no tremors or fits, nor does she seem to suffer from delusions or hallucinations or moments of lost time. At the hospital and on her admittance here to Fairview, she had refused to give an answer as to why she had tried to kill herself other than that she was tired of living. When asked whether she would try again if released, she had simply answered, "Probably." As to next of kin, she had answered, "None."

That to me was the most telling of Ursula's symptoms. She's an orphan. At one time she'd had parents, but now she does not. Her parents are both dead and she is only fifteen. I lost my mother at nearly the same age, so I knew how devastating the loss of one's mother could be. I still had Papa, though. And my sisters and Alex. Perhaps Ursula had lost her parents in a terrible accident that she'd unfortunately witnessed. Or perhaps they had been victims of the flu and she'd been bearing at an orphanage the awful weight of their absence before taking a job as a kitchen maid.

Whatever the true details were, I believed I had this grain of truth to begin talking with her: that she was alone and sad, and unable to cope any longer with either state of being.

Ursula is sitting in a corner of the women's dayroom, in a chair by a stretch of windows that runs the length of the back wall. Other patients of various ages are reading or playing cards or resting or wandering aimlessly about in conversations with the voices they hear in their heads. Sybil Reese is sitting at a table with three other women involved in a beading lesson. Beads and a length of string lie before Sybil, but she is staring out the same long set of windows as Ursula, though on the other side of the room.

I walk to an empty chair next to Ursula. As I sit down, she looks up at me. Dark circles rim her deep brown eyes. She looks wan, and I wonder if she is sleeping at all. Or perhaps sleeping too much. Her hair is chocolate brown like her eyes and she is petite and pretty. The bruising on her neck is now a circlet of mottled browns and yellows.

"Hello, Ursula," I say cheerfully. "May I talk to you for a bit?"

She shrugs and turns her attention back to the window.

"My name is Miss Bright. I am in my residency here. I'll be a doctor soon enough, though." I laugh lightly, wanting so very much to ease the somber mood she is projecting.

She looks back at me, slight suspicion in her tired eyes. "What kind of doctor are you?"

"I'm finishing up a course of study in psychiatry."

"I didn't know there were lady doctors like that."

"There are more of us now than there

used to be. I think that's a good thing. Don't you?"

Ursula's reaction to my statement is unreadable. She doesn't say a word.

"I'd like to try to help you, Ursula. I'm hoping we can chat about why you're here. I want you to know you can trust me."

She says nothing.

"Do you know why you're here?"

Ursula closes and opens her eyes slowly and then nods once.

"Can you tell me why you wanted to harm yourself? Whatever the reason is, you can tell me. I won't judge you. I promise. I just want to help you."

"Help me do what?" she says with what seems equal parts curiosity and disinterest.

I put one of my hands over one of hers. "Help you move past this great sorrow in your life. Help you find a way to accept what happened to you but move past it and live your life."

"Move past it?" she echoes.

"Yes."

Ursula looks down at my hand on hers and says nothing.

"You might be thinking right now it's too hard to do that, but if you —"

"I don't want to move past it," she says.

"Beg your pardon?"

She raises her head to look into my eyes. "I don't want to move past it."

I need a moment's thought before I can continue. "Right now the pain you carry might be all that you have, and it's probably scary to imagine having nothing at all, not even that, and I do understand that fear, but if you will just —"

"But I'm not afraid."

I hadn't expected this kind of response. I must attempt a different approach. If I can be allowed to see what she has suffered, perhaps I can convince her to trust me. "Ursula, can you tell me about your parents?"

"What about them?"

"Where are they?"

"They're dead."

"Can you tell me how they died?"

She inhales deeply as though to prepare to share with me something she hasn't told anyone else in a long time. "My father died in a construction accident when I was a baby. My mother died from that flu."

"I see. I'm so very sorry. My mother died from that flu, too," I say gently.

For a second, Ursula stares at me in disbelief that she and I could possibly have anything in common. But then she turns back to the window, and it's as if a cloud has passed over her.

"So you must have been a young girl when your mother died," I say. "Nine? Do I have that right?"

She says nothing.

"Any brothers or sisters?"

Nothing.

"Did your grandparents or other family take you in, Ursula?"

She blinks but does not answer.

"Do they know where you are?"

Ursula turns her head just a fraction so that she is now looking at Sybil Reese, sitting in her chair and staring out a window.

"Ursula, I really do think I can help you. But you must help me first. I need you to tell me if you have any family that we should know about. If they have hurt you or if you are afraid for them to know where you are, we don't have to tell them you're here. I promise you that. I just need to know if there is someone who can help us understand what you've been through."

For a second I think Ursula is done talking with me today. This happens. A patient suffering from mental illness will just suddenly shut down like a machine with its power cut off.

But then Ursula nods toward Sybil Reese. "What's wrong with her?"

I follow Ursula's gaze. "She . . . That woman has a sickness that has greatly affected her mind."

"A sickness? Like the flu?"

I shake my head. "No. It's not something that you or anyone else can catch from her."

"Is that what I have?"

"I don't think so." I say nothing else because I want Ursula to turn her attention back to me and she does.

"How do you know?" she asks.

"That woman has an illness here, in her brain." I touch my head. "I think where you hurt is here." And I place my hand over my heart.

Ursula studies me for a moment, contemplating my assessment, and I can see she is wondering how I can know this.

Then our attention is jointly commanded by movement just beyond us. Conrad Reese has arrived to visit his wife. He leans down to kiss Sybil's forehead, and she exhibits no response at all to his tender touch. When he straightens and lifts his head, our eyes meet. Heat rises to my cheeks, and I don't know why. I look away and turn back to Ursula.

Her gaze, however, is still tight on Sybil, as though she wishes she could trade places and be the woman in the room whose mind is so far gone she feels nothing anymore.

CHAPTER 52

Willa

Five years ago, if you needed rum to make punch at Christmastime, you just went to a store, bought some, and brought it home. I don't remember what it was like for someone to buy rum because I was nine back then, and rum didn't interest me in the least. I do remember the last day you could actually do that, though, because everybody was buying bottles of it — that and whiskey and Pabst Blue Ribbon and I don't know what else — to hide away in their cellars because there wasn't going to be any anymore. The next day it was illegal to make or sell or transport liquor. If you still had some in your house, you could drink it, but you weren't going to be able to buy more and no one was allowed to make more. That last afternoon, Papa and Roland Sutcliff sat on our stoop with cigars and glasses of port — in front of all the world, as Dora Sutcliff

425

described it — and talked about how the world was changing.

Dora, who was at our house and glaring through the glass at Papa and Mr. Sutcliff with her hands on her hips, told us girls that she was glad the temperance league got its way at last, and that those two men could puff and sip and commiserate all they wanted, but it was going to be a brighter day without all those inebriates ruining everything.

"What are inebriates?" I'd whispered to Evie.

She'd answered that they are people who drink too much. "And then they cause unbelievable trouble!" Dora had added.

"Like peeing in the street," Maggie chimed in.

She had Alex on her hip. He had only been two and he'd heard Evie say the word *drink,* so he started saying, "Grink! Grink peas! Grink peas!" And Maggie had to go get him some milk in a cup so he'd stop asking.

"My stars! It's not just the peeing in the street," Dora had continued. "They are putting their wives and children in the poorhouse. It's a travesty of the worst kind."

"Why do they drink too much?" I'd asked Evie, but it was Dora who answered.

"Because they are dirty dogs and scum!"

"But that's not why they drink too much," Evie said. She was in college then and she already knew pretty much everything about everything. "People who drink too much usually want to forget their problems. They want to escape some kind of pain or frustration or just the dissatisfaction of everyday life."

"They *create* the problem!" Dora had said. "They are the orchestrators of the pain and frustration."

"How does the drinking make them forget their problems?" I'd asked, very interested in Evie's answer.

"It doesn't really, lamb," Evie said. "After the drink wears off, their problems are still there."

"Except now they are worse, because they've put their wives and children in the poorhouse!" Dora said. "They are dirty dogs and scum."

I didn't care much for scum. But I have always liked dogs, even if they are dirty. I had gone outside then to sit with Papa and Roland Sutcliff as they drank their last glasses of port.

That was supposed to be the end of saloons and taverns and inebriates and peeing in the street, but it wasn't the end of anything. I don't read the newspaper much, but I see enough and I hear enough of the conversations between Papa and Roland Sutcliff and my teachers at school and the ladies at church to know there's plenty of bootleg liquor in this city and thousands upon thousands of speakeasies. That's what they call the saloons and taverns now. They call them that because you're supposed to talk quietly about them when you're out in public, and when inside them, too, so they can be kept secret from the law. A speakeasy is the only place where you can buy a drink now, and Dora says they are full of gangsters who control all the money and booze, and crooked cops and lawmakers who take bribes to look the other way. She says speakeasies are nothing short of the stoops of hell itself.

I don't know if Dora is right about all that. She's probably right about them being run by gangsters — who else but criminals can get ahold of something no one is supposed to have? She might even be right about there being policemen who take bribes not to arrest anybody. But that day with Howie wasn't the first time I'd heard beautiful music coming out of that speakeasy's grate. I'd heard it once before when Howie and I walked home that way so that he could buy me an ice cream at Spanky's.

So a couple days after Howie and I ran from that grate, I decided I would leave school a few minutes early on my own. That piano had called to me, and I wanted to go back and answer it somehow.

I hover now at the grate, hoping and wishing and wanting the piano man to somehow know I am here and start playing. I don't hear anything, though. I have no reason to be loitering here, and I know the longer I stay the more likely it is that someone might notice me and ask why I am here. There are fewer people walking about than there were the last time. Thankfully the vegetable lady is inside her store and not outside it. I decide that if someone does stop and ask, I will say I am waiting for a friend. I kind of feel like I am.

Please, please, I whisper in the direction of the grate. *Just one little tune.*

And then my wish comes true. I start to hear the notes of a song my mother used to sing to me. "Let Me Call You Sweetheart." The melody is faint, as though the vent is only partially open today. It is all I can do not to throw myself to the ground and pull up the grate so that I can fall into those notes and let them cover me. I close my eyes so that I can better concentrate on the music wafting up to meet my ears. I am only half aware that I'm singing the words just under my breath.

A hand is suddenly on my arm. The touch is gentle, but I startle anyway, nearly dropping the one schoolbook that I am holding — a volume of poems. I open my eyes, and there is the man in the suit who'd been smoking a cigar and leaning against the brick wall next to the grate the last time I was here. He wears a brown derby on his head today, and I decide he looks like he is made of sausages. He is big and round and has a crooked smile.

"It's you, isn't it?" he says. "You were the one singing here the other day, weren't you?"

Despite his polite manner, I am too afraid to answer him. Is he a cop in street clothes? Will he haul me down to the police station for hanging about a speakeasy grate?

"It's all right, missy. You're in no trouble a-tall. In fact, we were hoping you'd come back this way." His smile broadens. "My name's Mr. Trout."

"We?" I manage to say, my heart slamming in my chest. Why, oh why, hadn't I waited for Howie? I look about for a clear way to dash past this roly-poly man and take off running.

"Yes, Albert and me. He heard you singing the other day when he was playing. Why, you're a regular nightingale, missy. He told me to keep a lookout for you, and here you are!"

"Albert?" I say, unable to rein in my thoughts to come up with a better question.

"Yes." The man nods toward the grate. "He's our musical director, you might say. He lines up all the acts for our . . . club. He'd sure like to talk to you, Miss . . ."

"Adler." Mama's maiden name flies off my lips. I had no idea it had even been perched there. But I'm not afraid for my safety anymore. Mr. Trout said I sounded like a nightingale. Caution falls away as curiosity takes its place.

"Well, Miss Adler, Albert would very much like to speak with you about singing at our, ahem, venue." He looks at the book in my hand. "Just how old are you, Miss Adler?"

The dress code at the academy demands that we girls wear starched white blouses with ruffled collars with our midnight blue skirts, and our hair pinned up off our shoulders like married women wear theirs. It's to prepare us for life as respectable adults. I had always thought it was kind of

431

silly to dress this way until just now. Our uniforms and coiffures make us look older than we are.

"Eighteen," I say, as confidently as I can.

"Eighteen?" Mr. Trout echoes, his brows arched high. "You're a bit slight for eighteen, aren't you?"

"People come in all shapes and sizes." I nod toward his girth.

He tips his head back and laughs. "Right you are, Miss Adler. Right you are. I take it you're not married?"

I swallow a laugh. "I am not."

"And your father doesn't work for the government?" He says this in a quieter tone.

"He does not."

Mr. Trout leans in close. "Now, you strike me as a rising star, Miss Adler. You've always wanted to sing on a stage with an audience captivated by your every note, haven't you? You've longed for people to adore the very sound of your voice, yes? Aren't you ready to give up tossing your talent down dirty grates to sing instead for people who will pay good money to hear you?"

I can't answer him. I am transfixed by the images his words are planting in my head. He sounds like he is offering me rum punch, as much as I want, for the rest of my life. He is offering me escape from my everyday life. And not only that, but adoration.

The music below us suddenly stops.

"So, then," Mr. Trout continues, "might you consider lending your dulcet tones to our little stage? Albert is prepared to pay you the going rate for a vocalist of your quality."

"I might," I finally say.

He leans in even closer. "Come back tonight at ten o'clock so you can speak to Albert, then. Use the door around back. The password is *Cincinnati.*"

"Ten o'clock?" I gasp.

He frowns a bit. "Keep your voice down, Miss Adler. Yes, ten o'clock."

I look toward the grate. "Why can't I talk to Albert now?"

"Because it's not even four o'clock in the bloomin' afternoon!" He laughs again, but this time at my naïveté.

"Oh."

"Is that going to be a problem?"

By ten, everyone in the Bright household is usually in bed asleep. Usually. Sometimes I will see a seam of light under Papa's bedroom door. Sometimes Maggie is still awake. Alex is always fast asleep. Evie, if she's home, will have gone to bed long before then; she's always exhausted by the time she makes it back to us. "Not if I can sneak out."

Mr. Trout smiles conspiratorially. "Sneaking out will be good practice for you. You'll want to be good at keeping secrets from now on, if you know what I mean." He winks.

I suddenly want to get away from him. I need to think. I need for my heart to stop its wild thrumming. "I should be going."

He tips his derby to me. "See you tonight."

I start to walk away and he reaches out to stop me. "One more thing. What's your first name, love?"

Again, the name Mama was called when she was my age falls from my lips before I can wonder why. "Polly."

CHAPTER 53

October 1925
Maggie

A crisp autumn breeze is scuttling the leaves at our feet as Palmer and I stroll down Walnut Street. We have just left a lovely French restaurant, and though the food was delectable, Palmer wasn't his usual talkative self. His thoughts seemed far from me. He would ask a question about my day or the family or what I was reading, and I'd answer, but he wasn't hearing my replies. They seemed to float in one ear and tumble out of the other. At one point, I asked if he was feeling well, and he'd replied that he was fine. But I could tell something was distracting him, and I couldn't help wondering if perhaps he'd met someone else — another woman — and needs to break off with me. I would have asked him right then at dinner if there was something he needed to tell me, but I couldn't summon the courage.

And now we are out in the cool night air and the stars are twinkling and the noise and lights of the city surround us softly. My arm is on his, and his gloved hand rests atop mine.

"Thank you for dinner," I say, inviting him, I hope, to be frank with me.

"You are very welcome."

We take three steps in silence.

"I have some news, Maggie," he says.

I'm not surprised by his words, but I am surprised to realize that despite expecting him to have some news, I'm not ready to hear what he will say. It can't be good and I suddenly want to be home. I want to be with Alex and Papa and my sisters.

"Oh?" The tremble in my voice betrays my anxiousness.

He turns to me and stops. We are under a streetlamp and it bathes us in creamy light. Palmer smiles, as if he's heartened that I'm anxious. "It's not bad news."

My stomach does a somersault nonetheless. "Does that mean it's good news?"

"I very much hope so."

I can only wait for him to continue.

"I've been offered a position in New York. For the borough of Manhattan. It's a very good job, Maggie. Twice the pay that I'm getting now."

"New York?"

"Yes."

"New York." *How can that be good news?* I want to ask. I want to yell it. His moving a hundred miles away is not good news. Our courtship has been going well. Papa likes Palmer. Alex adores Palmer. Palmer's the first man I've ever been seriously interested in. This is not good news.

He takes my other hand now and draws me close. "I've grown very fond of you, Maggie. So very fond."

My mouth opens, but no sound comes out. My mind is spinning. Does this mean he will write so that we can try courting long distance? Or is he saying he's very fond of me but the job is too good to pass up and he must choose it over me?

"Do you hear what I'm saying?" Palmer tips his head to make eye contact with me. "I'm saying I'm in love with you. I want you to come with me. As my wife."

A buzzing in my ears commences, and for a second I can hear nothing but the sound of a thousand bees in my head. And then I hear this: *I'm in love with you. I want you to come with me.* These two thoughts muffle the imagined sound of whirring wings. I am loved by a man who wants me.

"Maggie, I'm asking you to marry me."

My voice is shuttered and I cannot push out any words. I'm speechless at the idea that all my life has been a journey to this moment when I make a decision that will change the course of my existence. Just like Papa and Mama did all those years ago in the curing barn when they chose to leave Quakertown and come here. Just like that day all of Philadelphia decided to go to a parade and the flu came down on top of all of us. Just like when Mama wanted me to show her where I found Alex and I decided not to tell her. And when I think of this, I realize I've not yet had that needed conversation with Palmer. I had thought it was too soon. The name comes out in a whisper.

"Alex," I murmur.

Palmer blinks. "Alex?"

"I can't leave Alex." The second I say this, I know in my core it is true. Alex is my one hold on anything truly wonderful in this world. How could I walk away from him?

Palmer closes his eyes for a second, and when he opens them, he breaks into a wide smile of relief. "Is that all that keeps you from saying you'll marry me? My darling, you needn't leave Alex. We can raise him together. You and I. Alongside our own children. He can come with us."

"He can?" But even as the words leave my mouth, I am overcome with how much Papa and my sisters would miss Alex if I were to do such a thing. In all my imaginings of a life with Palmer Towlerton, I never pictured us living anywhere but right here in Philadelphia. I even thought we might stay at Uncle Fred's spacious house, with Palmer and me sharing Mama and Papa's old room on the second floor and Alex keeping his room right across the hall. I wouldn't have had to take Alex away from anything or anyone then.

"Of course!" Palmer says. "Alex will love Manhattan. As will you."

The bees are returning to their strumming in my head. I need to think. I need to go home.

I look up at Palmer and he cups my face with one hand. "May I speak to your father, Maggie? Please say I may."

For a moment I wonder if it is possible to just run away instead. I imagine grabbing Palmer's hand and running with him headlong into the great unknown, like Jamie did. I imagine flying away from everything and everyone and beginning life anew, as though I'd never grieved a dead brother and dead mother, never taken a child from his home and kept him, never loved a man who had no need for me, never sung songs to cadavers as I combed their hair.

"Please?" Palmer says.

I hover a second between running away and running home, but then all that I am and have been pulls me back.

"Palmer?" I whisper, and I cover his hand on my cheek.

"Yes, my darling?"

"I need to think about what this will do to my family. Leaving and taking Alex. I need to think. It is no easy thing."

"But . . . do you love me as I love you, Maggie? Can you not answer me that?"

His gaze is hard on mine. There is love there in his eyes, but also determination.

I want to answer that he is not just asking if I love him; he is asking if I love him more than I love my home, my family, and my memories of the only life I've known. He is asking if I will leave it all for him. And I wonder if he would do the same for me.

"What if I asked you to stay?" The words come out of my mouth soft as gauze.

"What was that?"

"If I asked you to stay here with me, in Philadelphia, would you?"

He blinks, but his gaze never leaves mine. "You want me to decline the job?"

"No, I don't. I just want to know if you would if I asked you to."

"To marry you and live here?"

My heart is pounding at the thought. "Yes."

He puts his hands around my waist and draws me to him even though we are on the street and passersby are surely staring. "If you asked me, I would stay."

And then his mouth meets mine in a kiss. He has kissed me a few times before, but this is the first that hints of a greater passion, a deeper longing. An ache low in my gut nearly takes my breath away.

I could lose myself in this feeling and never want to be found, but I pull back before it sweeps me away.

Palmer is saying he loves me enough to turn down the job and stay here in Philadelphia. Maybe he does. Surely the woman deserving of that kind of love should cherish him enough to go with him to New York. I cannot ask him to give up the new job when I'm not sure yet that I do love him like that, only that I want to.

"I don't want you to decline the job."

He leans his forehead against mine. "Then marry me. Come with me."

"Will you let me think on it? Please?"

This time he kisses my temple before pulling back. "Yes. But I must leave before the end of the month. And I wish to speak to your father before I go. I can find a place for us and then come back for you and Alex."

I can only nod as again my voice has escaped me.

He takes my arm, smiling down on me. "Come. I'll take you home."

As we walk, Palmer tells me about the new position in Manhattan and about the legendary locale itself. It is small talk I appreciate because it leaves me free to quietly disengage to contemplate the choice I must make.

When we arrive at the house, he walks me up the stoop stairs and kisses my hand. "We could have a wonderful life together, Maggie. You and I. Alex, too."

I nod and say nothing.

"Good night, my darling." He steps away to hail a passing cab and then turns to smile at me as he gets inside it.

When I step into the house, I am enfolded by all that is comfortable and dear to me, and I at once feel the tugging of the two lives that beckon: the one I have and the one being offered me. I hear music in the sitting room. Willa is at the piano, singing and playing — something she is doing a lot these days. She seems lost in her beautiful music, playing as if to charm demons into benevolent supplicants. I cross the foyer to peer inside and I see Papa and Alex involved in a chess game. Papa is explaining all the moves and Alex is listening with rapt attention, fingering the ebony horse head of one of the knights. Behind me on the other side of the entry, I hear Evie in the kitchen at the sink. Everyone is home tonight. Even Mama's presence seems to warm the house as everyone goes about the evening's activities. It's as if she is right there, sitting in the armchair with a book. I long to tell someone what Palmer asked of me. My heart is bursting with the need to share it.

I imagine telling Papa and him being both happy and sad, and then the look on his face when I tell him I want Alex to come with me. Or telling Alex and having him stare up at me with equal parts excitement and apprehension and responding wide-eyed with "We're leaving?" I look to Willa and imagine telling her and hearing her say I'm selfish to even suggest taking Alex. Then I look at the armchair by the fireplace, and its emptiness pierces me.

I turn toward the kitchen, knowing it is Evie I must talk to first. Wise Evie.

I make my way quietly to the kitchen so

that the others in the sitting room will not hear that I'm home from being out with Palmer. Evie is drying her hands on a towel. The carcass of the chicken I had put in the oven earlier for their dinner still lies on its platter, now picked of its meat and ready to be thrown out.

She turns toward me. "Did you have a nice meal?" She looks tired. I cannot guess how many hours she spends at that asylum every week.

"I did."

Evie nods and picks up the teakettle. "Care for some?"

"Yes. Please."

She fills the kettle from the tap at the sink. As she sets it on the flame, I tell her. "Palmer is taking a new job in New York. He wants me to go with him."

Evie turns her head, an eyebrow raised.

"He wants to marry me."

For several seconds my sister says nothing. She is thinking. This is Evie's way, and it's why I've come to her instead of anyone else. She doesn't hear that I've said Palmer has asked me to marry him; she hears what I'm really saying. She hears that I don't know how I feel about Palmer and his proposal.

"Do you love him?" she asks.

"I might. I'm not entirely sure."

Evie reaches for the tea tin in the cupboard. "What did you tell him?"

"That I need some time to think."

"And what about Alex?"

Here again she knows without my saying it what burdens me just as much as not being sure if I'm in love with Palmer. What would my marrying and moving away mean for Alex? Can I take Alex away from his home here? Should I?

"Palmer says we can bring him with us. We can raise him as our own, alongside our own children."

Evie closes her eyes for a moment, her hand motionless atop the tea tin. She is imagining what I have been picturing in my head the last half hour. Alex leaving this house with me. Alex saying good-bye to her and Papa and Willa. And for whose ultimate good? Mine or his?

"I don't know what to do," I say. "I can't imagine leaving Alex, and I can't imagine taking him from Papa. And you and Willa. I don't know what to do!"

Evie exhales deeply as she opens the tin. "Don't you?" she asks gently.

"No! I don't. I think I love Palmer. But I'm not sure. Shouldn't I be sure? I don't even know what this kind of love between a man and woman is supposed to be like."

And there it is. This is what is perplexing me and tying my stomach into knots. The only love I had ever had for a man is the old one that belonged to Jamie Sutcliff, someone I barely know and whom I haven't seen or heard from in six years. In the first week after meeting Palmer, I'd spent more time with him than I had with Jamie Sutcliff in all the years I'd known him. And yet a buried part of me still yearns for Jamie.

"I don't know what this kind of love is supposed to be like," I say again, more to myself than to Evie.

My sister opens Mama's tea infuser in the shape of a cat and plunges it into the tea leaves.

"Yes, you do," she says, practically whispering.

I just stare at her.

Evie withdraws the infuser, fat with leaves, and clasps it shut. She stares at it for a second and then turns to me. "I think you do. I think we both do."

I open my mouth to ask her how she can know that, but Papa and Alex are suddenly there, having come into the kitchen so that Papa can make them both hot cocoa.

I wait for another chance to speak with Evie alone, but it doesn't present itself

446

before she excuses herself and goes to bed.

Later, when I have tucked Alex into his bed, the light in her room is off and all is quiet behind the door.

I head to my own room with her earlier words swirling about in my head, challenging me to believe they are true.

CHAPTER 54

Evelyn

The front parlor in this house is the finest room I've ever seen. The furniture is upholstered in expensive velvet brocade with satin trim, the wool rugs are Persian, the woodwork gleams, and the crystal chandelier above my head sparkles like it is made of starlight. Fresh flowers in Oriental vases grace every table even though it is October. The teacup in my hand is delicate bone china with gold filigree.

Agnes Prinsen, Ursula's employer, sits across from me, silver-haired and plump. The young maid who brought in the tea stands just to my left, her demeanor shy and hesitant. Matilda did not know she'd be asked to stay after she'd delivered the tray and I can see she very much wishes to be dismissed back to the kitchen.

But I've come to the Prinsen home for help with my patient. At Dr. Bellfield's direction, I've spoken with Ursula several times but have been unable to break through her armor. I've also had no luck in finding any of her extended family to help me piece together her history. I've searched all the school records and orphanages in Philadelphia for traces of Ursula's life before she became a maid for the Prinsen household but have found nothing. Ursula seems to be a young woman with no past, but I know that is impossible. Everyone has a past, and everyone's past matters. When I asked Dr. Bellfield if I might be allowed to go to the home where Ursula had been a maid to speak with those she'd worked with, he'd at first balked. He had never troubled himself to go to a patient's place of employment for insights the family could not supply.

"You're too impatient, Miss Bright," he'd said. "If you just continue your sessions with Ursula, I am sure in time she will reveal to you why she wanted to end her life."

"But if we could understand the reason why now, we could help her now," I'd replied. "She just stares out the window, surely trying to think up a new way to kill herself. What if she'd confided in one of the other maids? What if she had told one of them why she is so sad? If I knew what it was, I could help ease her past this heartache without her having to be the one to reveal its source."

"Sometimes it is part of the patient's recovery to be the one to reveal the source of her anguish," he'd replied.

"And the other times?" I had asked. "What about those other times?"

He was silent for a moment as he pondered this. Then he gave me his permission.

Agnes and Walter Prinsen, who'd made their fortune in the furniture business, were only too happy to allow me to speak to their other maid, Matilda, especially since they had little information regarding Ursula themselves. Agnes Prinsen had hired Ursula without references after they had met on the street. Ursula was selling sweets from a trolley and Agnes had taken pity on her and had bought some. They talked and Agnes soon found out the girl was an orphan sleeping on the floor of an overcrowded row house. Moved by compassion, Agnes had offered her a job as a kitchen maid and a place to live. She had not probed for more personal information because Ursula seemed guarded, as though she was hiding from someone. The Prinsens' cook had had minimal personal conversation with Ursula in the year she was there, and the housekeeper had had none. But Matilda, the upstairs maid who made the beds and did the laundry and served guests, had shared a room with her. Surely they had become friends, at least to an extent, and had perhaps talked at night as they lay in their beds.

Matilda stands before me now looking as though she thinks Agnes and I are somehow holding her responsible for what Ursula did to herself. She looks younger than her eighteen years. I try to reassure her that Ursula simply needs our help.

"She is feeling better, but she is still very melancholy," I say. "If we can discover what is making her so sad, we can help her find happiness again. You'd be doing her a great kindness if you could help me. Would you do that?"

Matilda looks from me to her employer and back to me again. "I don't know how I can help you, miss," she says, her face pale with worry that her job hangs in the balance.

"Just answer Miss Bright's questions truthfully, Matilda," Agnes Prinsen says, "even if you must reveal a secret Ursula told you to keep. Secrets will not help her right now. Surely you can see that."

"But . . . but she never told me any secrets."

"Did she say where she lived after her mother died? After the flu?" I ask.

"She didn't like to talk about her mother. Or the flu."

"She never mentioned an orphanage? Or who took her in? Or where she went to school?"

"No, miss."

"What did she like to talk about?"

Matilda bites her lip in consternation. "Nothing special. I did most of the talking. She just listened. I thought she was shy."

"Can you tell me if anything out of the ordinary happened on the day she tried to hurt herself? Anything at all? Or the day before?"

Matilda slowly shakes her head. "It was like any other day. Both days were."

"And she never had visitors or letters sent to her in the mail?" I ask this of both the maid and Agnes, and they shake their heads.

"You never woke to hear her crying in her bed?"

"No, miss," Matilda replies.

I am gaining no new ground here, and it perplexes me. I don't want to merely hope that someday Ursula will tell me why she wanted to end her life. I can't assume that I have the luxury of time. What if she finds another way to kill herself? What if she somehow escapes from the hospital and runs in front of a train or an automobile, or gets ahold of a pair of hospital scissors and slices her wrists? What if the second time she tries to commit suicide she is successful? She would be no different from Sybil then, a beautiful woman I cannot save. Every time I see Conrad Reese visiting Sybil, or holding her hand, or kissing her cheek, my heart feels riven in two. The devotion Conrad has for her is everything I want for myself. It is what I want for Maggie and Willa and even Papa were he to marry again. It is why I don't think Maggie should settle for marriage to a man she is merely fond of. It is why I can't keep my gaze off Conrad when he visits his wife. If only there was something I could do to restore Sybil to him. It angers and pains me daily that there isn't. But I know I can help Ursula. I know I can. If I can just figure out what happened to her.

I am pondering this when Matilda clears her throat.

"She . . . she did have a secret place in our room where she hid things." The maid practically whispers this, and her face turns crimson. Matilda had snooped into this secret place; this is obvious.

"It's all right, Matilda. It doesn't matter

that you know about it," I assure her. "Can you show us? Can you show us where it is?"

She looks to Agnes for approval, and when the woman nods, Matilda asks us to follow her.

The maid takes us through the kitchen and down a half flight of stairs that leads to two sets of quarters half aboveground and half part of the cellar. We enter one of the rooms. Inside the small space are two metal-framed beds separated by a nightstand and a hooked rug, along with a bureau, a washstand, and a wardrobe. A painting of irises hangs on the far wall. Only one bed is made up with linens; the other stands empty and available. Agnes Prinsen must expect Ursula to return to her. She has not filled the vacancy and given the bed to another girl. This adds fuel to my desire to help Ursula, to bring her back, to end her suffering. To do for her what I cannot do for Sybil and Conrad Reese.

Matilda turns to Agnes and me. "It's not my way to spy on other people. I was just curious, that's all."

"You're not in any kind of trouble, Matilda," Agnes replies. "Just show us the place."

Matilda crosses the room to the nightstand and kneels. She reaches between the legs of the table for a brick in the wall and shimmies it back and forth. The brick comes away from the cracked mortar around it, leaving a darkened rectangular space. She reaches in and pulls out a slender wooden pencil box. When she rises, she hands the box to Agnes, who opens it. Inside are a necklace, some dollar coins, a key, and several papers. Agnes removes the documents and flips through them. One is a single sheet of paper, a list of some kind, written in a foreign language that I don't recognize. Another is a photograph of a woman and a little girl of about five years. Ursula and her mother, perhaps? The last is an envelope addressed simply "Ursula." Inside is a letter and an expired train ticket from Camden, New Jersey, six miles away. The letter was written on a piece of stationery printed at the bottom with the name "The Franklin Hotel" and dated on the top: May 17, 1924.

"This date is just a few months before I hired her," Agnes says. She opens the letter and reads aloud:

Dear Ursula:
I know I can't change your mind about leaving us, but you need to know Cal didn't mean what he said. He knows it's

not your fault what happened to Leo. We all know it's not your fault. You were sick and you didn't know what you were doing. Sometimes the war and the flu and all that happened just gets to Cal and he drinks too much bootleg and then he says things he doesn't mean. He feels bad about what he said. He really does. You will always have a home here with us at the hotel, no matter what Cal said. So when your money runs out, and if you want to, come on back.

Rita

Agnes looks up from the letter. "Who is this Rita?"

Matilda shakes her head. "I don't know. Ursula never mentioned any of these names to me."

"She never mentioned living at a hotel in Camden?" I ask.

"No, miss."

Agnes stares at the letter for a minute. "Come with me, Miss Bright," she says. With the letter and pencil box still in her hand, Agnes leads me from the back of the house to a library across the house's marbled foyer and next to the drawing room we'd been in before. She stops at a desk made of polished cherry. A squat black

456

telephone sits atop it.

"Sit yourself down. I'm going to make a call."

I take a seat on a settee near a wall of books and Agnes lifts the telephone's handset. A moment later she is asking the switchboard operator to connect her to the Franklin Hotel in Camden, New Jersey. And a few moments after that, she is speaking to the woman named Rita.

I cannot help moving to the edge of my seat to listen to the half of the conversation that I can hear. Agnes gives her name and asks politely how the woman knows Ursula Novak. Then she explains that she is Ursula's employer and that the girl has had a difficult time — the vaguest of references to what actually happened — and that she's now recovering in a mental hospital in Philadelphia. Agnes mentions the letter she holds in her hand. Rita must now be asking what Ursula did that landed her in a mental hospital, because the next thing Agnes says is that Ursula tried to do herself mortal harm.

"And she has given her caregivers every indication she will likely try again if afforded the opportunity," Agnes says. "I was hoping you might share with me what happened to Ursula so that I can apprise her doctors.

They are at a loss how to help her. She won't tell them anything."

I am itching to jump off the settee and snatch the telephone out of Agnes Prinsen's hand. I want to ask the questions and I want to hear the answers.

"Well, what is it here that you mention in this note to Ursula?" Agnes says, apparently not happy with the entire answer Rita gave her. "What is not her fault? Who is Cal? Who is Leo?"

A moment later Agnes seems to have been turned to stone. All movement ceases. She stares at the bookshelf in front of her with wide eyes that are obviously picturing something other than books.

"Oh my!" Agnes says a few seconds later, her voice having lost some of its regal authority. "Oh, how dreadful."

"What is it?" I whisper, unable not to ask. "What happened? What's not Ursula's fault?"

But Agnes doesn't hear me. She is listening to more revelations.

"Yes, yes," Agnes continues. "I'll tell that to the doctor."

"Tell me what?" This I say at normal speaking volume.

Agnes turns to me, shaking her head slightly. Then she crooks an eyebrow and looks off in the distance again. "Wait. No one is demanding you pay for her care, Mrs. Dabney. That's not why I rang you. I called because —"

She stops and listens. "Well, all right. I will pass along the message. Good day."

I reach for the telephone to speak to this Rita Dabney myself even as Agnes lays the receiver on its cradle, the connection ended.

"I don't think that woman is entirely a very nice person," Agnes says, frowning. Then she turns to me. "She doesn't think it's a good idea for her and her husband to come to visit Ursula, and she doesn't want you or anyone else at the asylum contacting her. I think she's afraid you will force her to pay for Ursula's care, and she says they can't afford it."

"Who *are* they?" I ask.

"Rita and Maury Dabney took Ursula in when her mother died. They are her step-father Cal's parents. He was married for three years to Ursula's mother but was off fighting the war in France when she died. Ursula didn't have any other family but the Dabneys, such as they are. So they took her."

"What was so dreadful?" I ask, sensing that we are at last, at last making progress. "What wasn't Ursula's fault? What happened?"

Agnes inhales and exhales. "Very sad. Very sad indeed. Ursula had that awful flu, too. She was delirious with fever the day her mother died and she tossed her baby brother — Cal's only child at the time — into the Delaware River." Agnes shakes her head gloomily. "He drowned, Miss Bright."

CHAPTER 55

Willa

It's not that hard to do something you're not supposed to if nobody thinks you'd ever even contemplate doing such a thing anyway.

The first night I snuck out to the speakeasy, my heart was pounding as I climbed out Alex's bedroom window while he slept — my window in the attic is too high — and it pounded the whole time I was on the street trying to get there, and while I was meeting with Albert, and every second that I was sneaking back home. But when I tiptoed back inside my house, all was just as I had left it — everyone fast asleep in their beds. No one missed me because no one was awake.

My heart doesn't pound like a scared rabbit's anymore when I go. I've been back to the Silver Swan — that's the speakeasy's name and I like the way it sounds — seven

461

times now and haven't had a hint of trouble. But I've also perfected my technique. For my bed, I make a dummy out of pillows and rolled-up pajamas, and then I sneak out onto the ledge and down the trellis outside Alex's window after everyone else has gone to bed. You can't see his window from the street at night because it's too dark, so I can pop out from the little alley between our house and the apartment building next door looking like I just materialized out of the bricks.

That first night I went to meet with Albert, I had to get there on my own once I was on the boulevard, which meant I had to hail a cab like a businessman. That wasn't my favorite few minutes of the evening. But I did it, and since Albert liked my singing so much and wanted me to come back and entertain his patrons, he had a driver take me home. The driver's name is Foster. He now collects me on the opposite corner after I've snuck out the window and brings me back, like I'm a Broadway starlet. Albert doesn't want me meeting the wrong sort on the street, so he told Foster and Mr. Trout, who is like the Silver Swan's own policeman, that I am always to have a car bring me in and take me home.

Getting back into my room after I'm done

is easy, too. I have pocketed one of the spare keys to the side entrance where Papa brings in the bodies. I can slip in there at one o'clock in the morning and no one sees me or hears me. I can't chance going out that way because sometimes Papa's light is on. He might hear me walk past. Then I come through the kitchen, hang up my coat in the hall closet, and make my way up the stairs to my bedroom.

I always grab a glass of water on my way past the kitchen sink so that if I should see Papa or Maggie or Evie on the stairs for some odd reason, I can just say I was thirsty. I usually am thirsty after singing a dozen songs. I haven't quite figured out what I'll say if they ask why I have on street clothes if that should ever happen. I suppose I can say I fell asleep before I had a chance to put my nightdress on. They won't see any rouge or lipstick or face powder because I'm always very careful to take it off before I leave the Swan. Albert doesn't want me to wear too much paint, as he calls it, because my stage name is Sweet Polly Adler and he wants me to look innocent and childlike like Mary Pickford in *Pollyanna.* The costumes I wear are all ribbons and lace and bows — nothing like what I would choose to wear — but Albert says everyone loves it that I sing like an angel and look like one, too, because the world above can be a dangerous, miserable place. At the Silver Swan, however, people can forget their troubles, drink some fine bootleg whiskey, and listen to Sweet Polly Adler sing their woes away.

I'm not the only singer at the club. There is a lady named Lila who has the reddest lips I've ever seen. She wears her black hair in a cute bob and smokes cigarette after cigarette from a skinny ebony holder. Her long, lacquered fingernails — the shiniest crimson — click on everything she touches. Lila's costumes are all fringe and feathers and sequins. I'd much rather wear her dresses. Lila is the one who puts my lipstick and rouge on and curls my hair with a hot iron.

Sometimes when I'm done singing, men want to come back to where we get dressed or they want me to come sit at their tables, even on their laps. Lila always tells them she'll kill them if they so much as touch a hair on my head. And then she always adds, "But you'll already be dead because Albert'll kill ya first." Those men laugh like it's a joke, and Lila does, too. But everyone can tell she's not joking.

I think Lila likes me all right. It's hard to tell. She told me a few days ago that she always wanted to have children but never did. She said if she'd had a little girl she would have named her Winnifred. But then after she told me that, she ignored me the rest of the night.

I usually do two shows. One at eleven and one at midnight. And I get three silver dollars every night that I sing. I must hide my money, of course, and I can't buy anything with it because there would be questions. But someday, when I'm older and on my own, I am going to buy Papa something wonderful with all the money I'm making right now. I don't know just what I will buy, but something amazing. Like maybe a solid gold watch or a horse that he can board in the country, or passage to England so that he can see Big Ben and the Tower of London and the lions in Trafalgar Square. He told me once he'd like to see London someday. Maybe I'll have enough money to go with him. And we could take Alex. Maggie will probably be married to Palmer by then and who knows where Evie will be. But I can see Papa and me and Alex sailing on a ship as beautiful as the *Titanic* had been and then riding around London in a horse-drawn carriage like we haven't a care in the world.

This is what I am thinking about as Foster brings me home tonight, what I might buy for Papa with all my silver dollars. It was a good night, Albert said. Standing room only. Everyone seemed to enjoy my show. There's a four-piece band that plays and there's Lila, of course, and there's a man who tells jokes, and there's me. I can tell when the customers enjoy a show by how quiet the room gets. It's never completely quiet; there's always a group of people laughing or talking. But sometimes when I'm singing, a hush falls over the room, and it's as if I'm not a girl pretending she's Sweet Polly Adler, and all the people aren't stuck underground drinking illegal liquor, and above us isn't some broken, tired old city run by mobsters. It's as if I am just me and they are just them and the world is still a lovely place. That's the way it was tonight when I sang "Look for the Silver Lining." When I sang the line that somewhere the sun is shining, it was like everyone in the smoke-filled room wanted to believe it.

The moment ended, of course. When my show was done, the band came on to join Albert, who always plays for me, and the people started to dance, and it got noisy again.

Still, I have three new silver dollars in my coat pocket, and for a second there, everything seemed right.

Foster lets me out on the corner so that I can make my way quietly and slip unnoticed into the house. I go to the back stoop like usual and I fish the key out of my handbag, and all the while I am wondering how I can somehow trap this lovely lingering feeling inside me. When I step up on the stoop, I nearly trip over a body in the dark.

How dare someone drop off a corpse in the middle of the night? I'm thinking, but then the body moves and my breath catches in my throat.

"Who's there?" I sound braver than I feel. The last thing I want to do is fight my way past a drunkard or a hobo sleeping on our stoop. Or worse, have to yell for help and wake up the house.

"Willa? Is that you?"

I do not recognize this man's voice. He raises himself to his knees and then stands. As he does, the sallow light cast by a gas streetlamp a few yards away falls across the top half of his body. The man's face is vaguely familiar, but I cannot place him.

"Who are you?" I demand.

The man takes a step toward me and is now fully visible. "Willa. It's me. Jamie Sutcliff."

For a couple seconds, I just stand there in wordless shock. The last time I saw Jamie

Sutcliff, I was eight years old. He had just come home from the war. His brother, Charlie, had died of the flu a few months back and then Jamie had crept off in the half-light of dawn with a duffel over his back without telling anyone — not even his parents — where he was going. He looks the same now, but different. His hair is longer, he seems a mite taller, and he looks more like a man who's been places. I suppose that's exactly what he is.

"Willa, what are you doing out here?" he says, worry splashed all over his face.

"What am *I* doing out here?" I answer. "What are *you* doing out here?"

"I hitched a ride into town," he says. "It's late. My parents' place is dark, and I didn't want to wake them by pounding on the door. They don't know I'm coming. I thought I'd just sleep here on your back stoop until daylight."

If I hitched my way home after being gone six years, I'd pound on the door of *my* house — that's for sure. "You really think your parents would be upset if you woke them up to let you in?" I ask.

He shakes his head slightly. "I don't want to come home that way. Pounding on the door in the middle of the night."

"So you're coming home?"

"Maybe."

"Why'd you leave in the first place?" I know it's none of my business, but the question just tosses itself out of my mouth. I suppose it's because I've always wondered. I'd bet lots of people have.

He doesn't need time to think up an answer. "I had to take care of some things."

"What things?"

"Things inside me. Broken things."

We stand there looking at each other for a moment. Jamie must have taken care of whatever was broken inside him, because there he was, on my stoop and only a few steps away from the life he left. I'm one second away from asking him how he did it when he asks me what I'm doing outside at one o'clock in the morning.

"Sometimes I can't sleep," I say, the lie coming out fast and smooth, but he just nods like he understands perfectly. "I'd appreciate it if you didn't mention to my father or sisters that I was out for a walk just now," I add.

"These are not safe times to be on the street in the middle of the night," he says.

"I didn't go far." Not a lie. I had been inside a nice automobile with squeaky leather seats that had just let me out across the street. "And I came back. So I'd appreciate it just the same if you didn't say anything. I can tell everyone I was getting a drink from the kitchen and heard a noise outside on the back stoop and found you. Please don't say anything."

He thinks on it for a second before saying, "All right."

"Come on in," I tell him. "Papa wouldn't want you outside like this when I know you're here. You can sleep on the sofa in the sitting room."

It's cold and damp, and he doesn't argue.

I unlock the door, and Jamie Sutcliff follows me in. As we step into the mudroom, I ask him if I haven't changed all that much and that's how he recognized me so quickly.

"Your eyes are the same," he says.

I guess our eyes don't change much from when we were young. Perhaps it's just how we see things that changes.

CHAPTER 56

Maggie

I know I've overslept when I hear a voice downstairs that is deep like Papa's but does not belong to him. I look at the clock on my night table and am chagrined that it's after seven, and yet I wonder who has called on us so early in the morning. The two hours that I'd lain awake in the wee hours of the morning — my thoughts in a tumble — had no doubt caused me to sleep past my normal waking time. In the hours before dawn, and while the rest of the house had slept, my brain kept reminding me I had said yes to Palmer.

It had been a week since he asked me to marry him, and I'd finally concluded that being loved by him was surely the most marvelous thing to have happened to me in a very long time. Not only that, but he wanted Alex with us. And while it would be hard to take Alex away from Papa and my sisters, he would at last have the benefits of a typical family with Palmer and me: a father, a mother, and one day, siblings. I would even allow Alex to start calling me Mama if he still wanted to.

So, last night I had told Palmer yes, I would marry him and he could speak to Papa. We'd been alone in the sitting room, as Alex and Evie were already in bed and Willa had gone up to her room early, too. Happy to finally have the answer he wanted from me, Palmer hadn't wanted to wait a minute. He'd happily kissed me, and then he'd taken my hand to accompany him to the office where my father often retired in the evening to smoke one of Grandad's cigars and read.

Papa had the reaction I thought he would when Palmer told him he wanted my hand in marriage. He was happy that I had won the love of such a fine, accomplished man as Palmer, and relieved that I would always be well taken care of.

"New York's not so far," Papa had said, when he heard the extent of Palmer's plans, and he stroked his chin in that way he does when he's contemplating something.

Then he said he didn't know much about how to pull off a proper wedding, and I assured him that Palmer and I didn't need a lavish ceremony that would take months to plan. Something simple would be just fine.

"I suppose Dora Sutcliff might be able to help us with the preparations," he'd said, his mind obviously still whirling with how the bride's father was supposed to handle the details of a wedding when he was a widower. "Or your grandmother."

Papa had mended his relationship with my mother's parents to a point. He still hadn't fully moved past the notion that Mama would quite likely be alive if they had just let her and us girls come back to Quakertown when she'd asked. Anything having to do with Grandma Adler was always a pondered thought.

"I'm sure if we need any extra help with anything, Dora will be happy to lend a hand," I'd assured him.

Papa then visibly relaxed. It would have been kind to let him enjoy that moment a little bit longer, but I had to tell him the rest.

"Palmer and I would like to take Alex with us," I said, startling myself with how sharp those words sounded out loud.

Papa didn't say anything for a second. "You want to take Alex?" he said a moment later, echoing my words as though he hadn't quite heard right.

"It would be our privilege to raise him alongside any children we may have of our own, Mr. Bright," Palmer said.

"He'd have a home like all the other children in school," I went on. "A home with two parents and brothers and sisters closer to his own age. And he and I could come down on the train on Saturdays and we could spend the whole day here with you and Evie and Willa. I can't imagine leaving him, Papa. Nor can I envision him here without me. I'm already like a mother to him. . . ." My voice trailed away as my throat tightened.

Papa had started to stroke his chin again, deep in thought. "Yes . . . ," he said, but I wasn't sure what he was saying yes to. Perhaps it was to this unspoken thought that no child should have to say good-bye to his mother.

"Papa?" I needed to know what he was thinking. Alex was not my father's adopted son. Alex was a member of this family as a ward of the state. He had our last name because no one knew what his last name was. Even I didn't know what it was. We had been told that at some point the court would declare Alex adoptable. Surely after six years of no one coming forward to inquire about Alex, Palmer and I could now petition to adopt him and be accepted. If my father would consent to it.

Papa took another moment to ponder and then he nodded as he sat back in his chair, the move of someone who has just decided something. "Every child deserves a home like that," he said, a quiet sigh escaping at the same time.

"We'll give him everything a child needs," I said.

"I know you will. You have from the very beginning, Mags."

The moment grew so tender that Palmer excused himself. He said he needed to telephone his parents in Delaware and that we'd go shopping for a ring the next day and that I could pick out whatever kind of gem I wanted. I walked him to the front door. His kiss good-bye was long and deep.

I locked the door, turned off the lights, and saw as I neared the staircase that Papa's office door was still open and light spilled out of the room. He was sitting where I'd left him, but now he had opened a bottle of cognac that he'd retrieved from some hidden place and he'd poured two glasses.

He looked up and offered one of the glasses to me. I'd never had cognac or any other kind of liquor before. I moved forward to take it and I sat in the chair next to his.

"It's the last of it," he said. Then he'd lifted the little glass toward me. "To your happiness, Maggie. To yours and Alex's and Palmer's."

The cognac felt like a cleansing fire as it slid down my throat and into my body. We didn't say anything else as we sat there and sipped.

"I want to pick the right time to tell Alex that we're taking him," I said when the drink was gone. I felt warm and loose and sleepy. "I don't want to tell him until I can tell him everything. Like when the wedding is. When we're leaving. All that."

Papa took the glass from me and set it down by his own. "News of an engagement doesn't stay quiet for long. Especially when plans are being made. And the bride-to-be is wearing a ring."

"I know. I won't wait too long."

Papa smiled at me. "I'm happy for you, Maggie. Happy and sad. Your mother would have loved to be a part of all this."

We were both quiet for a moment, each lost in our memories of Mama.

"Might you marry again, Papa?" I had been wondering this for a long time.

He didn't stroke his chin in contemplation. He answered me straightaway like he'd known the answer to this all his life. "Your mama is the only woman I could ever love, the only woman I was ever meant to love."

I carried those words up the stairs with me.

They plucked at my dreams as I slept, and they tugged me awake at two thirty in the morning and kept me sleepless until sometime after four. I didn't think I would get back to sleep at all, but I guess I did.

I hear another voice downstairs now, and this time I recognize it. Alex is down there, too. Perhaps a person Papa knows well died during the night, and now someone from the family is at our door to let him know they need him as soon as he can come. He will need breakfast.

I rise and dress as quickly as I can, working my long hair into a loose braid. When I step out onto the landing, I see that Evie's door is ajar, and I catch the aroma of coffee and toast. She is up, too. I descend the stairs, all the while trying to place the voice that I hear. Papa is asking the visitor if he would like to use his washroom to shave and the man says no, thank you. I reach the bottom of the stairs and turn toward the sitting room, where the voices are coming from. Papa is kneeling on the hearth and feeding the fire. Alex is standing at the sofa in front of our visitor. I don't see the man's face until I am at the doorway.

And then I see him. Jamie Sutcliff, sitting on the sofa next to a bed pillow and a rumpled blanket. He turns toward me as I enter, and I see a softening in his eyes and face that I can only describe as hinting of regret. Or gratitude. Maybe both.

"Jamie." I say his name and it feels like I had last said it out loud only yesterday.

He stands. "Hello, Maggie." His hair is long and a bit mussed; his trousers and faded flannel shirt are wrinkled from travel and sleep. The wool socks he wears are threadbare. At his feet is a tattered rucksack, half-open. But underneath all these evidences of a roving life, I see in his gaze tiny traces of the man I met when I was young, before he went to war, before the flu killed people we loved, before he returned from the trenches a hollowed-out soul.

There is so much I want to ask him, and it seems by the way he is looking at me that there is so much he wants to tell me. But I can't think of what I want to say, so what comes out of my mouth next is laughable.

"You're here."

He cracks a smile. "I am."

"Willa found him sleeping on the back stoop last night," Alex offers.

"Willa?" I murmur, but not to Alex. To Jamie.

Papa stands and turns from the fireplace. "She'd gotten up to get a drink from the kitchen and heard a noise. Found our old friend here trying to take shelter for the night and wisely asked him to come in and sleep on the sofa."

Willa comes into the room. "Hello, sleepyhead," she says as she walks past me. She holds a coffee cup on a saucer that she hands to Jamie. He thanks her for it and takes a sip.

"Didn't think Papa would be too pleased with me if I just left him there," Willa says. "And he didn't want to wake his parents up to let him in."

"He's come from California," Alex adds. "He's seen a whale."

"You were sleeping on our stoop?" I am still trying to grasp that Jamie is standing a few feet away from me. He had slept in this room. While I lay awake last night pondering the abrupt turn my life is about to take, he was just below me, sleeping on the sofa.

"I got into the city late. I didn't want to wake my parents in the middle of the night." He breaks into another smile. "I've actually slept on a stoop before, many times actually, so I was perfectly fine with the idea of sleeping on yours. Daylight would have come soon enough."

Evie now enters the room with a plate of toast cut into triangles and offers it to Jamie. He doesn't reach out to take it.

"That's so very kind of you, but I should probably get going."

"It's just some toast, Jamie. You should eat something," Evie says, in a half-motherly, half-doctorlike way.

She sets the plate down on the sofa table in front of him, and a second later he places his coffee cup next to it. "It's not that I'm not grateful, because I am. I just know my mother will be wanting to feed me, too. And it's been a while since I ate a great deal of food all at once." He turns to Willa. "If I could have my coat, I'll be on my way and out of yours."

"You're not in our way, son," Papa says.

"I know where his coat is!" Alex scampers past me and out of the room.

Jamie moves forward to follow him, but he stops as he's right next to me in the doorway. "It's good to see you again, Maggie."

His eyes are telling me something. I don't know what it is and I am unable to say anything in return. A second later he is at the front door putting on his coat and then slipping his feet into worn boots that had been left in the foyer.

Papa, Willa, and Evie have followed Jamie. He thanks us again for our hospitality and Papa tells him as he lifts the latch and opens the front door that we're all glad that he's come home.

I am watching him about to step out of the house when I see out of the corner of my eye his rucksack where he left it.

"Wait, Jamie!" I call out.

I cross the sitting room to the sofa and lift the rucksack up off the floor. Some of the contents start to spill out the opening and I pause to coax a pair of socks and a shaving brush back inside.

It's when I do this that I see them inside the rucksack, tied loosely together with a piece of twine — all the letters I ever wrote to Jamie, from the very first one to the last.

CHAPTER 57

Evelyn

The contents of Ursula's pencil box are spread out before me. The photograph. The list. The train ticket. Rita's letter. The key. The coins. Perhaps I ought not to have brought them home with me, but I don't have the time at the hospital to ponder them like I want to. Like I need to. Downstairs, Willa and Alex are playing some kind of game where she plays a song on the piano and Alex must run around the room tagging things. Maggie is out with Palmer planning her wedding and Papa is at a businessmen's meeting.

Another week has gone by, and while I'm now sure I know why Ursula tried to hang herself, I am no closer to having her tell me the reason for it herself. When I brought the pencil box to the hospital from the Prinsens' and shared with Dr. Bellfield what Rita Dabney had said about Ursula's baby brother, I asked him what he thought we should do with this information. He, of course, turned the question back on me.

"What do you advise?" he said.

"I want her to trust me with her past," I said, thinking out loud, "so that she will trust me to help her with her future. So I don't think I should tell her yet that I went into her private space and took her things."

"Continue," he said, giving me no indication if he agreed with me. Maybe he didn't. Maybe Dr. Bellfield is the type to produce the pencil box at a session and see what kind of reaction he gets.

"I'm thinking I should start with where she last was — at the Prinsens' — and go backward one step at a time, rather than yanking her all the way to the beginning of her troubles and trying to move her forward from there."

"And how do you plan to sustain this protracted backward momentum?"

He asked it nicely enough, but I could see what he was getting at. To keep Ursula taking backward steps to the moment she stood at the river's edge with her baby brother, I would have to have compelling reasons for her to keep moving.

"I need to ask the right questions," I said.

"And if she does not answer them? What

is your plan then?"

"I . . . I don't know yet."

"I am intrigued by what you have uncovered, Miss Bright. And I will allow you to move ahead as you have suggested — for the time being, anyway. Let's see how the patient is in two weeks."

I knew two weeks would not be enough time. I needed more information to ask better questions. I needed to talk to Rita Dabney myself instead of guessing at what her letter meant. "May I travel to Camden to speak with Ursula's family?" I'd asked.

"You told me they did not wish to be contacted."

"Yes, that message was passed on to me by Agnes Prinsen, but I did not agree to that request."

"I am guessing they will decline to speak to you."

"They might."

Dr. Bellfield had crinkled his brow. "You have other patients, Miss Bright. You will always have other patients. You cannot become involved to this depth with each one. You will exhaust yourself."

"But this is one I think I can help."

He had said I could go. I finished with my other duties and then grabbed my coat and umbrella to walk up to the station and catch the next train across the river into New Jersey. A steady rain was falling and I knew despite my umbrella I would likely be soaking wet when I got to the platform, but I didn't want to wait until a drier day to go to Camden. Dr. Bellfield had given me only fourteen days.

As I stepped through the front doors, Conrad Reese was coming inside to visit Sybil, and he was shaking the water off his own umbrella.

"Good afternoon, Miss Bright." Raindrops glistened on his black wool coat like tiny shards of glass. "You have to go out in this?"

"I'm afraid so. Not far, though. Just to the train station."

"That's six blocks!"

I only have two weeks! I wanted to say. "I've got an umbrella," I said instead.

"Please allow me to drive you to the station. You can't walk in this. You'll be drenched before you get to the cross street."

His kind offer was so unexpected I fumbled for a response. "That's . . . that's too much trouble."

"It's no trouble at all. My car's right here and I've only just arrived."

"But you've come to see Sybil."

He looked at me for a long moment, and I could read the unspoken words in that look. Sybil didn't know he was coming, and she wouldn't be put out that he'd been detained. She wouldn't recognize him when he did finally get inside the hospital. And she wasn't going anywhere.

"Please," he finally said. "It's the least I can do. You've been so kind to my wife. I see the extra care you give her. It would be a mere token of my gratitude."

A minute later I was inside his Buick touring car and we were headed to the station.

"Where do you need to go, if I may ask?"

"I must consult with another patient's family. In Camden."

He took his eyes off the road to glance at me. "New Jersey? In this weather? It will take you forty minutes to get there."

I shrugged. "I have to go."

"I'll take you across. It's only eight miles or so. Let me take you."

"Mr. Reese! I couldn't possibly have you do that."

"I insist. This is no kind of weather in which to be out."

"But I don't know how long I will be."

He turned east in the direction of the Delaware River and the newly constructed bridge to New Jersey. "All the more reason for you not to be out in all this."

I could see that he would not be persuaded, and in truth, I didn't want to spend the next few hours dashing through driving rain onto train platforms. "This is so very kind of you."

He shook his head. "It's nothing."

But it wasn't nothing. Not to me.

On the way, he told me about the book printing business he owns with his mother, and that he is the oldest of five children but the only son. Three of his four sisters are married, two with small children. The last at home is sixteen. He and Sybil had been married five years, but I already knew this. I knew she had started to drift just a few weeks after their wedding. All this was in Sybil's file. I told him the names and ages of my sisters and our ward, Alex; about losing my mother and great-uncle to the flu; and my lifelong desire to be a doctor. He shared that he, too, had lost a parent to the flu. His father.

Conrad was easy to talk to, and it seemed in no time we were pulling up in front of the Franklin Hotel, a four-story building, white brick with green trim, that had seen better days. The striped awning out front sagged with the weight of water and too many years.

"Shall I just wait right here for you?" Conrad asked.

I looked up at the tired-looking structure from a rain-streaked window. "I actually may be back out rather quickly."

"Oh?"

I turned to him, feeling a little guilty for not telling him up front that the Dabneys might not give me even five minutes of their time. "I'm not sure how much help this family is going to want to be."

He frowned. "Want me to come in with you?"

"No. It's not that. They just . . . They don't want to get too involved. I don't think I'll be long. But if you need to get back . . ."

"I'll wait," he said.

I got out of the car and ran through the rain to the front door. The foyer inside was carpeted in a floral print that had mellowed to a subtle brown. Two green leather chairs were situated around a table and a coal fire. A woman of ample size with streaks of faint silver in her hair sat behind a desk. Behind her, room keys dangled on a felt-covered pegboard lined with hooks.

"May I help you?" she said.

"Mrs. Dabney?"

"Yes."

I took a breath. "My name is Evelyn Bright. I am a medical student and one of the care providers for Ursula at the Fairview Hospital. I'd appreciate it very much if I could ask you a few questions about what happened to her and her baby brother."

Rita Dabney's eyes widened a bit. "I told that other lady that we don't have the money to pay for a mental hospital. I made that very clear!"

"I'm not here for money, and no one is going to ask you to pay for anything. I just have some questions."

"She's not really our problem, you know. I feel sorry for her. I always have, but she's not really ours. If you ask me, we've been more than kind to her. Especially after what she did. She killed our first grandchild, you know."

My hackles rose at the callousness of this woman's words, but I reined in my indignation and continued with my calm questioning. "Yes, so I've heard," I said. "I just want to know what happened that day her brother died. And then what happened after it."

"Well, none of us were there. We were here, and Ines and the children were over the river in Philadelphia."

"Ines?"

"Ursula and Leo's mother. Cal's first wife. She and he had that little apartment off South Street in as derelict an area as I've ever seen. I told Cal when he was about to be shipped off to the war that Ines and the children should come here to live with us, but Cal and his father weren't on speaking terms then and he didn't want any part of that. Maury and I weren't even invited to the wedding. Cal married this Croatian widow with a five-year-old daughter and we weren't even consulted or invited."

The woman stopped and grimaced angrily, like the offense still stung.

"And then Ines and Cal had a child?" I asked so that Rita Dabney would go on, even if it was to continue talking about herself when it was Ursula I was asking about. I was beginning to see more and more the dark depths of Ursula's world.

"Cal didn't even tell us she was pregnant until the baby was born, and even then I had to beg to see him. Ines convinced Cal I should at least be able to see the baby. But then he was shipped off to France two weeks after Leo was born. Next thing I know there's a killing flu all over the face of the earth. I didn't know Ines had it. And I didn't know she had given it to Ursula. If I had known I would have come for them no matter what Cal had told her before he left. I didn't know!"

"I'm sure you didn't," I said empathetically.

"Then I come to find out from the police that Ines is dead and Ursula was found wandering around the river, blood all over her, sick with the flu, and carrying on about an angel coming for Baby Leo in a little brown boat. She tossed him into the river. A helpless baby. She drowned him."

Rita Dabney's eyes had misted over.

"I'm so very sorry."

"The worst of it is, she says she doesn't hardly remember that day."

"I think maybe she does," I said.

"Well, I've asked her time and again what on earth made her think an angel had come in a little brown boat for that baby, and she could never tell me."

"Maybe the baby had died. Their mother was dead. Maybe the trauma of losing both her mother and her brother in the same day was too much. Maybe Ursula's mind created the image of the angel taking Leo to soften the blow of seeing them both dead."

"But she threw him in the river!"

"If the child was dead already, then she didn't drown him."

"Then why is she the way she is? Why did she try to kill herself? He was alive when she threw him in. If he wasn't, she wouldn't be carrying the guilt that she is. She is the way she is because deep down she knows she killed that baby. Probably because she was jealous of him."

"She was sick with fever."

"But my grandson is dead just the same."

I paused for just a moment to collect my thoughts. "You and your husband took her in then?"

Rita Dabney's nod was accompanied by a half-concealed snort. "What else could we do? Ines had no other family that we knew of. The city was plumb full of orphans. They didn't want another one. And I did feel sorry for her. I did. Ursula was the saddest child I'd ever laid eyes on. When Cal came home some months after the war, he didn't even want to see her. It was several years before he'd even look at her. And he had his own problems from the war. He softened up after a while, but there were times before he met his second wife and she gave him a new baby when he'd get ahold of liquor, and when he did, he always lit into Ursula and blamed her for everything bad in his life. It wasn't her fault Ines died or that Cal had to see what he did in the war, but he heaped the blame for it all, and Leo's death, too, on her. I don't blame her for having left."

"Left? Didn't she run away at fourteen?"

Rita opened her mouth and then closed

it. A second later when she spoke again, I knew we were finished. "She left. You apparently read the note I wrote to her. I told her she always had a home here. But she wanted to go. And now I think it's time you went."

I thanked Rita Dabney for her help and she merely tipped her head to acknowledge she'd heard me.

It was raining harder as I stepped outside. I ran to Conrad's automobile, so grateful that he had wanted to wait for me.

"Did you get what you needed?" he asked as he pulled away from the curb.

"More or less," I said.

He needed to concentrate on the slick street as we made our way back across the bridge into Pennsylvania, and the easy camaraderie that we had on the way to Camden was gone. The silence as he drove seemed to emphasize the fact that we were alone in his car.

We pulled into the gravel driveway of the hospital some minutes later, just as a break in the clouds appeared.

"Thank you for taking me," I said as Conrad set the Buick's brake. "I so appreciate it."

"I'm the grateful one. You're the only person who has shown any real interest in helping Sybil."

"I wish I could do more. I truly do."

He had held my gaze from across the seat. "I know you do."

I stayed for only a second more. Then I went into the hospital ahead of him, my face warm despite the chill.

And now, several hours later, I sit with Ursula's secret possessions lined up on my bureau and the memory of that look Conrad gave me.

I don't know what to make of any of it.

A knock at my door pulls me from these thoughts.

"It's Maggie. Can I come in?"

She opens the door and her face is flushed. I can't tell if she's happy or terrified. I haven't seen much of her since Jamie's sudden return.

"Everything all right?" I ask.

She extends her hand toward me. On the ring finger of her left hand is a shining sapphire rimmed with little diamonds.

"You said yes."

"I did." Tears glisten in my sister's eyes. "Two nights ago. But he gave me the ring tonight."

"It's official, then?"

Maggie exhales nervously. "I suppose it is," she says.

"And Papa?"

"I was there when Palmer asked him. He couldn't be happier for us. And he understands about Alex. He *wants* us to take him." She shudders a bit, as if a frosty gust has just swirled about her. She reaches up with the hand that wears Palmer's ring to catch a tear that has started to fall. "This is the best thing for Alex, isn't it? Taking him?"

"It's not always easy to identify the very best thing to do until you do what you think is best," I tell her, with Ursula's pencil box in my peripheral vision. "I do know Alex loves you like a son loves his mother. And he is obviously very fond of Palmer."

"Then it's the right thing to do, isn't it?"

I'm instantly whisked back in time to the day Mama lay dying and I stood at her door listening as she told Maggie she did the right thing by bringing Alex home. And I wonder, not for the first time, if the right thing to do is always the best thing. When I don't answer right away, Maggie continues.

"You're so busy with your work and studies, and Willa is only fourteen and still in school. Papa can't take care of Alex by himself. He'll be having to ask Dora to take Alex during the day, and now that . . . that Jamie is home, she may not want to."

I hear the way Maggie says Jamie's name.

I hear the buried wound there. The long-ago yearning for his affections.

"Please tell me this is the right choice to make, Evie."

"Which choice are we talking about?" I ask her. I know my sister well enough to see she is conflicted about other decisions she has made besides the one regarding Alex's future.

Maggie holds my gaze for a moment, relieved, I think, that I have seen through her questions.

"Jamie kept all my letters," she finally says. "Every one for the last seven years. I saw them in his rucksack. He had hardly anything in it, after all these years away, but he had my letters. He kept them. Why would he do that?"

The answer is obvious to me. Surely it is to her as well. "You need to ask him, Maggie, if it matters to you that he kept them. You can't guess or wonder."

I can see in her eyes that she knows I am right.

And now I know, too, what I need to do.

CHAPTER 58

Maggie

It doesn't take long for news of my engagement to Palmer Towlerton to spread. I told Ruby the day after Palmer gave me the ring so that I could ask her to be my witness, and she told everyone we'd ever known in school, even if they were only acquaintances. In a matter of days, it seems everyone has heard, including the coroner of all people, whom Papa knows on a first-name basis.

The words of congratulations have been followed by the question "So, when is the big day?" Palmer has already looked at the calendar, and suggested the day after Christmas, a Saturday, because if any extended family have come to town — meaning his — they will still be here on the twenty-sixth. He hasn't asked if I agree; he's merely thinking it's the date that makes the most sense, so how could I not be in favor of it? He'll be in town; his sisters and their families will be in town. It's the perfect day for a wedding.

When people ask me when the big day is, I keep saying we're still looking at dates. Palmer laughs when this happens and tells the inquirer that it will likely be the last Saturday in December. Then when whoever has asked has walked away, Palmer says something like "People just want to wish us well, Maggie. They aren't fishing for an invitation to the ceremony." Then he will bring my hand up to his lips to kiss it.

Palmer and I told Alex yesterday that we want him to come with us to New York after we marry. He seemed cautiously pleased by the plan, and he asked more than once how far away Manhattan is. He has no frame of reference for distance. We don't get to Quakertown very often and that's the farthest he's ever been from home. He also asked if the rest of the family is coming, too, and he seemed sad when I said Papa, Evie, and Willa are staying here. Willa wasn't that happy about the idea, either.

"So, why, again, are we leaving?" Alex said after we'd answered all his queries. I wanted to turn to Palmer and ask the same question.

With all the fuss over the engagement, I've been too busy to talk to Jamie and it seems the Sutcliffs have been happy to have Jamie all to themselves. Dora hasn't been over since Jamie came home, other than to bring us a plate of pralines as a thank-you for letting him spend the night. She didn't stay for a visit, though, so I couldn't ask her anything about how Jamie is doing now that he is home or why he came back or if he is planning on staying. And while I've kept my eye on the Sutcliffs' home and business, I haven't seen much coming and going. I am guessing that Dora perhaps wanted to make a celebration out of Jamie's return and he'd asked her not to.

I've been pondering Evie's advice to me, though, every spare second. And I know I need to talk to Jamie and that it cannot wait. Today, after the morning's restorative work, and while Willa and Alex are at school, and Evie's at the hospital, I will walk over to the Sutcliffs' to return Dora's plate and ask to speak to him.

Dora answers the bell, happier than I've seen her in years.

"You didn't have to trouble yourself to bring this old plate over!" she says as I stand at the threshold of their apartment above the accounting office.

"It was no trouble. The pralines were

wonderful. Thank you."

"My mother's recipe! And what's this I hear about you and Mr. Towlerton?" She beams at me but doesn't invite me in.

"Oh. Yes. He proposed."

"Lucky you! And I hear you'll be setting up housekeeping in New York City after the wedding. My, my. Manhattan!"

"Yes. Um, do you think I could speak to Jamie for a minute?"

"He's downstairs in the office." Dora leans toward me in glee. "He's back at his old desk, Maggie. Working! He's home. Home to stay!" Her gray-blue eyes flood with tears.

"I'm so happy for you. For all of you."

"I know! It's the only thing I've wanted since the day he left. It's all I prayed for. And now? My prayers have been answered." She hugs the plate to her chest.

"How wonderful after all these years."

"Yes, yes!"

"Has he . . . mentioned why he decided to come home?"

Dora cocks her head to the side. "You know, I haven't asked him. I don't care why he came home. Only that he did. That's all that matters to me. He wanted to come home. And he did."

"Right." Any hope that Dora Sutcliff might shed some light on the situation vanishes. "So, I'll just head downstairs, then."

I start to turn, but she reaches for my arm. "Here. Come in through the apartment and use the indoor stairs."

I follow her inside, through a tiny entryway and to a set of stairs that lead to the office below.

"Want me to take you down?" she asks.

"I'll be fine. Thank you, though." I take the first couple steps.

"We should have an engagement party," Dora calls out from the top of the staircase.

"Oh. Um. Well, that's a nice idea," I answer.

"Let's talk later."

"Certainly."

I get to the bottom of the stairs and open the door that leads to the office space. I find myself in a back room full of file cabinets and shelves of ledgers that reach to the ceiling. The door to this anteroom is ajar and beyond it I hear the clicking of an adding machine.

"Jamie?" I poke my head through the door's opening.

Jamie is seated at his old desk, working the machine, with an open ledger in front of him. The desk where his father sits is empty. Beyond him is the counter that separates his and his father's offices from the reception area. Beatrice's chair is empty, too.

He looks up as I come into his office. He's had a haircut and is clean-shaven. The clothes he's wearing are new and tailored.

"Maggie!" His smile is one of surprise but also of obvious delight.

"Your mother let me come down the stairs from the apartment. I need to talk to you for a minute if that's all right."

He stands. "Of course. Please. Come in. Have a seat." He moves newspaper pages off a chair directly across from his desk. He motions for me to sit and then he takes an identical chair next to it.

I look past him to his father's office. "So, your father is away at the moment?"

He glances behind him and then back to me. "Yes. He's meeting with a client."

"And Beatrice?"

He slightly crinkles one eyebrow. "I'm afraid she's out sick today."

I nod. The conditions are perfect for what I want to ask, but I don't know how to say it.

"It's true, then? You're getting married?" He is looking at my ring.

I gaze down at the sapphire on my finger. "Yes."

"Congratulations. I'm sure you'll be very happy."

I lift my head to look at him. "You are?"

He blinks. "Pardon?"

"You're sure I'll be very happy?"

"You're not?"

"I don't know how any of us can be sure of anything."

He studies me for a moment, and I know he's wondering what in the world I am talking about. I close my eyes for just a moment to dispel the notion that I might not love Palmer like he loves me.

"Maggie?"

"I saw the letters." The words tumble out too soon. But once they are out, they are out. I open my eyes.

Jamie is looking intently at me. I cannot read his expression.

"I didn't mean to look inside your rucksack. It just happened. You were leaving my house to come here and you'd forgotten it in the sitting room. I went to get it for you and because it was open, a few things started to fall out when I picked it up. I merely wanted to put everything back inside. And that's when I saw them. My letters."

He is quiet for a second and his unreadable thoughts are making my heart pound.

"I'm not angry you saw those letters," Jamie finally says. "I was going to tell you myself that I still had them. I figured at some point I'd have the chance."

"You were?"

"Yes."

"Why did you keep them?"

"Because they are precious to me."

I can't make sense of those six words strung together like that. How could my letters be precious to him? How?

"You never wrote to me after you came home from the war," I say. "I sent you all those letters after you left and you never wrote back. Not once."

"That doesn't mean your letters aren't precious to me."

My mind is whirling with confused thoughts. I want to reverse time and spin the earth back to before I had decided I meant nothing to him. Before he made me feel like I had meant nothing to him.

"I don't understand," I say. "You left. You wanted nothing to do with any of us. You *left*!"

"I know. I'm sorry. I was a broken man when I came home from the war. I hated who I was, who I had become. I hated what I had seen and what I had done. I didn't want to be here where life had been beautiful. When I was in France, everything I believed to be true was turned on its head. It was like waking up every morning in an upside-down world where everything that had been sacred had become profane. Every time a shell knocked me to the dirt or blew apart the man next to me or I aimed my gun and fired, I felt myself disappearing. Some of the other soldiers found a way to navigate the upside-down world. I never figured out how I was going to stay me. When I was shipped home, I didn't know how to be the man I was before. That's why I couldn't stay here."

I'm not aware that tears have gathered in my eyes until he reaches into his vest pocket and offers me a handkerchief.

I blot my eyes and I smell the closeness of his skin on the fabric. "I still don't understand why you saved my letters."

He leans forward and takes my hand. "Because every time you penned a letter to me, you wrote to the man I had been, the man you thought I still was. Every time I read or reread one of your letters, I was given a glimpse of the person I used to be. You made me believe I was still in there somewhere, past all the regret and the wounds and the self-loathing. There were many times I wanted to give up, times I wanted to point a gun to my head and just be done with it, but I'd see your letters in my rucksack and I'd find the will to live another day. All these years that I've been roaming about, doing odd jobs here and there and waiting to see if my world was ever going to turn right side up again, it was your letters that gave me the hope that one day it would. Your letters saved my life, Maggie. I wouldn't be here if it weren't for you. I'd be dead."

"But . . . but I stopped writing." My voice is tight in my throat and feels leaden. I do not feel like anyone's savior.

"It didn't matter. All those years that you did were enough for me. And after your letters stopped coming, I found myself wanting to live so that I could come home and show you that you hadn't been a fool for writing a man who never wrote back."

I was in love with you, my heart whispers. *That is why I kept writing. And why I finally stopped.*

He squeezes my hand before letting go. "I'm glad you came over, Maggie. I wanted to find the right time and place to tell you all this. I wish . . ." His voice falls away.

"You wish what?"

He smiles and shrugs. "I wish I had come home sooner."

"I wish you had, too."

For the first time ever, the eight years that separate Jamie and me seem like nothing more than a day. Unspoken words hang between us. He leans forward slightly, and I want to think it's the posture of a man about to kiss the woman who saved his life.

And then Roland Sutcliff throws open the front door to the accounting office, jangling a bell to announce his entrance and breaking the spell.

CHAPTER 59

Willa

Lila enters her dressing room wearing a silky black robe trimmed with glittering gold lace. Her ever-present cigarette holder is in one hand, and a cocktail glass is in the other. A man wearing a pin-striped suit, with gelled hair and a pencil mustache, is laughing behind her, spilling his own drink on his polished shoes.

When she sees me, Lila puts up a hand to the man's chest. "We'll have to do this later, Frankie."

"What?" the man says as he stumbles against her raised arm.

"You heard me. Later." She is looking only at me.

The man named Frankie unloads a string of curses.

She turns to him and tells him to shut the hell up or there won't be a later. He sighs and ambles off, his shoulder hugging the wall as he disappears down the hall. Lila shuts the door and pivots to face me.

"What are you doing here, love?" she says.

It's a Sunday. I don't sing on Sundays. "I want to work tonight."

She crosses the room to stand by me, folding her arms and leaning her backside against her dressing table. The top of the table is covered with lipsticks and pots of rouge and eye color, bottles of perfume and tins of scented talcum. One of the tubes of lipstick falls over. "Does Albert know you're in my dressing room?"

"No."

"How'd you get here?"

"I took a taxi."

"A taxi dropped you off here?" she says, her perfectly painted eyebrows raised.

"A block away. I'm not stupid."

She cocks her head, and her perky bob falls away from the left side of her face like fringe on a curtain.

"What are you doing here, Willa?" She never uses my real name even though I told her what it is. She always calls me Polly, or love, or doll.

"I told you. I want to work tonight."

"That's not going to happen. Look, Albert likes you, but he doesn't like surprises. You here right now is a surprise. You say you're not stupid. I'm telling you, the smartest thing you can do is go back home and come back on Friday like you're supposed to."

I want to sweep my hand across her table. I can feel the muscles in my arm tensing with the desire to send everything clattering to the floor.

"Like I'm supposed to." I echo her words, but she said them gently and they come out of my mouth hard and angry. I'm tired of people telling me what they're going to do no matter how I feel about it.

"Hey, we all have to live by someone's rules," Lila says, as if reading my thoughts. "You work here, you live by Albert's rules. I don't know who at home you're mad at, but you can't be here right now. Every time you come to the club, Albert takes a risk. You know that, don't you? He takes extra precautions on the nights you're here."

I don't know what she means and she can see that I don't.

"You're young," she says by way of explanation. "You're still a child."

"I'm eighteen."

"You're fourteen. You live at home with your father. You still go to school. You —"

"How do you know all that?" I hadn't told

Albert my real name or anything else about me.

"Albert knows everything about the people he hires. He knows you want to be here and that you can be trusted to keep your mouth shut. But other people can be idiots. Other people can cause trouble. He makes special arrangements on nights you sing. Financial arrangements. You're good for business, kid. People like you. They're coming special to hear you. So don't mess it up, okay? Go home."

"I don't want to go home." I don't. I don't want to hear any more of Maggie's plans to leave Philadelphia and take Alex. I can't believe Papa is letting her do it. She has no right to take Alex from him. And he's just letting her. Maggie knows how much Alex means to Papa. After all the losses he's suffered, how can she take that boy from him? She's only thinking of herself. I don't want to go home. I want to wear the bows and lace and sing like there are only good things in this world.

Lila inhales from her cigarette and blows the smoke over her shoulder. Then she slides onto the bench where I'm sitting. Her robe feels cool and silky against my skin. "Who'd you get in a fight with?"

"No one."

"Go home."

I sit there for a minute, staring at my reflection in the mirror inches away from us, wishing there were a way to disappear into the glass like in the story by Lewis Carroll. "Why do people hurt other people?" I murmur.

Lila laughs. "Because they can, sweetheart."

I look at the face in the mirror, at that sad face. "That can't be the reason."

Lila leans in. Her face is next to mine. Our temples touch and our eyes meet in the mirror. "Sometimes they just can't help it," she says. "They don't mean to hurt anyone. It just happens. And there's nothing you can do about it."

"Nothing?"

"Not unless you've got a magic wand, love."

We sit there a minute longer as the smoke from her cigarette twirls about our heads like a halo.

"I'll get you a cab," she says.

Fifteen minutes later I am standing at the front stoop of my house. It's only a little after midnight, but the house is dark and still. No one sees or hears me come in brazenly through the front door.

I cross the foyer to the staircase and stop

to look down the little hallway toward Papa's room. The seam under his door is a ribbon of mellow light. He is still awake. He didn't hear me come in. Didn't hear the front door open and close.

I stand there for a second or two longer, looking at his door and thinking of all the things I would change if I had a magic wand.

CHAPTER 60

Evelyn

I have been preparing for this day for nearly a week. Since the evening I told Maggie that she had to ask Jamie about those letters, I've known I would have to be equally honest with Ursula. Maggie told me she had spilled her question to Jamie in a moment of anxiousness, and while she had gotten the most tender of answers, I could not spill anything to Ursula in a likewise kind of temperament. I had to formulate what I was going to say, how I was going to say it, and how I would respond to every possible kind of reaction from Ursula, including no response at all. Maggie hadn't prepared herself for what Jamie would tell her about those letters. I can see that she's confused about her feelings for Palmer now that Jamie has come home, and especially so since learning the reason he kept them. She hadn't contemplated the response she would get or what it might mean for her future with Palmer. I couldn't be as unprepared when I met with Ursula.

I told Dr. Bellfield that I had decided I was going to do it his way — lay it all on the table, so to speak — but that I wanted a couple days to study case files and practice what I would say to Ursula to get her to open up to me. I think he's grown tired of my little crusade and he waved me off to indulge in whatever approach I wanted, reminding me, though, that I have other patients.

But I am ready now. The time is right and I'm well-prepared. Today's the day.

I take Ursula's pencil box, wrap it in a cloth napkin I took from the dining room, and head to the solarium, where many of the patients spend the afternoon now that the weather has turned.

When I step inside, I see Ursula in her usual corner by the window. Conrad Reese is also there, sitting by Sybil in the opposite corner. He appears to be reading to her. He nods hello to me and I return the silent greeting. I make my way to my patient, hoping that I've chosen wisely to produce the pencil box when she's in the solarium with other people about.

I take the chair next to her, glad that no other patient is too close by. She is alone in her corner. We have a measure of privacy.

"Hello, Ursula."

She looks up at me. "Hello."

"How are you feeling today?"

She lifts and lowers her shoulders. "I don't know. All right, I suppose."

I clear my throat and position the fabric-covered box on my lap so that it is easy to reveal. "I need to ask you something, Ursula. It's actually fairly important."

Her gaze registers interest.

"I need to ask for your trust. I know we haven't known each other very long, but I am asking you to trust me."

"Trust you for what?" Her tone suggests maybe she has had bad luck trusting people.

"That my sole desire and aim is for you to be well and happy."

"I guess," she says, sounding dubious.

I reach out to squeeze her hand in gratitude. I want her to think of it as a handshake — like we've agreed on this. She doesn't flinch, but neither does she show any signs that she and I have struck a deal.

I take back my hand. "I need to show you something." I peel back the napkin from around the pencil box.

Her eyes widen only slightly. "Who gave

that to you?"

"Your roommate, Matilda, happened to know you kept it hidden in your room. She showed it to me."

Ursula blinks languidly as she stares at the box, and then she turns her gaze back to the window. "I don't care that she did. I don't need it anymore. I don't need anything inside it. She can have it if she wants."

I steel myself for what I will say next and for whatever Ursula will say or do. "Ursula, I spoke to Rita Dabney at the hotel. She told me what happened. I know about your baby brother. I know you think it's your fault he died."

Ursula doesn't move. She swallows with effort and then two tears track down her face like silver strands of light. "It *is* my fault."

"You were ill. You had the flu and were delirious with fever. It wasn't your fault."

She shakes her head and more tears fall. "You weren't there."

"It doesn't matter that I wasn't there. The facts are the facts regardless. Your mother had just died, Ursula. I know you loved her. I saw the photo of you and her in this box. I saw the list of hers that you saved. The necklace. She had just died, and you were very sick with the same thing that killed her.

And maybe Leo was sick with it, too. Maybe he was already dead. Maybe you took him to the river because it was just too sad to see his dead body alongside your mother's. And then your mind created the angel and the brown boat so that you could imagine him safely traveling to heaven."

"He wasn't dead," she whispers, the tears suddenly falling freely. "He was alive."

She makes no move to wipe the tears from her face. I reach into my skirt pocket for a clean handkerchief and offer it to her. But she seems not to see my hand in front of her.

"I saw the angel in white," she continues softly, almost as if she is recounting the day to herself, not to me. "I saw the little brown boat in the angel's arms. I don't remember going down to the river with Leo. But I remember he was alive in the angel's arms. He was alive."

Her voice falls away.

"Are you sure he was, Ursula?" I ask, again offering the handkerchief. "Perhaps he wasn't."

"The angel told me I didn't have to worry, that Leo was safe with her," Ursula continues, but not to me. She is speaking to her reflection in the window glass. "I saw him crying, reaching up to touch the angel's face, and I saw the little heart-shaped mark on his stomach as he wriggled in her arms. He was alive."

My breath catches hard and cold in my throat. "What did you say?"

"I tried to follow them," Ursula says, numbly. "I wanted to go with them to heaven. I tried. The angel was too quick. She flew. I tried to follow them. . . ."

She continues to weep quietly, but I am barely aware of anything but the bolt of dread hammering its way through me. Ursula's memories are colliding with my own. No, not colliding. Coming into focus. They are layers of the same truth. Hers. Mine. The same. I see them folding in on themselves to reveal one reality, not two.

The heart-shaped birthmark.

Alex.

The angel in white.

Maggie wearing Mama's lace scarf as a mask.

The little brown boat in the angel's arms.

Maggie's coat bundled to carry the naked, crying infant away in the chilled October air.

Ursula, struggling to her feet to follow them out of the building. Maggie, walking too fast. Ursula, losing sight of Maggie and the baby in the warren of tumbledown row houses. She ends up at the river, too dazed and fevered to even realize she's there.

When the authorities are called in by passersby who see the sick girl wandering about, they figure out who Ursula is and where she lives. They take her home and find a dead mother and an empty cradle. They ask this nine-year-old girl found delirious by the river where the baby is and she tells them about the angel with the little brown boat who took her brother to heaven.

I'd always known Maggie was lying when she said she couldn't remember in which row house she'd found Alex. But now I knew why. It was because she had seen Ursula. And Ursula had seen her.

Alex is Leo.

For a second I cannot breathe. And then I feel all that I am inside wanting to vomit itself out of me. I let this happen. I am the one who put Ursula in this hospital. I'm the reason she tried to kill herself. Maggie lied about how and where she found Alex. And I knew she had lied. I have always known. I put a hand to my mouth.

Ursula, in her own private hell, doesn't seem to notice.

"Ursula, I need to take care of something," I say, mechanically. "I'll be back in a little bit." I grab the pencil box and rise on shaking feet, wondering where I will go.

I must get out of this room. Out of this building.

My first steps away from Ursula are even and measured. But a guttural wail is soon tearing its way to the top of my throat and I quicken my pace as I enter the main corridor. My eyes burn with tears that I simply must not release until I can get out of the hospital and away from the patients and my coworkers. With effort, I swallow the cry that wants to erupt from the core of my being. I insert my key with a trembling hand into the locked door that leads to the hospital's main lobby and which prevents the patients from wandering away. In my haste, I don't wait for the door to close behind me. I can barely keep my mouth shut as I cross the foyer. A few people in the waiting area look my way, as does the nurse at the front desk. I disguise my behavior as a bit of a coughing fit, soon to be brought under control by a breath of cool autumn air.

I burst from the building into the frosted afternoon, and the tears immediately begin to course down my cheeks. I must find a place to let them have their way, for there will be no reversing them now. The full weight of what Maggie had done — what I let her do — is falling on me heavy as iron and blistering as fire. Ursula Novak's pitiful existence is because of us. We are to blame for the last seven years of her tormented life. Only us.

I race for the hospital's garden shed at the far end of the front lawn. It is set back from the pea-gravel driveway and partially hidden by trees that have lost their leaves. In the spring and summer, the shed disappears into the landscaping. The tools inside are too dangerous for it to be located on the back lawns where the residents are encouraged to spend part of their day.

I had seen the groundskeeper raking leaves earlier that afternoon, so I am confident the shed will be unlocked. My heels crunch on the frozen grass as I half run, half walk toward it. I throw open the door and pitch forward toward a chest-high shelf loaded with clay pots that have been brought in for the winter.

I toss the pencil box onto the shelf and release the pent-up sob through clenched teeth. My torso begins to shake with the force of my tears. The image of Ursula Novak slipping the noose over her head, kicking out the stool, and then her anguish wanting to wrench the life out of her plays relentlessly in my head. It is my fault Ursula tried to hang herself and now sits in the asylum wishing she was dead. My fault. I should have demanded that Maggie tell me the truth about where she found Alex. I was the older one. I was the wise one. I was the one who knew she was not telling the whole truth.

God, help me, I whisper. And it's a prayer and a confession and a cry for help. I must gain control of myself and return to the solarium. I can't leave Ursula in the room the way I did. But I have no idea what I will say to her when I go back in. I need to talk to Maggie. I need to know the truth at last.

In my turmoil, I don't hear the footsteps behind me. The voice is the first thing that lets me know I am not alone in the garden shed.

"Miss Bright, are you all right?"

I spin around, nearly losing my footing. Conrad Reese reaches out to steady me. There is only one explanation for why he is here in the shed, asking me if I am all right. He had been watching me in the solarium as I spoke with Ursula. He had been watching me like I watch him. He had seen that Ursula had said something that upset me. Me, the psychiatrist. The one who is supposed to be in control. The one who is supposed to be listening to the patient and offering wise words in response. He had seen me leave the room with my hand over my mouth. He had followed me down the hall. He must have caught the inner door that I'd failed to secure and trailed me out the front door, across the lawn, and into the garden shed.

I want to know why he would do that and yet I think I already know why he would do that.

He takes a step forward. "Miss Bright, what has happened? Is there anything I can do to help you?"

He has never looked more beautiful to me than in this moment. His gaze, alight with compassion and longing, is tight on mine. He is standing so close to me that I can smell his cologne, the scented pomade in his hair, and the starch in his collar. I fight for the words to tell him that I am fine, I just needed to clear a cough, and that I'm so very sorry to have alarmed him. But those words don't come.

"I've done something terrible," I whisper.

"Oh, I'm sure that's not true." His eyes don't widen even a fraction. He doesn't believe such a thing to be possible of me.

He's been watching me like I've been watching him.

"But it is true. It is!" Fresh tears spill from

my eyes and I want him to pull me into his arms and whisper that all will be made right in time. *Not to worry. Everything will be made right. You'll see.*

"We've all made mistakes, Miss Bright." He roots about in his coat and trouser pockets for something. A handkerchief, no doubt. But he doesn't have one.

"Not like this." A fresh vision of Ursula swinging by a rope, her brain causing her legs to jerk and flail, fills my mind. "Not like this."

Lacking the handkerchief, Conrad extends his hand tentatively toward my face and catches my tears with his fingertips. "We've all done things we wish we hadn't," he says, so gently.

I look up at him, in awe and wonder and agony. I see the ache he also carries, the grief at the slow loss of his wife, at the death of the dream he'd had for their life together. We had wanted happiness for our lives. We'd pursued it the way everyone did after the flu and after the war, and we thought we'd caught it. He'd done nothing wrong, though. His pain was different than mine because it was undeserved. I tilt my head into his palm and before I know what I'm doing, I am kissing it. His strong hand is wet with my tears and I taste salt. A second later Conrad's arms are around me and his lips are on mine, tender and hesitant. It's as if we both sense that we're poised above a dam about to burst, and the water could sweep us away if we let it. If we want it to.

A second later I am returning his kiss, and then his hands are everywhere on my upper body and his lips are finding me in places I have never before been found. Behind my ear, along my jaw, on the chevron between my clavicles. His chest muscles are tight under my fingertips, tensing with desire, and I hear a small voice in my head telling me nothing good can come from continuing this. Nothing. Conrad is married. To my patient. Conrad is married to Sybil. Sybil is his wife. But I cannot hold back the floodwaters. I'm in love with Conrad. I have been for weeks and had refused to admit it. I would do anything for him. Live for him, die for him. I would do anything, including cure his wife, if I could, and if it would make him happy.

His wife. He is married. Sybil is his wife.

I pull away. We are both breathing as though we've just run through a great stretch of woods. His hair is askew where I've run my hands through it. His coat is off and lies at my feet, his vest unbuttoned, and his shirt untucked. Three buttons on the front of my dress are open, and cold air stings my bare flesh.

Conrad is staring at me with tears in his eyes, and I don't know if he's sad that we'd started on each other or that we stopped.

"I'm so very sorry," he says a second later, his words cutting across the space between us. "Please forgive me. Please. I'm so sorry."

I don't want him to be sorry. And I can't utter the words that I forgive him, because I don't. I can't forgive him. I'm in love with him.

Conrad doesn't know what to make of my silence. He stoops for a second to pick his suit coat up off the dirt floor and then he lays it across his arm. "Are you all right?" He doesn't look at me. "Are you hurt? Did I hurt you?"

Hurt me? Has he hurt me? All I feel at this moment is an ache for everything in my life up to this point to have gone differently. I feel anew the scorching loss of Henry, my mother, Gilbert, and even my own innocence at embracing without question Maggie's deception, year after year after year.

Conrad raises his head. I am still only partially buttoned and tendrils of my hair have fallen about my face. He looks away from my body for just a second and then returns his gaze, focusing on my eyes only.

"Please, Miss Bright. Tell me you are all right."

I'm not. I'm not all right. Maggie and I have taken a child from his family, have caused his sister years of merciless suffering, and the man I love is married to someone else.

"Miss Bright?"

"Evelyn," I say as new tears rim my eyes.

"Please. Did I hurt you?" His voice sounds pained.

"You could never hurt me, Conrad."

His intense stare softens as he realizes that I'd *wanted* him to touch me and kiss me and take me. I wanted him. I want him. I have been watching him like he's been watching me.

Conrad closes his eyes at the impossibility of our situation. Then he turns, puts on his suit coat, and tucks his shirt into his trousers. I refasten the buttons on my dress and slip the fallen locks of hair back into their hairpins.

He moves toward the door. "I won't take advantage of you again, I promise," he says over his shoulder.

He takes another step and I rush forward. "Conrad, wait!" I grab his hand, and my fingers touch his wedding ring. We both look down at the circle of gold. He pulls his hand away but then reaches up to touch my face for the merest second before he steps outside.

I watch him walk across the lawn to the driveway, and to the rows of automobiles parked in front. He climbs into his Buick and drives off slowly. I don't move until he is gone from view. Before I leave the shed, I retrieve Ursula's pencil box and I check to make sure that I've seen to every detail on my clothes and every hairpin.

It is only a few minutes after three, but I must find Dr. Bellfield and ask him if I might have the rest of the afternoon to take care of a family matter. I cannot think of Conrad right now or what almost happened in the shed or what *did* happen in the shed. I must first see that Ursula is all right in the solarium, and then I must talk to Maggie.

We must tell Alex the truth.

We must tell everyone the truth.

CHAPTER 61

Maggie

Samples of engraved wedding stationery are splayed across the dining room table, each piece of paper bearing names and details of people who do not exist. Palmer's mother wants us to decide on a style so that the invitations can be printed next week. November is just around the corner and then it will be December in a blink, so Imogene Towlerton says. My future mother-in-law has stepped in where my mother would have, had she lived to see me marry, securing the wedding chapel at the church for the day after Christmas, ordering a cake, and supplying Palmer with the samples so that we can select the paper and ink for the invitations before he leaves.

I have been numbly agreeing to everything, including Imogene's offer to take me shopping for a dress. When Palmer asks me which invitation I like best, I say, "How can

I choose? They are all beautiful."

I feel like I am planning someone else's wedding, not mine. Palmer thinks I am a nervous bride, that's all. Perfectly understandable. But it's not nervousness I feel; it's the sense that I'm being torn in two. Half of me wants to marry Palmer, take Alex to New York, and build a life, the three of us, far away from old heartaches. The other half wants to believe Jamie was leaning forward to kiss me when his father opened the door to the accounting office, wants to believe it wouldn't have been any ordinary kiss. Wants to believe it would have been the sealing of a truth I have long known and that Jamie had finally realized and come home for, that we were destined to love each other.

Just thinking of that almost kiss now makes me blush.

"Mother and I will take care of it," Palmer says, kissing my forehead. He scoops up the papers and slides them back inside the leather portfolio in which he brought them. "All right, then. I think that's all we need to attend to for now." He stands, almost triumphantly. He's heading up to Manhattan in the morning, a day before he starts his new job, to scout out an apartment for us. I stand, too. "Hopefully the next few weeks will fly by and I can come home with good news about where we will be living," he says as I walk him to the door.

"I hope so," I say absently.

In the sitting room just a few yards from us, Willa, who has just gotten home from school, begins to pound out a tune on the piano, loud enough to wake the cadavers down the hall. Palmer nods toward the sound.

"She still angry with us for taking Alex?" he asks.

I haven't given the situation with Willa much thought even though she was rather upset to learn that Alex is coming to New York with Palmer and me. Willa's ire is understandable this time, but I have had more pressing matters to ponder than how to ease her displeasure. "I suppose she is," I answer.

"Well, try not to let it bother you too much, hmm?" He kisses me and then opens the door, letting in a chilly blast of cold air. Evie is just coming up the stoop from her workday at the asylum. It's early, though. Not yet even four o'clock. Her cheeks are crimson from the cold.

"Good afternoon, Evelyn," Palmer says genially, tipping his hat.

"Yes. Good afternoon, Palmer," she says

quickly, walking past him and coming straight for me. "I need to talk to you, Maggie."

"She's all yours," Palmer says cheerfully. "I'm off."

I wave good-bye, watch Palmer walk away, and then close the door. In the foyer, Evie has taken off her coat and is now unwrapping her muffler. Her hands are shaking.

"Is it that cold outside?" I ask.

She turns to me. Her eyes are alight with what I can only describe as fear. "I need to talk to you alone."

"Evie, what is it?"

"Where's Alex?"

"He and Papa went to the hardware store. Why?"

She pulls a small wooden box out of her handbag and then grabs my arm. We pass Willa, whose fingers are attacking the keyboard like hammer strokes, and head for the stairs. Seconds later we are in Evie's room on the second floor and she has closed the door, bracing her back against it.

"Evie! What in God's name has happened?"

My sister closes her eyes for a moment, as if she can't find the words to tell me her terrible news. I feel my heart thrumming in my chest. I'm afraid and I don't know why.

"Evie?" I murmur as I sit on her bed, afraid that I may topple.

She opens her eyes and they are rimmed in silver. "I know who Alex belongs to."

Heat immediately fills my head, and a roaring starts in my ears. "What?"

"I know your secret. I know why you pretended not to know in which house you found him. Because there wasn't just a dead mother inside it. There was a girl inside, too. A sick girl. His sister."

I am at once nauseated and hot and cold and flattened. I must be dreaming. Must be. This nightmare where what I did is exposed is one I've had before, many times, but it has been a number of years since the last occasion.

I am dreaming, so I close my eyes that I might wake.

Evie is suddenly kneeling before me, her hands tight on my arms, her nails biting into my flesh. "That girl thinks she killed him! His sister thinks she threw her baby brother in the river because everyone told her she did. She's lived the last seven years thinking she killed Alex! She tried to kill herself because of the horror of it. And now she sits in my hospital after trying to hang herself. For the love of God, Maggie, tell me the truth! What did you do?"

And then the other me, the one who has been agreeing to all the wedding plans, tells Evie what I did. How I saw the dying girl on the sofa and how I'd assured her I'd take care of her brother, how I had run back to Mama with the baby, how Mama and I retraced my steps, and how I had seen through the broken window that the girl on the sofa was gone. And how I only had a second to decide what to do.

"When I found Alex, I thought that girl was dying, and then when Mama and I walked back, I saw she was gone. I told myself she must have crawled into their mother's bedroom to tell her the baby had been rescued and had died there on the floor where I couldn't see her. But I didn't want to look inside and find out if I was wrong. I pretended I couldn't remember which building it was. I didn't want to go back with Mrs. Arnold the next day and find out there were other family members. So I lied to her, too. I wanted the baby for us because we had lost Henry and that baby needed us. And we needed him. I thought that girl had died. And no one came for Alex. No one went to the police station asking about him. We waited and waited and no one ever asked."

"Because everyone thought Ursula had

thrown him in the river," Evie says, her voice husky and her face wet with tears. She is looking down at my hands, limp in my lap.

"Ursula?" I say.

"That's her name."

"Why? Why did everyone think she did that?"

Evie then tells me how this girl named Ursula had been so feverish everyone believed her to have been delirious when she said an angel in white lace — me — had taken her baby brother away in a little brown boat — my coat. Ursula had seen the heart-shaped birthmark on his tummy as he wriggled — alive — in my arms. This is how Evie knew Ursula's baby brother was Alex. Ursula had tried to follow me and couldn't, and she'd been found wandering down by the river, mumbling that she was looking for the angel who had taken away her baby brother in a little brown boat.

"She thinks she killed Leo," Evie says as she wipes her face with the back of her hand.

"Leo?"

"That's Alex's name, Maggie. His name is Leo. And he has a sister named Ursula. And a father named Cal. And grandparents named Rita and Maury."

For a moment I can only sit on Evie's bed and try to allow these names to have a place in my head. But I can't. Alex is ours. He has sisters named Maggie and Evie and Willa. And a father named Thomas Bright. Alex is ours. Alex is ours. Alex —

"Maggie, we have to tell Papa."

I snap my head up to look at her. "No," I say plainly.

"We must!"

"No."

"He's not ours!"

"Yes, he is."

Her hands are on my shoulders again. "Maggie, listen to me. You did what you thought was best. No one will fault you for that. You thought Ursula was dying. And then when no one was looking for Alex, you thought she *had* died. You were young and it was a terrible time for everyone. You did what you thought was best for him. And now we need to do what is best for him again."

I free myself from her grip. "How is telling him all this going to be best for him? He doesn't know any of those people! They are strangers to him. We're the people he loves! We're his family. How can you even think of letting complete strangers come and take him!"

"Can you tell me you can go on pretending you don't know who he really is?" Evie says, her voice splintering. "That you can live knowing he has a sister who spends every moment of her miserable life thinking she killed him?"

I want Evie to stop talking. Just stop. Stop.

"He's not ours, Maggie," she says.

My mind conjures a horrible image of Alex's face when I tell him. Of Papa's. And then I see the shattering image of Alex screaming as people he doesn't know drag him out of this house. The contents of my stomach rise like a fountain, and I dash off the bed, throw open the door, and run to the bathroom. I heave into the commode, and it seems like my very heart and soul are being expelled out of me.

Evie is at my side, stroking my back and crying softly. A moment later Willa is at the doorway, too, having heard my retching in between the measures of her music.

"What's wrong with her?" I hear Willa asking. And then, "Evie, why you are crying?"

"Are Papa and Alex home yet?" Evie asks, ignoring both questions.

"Only just," I hear Willa say. "They're in the mudroom, I think, taking off their coats."

"We need you to take Alex for a little bit

so that Maggie and I can talk to Papa alone. Will you do that, Willa? Can you take Alex to the sitting room and play one of your piano games?"

"Why? What has happened? What's wrong with Maggie?"

"Please, Willa. You will know soon enough. Just tell Papa that Maggie and I need to talk to him. Tell him to wait for us in the viewing parlor. Then take Alex to the sitting room and close the doors. Please?"

There is a pause. I can't raise my head to look at Willa. She will hate me after this.

"All right," Willa says.

A moment later she is gone. Evie moistens a washcloth and then helps me to my feet. She wipes away the vomit and perspiration from my face.

"I need to get something from my room," she says.

I put a drinking glass under the tap and then force myself to swallow some water. When Evie returns a minute later, she has in her hand the little box that she'd taken out of her coat pocket when she got home.

"What is that?" I say, loathing it even though I don't know what it holds. It's somehow related to Alex being a boy named Leo — I'm sure of that at least — and I hate it.

"It's Ursula's. There is a picture of their mother inside. Alex deserves to see it."

We hear the pocket doors to the sitting room close, our cue that Willa has taken Alex inside. He won't see our ashen, tearstained faces as we come down the stairs.

"Come," Evie says to me, taking my hand.

"I can't," I whisper.

"Yes, you can."

I look at the box in her hand. "Can I see it? The picture of their mother?"

Evie opens the box and withdraws a sepia-toned photograph of a dark-haired woman with long curls and kind eyes. She is sitting on a chair with her hands in her lap. A little girl with ringlets stands next to her with her hand on the mother's left shoulder. The mother's torso is angled toward the girl, as if perhaps she'd wanted to have her arm around the girl's waist but the photographer told her to leave her hands folded in her lap. The woman is pretty and young and her slight smile is serene.

This was the woman I saw dead on her bed the day I found Alex. This woman.

His mother.

I hold the photograph to my breast as Evie and I descend the stairs and make our way to where Papa waits for us.

CHAPTER 62

Willa

I found out at breakfast that Papa was going to let those people come for Alex while I was at school.

While I was conjugating French verbs or solving algebraic problems or reciting Longfellow, Alex was going to be taken from us to become a boy named Leo who lives in New Jersey, as though this was just any old ordinary day for the Brights. I'd smashed several cups and plates before Papa had relented and said I didn't have to go to classes today. I could stay home and watch Alex's real family come and take him.

"If that's what you really want," Papa said. He was crying, too, though not like me. His tears had been falling slow and silent.

"So we're talking about what I *really* want?" I'd yelled, and I think I swept another dish off the dining room table. It's hazy now, at what point I'd run out of dishes. I think Evie may have removed some before I got to them all. She kept saying, "Willa, please! Don't make this harder than it already is." Maggie sat in her chair like a statue. Like a gargoyle. Alex, thank God, was across the street at the Sutcliffs'. Dora had wanted to say good-bye and make him banana pancakes for breakfast. His favorite. Alex had spent a lot of time with Dora when he was little and we girls were in school.

Yesterday, when word had gotten out that Alex's real family had been found, Dora and Jamie and Roland had come over to our house pale-faced and distressed, like there'd been a death in the family.

"How did all this come about?" Dora had said as she cried and twisted a handkerchief in her hands.

Evie had to tell the Sutcliffs all the terrible details because I was too mad to explain anything and Maggie was holed up in her room like a coward. Papa and Alex were at the county offices or the police station — I didn't know which and I didn't care — because the authorities needed to talk to him and Alex, and Alex's real father and grandparents were coming to meet him and to discuss when to turn him over. Like Alex was a lost dog we'd found.

Evie told them about her patient Ursula

Novak and how she figured out Alex is Ursula's brother. Then Evie told them what Maggie had done all those years ago during the flu when she found Alex. "Maggie honestly thought Ursula was dying," Evie had said. "And when no one reported Alex missing, she was sure that's what happened."

"Oh yes, I do remember that," Dora had replied, wiping her eyes. "I remember how we kept waiting for the police to say Alex had family looking for him."

Then Jamie had asked how Maggie was doing, as if she's the only one whose heart is breaking. Evie said the police aren't going to charge her with any crime because she was only thirteen when it happened, and Papa wasn't going to be charged, either, because we'd duly reported that we had found the baby and were caring for him. It should have been the authorities who connected the dots, not us. We did mostly everything right. Mostly. Maggie's not being truthful about where she found Alex was the wrong thing to do. The police didn't know if the family would bring civil charges, but everyone is hoping — the authorities included — they won't.

Jamie had then asked if he could see Maggie, and Evie said maybe another time.

Imogene Towlerton wanted to see Maggie yesterday, too, and Maggie had said she didn't want to see or talk to anyone. Palmer called her from New York, and she wouldn't even talk to him on the telephone.

"Oh dear," Dora Sutcliff had moaned. "What a sad time this is. Except for that other family, I suppose. They are probably thinking this is the happiest news ever."

And Evie said, yes, it has definitely changed one life for the better in an immeasurable way. Ursula Novak no longer wants to die.

"She'll be getting out of the asylum, then?" Roland had asked.

And Evie said Ursula's discharge would likely take place soon, provided the upheaval from Alex returning didn't send her spiraling into a different kind of mental trauma.

"The mind is a delicate thing," Evie had said.

An hour later Papa and Alex had come home. Alex looked like he was walking around in someone else's dream. He didn't appear to be sad or happy. He just clutched his mother's photograph like it was a train ticket he'd been told not to lose or he'd be scolded.

He wanted to go upstairs and see Maggie when he got home, and Evie didn't tell him not to bother her. Alex was the one person Maggie still wanted to see.

When he was out of the room, Evie asked Papa how it went. She had met Alex's grandmother before, but not the grandfather or Alex's dad, and she wanted to know what they were like.

We were in the sitting room. Papa had eased himself down onto the sofa. He looked twenty years older.

"They seem like good people," Papa said. "I don't know. Alex's father is . . . He seems to be still in a state of shock. He's not taking Alex to his house, because his new wife just had a baby, so Alex will be living at the hotel with his grandparents. As will Ursula, when she's released."

This made my blood boil. "His father doesn't want him?" I said.

Papa ran his hand across his face. "I think it's complicated for him."

"Complicated for *him*?" I yelled. The china dancer on the end table looked ripe for hurling, and I had to sit on my hands so that I wouldn't reach for it.

"Keep your voice down!" Evie had said, shushing me like a mother might.

"How can you even let them take Alex?" I continued. "Do they have any idea how complicated this is for *us*? For Alex?"

"Willa —" Evie began, but I'd just moved on to my next objection.

"How dare they think living in a hotel with grandparents he doesn't even know is better for Alex than living here with us?"

Papa had taken his hand away from his face. "He's their flesh and blood, Willa. What would you have me do? The law is on their side."

Evie had asked when they wanted him. And Papa had said, "Tomorrow."

Which is today.

Alex's grandparents came for him at two o'clock this afternoon. Maggie and I helped him pack his things, although I said nothing to my sister the whole time. He was putting things from his bureau in a box when he picked up the picture of Mama that he'd had for the last couple years.

"Do you want this back?" he said to Maggie.

She put a hand to her mouth and started crying. It's hard to talk when you're crying, but she pulled her hand away a second later and managed to tell him that if he wanted to keep it awhile, he could.

"I don't know what I should do," Alex said numbly.

"I don't, either," Maggie said.

"If you want to take it, take it," I said.

"They don't get to decide everything."

He held the photograph for a second, looking into the eyes of the mother who'd carried him home the day Maggie found him. *My* mother. He put the photograph back atop his bureau. Then he reached for something behind the lamp, next to the photograph.

"What about this?" He held up the rocking horse rattle that we told him he'd been found with when we made up the story of how he came to us. "Was this mine?"

"Of course it was yours," I said before Maggie could say something stupid like it had been Henry's.

He looked at it for a second and placed it carefully on top of his socks and folded pajamas.

When the room was all packed up, Alex looked empty of all sensation, like his own soul was now in one of the boxes.

We heard the doorbell chime, and we all knew Alex's grandparents had arrived. Evie came up to get us.

Maggie said she needed to say her good-byes right there in Alex's room. We'd been advised there would be no visits for a while so that Alex could get used to being Leo Dabney. We didn't know how long *a while* was going to be. No one knew. As long as it took, we'd been told. Maggie hugged him close and tight. As mad as I was at her, my anger melted a little as I witnessed Maggie's heartache. She loved Alex like a mother loved a child. Mama had made us promise to care for Alex like he was our own, and we had done so, and yet none of us love him like Maggie does. All the love she'd had for Henry and Mama had been funneled into her devotion to Alex, the little boy she'd saved.

Maggie pulled away, told him to be good, to mind his manners, and to come visit as soon and as often as his grandparents would allow. Alex nodded wide-eyed at Maggie's parting words. I could see he had no way to appreciate what was happening. He'd never had to say a good-bye like this one.

Papa had asked Jamie to come help take down the boxes, and they were at the doorway. They'd probably seen and heard Maggie's farewell, as Jamie's eyes were glistening. Maggie took one look at Jamie and then she bent and kissed Alex's head and fled to her room.

We each took a box down the stairs, Papa and Jamie taking the bigger ones.

Rita and Maury Dabney were standing in the foyer looking like they didn't know what to do with themselves. They are probably a bit older than Papa, with faces that are wrinkled from time and trouble, it seemed to me — not from smiling for too many years. Papa introduced Evie and me to them. Evie said, "How do you do?" I said nothing.

"And the one who found Leo?" Rita Dabney asked.

"His name is Alex," I muttered. Only Evie seemed to hear me. She shot me a hush-up look.

"I'm afraid Maggie is taking this hard," Papa said. "Perhaps you could meet her another time?"

Rita seemed relieved *and* put out that the girl who had both rescued and abducted her grandson wasn't coming downstairs to meet her. It was like she wanted to thank Maggie and wring her neck.

The boxes were loaded into a truck the Dabneys had parked at the curb. It was an older truck, green and rusty.

Rita Dabney said, "Well, we'll let you say your good-byes, then."

Evie knelt to Alex's level and wrapped her arms around him. "We'll see you often — I just know it. And soon you'll get to meet your sister, Ursula. She's so looking forward to seeing you again. You'll like her, Alex. And she loves you so much."

"All right," Alex mumbled. He didn't even know what he was saying *all right* to. Nothing was all right. That was obvious to all of us. Except to the Dabneys, I suppose.

I had no intention of saying good-bye to Alex. I wasn't going to call him Leo. And I wasn't going to move Mama's photo off his bureau. I bent down and hugged him. "I'll be seeing you," I said, knowing I would do whatever I must to see Alex after this. If I was of a notion to go see him, I'd just go do it. I knew how to take a train to New Jersey. I knew how to sneak around.

I let him go and stood up, feeling very proud of myself for how I was handling the situation.

Alex, who had been quietly composed all this time, turned to Papa now and burst into tears. I couldn't watch as Papa embraced our boy and fought back his own emotions so that Alex might find the courage to go with two people he'd only met yesterday.

I looked away as the Dabneys peeled Alex out of Papa's arms and put him in their truck while he cried and yelled, "I don't want to go! I don't want to go!"

Evie, wise Evie, kept her smarts about her. "We'll see you soon! Before you know it, my darling!" she said, her voice sounding a bit shrill as she forced a happy tone into it.

I heard the truck door slam shut against Alex's sobs and then the puttering of the engine as the truck eased off into traffic. And all the while Evie shouted, "It'll be all right! It'll be all right!" while Papa just stood there and said nothing at all.

I opened my eyes and stared at Evie, hating her for becoming a doctor and working at an asylum and for figuring out why one Ursula Novak wanted to kill herself.

If only she had become a teacher or a chemist or a librarian.

Why, of all the lunatics at that hospital, did Evie have to get paired up with Alex's real sister? Dora had said earlier that surely it was fate, the heavens trying to make right what had gone wrong seven years ago.

Don't talk to me about fate, I wanted to say to Dora. *Fate* is just another word for saying we're all powerless. Me. Mama. Papa. Maggie. All of us.

Love something long enough and true enough and fate will tear it right out of your hands if it chooses, and there's nothing you can do about it.

Chapter 63

Evelyn

Ursula took the news that not only was her little brother alive, but he'd been living for the last seven years in my house, surprisingly well. I was prepared for every response, from full-blown hysteria to catatonic stupor, but when the full truth was laid before her, the tears that fell were accompanied by no additional physical response other than that she laid a hand across her heart, perhaps to feel beneath her skin her splintered soul becoming whole again.

After Maggie had escorted the police to the row house where she'd found Alex, and Rita Dabney had confirmed that was where Ines Novak Dabney had lived with Ursula and Baby Leo, there remained no doubt who Alex was. The heart-shaped birthmark was proof enough to me, but the authorities were convinced only after Maggie took them to the building and Rita Dabney independently identified it as the home she'd visited when Leo was first born. How to share this news with Ursula kept me awake for two nights.

It wasn't exactly my news to share. The police, or the child welfare people, or even her step-grandparents probably had the right to tell Ursula that Leo was alive more than I did. But Dr. Bellfield believed if I was up to the task, Ursula might better receive the news if she heard it from me. The police, the child welfare authorities, her step-grandparents, they had all spent the last seven years fully persuaded Ursula was responsible for Baby Leo's death. I had not spent the same amount of time thinking she had killed her brother. I was not in that mix of people who'd believed she had drowned Leo in the Delaware River. Not only that, but I had refused to let her waste away in the asylum. I had been doggedly pursuing a way to help her. It was decided by Dr. Bellfield and the other senior staff that I could be the one to tell Ursula the remarkable news that Leo was alive but that Dr. Bellfield would be present in case Ursula became distraught, especially at my family's part in what had happened.

For two days I did nothing else, thought of nothing else, except for how to tell her.

Dr. Bellfield graciously gave me time off to prepare and also deal with the turmoil happening in my own family. Losing Alex was like losing Henry all over again. And yet I'd lain in my bed pondering the turn of events, and Dora Sutcliff's observation that fate had brought Ursula to my hospital, fate had caused my heart to be stirred for her, and fate had pressed Dr. Bellfield into assigning me to her case.

I couldn't get past the notion that I was meant to be Ursula's doctor. It had been my destiny that her life and mine would meet at this precise moment in time, just like it had been Maggie's destiny to find Alex, like it had been Mama's destiny to die from the flu but Willa's to survive it. Just like it was my destiny to love Conrad even though he can never be mine. These truths seem wholly inevitable to me now. Unavoidable. They'd been woven into the fabric of our existence long before we were even aware of the fibers.

When I arrived at the hospital on the morning I was to tell Ursula, the same day Alex was taken from us, I wanted to find Conrad first. I wanted to see his face and hear his voice and catch his scent. I wanted the truth of his inescapable presence in my life to uphold me as I walked into Ursula's room to tell her things that would forever alter her world. I didn't see him, though. He was not in the solarium where Sybil sat listening to — without hearing — a retired church pianist play hymns.

I was shaking as Dr. Bellfield and I entered Ursula's room. Just outside the door, a nurse waited with a hypodermic in case Ursula needed to be sedated after I told her. But perhaps the truth feels so right when we at last hear it that it is its own calming agent. Ursula did not fall apart or lunge at me or faint dead away.

When I told her everything, when all the pieces at last made sense, especially Maggie's white lace mask and her brown coat, Ursula looked at me with tears shining in her eyes and her trembling hand over her heart and said, "Thank you."

Words failed me then. I could not find my voice to say anything else. When she asked when she could see Alex, I could not answer. Dr. Bellfield told her a meeting would no doubt happen very soon. "We need to think of his emotional state as well," Dr. Bellfield had said. "He's been well cared for by Miss Bright's family and it's the only home he knows."

"Oh. Of course," Ursula had replied, casting a glance at me and seeing the single tear sliding traitorously down my cheek.

Rita and Maury were now only too happy to reassume their guardianship over their step-granddaughter and called that same afternoon to arrange for Ursula's release. Dr. Bellfield was able to convince them to let the news settle first, and then to allow Ursula to be reunited with her brother within the safe confines of the hospital. They agreed somewhat reluctantly to arrange for Ursula's discharge after she and Alex had a chance to meet. Alex had been told only that his sister had recently been ill but was much better and that she was very much looking forward to seeing him again. It was agreed that two days after Alex had been returned to the Dabneys, they would bring Alex in to see her. Only they called him Leo, of course. They had also asked that I not be present for that meeting.

And I was told by Dr. Bellfield that I needed to honor that request.

I did not go into the hospital the first day we woke to a morning where Alex was not a part of it. I might have stayed home today, too, but I know the Dabneys are bringing Alex in to see Ursula this afternoon. Perhaps the Dabneys will suddenly change their mind about my being there for that reunion. I don't want to be twenty minutes away if that should happen. I want to be just down the hall or in the next room. What if Alex asks for me? What if he cries for me? I must be there.

I arrive at the asylum at the usual time and attend to my routine duties, but my thoughts are scattered. The other residents, the nurses, the orderlies, everyone who works at the hospital knows what has happened. They glance at me with questioning eyes, some clearly astounded and moved by my situation, others seemingly skeptical that I hadn't known Ursula Novak existed before this and that I somehow arranged her stay here.

Dr. Bellfield looks for me fifteen minutes before the Dabneys are to arrive and tells me I am to avoid the entrance to the hospital, his office, and the main corridor.

"It's important that you stay out of sight," he said.

"You will keep an eye on Alex, too, won't you?" I ask him, flinching a little at the sting of his words. "This has been very hard for him."

"I know how much you care for this child. If I see anything amiss, I won't ignore it. But, Miss Bright, this situation *is* going to be hard. For everyone. Surely you know that. An extended time of adjustment for everyone involved is to be expected."

"He's just a little boy," I say, reining in my emotions.

"Yes, I know. But the law says he's *their* little boy. That's why it's best you honor their request to stay away. I'm agreeing to this for him. Not for Ursula. Not for the Dabneys. And not for you."

I had wanted to find a way to view the reunion from some hidden vantage point. But now that I know the meeting will take place in Dr. Bellfield's office, I see that will be impossible. And while it hurts, I see Dr. Bellfield's point. Even if Alex were to ask for me, it won't help him to see me. It will only make it harder for him today than it was when the Dabneys came to the house for him. Perhaps I could find a way to listen in, though.

When Dr. Bellfield leaves me for the meeting, I hover at the door to the wards until I see through the glass that Ursula has been escorted to Dr. Bellfield's office to wait for Alex to arrive. I make my way through the main lobby and then the corridor to the administrative wing, letting myself into a broom closet close to Dr. Bellfield's office that I know is vented. I close the door quietly and get myself as close to the vent as I can, overturning a metal bucket so that I can stand on it and hopefully hear better. But when I finally hear the telltale sounds of multiple voices in Dr. Bellfield's office, I can't distinguish them. The venting garbles the words and the intonation. All I can hear is a deep voice, followed by a soft, feminine one, followed by one belonging to a young child. Dr. Bellfield. Ursula. Alex. But I can't make out what they are saying. I hear slight laughter, happy tears, more voices, more laughter, more happy tears.

But I can't hear the words. This moment is not mine. I don't belong to it.

I don't want to be in the closet anymore, struggling to make myself a part of what is happening in Dr. Bellfield's office. I climb off the bucket, aware of fresh tears that threaten to fall, and open the door slightly to make sure no one will see me leave. I make my escape and look for a corner of the hospital where I don't have to think about the fact that Alex is here and I can't see him and everyone is telling him his name is Leo, but where is such a place? There is no place I can escape to where I will stop thinking about what is happening.

As I near the main entrance, I see Conrad at the reception desk, leaning over it and signing something. I am overcome with the desire to run to him and throw my arms around his neck and relive the memory of his kisses. I want him to soothe the burn of losing Alex, of being responsible for Ursula's years of suffering and now Alex's misery, of missing Mama, and of facing my existence alone. My feet are moving toward him and I don't know what I will say; I only know I can't walk past him and say nothing, not after what happened in the shed and what is happening right now.

He makes it easy for me by looking up as I approach. He smiles slightly, but it is a troubled, conflicted smile.

When I reach the desk, I look down at the document he is signing. Discharge papers. He's taking Sybil out of the asylum. He pushes the document toward the nurse behind the desk.

"What are you doing?" I murmur.

"I'm taking Mrs. Reese home, Miss Bright," he says cordially, for the nurse's sake.

"But . . . but Sybil needs constant care. She will not get better." My voice sounds strained. Childlike. The nurse looks up at me.

"Yes, I understand that. I'm going to be arranging for a live-in nurse," Conrad says, and then he turns to the nurse. "If you could collect my wife and her things now, that would be most appreciated."

"Certainly, Mr. Reese." The nurse turns toward an orderly to give him instructions.

Conrad touches my arm and leads me away, around the back side of a nearby marble pillar that affords a modicum of privacy; at least it is out of the line of sight of the reception desk. "I can't keep Sybil here," he says. His eyes are pleading with me to understand. But I don't want to.

"Please don't take her," I whisper. "Please?" I feel like my world is crumbling beneath my feet. I lean against the pillar to steady myself. If he removes Sybil from the hospital, I will likely never see him again.

"I have to. I can't . . . What happened the other day . . ." His voice drops away.

I can't let him disappear from my life. I can't. "It doesn't have to happen again. I promise. Please don't take her, Conrad."

"But don't you see? I *want* it to happen again! I want it to. And I can't. . . . Sybil is my wife! I know there isn't much of her left, but I can't abandon her, Evelyn. I can't. That's not the kind of person I am. It doesn't matter that she doesn't know who I am anymore. *I* know who I am. I can't abandon her. And I can't come here every other day and see you and not wish things could be different. I have to take her and go."

I hear everything he is saying and I understand it, but I can't accept it. The world is tipping off its axis. What is happening is not supposed to be happening.

"Stop," I say. It is the only thing I can say.

He reaches up with one hand to touch my cheek. "It's best this way. To stay would be too difficult. You deserve to be happy, Evelyn. Good-bye."

Conrad pulls his hand away, and before I can say another word, he has moved away from the pillar. Sybil is being wheeled toward the reception area, her expression as vacant as an empty room. A nurse is pushing her, and an orderly carries a small case of her private belongings.

Conrad doesn't look back at me as he meets up with Sybil, and the four of them make their way toward the front door.

I can't stay to watch them drive off. I am not supposed to be in the main entrance. Alex might see me and throw himself into my arms. It takes Herculean effort to walk calmly to the staff washroom, where I let the tears fall at last.

CHAPTER 64

Maggie

Papa is bent over a dead man, shaving the enormous pale face with a steady hand. He's doing my job. He looks up when I step inside the embalming room.

"You don't need to be in here right now, Mags. I can handle this."

But I do. I do need to be in this room where the terrible things that can kill a person are covered up, plastered down, brushed away.

"I don't want to be wandering around the house today, looking for something to do," I tell him. I don't need to add that Alex's absence is everywhere inside the house, along with Willa's ever-accusing eyes when she's not in school.

He slides the straightedge down the man's face. It makes the same scraping sound that Papa's razor makes when he shaves. The dead man is huge. He barely fits on the table. "Wouldn't you rather be planning your wedding?" Papa asks.

"No."

He tips his head in my direction. "No?"

I shake my head.

"It might take your mind off all this."

"No, it won't."

"Have you talked to Palmer?"

I'm not sure how to answer this question. Palmer and I have spoken on the phone, but he did most of the talking. Was I all right? Yes. Was I going to be arrested? No, I wasn't. Was Alex all right? We don't know. Either they haven't allowed him to call or he doesn't want to, and there have been no invitations yet to come visit him. Probably too soon, Palmer said. It's only been five days. I had no response to this. He went on to describe his new job and the little apartment he'd found for us on the Upper West Side. He told me he'd be home in a week for a visit, and then he'd take me out and spoil me and kiss my woes away.

"Don't worry, my sweet. I am very fond of Alex, but we'll soon have our own children," he'd said. And I knew he meant well. But I wanted to slam the telephone down on its cradle.

"We've talked," I reply to Papa. "Let me

finish with this fellow. Please? I need to stay busy."

Papa regards me for a moment and then sets the straightedge down on a tray. "All right. Don't try to change him into the suit. He's too heavy. I'll take care of it."

I look at the dead man. There isn't a hint of injury anywhere. "What happened to him?" I ask as I put on my apron.

"Alcohol poisoning. He drank some bad bootleg. A lot of it. It's a shame. He's younger than me."

Yes, it's a shame.

Papa pulls off his own apron as I tie the strings on mine. "I've got some telephone calls to make. I'll be back in a little bit." He leaves me to it.

I finish shaving the man and then groom his mustache and wax it into place. The family provided no photo, so I decide to part his hair down the middle and tame his stubborn curls into place with pomade. I add a little stage makeup to his face to brighten the pallor and a little rouge to his cheeks. One eye has popped open, and I am easing it back into the closed position when I hear movement behind me.

I look up. Jamie is standing at the doorway. "Good morning, Maggie."

I haven't seen him since Alex was taken

away, and I haven't talked to him since he and I were alone in his father's accounting office. I should return his greeting, but I'm bewildered by his presence. I don't know that he's ever been in the embalming room. He seems to read my thoughts.

"Your father asked me to come over this morning to help him move this man. I knocked at the back door, but I guess he couldn't hear me."

"Oh. Papa's making some phone calls in the other part of the house. I'm sure he'll be finishing up soon."

Jamie nods and steps in all the way. He looks at the cadaver. "You did a nice job," he says. "He looks like he's sleeping."

"You couldn't tell what killed him," I reply, downplaying my restorative work. "I've worked on far worse."

He smiles a gentle grin. "You always did like to fix things."

I'm sure Jamie intends for it to be a compliment, but it feels like some kind of indictment. "Is that a bad thing?"

"Not at all. It's one of the things I've always liked about you." He steps closer to me so that he is now standing at my side, our elbows nearly touching. "I'm so sorry about Alex. I wanted to come see you a few days ago. Evie didn't think it was a good idea."

A lump instantly materializes in my throat at the mention of Alex's name while my heart begins to beat a little faster at Jamie's concern for me. "I don't want it to be like this," I whisper.

"Of course you don't."

"No one ever came for him," I continue, almost as if I am saying this to the dead man who doesn't know me at all rather than to Jamie, who seems to know everything about me. "I thought Alex was ours. I thought God had given him to us in exchange for taking Henry."

"I know."

"I thought that girl was dying. She looked like she was dead already. I thought she'd crawled off the sofa where I had first seen her and died on the floor in her mother's room. I didn't want to go in and see. You wouldn't believe what I had seen already. The bodies in Uncle Fred's hallway and on the stoop and in the viewing parlor. Always more and more."

Jamie puts an arm around me, like we are comrades on the battlefield, like he knows exactly what I mean, because surely he does.

But he hadn't lied like I had.

"I told my own mother that I didn't

remember where I had found him," I say, my voice breaking and hot tears filling my eyes.

"Yes," he says.

"I lied. To Mama. To Papa. To Evie and Willa. To Mrs. Arnold. The police. I lied to everyone. And look what my lying has done. I can't fix this. There is no fixing this." A sob escapes me.

He turns me around to face him. "Look at me, Maggie."

I swallow a sob and force myself to meet his gaze.

"It *is* being fixed. Slow but sure, it's being fixed, right now, right as we're standing here," he said. "It won't happen in one day or one week or even one year. I've learned that in my years away. I came back from the war wanting everything to go back to the way it was before I'd left, the very moment I got home. But the war was real and terrible, and I was swept up into every ugly aspect of it. It is now a part of the story of my life, just like finding Alex is part of the story of your life, as is having to give him back. You want to fix what hurts the moment it starts hurting, but this time you're going to have to embrace the slowness of healing. You'll never be able to live with this part of your story until you realize you must make peace with what happened to you and your part in it. And that takes time."

I know he is right. I know he is speaking to me out of his own experience, which was surely far more hellish than my own. But I don't know how to go slow. I see something shattered and I want to glue it back together this second. And I don't know how to accept my own part when it caused so much suffering.

"But what I did . . . ," I begin, but I can't continue.

"What you did may have had consequences that pierce you now," Jamie says, "but just think for a moment what might have happened if you hadn't found Alex that morning, if you had stayed home instead of going with your mother."

"I don't know. No one knows!"

Jamie tips my chin up so that I must look into his eyes and hear his words. "Isn't it possible, even probable, that Alex would have died? Isn't it likely he would have caught the flu from Ursula? Who would have come to his house that day if you hadn't? Not the father — he was away at the war. Not the grandparents — they were estranged from their son and his family at the time. Not the dead mother's extended family, because she didn't have any. Evie told me this is how it was. I don't think anyone else would have come that day."

I had to ponder this a moment. I *had* saved Alex. Perhaps he was alive today only because I'd taken him back then. Perhaps, for now, the knowledge of that would have to be enough.

"You see?" Jamie said. "We only see a little bit of our stories at a time, and the hard parts remind us too harshly that we're fragile and flawed. But it isn't all hard. Your story isn't all hard parts. Some of it is incredibly beautiful."

He's looking into my eyes now, and his hand is still on my chin. I can almost taste his lips on mine. When he doesn't move in, I do. I bend toward Jamie to kiss him, and when I am mere inches away, he turns his head.

"You belong to another," he says hoarsely, as though it hurts him to say it.

This time *I* turn his head so that he must face me. "I've only ever belonged to you," I say, knowing without a speck of doubt that it is true. It's always been true. "I've only ever loved you, Jamie. From the very first day I met you, and all the years you were away. I wanted to learn how to love someone else. I thought maybe I'd figured out how I could with Palmer, but I knew the moment you returned home that there will never be anyone for me but you."

His gaze is tight on mine as he considers this, and then he finishes what I started. He kisses me in the embalming room with a dead man at our side, and I begin to believe he may be right about parts of our stories being incredibly beautiful.

CHAPTER 65

Willa

The Silver Swan is packed. Through the haze created by smoke and stage lights, I can see that people are lined up against the wall in the back, sipping drinks that they must hold in their hand because the tables are all full. Albert at the piano leans toward me and tells me I sound particularly beautiful tonight. He points to a couple people wiping their eyes with handkerchiefs after I finish singing "Danny Boy" and he says, "And they're not just drunk."

"Sing it again," someone yells, and then others call out. So I do. And this time, when I sing about the summer ending and all the flowers dying and that the one I love must leave and I must stay, I think of Alex — gone from us for a week now — and tears are soon slipping down my face, and the room full of people is silent as I start the second verse.

We've heard nothing from Alex. Papa told me the child welfare people have said it will be easiest for him if we leave him be to get to know his family. Evie said if we were to see or talk to him now, it would be like starting all over again for him. It would be too cruel.

There is a man at the back who's staring at me now like he knows me. But it's shadowed where he's standing, and I can't quite make out his features. Albert told me if I ever saw someone I recognized in the audience, I should let him know so that he can be ready to pay that person to keep his mouth shut about me, but I'm not entirely sure I know this man.

I continue to sing, despite the tears that have fallen, and when I am done, the place erupts in applause. I take my bow and step off the stage. A man in a tuxedo with gold cuff links declares that drinks are on him, and there is more cheering. I part the beaded curtain that leads to the backstage area, and Lila meets me on the other side. She'd been listening.

"Damn, you're good," she says. "You had them eating out of your hand, doll."

"Thanks, Lila."

"Were those tears real?"

"Aren't all tears real?" I answer, and she

smiles and takes a puff on her cigarette.

All of a sudden there is a loud noise behind us on the club floor, followed by shouts and the sounds of breaking glass and overturning chairs.

I wonder if there is a fight or if someone has fallen off the stage. I hold back a portion of the separating curtain to look, and a wall of people is running toward me like the place is on fire.

From behind me I hear Lila ask what has happened, and someone running past me yells that it's a raid.

I am pushed to the wall and then flattened against it as patrons fly past me to get to the club's back entrance, which we entertainers use. A man twice my size spills a drink on my head and then slams into me as another fleeing patron pushes into him. I am about to topple to the floor to be trampled when I feel a strong hand take my arm and hoist me to my feet. I'm thinking it's Mr. Trout or Foster or maybe even Albert, but I can't tell because the hallway is suddenly plunged into darkness when someone smashes the electric light above us so that the raiding police can't see who is escaping out the back door.

"Lila!" I yell, but I can't hear my own voice above the noise and chaos.

Whoever has my arm has a firm hold and is pulling me along with such force that I can't stop to see if Lila is finding her way out, too. We are on the narrow staircase, nearly out, but not quite. I don't know what will happen if the police catch us. I will be arrested, I suppose. Papa will have to come down to the police station and get me out of jail. I feel the color drain from my face as I picture him looking at me from his side of the bars.

"How could you do this to me?" he will say. Or, worse, he won't say it.

For a moment, I can't breathe. There are too many people pressing in on me and there's too much grief at the thought of Papa looking at me that way. And then we are bursting onto pavement that is shining wet with recent rain and glowing under a now-happy moon. The man who holds my arm begins to run, like everyone else, even though at the other end of the alley, police are shouting at us to stop. He keeps hold of me, yanking me down side alleys and back streets, ever farther away from the shouts behind us. My feet and ankles are soon drenched from splashing in puddles. The baby blue dress that is Sweet Polly Adler's signature frock is soon flecked with mud and dirty rainwater.

We round a corner, and the man stops and pulls me to the side of a building so that we are pressed against the bricks. When he turns to me I see that I was wrong. It's not Mr. Trout or Foster. It's Gretchen's father, Mr. Weiss. He's the man who'd been at the very back whose face looked familiar to me. He's the man who looked like he knew who I was.

"What were you doing in there?" he gasps, in between breaths. His voice sounds so ordinary. All these years I expected Gretchen's father to have a thick German accent. But he sounds just like me, as American as I am. He has the same kind of fatherly look in his eye that Papa would have, but without the devastated hurt.

"I was singing," I said, unable to think of a better answer.

"I know that, but why? Why in such a place?" He shakes his head, incredulous.

"I wanted to."

Mr. Weiss leans against the bricks and takes in a deep breath. "You were nearly arrested tonight."

"So were you."

He turns his head to look at me. "*I'm* not a girl who should be home in her bed." He sounds angry. Like he's planning to tell Papa where I was, which means I may not be on my way to jail at this moment but I am going to get found out anyway.

"I know who you are." I don't mean for it to sound like a threat, like I plan to see if I can get him in trouble, too. But it sounds like that.

"I know who you are, too," he says, but not in a mean way. In an irritated way. He pulls me away from the wall, and we start to walk south toward our part of downtown. "You're the schoolgirl who is always looking in my front window and making my dog bark."

"I don't *make* him bark!" I snap back, but at the moment I say this, I realize he doesn't seem to know I am the mortician's daughter who lives down the street from him. I am just the girl who makes his dog bark. I may not be in danger of Papa finding out after all. I can't think of anything worse than Papa having to bear another crushing blow. Not now. Not after losing Alex. I soften my tone. "I'm not trying to make your dog bark. I'm just saying hello."

"Well, it makes him bark. Why must you say hello to him?"

"Because he was Gretchen's dog."

He stops and turns to look at me. In the cheery light of the moon, I can see his eyes have gone glassy. "You knew my Gretchen?"

"Gretchen was in my class at school. I used to watch her play with that dog. He was so cute and he loved her so much. I could tell by the way he'd jump and prance and play when she was with him."

"Yes," he says in a dreamlike voice. "He loved her."

"And then after Gretchen died, I'd see you walking him and I wanted to run after you so that I could pet him and play with him, but I didn't know if I should. Or if you would let me. So I never did. But I'd walk past your bakery all the time, and I'd see your dog in the window above and he'd see me. He'd bark and it was like we were saying hello to each other."

"You're one of Thomas Bright's daughters," he says slowly, as though all the details are becoming more clear to him.

I don't say anything.

"You lost your mother to the flu."

A hot lump immediately forms in my throat. "She caught it from me."

He blinks. "What?"

"I gave it to her. I had the flu, too. I got better. She didn't."

"Who told you you gave it to her?"

"No one had to tell me. I had it and she took care of me and then she got it. From me."

Gretchen's father looks down at Sweet Polly Adler's dress. At my disguise.

"You can't be out like this in a place like that," he says, nodding in the direction we came. "What you're doing won't bring your mother back. She wouldn't want you to be doing it. And I'm sure your father doesn't."

We stand there looking at each other, both with our losses raw and new and out in the open like they just happened.

"What's your name?" he says.

"Willa," I whisper.

"I'll walk you home now, Willa," Mr. Weiss says. "And tomorrow, you come up to the bakery to meet Louisa, Gretchen's mother. You can have some apple strudel and then you can take Fritz for a nice long walk and you can play with him as long as you want. You can come back to play with Fritz every day if you wish, and I won't say anything to your father about where you were tonight if you promise you won't ever go back to that place. Do we have a deal?"

It suddenly occurs to me there won't be a Silver Swan after tonight. I won't know what has become of Albert or Mr. Trout or Foster. Or Lila. A peculiar sadness envelops me. Everything I love always gets taken from me in one way or another. Even that little dog will someday be taken from me.

"Do we have a deal, Willa Bright?" Mr. Weiss asks.

I tell him yes.

It is easy to make promises in a world where nothing lasts.

CHAPTER 66

December 1925
Evelyn

Oddly enough it was when Maggie told me that she broke off her engagement to Palmer back in November that I first began to see the slender strands of the solution to my own predicament.

We were all of us — Papa, Maggie, Willa, and I — living in the same house but isolated and alone in our remote mental wastelands of sorrow. Our shared grief was that Alex had left us, but we were all suffering from private wounds we did not speak of to one another. We were getting a taste of what it would have been like if Mama had died and we hadn't had Alex to soften the blow.

Papa has always been a quiet man, never one given to expressing his feelings aloud, and with Willa, it was always better just to let her vent her anger and be done with it.

She was never one to seek solace from us anyway. If I had asked her if she wanted to talk about how she was feeling regarding Alex's absence, she would have told me to mind my own business.

But Maggie is different. She is neither reserved like Papa nor unreceptive like Willa regarding any consolation I might be able to offer.

When she came to my room to tell me she'd given Palmer back his ring, I was fairly sure I knew why.

"It would have been a terrible mistake," she'd said, sitting down beside me on my bed. "I couldn't marry him when I loved someone else. When I will always love someone else."

It was this little string of words, which my sister had practically whispered, that sounded like clarion bells within me. I loved Conrad. I would always love Conrad.

"Does Jamie know?" I'd asked.

"Does Jamie know that I broke off my engagement or that I have always loved him?" Maggie replied.

Before I could answer, she continued.

"He's always known I was in love with him when I was younger. He thought it was sweet. And he knew I must have continued to love him when I kept writing to him after he left and was gone all those years. He came home wondering if I still loved him, hoping maybe I did. And then he thought he was too late."

"He almost was," I said.

"No, not really. I'm the one who almost got it all wrong. Not him."

"What will you do now?" I'd asked her, hoping her answer would help me choose my own next steps.

She'd shrugged. "He wants us both to settle in to the way things are right now. Him being back, Alex having been taken from me, my breaking off the engagement, us being more than just friends. These things seem more like a season I need to abide patiently rather than something I need to do. So what I'm going to do is go on loving Jamie because I can do no other."

I knew then, as sure as I knew my own name, that my heart would only ever belong to one man. What I lacked now was not a single-minded purpose, but the courage to believe the bold plan forming in my head was attainable.

The next morning at the asylum, I retrieved Sybil Reese's file from the archives. I flipped to her admission papers and noted her place of residence, memorizing the address for the soon and coming day when I would have no doubts.

December's first snow is falling like dandelion cotton as I step out from underneath a towering elm across the street from Conrad and Sybil's house. The sun is just starting to set. Conrad is home from work; I made sure of it. I had earlier watched as he left his printing company. I saw him get into his car and head for home. I'd hailed a taxi and followed him, getting out on the opposite side of the boulevard and waiting twenty minutes before coming out from my place of cover.

His house is a redbrick Colonial with white trim. Empty flower boxes hang from all the windows, and a hearty hedge all around the house sports a feather dusting of snow. Warm lamplight shines mellow through window sheers. No one has pulled the heavier curtains closed yet. I sense welcome and it makes me smile.

I ring the bell at the front door, and my hand does not shake. Nor does my voice tremble when a housemaid in a black frock and white cap answers the door and I tell her I wish to speak to Mr. Reese. I have never been more sure of anything. Four weeks after memorizing Conrad's address, I am fully convinced of my destiny. It begins here on this doorstep.

The maid invites me in out of the cold. She asks who she may say is calling and I give her my name. I have no sooner spoken than I see Conrad appear at the doorway of a room just off the tiled entryway. He heard me come inside, heard my voice.

The maid is about to announce me when Conrad thanks and dismisses her. But he doesn't quite know what to do with me. For several seconds we just stare at each other. Then he realizes he let the maid go before she had a chance to take my coat.

"May I . . . that is, shall I take your coat?" he asks, hesitantly.

The question is really: "Why are you here?"

"Yes, thank you."

He helps me off with it and then hangs it on an enormous hall tree with cherubim and ivy carved into its frame and which sports a bench to sit on to pull on overshoes. Or take them off.

"Please?" Conrad motions to the room he just came out of. It is a sitting room paneled with bookshelves. A cheery fire is blazing. Pages of a newspaper lie open on a mahogany desk, and the chair is pulled out. A pipe sits on a brass holder, ready to be lit. The room is warm and wonderful.

If I had been any other caller, Conrad would have no doubt asked me to sit down and perhaps rung for tea. But after I admire the room, I turn to see that he is standing in the middle just like I am, looking at me. I don't care. I don't want to sit and pretend this is just an ordinary social call.

"I had to see you," I say, in answer to his unspoken question.

"Is everything all right?" he asks, but I can see that this isn't what he is most curious about. He wants to know why I have come, unbidden, to his house.

"Perhaps." I want to say that I have come with a proposition. A solution to our dilemma. A way for us to have what we want. All that we want.

He finally remembers his manners. "Would you like to sit down?" he says, wide-eyed but polite.

What I must say will not entail a long visit that requires chairs or tea. I move toward him, and I take his hands in mine. "What I would like, Conrad, is to spend my life with you."

He sucks in his breath, fully unprepared for this answer I've given him, but not completely surprised and definitely not repulsed by it. I see in his eyes he has already thought of this, too: what it would be like for him and me to be together. For a second he imagines it again, but then he shakes his head. "That is impossible."

"No. It is not impossible," I reply. "It might be difficult. Certainly different. But it's not impossible."

"Evelyn." He says my name but nothing else. What I am about to propose has not occurred to him. And why should it have? It is the most outlandish, unheard-of, remarkable, singularly amazing answer to the question that has been haunting us both. I swallow back any trace of fear and I tighten my hold on his hands.

"I will help you take care of Sybil," I say. "We can watch over her together. Here. In this house."

"What are you saying?" Conrad's voice is airy with surprise.

"I'm saying you and I can care for her. For as long as she draws breath. I'll be yours and you'll be mine and together we'll care for her."

He stares at me as the full weight of what I am suggesting begins to fall on him. "I don't understand. How would you be mine?" he says.

I am already yours, my heart replies. "I would be yours to whatever extent you would want me to be," I say aloud. "You said the other day at the asylum that I deserve to be happy. I can't be happy if I am not with you."

Conrad closes his eyes and swallows hard. "But —" he begins.

"But you can't abandon her. I know you can't. I'm not asking you to. I can care for her. I know how to care for her."

His gaze is intense as he studies the features of my face. I can't tell if he's imagining his lips on every part of me or memorizing my contours before he refuses me and sends me away. His eyes glisten.

"I love you, Conrad," I tell him, when he says nothing. "I won't love anyone else. I can't."

He pulls me to him then and kisses me and I taste salt where his tears and mine mingle. It is not the kiss of raw, physical desire that we shared in the shed. It is instead the melding of two wounded hearts that somehow, after all that has happened to both of us, can still love. I could die this moment and be happy.

Conrad breaks away first and kisses my forehead. "I can't ask you to live here, with me and Sybil, as . . . as my mistress, Evelyn."

"You're not asking me to."

"But I could never debase you that way. I

just couldn't."

I place my hand over his heart, and I can feel it pulsing beneath his shirt. I was destined to love only this man just as Maggie was destined to love only Jamie. It is inevitable that he and I will be together. "Then don't."

Chapter 67

Maggie

Papa and I are getting the viewing parlor ready for an afternoon service when the front doorbell rings. It's the week before Christmas and Willa's at school, so I offer to answer it. Papa, who always wanted me to think of my job at the funeral parlor as temporary, is nevertheless happy that I'm no longer preparing to move to Manhattan.

He was only momentarily disappointed when I called off the wedding. When I explained to him that I'd only ever and always loved Jamie Sutcliff, he understood. He understood probably better than anyone, because that's how he felt about Mama. He still loves Mama. Her being gone hasn't changed anything.

Palmer, on the other hand, did not take the news as easily as Papa did. God knows I never wanted to hurt Palmer. I tried to tell him this. I tried to explain that I would only be injuring him further if we went through with our plans to marry. I could never return the love he had for me. He should not want to marry someone who could not. I've heard nothing from Palmer since I called off the wedding, not that I would expect to. He returned to Manhattan angry and disappointed and wounded. But at least he has not called or written begging me to change my mind. I believe he will move on from me to love another. I am counting on it.

Jamie isn't one to rush anything, so even though I know I'll be marrying him someday, there is no ring, there is no wedding date, and he hasn't come to Papa like Palmer did. We are becoming acquainted with each other on the ordinary, day-to-day level. So in the meantime, I am still Papa's assistant.

I pass through the kitchen and into the entryway. I don't recognize the man who stands on the other side of the front door glass. I wonder if he is a visitor who's been given the wrong time for the funeral today. I open the door, and a swirl of frigid air blows past me. I ask if I can help him.

He takes off his hat. "Yes, ma'am. I'd like to speak to Thomas Bright, if I may."

"Is my father expecting you?"

The man turns the hat by its brim. "No, he's not."

"Oh. And you are?"

"My name's Cal Dabney."

For a long moment I can only stand and stare at Alex's father. I know the blood drains from my face because I feel it.

"Look, I'm not here to raise a fuss over what happened. It was a long time ago and nobody's to blame."

"What do you want?" My voice sounds stiff.

"Are you one of the girls? Are you Maggie?"

I nod once.

"I just want to talk to your father."

I open the door wide, a silent gesture for him to come inside.

"May I take your coat?" I say, mechanically.

"I don't reckon this will take long."

I show him to the sitting room. Papa and I have let the morning fire die down and the room is chilly. Unwelcoming. Cal Dabney doesn't seem to notice.

I excuse myself and retrace my steps to the viewing parlor. When I tell Papa who is at the door, he says, "What does the man want?" I recognize the fear in his voice.

"He said he just wants to talk to you. He

said it wouldn't take long."

I return to the sitting room with Papa. Cal Dabney is looking at the family photographs on a table by the bay window. Alex is in one of them.

Papa thrusts out his hand. "I'm Thomas Bright. How do you do?"

Alex's father shakes Papa's hand. "Cal Dabney."

I start to leave the room, though I am planning to stand where I can hear everything being said. But Cal calls out to me.

"You don't have to go. It might be better if you stay."

"Is Alex all right?" I ask as I turn back around. "I mean, Leo. Is he all right?"

"You can call him Alex. That's what we're calling him. We found out pretty quick he doesn't like the name Leo."

I want to laugh. To smile. To cry. To scream.

"How are things working out?" Papa says kindly but with a measure of displeasure. It's been eight weeks since Alex left us, and we've heard nothing from him or about him.

Cal shakes his head. "Well, that's why I'm here. They're not exactly working out."

"What do you mean? What's happened? What's wrong?" I practically shout these three questions. I am picturing Alex cowering in a closet, or wasting away because he's not eating, or crying himself to sleep every night.

Papa touches my arm to calm me. "How can we help?" he says.

"It was wrong what happened to my boy all those years ago. But it was wrong what happened to him now, too. I see that," Cal says. "He doesn't know us. He doesn't love us or trust us. You're the people he loves and trusts. My parents got no call to raise that boy just because they want back what they think is theirs. Fact is, he's not theirs. Alex is mine. Only mine. And if Ines was still alive and she and I had spent the last seven years searching for our son, it'd be different. But she's gone, and I had to move on. I have a new family and a new life now. Just like this boy was given a new family and a new life when you took him in. I'm not saying I don't want to be a part of Alex's life. I do. I want to take him fishing and maybe to a baseball game now and then. I want him to grow up knowing his little brother. I want him to learn to love me and trust me." Cal turns to face me. "But I want him to live here with you. With all of you. This is where he wants to be." He turns to Papa again. "So what I'm asking you is, will you take him back? Can he live here?"

I want to slap this man for not wanting Alex and hug him for the same reason, even though I know what he truly wants is for Alex to be happy. I don't know if he's making the right choice or the easy choice. All I know is he wants Alex to come home. I wait to see what Papa says.

Papa rubs his chin for a second. "Alex will always be welcome here," he finally replies. "This is his home for as long as he wants it to be. I'm sure we can work out the finer details."

Cal exhales a breath of relief. "I'm so glad to hear that. I'd like to tell him and my parents today if that's all right. Maybe bring him over tomorrow?"

"Of course," Papa says.

Cal puts out his hand for Papa to shake it. "Thank you. You all did a fine job of raising my boy. Better than I was raised, I can tell you. I don't mind that I'm having to call him Alex."

Papa swallows a knot of emotion. "He's a wonderful boy. I hope you know we love him like our own."

"See?" Cal says. "That's just the thing. You all love him. And he loves you." Then he turns to me. "And I want to thank you for saving him back when you did. I used to be an angry man at what I'd lost over the years. I'd forgotten how to see anything good in my life. But I'm seeing the good more and more these days. I realize now that Alex surely would have died of that flu if it weren't for you."

"I'm sorry I was part of the reason you were so angry," I carefully reply.

Cal shrugs. "I guess all of us are just doing the best we can with what life hands us."

We walk Cal Dabney to the door. He tells us he'll be back tomorrow around five o'clock if that's all right. Papa asks him if he'd like to bring his new wife and baby to dinner the following weekend, and he says, "That sounds mighty nice."

When the door closes, I turn to Papa. "Did that just happen?"

He smiles. Then laughs. Strokes his chin. Shakes off a silver line of tears glimmering at his eyes. "We'd better get back to getting the parlor ready. The family will be here any minute."

He heads back to resume the work we were doing when the doorbell rang, but I want to fling open the door and run across the boulevard to the accounting office. I want to tell Jamie. Because this is what lovers do. When something good happens, and even when something bad happens, you want to share it with the person who holds your heart.

I will help Papa move the deceased woman into the parlor. I will make sure she looks as peaceful as a dreamer. I will position the flowers so that she will appear to have merely been found napping in a garden among the butterflies, and then I'll run across the street to Jamie. When Willa comes home from school I'll tell her that Alex is coming back to us, and maybe she will at last let go of the anger she guards like a prized possession. And when Evie comes home tonight, I will tell her, and I'll ask how her grand experiment is going so far.

I don't know what Alex's return will mean for me and Jamie. Who can ever say to the letter what the future holds? It is the same with Evie and this man named Conrad whom she loves. We are all doing the best we can with what life hands us. That's all we've ever been able to do. This is how we live our story.

Papa and I move the deceased woman into place. I look down at the body in the casket and tighten a curl on her forehead, straighten a fold, reposition a hand. There.

She is ready.

CHAPTER 68

February 1926
Willa

I set Mama's hairbrush down on my dressing table as I stare into the mirror at my fifteen-year-old self. Fifteen! Finally. I used to think the space between the beginning of a year and the end of it stretched across time as far as one end of the sky to the other. But here I am, saying hello to fifteen, and it seems like just yesterday I was turning fourteen. I remember Mama saying to me once, when I told her everything took too long, that there'd come a day when I thought time went by so fast, I could barely catch my breath.

I didn't believe her then, but I'm beginning to think maybe she was right. The new year is only a month old, and already it seems like it's a vast improvement over the year we just had.

For one thing, Alex is back where he

belongs. And not only that, but Ursula lives with us now, too. When Papa told me he was going to invite her to come take Evie's room, my first thought was I didn't want to have to share Alex with her. She is his actual sister, after all. But Papa said — and Evie and Maggie agreed — that Ursula had suffered too much in the past to be stuck with Rita and Maury in New Jersey all by herself. They're not even related to her. The whole point of reuniting Alex with his family was to reunite him with her. And so it just made sense to ask her if she wanted to come live with us, too. And of course, Ursula did. She came two days after he did. And now that she no longer must work for a living, she's not somebody's maid anymore. She's back in school. She's way behind, though, so she's in the same classes with me, even though she's a year older.

Truth be told, I like Ursula. She's kind of like Maggie, only not as bossy, and kind of like Evie, only not as smarty-pants. Since we have the same classes, we can study together, and she can help me with geometry, which I hate, and I can help her with French, which she's terrible at.

And Alex? He's just so happy to be home and to be Alex again — not Leo — and to have Ursula right next door in Evie's room, and to be able to go across the street to the Sutcliffs' for banana pancakes on Saturdays. He sees his father on Sundays, sometimes for overnights. His stepmother's name is Trixie, which is a pretty fun name if you ask me, but she's shy and quiet. I don't think she knows what to make of all us Brights. Still, her and Cal's baby is adorable. His name is Steven. I thought seeing Alex go off with Cal on weekends would make me mad, but it doesn't because he always comes home to us.

Maggie and Jamie are courting now, which would have been weird when she was thirteen and he was twenty-one. But now that she's going to be twenty-one in May and he's already an old man at twenty-eight, no one cares. I can see why she loves him, though. He's nice to her and Papa likes him. I think Papa likes him better than Palmer. Poor Palmer. Maggie broke his heart like you wouldn't believe. Good thing there are plenty of eligible girls in Manhattan to help him forget her. Maggie feels bad about hurting him; I asked her if she did. But she told me it would have been more cruel to marry him when she loved someone else. I think when Maggie and Jamie marry, they will get their own place, but it won't be far. Like maybe just down the street. I don't think

Maggie can be happy without Alex around. He's more than just the baby she found all those years ago. He's the proof that out of a great pile of ashes you can still find something that the fire didn't take.

Evie just got married to that man whose first wife was a patient at the asylum. It was the shortest, quietest ceremony ever. Evie and Conrad just showed up at the courthouse in some new clothes, said their vows, and voilà, they were married. But first Conrad had to go all the way to Mexico to get a divorce so that he could marry Evie. His first wife, Sybil, is as crazy as they come. I've met her. Evie — if you can believe this — takes care of her when she's not working at the asylum. In their house. Do you understand what I'm saying? Sybil, the first wife, lives in the house, too. Right there with her former husband and his new wife, who is Evie. Sad, pathetic Sybil sleeps down the hall from where Conrad and Evie sleep, in the room that used to be her bedroom. But Sybil is so far gone, she doesn't care. Can you imagine? She is like a walking paper doll. She's flat and empty.

I asked Evie, how long can she do that? Take care of that woman? Isn't she jealous? Doesn't she wish Conrad would put Sybil back in the asylum? Evie said Conrad's devotion to Sybil is one of the things that drew her to him in the first place. I told her that was plain weird. And she said the little bit of Sybil that Conrad still loves is so small, it's no trouble to love that part of her, too.

I can tell you right now, when I fall in love it's going to be with someone who is mine and only mine. But I don't know if I will ever marry anyone. Maggie is always thinking only about Jamie and his happiness, and Evie's over the moon about Conrad and his. I'd rather concentrate on my own happiness, thank you.

The Weisses have been very nice to me since the night of the raid. And Mr. Weiss never told Papa about the Silver Swan. I don't think it's because telling Papa would mean he'd have to admit he was there. I don't think Mr. Weiss cares if Papa learned he had been at that speakeasy, too. Mr. Weiss decided not to tell because he doesn't want my relationship with Papa to suffer. He still misses Gretchen just like I miss Mama. She was their only child. I think he and Mrs. Weiss like having me over to play with Fritz because I remind them a little bit of her. Mr. Weiss takes care to remind me now and then that it's not my fault Mama died. It's sweet how that matters to him.

Maybe he's right that the flu randomly took whoever it wanted, no matter what any of us did or didn't do.

I let him say what he wants. I like going over there and Fritz loves it when I come. Louisa makes the most delicious things in their bakery, and she always gives me something yummy to take home with me.

So I'd say 1926 is starting out rather nicely, especially when you compare it to other years. Evie and Conrad are happy, Maggie and Jamie are happy, and Alex and Ursula are happy. Even Papa seems relatively happy, though his happiness will always be a little thinner compared to everyone else's.

I look into the mirror again, closer this time. I may be fifteen, but I sure look the same. At least to me. No matter. I glance up at the clock on the wall. It's getting late. Just a few seconds before midnight. Time to stop all these contemplations.

I slip Mama's butterfly hat pin into the knot of ribbon that holds my curls so that it looks like the little thing just landed there to listen to me sing.

Then I step out of my dressing room at the Landmark Club, just five blocks away from where the Silver Swan had been. Lila meets me on the other side of the door.

She'd made it out of the raid and wound up at the Landmark a week after the Swan was shut down. Her new employers had heard about me. Can you imagine? They'd asked her to see if Sweet Polly Adler was interested in working at the Landmark, too. Lucky for me Alex is still a sound sleeper, so sneaking out his window is still easy. Some things just don't change.

"They're calling for you, doll," Lila says.

I hear the patrons shouting my name as I part the stage curtain.

The piano music begins for my entrance and I imagine that I'm not in some speakeasy owned by gangsters but in a concert hall and my papa is in the front row with Mama beside him. They are cheering for me, their heads close together. Then Mama whispers something to Papa, and he grins and kisses her temple. A smile breaks wide across my face as the curtain falls away behind me, and I step into a flood of light, bright as heaven itself.

ACKNOWLEDGMENTS AND AUTHOR'S NOTE

Deepest thanks are extended to my insightful editor at Berkley, Claire Zion, and literary agent extraordinaire, Elisabeth Weed, for all the wise counsel regarding both the big and little details of this story. I am also so very grateful to everyone at Penguin Random House — Ivan Held, Craig Burke, Danielle Dill, Roxanne Jones, and Fareeda Bullert, to name a few — for coming alongside this book so enthusiastically. Thanks also to my mother, Judy Horning, for careful proofreading and unflagging affirmation and for just being my mom; to the Free Library of Philadelphia and specifically map curator Megan MacCall; to the staff of the Kimpton Hotel Palomar, the Philadelphia History Museum, the Historical Society of Pennsylvania, and the kind citizens of Philadelphia for always being ready and willing to answer my questions. And thanks are extended to everyone who, when I said my next book would be set during the 1918 Spanish flu pandemic, told me about the long-ago aunt or cousin or great-grandfather whose life was irrevocably changed because of it.

I read a great many articles, books, and excerpts as part of my research for *As Bright as Heaven,* but I could not have written it at all without the following resources, and which I recommend for further reading: *The Great Influenza: The Epic Story of the Deadliest Plague in History* (Viking, 2004) by John M. Barry; *American Pandemic: The Lost Worlds of the 1918 Influenza Epidemic* (Oxford University Press, 2012) by Nancy Bristow; *America's Forgotten Pandemic: The Influenza of 1918* (Cambridge University Press, 2003) by Alfred W. Crosby; and *Embalming: History, Theory, and Practice,* Fifth Edition (McGraw-Hill, 2011) by Robert Mayer.

While I endeavored to stick to the facts wherever I could, I made use of literary license with regard to a few details. There is no Broad Street Methodist Church, but there is a beautiful Gothic Revival–style church on South Broad Street that was known in the nineteenth and twentieth centuries as the Chambers-Wylie Presbyterian Church, and which is now the home of Broad Street Ministry. I wanted to be able to control the particulars regarding where the Bright family attended church and thus invented one for them, but I patterned it after this one. The asylum where Evelyn works in the later chapters is also fictional, but loosely patterned after Dr. Thomas Kirkbride's Pennsylvania Hospital for Mental and Nervous Diseases, which in 1918 was located along the north side of Market Street at Forty-ninth Street. Lastly, while in the story Evelyn and Conrad traveled by car to Camden, the bridge that spans the Delaware River and connects Philadelphia to New Jersey did not officially open to traffic until a few months later, in the summer of 1926. The day-to-day details of the pandemic as it swirled about Philadelphia in the fall of 1918 are as factual in the pages of this story as I could make them. The official count of Philadelphian lives lost to the Spanish flu is 12,191.

You might be wondering what prompted me to write a novel with the Spanish flu pandemic as a backdrop. As a lover of historical fiction — both reading it and writing it — I am always on the lookout for untold stories from the past that reveal the resiliency of the human spirit despite incredibly difficult circumstances. In 2016, I began to study the 1918 Spanish flu as a possible setting for a novel, as I was aware its centennial was fast approaching. I realized rather quickly this historic pandemic is an untold story. It is millions of untold stories. Until I started researching, I had no idea how globally devastating this event was and how much it changed the human landscape of the entire world. The Spanish flu pandemic of 1918 was arguably one of the deadliest diseases in history, second only to the Black Death, yet few people living today are aware of its impact. Fifty million people worldwide are estimated to have died from Spanish flu. That's a staggering number, far more than the number of lives lost in World War I. This pandemic is more than just a sad moment in history; it is the untold stories of people just like you and me — and our parents, our brothers and sisters, our children. It is millions upon millions of stories of people just like us.

I could have chosen any number of American or European cities in which to set the story, and I likewise could have given the setting to a variety of individuals. This flu killed the poor and the affluent with equal indiscriminate force. I selected Philadelphia because it was one of the hardest-hit American cities, with more than twelve thousand dead, and I chose to give this story to the wife and daughters of a newly installed undertaker because theirs would be a unique perspective on a world turned upside down by such a cavalier killer.

Death comes for us all in one way or another. It is a certainty. Our lives will one day end, and most of us never know when. Interestingly enough, it is our mortality that gives our existence its value and beauty. If our days were not numbered, we probably wouldn't care how we spent them. How does this knowledge that we are mortal affect our choices? The risks we take? The risks we don't? These were the questions I wanted to explore as I wrote this book and that I wanted you to ponder as you read it. We are, all of us, living out the stories of our lives. Each of our stories will end, in time, but meanwhile, we fill the pages of our existence with all the love we can, for as long as we can. This is how we make a life.

I would love to hear from you via e-mail or via one of my social media platforms after you've read this book. Tell me your thoughts and insights, dear reader. You are the reason I write. . . .

ABOUT THE AUTHOR

Susan Meissner is a former managing editor of a weekly newspaper and an award-winning columnist. She is the award-winning author of *A Fall of Marigolds, Secrets of a Charmed Life, Stars over Sunset Boulevard,* and *A Bridge Across the Ocean* among other novels.

The employees of Thorndike Press hope you have enjoyed this Large Print book. All our Thorndike, Wheeler, and Kennebec Large Print titles are designed for easy reading, and all our books are made to last. Other Thorndike Press Large Print books are available at your library, through selected bookstores, or directly from us.

For information about titles, please call:
    (800) 223-1244

or visit our website at:
    gale.com/thorndike

To share your comments, please write:
    Publisher
    Thorndike Press
    10 Water St., Suite 310
    Waterville, ME 04901